Kat's Kosmic Blues

an "almost-but-not-quite-true story"

PATRICIA J. PARSONS

MOONLIGHT PRESS | TORONTO

ISBN 978-1-7772431-5-9

For information or permissions:

Visit www.moonlightpresstoronto.com

Or email moonlightpressinfo@gmail.com

Author's Note

Kat's Kosmic Blues is another "almost-but-not-quite-true story" and the prequel to The Year I Made 12 Dresses. It is book number two in a three-book series. This is a book that can be enjoyed as a stand-alone story, but if you haven't read the first "almost-but-not-quite-true story" and want to get to know Charlotte "Charlie" Hudson and where this story all began, you might want to read that one first. Either way, I hope they both bring you laughter and tears. ~PJP

"Life isn't about finding yourself. It's about creating yourself."
~ George Bernard Shaw

"You're only as much as you settle for."
~ Janis Joplin

"No daughter of mine is going to an art college!" My father crumpled my acceptance letter from the Nova Scotia College of Art and Design, which only a moment ago, I had shared so proudly with him. Then he threw it against the wall. "You'll accept the offer from the University of Toronto. You'll study to be a teacher like any proper young woman." The emphasis was on "proper."

His face was red, his eyes bulging. "If you're lucky, maybe you'll even find a husband."

I just stood there without saying a word. What was there to say? I knew anything I said would be pointless. I clenched my fists and wished, ever so briefly, that he'd die. Right this moment. Right there in front of me. But he didn't.

It was 1965. I was nineteen years old. And I was angrier than I had ever been in my life. I was still outraged three months later when I unpacked my suitcases and settled into my residence room at Ardmore Hall. At least Toronto was 1000 miles from my father.

My name is Kat Wilson Hudson, and you need to hear my story.

Charlie

Try to Remember

The Brothers Four, 1965

THE EMAIL FROM THE ESTATE LAWYER WAS CRYPTIC. Mom had been dead for just over a year, the house cleaned out and sold, and the estate finally settled. Now it seemed that there was a loose end—one that neither my older sister Evelyn nor I had known anything about.

> *"Dear Ms. Hudson. We trust this finds you well. With reference to the estate of your mother, Katherine Wilson Hudson, we are writing at this time to inform you that we have been contacted by one Mr. Edmund Lancaster concerning a matter of some urgency vis a vis your mother's estate. We are troubled that this matter has come to our attention so late and with probate nearly complete. As the executor of your mother's estate, you are asked to contact Mr. Lancaster at the address below as soon as possible, after which we will expect to hear from you should there be anything further to be added to the estate..."*

1

What in the world? Add to Mom's estate? What could there possibly be? We (or mostly I) had been through every inch of Mom's belongings over the past year. Although to tell you the truth, I'd had more than one surprise about my mother since she died on Christmas Eve just over a year ago. At this point, I could not even imagine what this could be about. And I had never heard of someone called Edmund Lancaster.

Mom's estate had been settled over the past year while we (or mostly I) readied the house for sale, which had been completed a couple of months earlier. And now life had moved on. Evelyn, my overachieving and up until this minute childless-by-choice sister, had recently reconciled with her uptight, neurotic, workaholic husband Michael, and she was—wait for it—pregnant! The whole idea of becoming a parent seemed to have resulted in a personality change for both of them—a personality change for the better, I might add. What did I know, though? I didn't see either of them often since they lived half-way across the country. And me? Well, I had just moved in with Tom, the love of my life. When the email arrived, I was deep into the first few weeks of a new job. I was now the writer-in-residence and creative writing teacher in a private high school while I toiled, as I had always done, in my free time on the great Canadian novel. At least I hoped it would be. Oh, and there was a January blizzard swirling outside. Regardless of any of this, I would have to follow up.

It was two days later before I had a moment and remembered to contact Mr. Lancaster. He answered my phone call on the first ring.

"Miss Hudson? Thank-you for getting back to me so quickly." He coughed slightly. "I've been waiting to hear from you. I have some of your mother's things. They're yours now."

I had no idea what he was talking about. What "things" could he possibly have? "Mr. Lancaster, perhaps you could give me a bit more information about the things."

"I'm not sure I can do that. This is between you and your late mother."

It was all too mysterious. It occurred to me that since he told me these things were mine now, I would surely be privy to more detail. However, it appeared that I wasn't going to get anything more out of him. So, I arranged to meet with him on Saturday.

"If I could make a suggestion," he said just before hanging up. "You might make plans to be here a while." *Cryptic*, I thought.

On Saturday morning, I was pouring myself a cup of coffee in our large, bright kitchen where Mom's old red Formica table with its red vinyl-covered chairs now had pride of place, when Tom rolled in. He was dressed to impress.

"Where are you off to so early on a cold Saturday morning?" I said as I poured coffee for him and pecked his cheek.

"I was just about to ask you the same thing."

"You first."

"I have two showings this morning." Tom was an uber-successful real estate agent who seemed to have clients even in the dead of winter. Not that he needed them, though. When he and I started dating, he had already sold his internet business, which explained this extraordinary, newly renovated Victorian house we lived in and his Tesla in the garage. "Your turn."

I handed him a print-out of the email I'd received from the lawyer. I had been planning to tell him about it the day before, but we'd been so busy, it slipped my mind. "What do you suppose it's all about?" I said, buttering another piece of toast. Toast happens to be one of my personal weaknesses. Odd, I know.

"Beats me," Tom said when he finished reading the lawyer's email. "But it does sound intriguing. Sounds like the makings of a great story for a writer."

Oh, he knew me so well. My struggling writing career seemed to be taking off just as I embarked on the new teaching job. Each seemed to feed off the other. That's why time was a rare commodity for me right now. However, a mysterious communique like this did set off my writer's antennae.

"Well, call me later and let me know what's going on. Especially if it's exciting." He looked at his watch. "Gotta go! See you later this afternoon. I'll make you a martini, and you can tell me all about it. Oh, and remember, we have dinner plans." He kissed me good-bye and was off. "Love you, Charlie!"

An hour later, I was driving south on Maxwell's Park Road, inching my way through the snow that had yet to be removed from this side street. I was also thanking my lucky stars that I was driving a four-wheel drive. I'm not at all sure what I thought I was looking for. The address turned out to be a sprawling storage facility with a gated entrance that seemed to lead into a massive multi-acre property. It looked like it had been there for decades. It must have been one of the very first of these facilities. It seemed to me that the attraction to hoarding stuff was more of a twenty-first-century phenomenon. There were garage doors as far as the eye could see. *Dear god,* I was thinking, *please don't tell me that Mom and Dad had stuff in a storage locker here.* I spent months after Mom's funeral living in our old family old house, trying to make it through the accumulated masses of belongings that made up the life of a semi-hoarder. I wasn't sure I could do it again.

I buzzed the intercom at the gate.

"That you, Miss Hudson?" came the disembodied voice that sounded like Mr. Lancaster.

"Yes, sir," I said.

"Welcome to the fort!" And the gate magically opened.

I drove inside, and it closed behind me like some kind of secure compound the feds might use—at least that's what they looked like on TV. I pulled up in front of the office, where a large man with a grey-streaked beard wearing a parka and wool toque stood in the door. He waved as he crunched through the snow toward where I was still sitting in the car.

"Hello there, Miss Hudson. You have no idea how happy I am to meet one of Kat's little girls finally. I've waited a long time for this! I don't suppose you have a key to the unit?"

I told him I did not. He ducked back inside for a moment, presumably to retrieve the key. This could not have been more peculiar. How in the world did my buttoned-up, perfectly coiffed, late mother know this man well enough that he knew about her daughters? However, an even more pressing question was why he had called her Kat. No one except Mom's closest friends even knew that she was called Kat at one time. She was most assuredly Katherine to Dad and everyone else in Mom and my late father's social circle. Surely, she hadn't spent any time here. But he did seem to know about me. "Don't bother to get out of the vehicle," he continued. "Just follow me down the roadway here, and I'll let you in."

So, I did as I was told and followed him slowly down the road in my Jeep while Ed walked through the snow. We took the first right past a long row of storage garages, then stopped in front of the fifth one down. It was a large double garage door with a regular, single door beside it. There was no one else around, making the place seem just slightly creepy. I reluctantly got out of my car. I supposed he was harmless, but I'd be on my guard, nonetheless. What was this all about, anyway? I was about to find out.

"Mr. Lancaster," I began when he interrupted me.

"Please, call me Ed," he said.

"And please call me Charlie, Ed." I looked at the imposing garage doors. "Are you sure that this space was my mother's? Mrs. Katherine Hudson?"

"No doubt about it," he said as he unlocked the door. There was something about the way the corners of his mouth turned up—almost, but not quite, a smile—that made me wonder what he knew that I didn't. "I'll just go in ahead of you and turn on the lights," he said, stepping inside. "There you go. I'll be in the office

5

if you need me. If you need a break, I have a Nespresso coffee machine."

I had no intention of taking a break. I planned to load up my car with whatever was in there and get away. I hoped there wouldn't be much that I'd have to discard.

"Your mother was quite a woman. I miss her."

"About that," I said as I followed him. "Was there some kind of rental agreement on this storage space?" I was so confused.

"Of course. Your mom had it paid up until the end of this past year. I make that to be two weeks ago. I know I should have gotten in touch with you before this, but I almost didn't want to let it go."

I was getting more confused by the minute. It occurred to me that he should have contacted me the minute Mom died a year ago, but I decided that there was nothing to be gained from that conversation, and maybe he hadn't known. However, he seemed to know more about my mother's storage life than I did since I couldn't think of a single reason why Mom had this storage space that Evelyn and I had been entirely in the dark about.

"Anyway, the place is heated, so you'll be nice and toasty. There's an intercom on the inside. Let me know if you need anything. I'm here all day." With that, he gestured for me to enter, handed me the key, turned and made his way back through the snow in the direction of the office.

I stepped inside, expecting to have to let my eyes become accustomed to the gloom. I could not have been more wrong. As I entered and closed the door behind me, I felt as if I were falling through a rabbit hole. Or maybe I'd just stumbled through the looking glass. As I unwound my scarf, I said out loud, "Well, Charlie, you're certainly not in Kansas anymore." Mixed metaphors be damned.

The dazzling light made me think that there must be a hundred skylights in the place. There were, in fact, two, but the snow coating filtered the sunlight. The interior lighting was daylight LED light, but it did little to explain what I was looking at. I had expected to see boxes—there had been hundreds of them in Mom's basement and attic, so I was expecting more of the same. There wasn't a cardboard box in sight. I removed my coat and hung it on a dazzlingly shiny brass coat rack tucked in beside the door. I had expected the floor to be bare concrete, but it wasn't. It appeared to be some kind of wood laminate, so I took off my boots. The floor was so cold, though, that I quickly put them back on. Then I stood in the doorway to try to figure this out.

I looked across at the back wall, which was covered with shelving and file drawers. In the middle of the space was a vast, marble-topped counter with a drafting table at one end. There were two stools at the counter, one on either side.

Along the wall to my immediate left that should have been just one big, double garage door, the wall was covered with corkboard and a whiteboard. There were dozens of pieces of paper pinned to the corkboard and notes written on the whiteboard—all in Mom's peculiar all-caps printing. It looked as if she had just finished it and put her marker down. I felt a shiver run down my spine. I could almost feel her presence. I took a deep breath and continued to look around.

All along the left wall, there was a built-in desk of sorts with drawers and shelves beneath. On top of the long desk was what appeared to me to be a heavy-duty, industrial sewing machine and what I recognized from my recent foray into making dresses, a serger. What I knew about sewing I had learned over the past year since Mom died. I continued my perusal.

Snaking along the wall immediately facing me was a long clothes rail filled with brightly coloured clothing pieces on wooden hangers. There were three dressmakers' dummies in the far corner—one was naked while the other two were wearing what appeared to be half-sewn pieces of clothing.

I had two thoughts. The first was, *this is going to take forever to clear out*. The second thought, and perhaps more important if less practical, was: *what in the world was my mother up to here?*

I turned back toward the door and saw the intercom hanging on the wall. I tapped it. When Ed's voice came on, I said, "Ed, how long has Mom been renting this storage space?"

"Let me think a minute." He whistled softly. "I guess since sometime in the early 80s."

How was that possible? How was it possible that Mom had been doing whatever she was doing here since before Evelyn and I were even born?

"Everything okay, Charlie?"

I told him it was, then I turned and took a deep breath. Where in the world would I start?

This past year since my mother died had been one of the most extraordinary of my life. The most important lesson I learned from clearing out my mother's house was that I didn't know people as well as I thought I did. The truth was that I didn't even know myself as well as I thought I did. I learned that my mother had been a budding or at least wannabe designer back in the 1960s, but that had never been the direction of her life as I knew it. She was an accountant's wife, the mother of two daughters, a substitute English and history teacher as far as I knew. She had also been the perfect suburban housewife and the ideal widow after Dad died more than ten years ago. What, then, did all this mean? My eye immediately moved toward the filing cabinets. If anything could shed some light on this, maybe their contents could. Ed had been right. This was going to take a while.

I turned back to the whiteboard for a moment. What had Mom been writing there before she died? I felt as if I were no longer alone in this peculiar space. I turned quickly, but there was no one there. I turned back to the whiteboard and realized I couldn't even read a single word. Not through my tears.

I wiped my eyes with the back of my hand and, for the first time, noticed a cabinet in the far corner. It looked to me like it might be a record player. You know what I mean? It looked like it was one of those things that played old vinyl records. I walked over to it and lifted the top. I was right. Beside it was a shelf unit filled with those large vinyl records from back in the day. I pulled one off the shelf and looked at the jacket.

Try to Remember. The Brothers Four. I slid out a second one. The album cover was a riot of cartoon-like colour. *Cheap Thrills*, it said. Big Brother and the Holding Company. Dear god, these couldn't possibly have belonged to my mother. When I was a child, the only music I ever heard in our house was Dad's classical music and a bit of standard jazz.

I looked down at the turntable and flicked the first switch I saw. The big, flat disc started turning. I flicked it off. Then I slid the black vinyl record out of The Brothers Four jacket and placed it on the turntable like I'd seen people do on TV. I turned the switch on again and lifted the needle, placing it gently on the record. It didn't catch at first. I figured that it would have to be in one of those grooves, so I moved it in slightly. Suddenly, four-part harmony filled the room from speakers in all four corners. Try to remember, they said.

I was feeling slightly creeped out by this point. I took a deep breath and wandered around the periphery of the space, listening to the sounds of music from decades ago. I ran my hands over the marble top of the counter in the centre of the room, feeling the cold hardness beneath my fingertips. Then I walked over to the corner and stood in front of the mannequins.

"If you could talk," I said to them, "I wonder what you'd tell me. What in god's name were you up to, Mom?"

I lifted the edge of the half-finished jacket that one of them was wearing. Suddenly, it occurred to me that today was exactly one year since I'd found Mom's dusty old sewing machine hidden among the detritus in the basement of our old house. Until that day, I hadn't the slightest idea that my mother was interested in sewing, and I had no idea how that sewing machine ended up hidden in the basement. As I examined the stitching on the jacket, I ran my fingers down the bumps and could almost feel my mother's presence in the room. I could picture her here at that sewing machine, motoring her way along the seams. But why? And why here?

I then crossed the room to see if I could garner any further information from the pieces of clothing hanging on the rail. I walked along slowly. These were certainly not my mother's clothes. I pulled a jacket off the rack and held it up in front of me. There was something familiar about it. Not the piece itself, but there was something about the style. Something about using three different fabrics to make up the jacket caused me to think I might have seen it before, or at least, one like it. I wasn't a fashionista, by any means, but since I'd found Mom's sewing machine, I'd learned to sew, and, with the help of a fabric store clerk called Al (who I had come to refer to as my fabric guru) I had learned a lot about fabrics. These were high-quality, and they were familiar. I lifted the jacket closer and looked at the label.

"*Kosmic Kat.*" That's what the label said. What?

I put it back on the rack quickly. I shrugged off the zippered sweater/jacket I was wearing. I looked at the label. "*Kosmic Kat.*" I was so confused. I'd bought this very functional piece of winter clothing at a boutique near the Hydrostone Market. It was one of those tony little places that stock only the chicest cult-favourites. *Kosmic Kat* was one of those brands with a cult-like following.

I began frantically checking the labels on the other pieces hanging on the rack. They were all *Kosmic Kats*. I then turned toward the desk to the left, where I could see stacks of papers. It didn't take me long to realize that I was looking at a pile of invoices—all with the *Kosmic Kat* logo prominently displayed in the upper left-hand corner. Had my seventy-plus-year-old mother been secretly working for this company? That's when I saw them.

There were two envelopes on the desk. They were regular letter-sized envelopes. They were addressed in Mom's distinctive printing. One said, "EVELYN."

The other one said, "CHARLIE."

I Am a Rock

Simon and Garfunkel, 1965

MY HAND WAS SHAKING AS I REACHED FOR THE ENVELOPE with my name on it. I slumped into the desk chair, and as I lifted the envelope, a faint scent of a spicy perfume reached my nose. It was very soft, but it seemed I'd smelled it somewhere before. It seemed to conjure a memory of Mom when I was a child. But it wasn't what Mom regularly wore in recent years. Every year, for as long as I could remember, my father had given her a bottle of Chanel No. 5. This was not it. This one was slightly exotic, evoking images of stealth and secretiveness. *How appropriate*, I thought. The scent conjured a fuzzy image in the back of my mind, but I couldn't put my finger on it. *Oh well*, I thought, *probably not important*. I put the envelope back on the desk and sat back, wondering if I dared to open it.

I could almost hear my sister Evelyn's voice in my ear saying, "Well, for god's sake, Charlie, of course, you should open it. Why do you think Mom left it there with your name on it?" I knew that she was right.

I felt as if I probably shouldn't just rip it open, though. It seemed wrong. It seemed to beg for a more finessed approach. I wondered if Mom had a letter opener anywhere around. I opened the centre drawer in the desk. Of course, there was one there—a large-menacing-looking, silver letter opener with initials on it. "SXC." I had no idea whose initials they were.

I took a deep breath and was about to open it when my phone rang. It was Tom.

"Hey, Charlie! How's it going?"

"Oh, Tom. I honestly don't know."

"What's going on?" I heard him take what was probably a sip of coffee. "Is there a lot of stuff?"

"You could say that," I said, looking around. "I'm not sure how to attack it."

"Well, remember how you did it a year ago when you faced your Mom's overflowing basement—like the old saying about how to eat an elephant."

"One bite at a time," I said. "You're right. But, Tom, this is way more than a pile of boxes filling a basement." I heard a phone ring in the background. Tom must be in his office.

"Damn, Charlie, I gotta go. Will you be finished up by lunch?"

I checked my watch. It was ten a.m. "Not a chance. In fact," I said, "I think I'll order in some lunch. I'm going to be here a while.

"Not a problem. I'll check in with you later, and I'll make you that martini before we have to meet Andrea and Richard for dinner."

Damn! I'd forgotten that we had dinner arrangements tonight. On this January Saturday night, all I really wanted to do was have someone (Tom) pour me a dry martini with three olives and hole up on the couch in the family room to do some serious Netflix catching up. Today, more than ever, with what I was facing here, I wasn't at all sure I'd be up for socializing this evening. And the worst thing was that I couldn't bring myself to give Tom any more details about it. And I didn't know why. I only knew that there was a lot about my mother I still didn't know. And I had to find out.

I pretended that I hadn't forgotten and promised to finish up here in time for a pre-dinner drink. Then I hung up and looked at the envelope that was still staring up at me from the middle of the desk. Mom's desk. A desk I didn't know she had.

"For the love of god, Mom, what's this all about?"

As if she had somehow heard me, a sudden gust of wind blew across the desk, and I shivered as I watched the envelope as it was picked up by the breeze and settled down closer to me on the edge of the desk. I let out the breath I realized I'd been holding, then jumped.

"Sorry to startle you, Charlie."

I looked over toward the voice. Ed was standing there in the doorway in his heavy coat, holding his toque. Of course, the gust of wind had come from the open door.

"Ed. I didn't hear you open the door."

"I knocked, but I guess you were too engrossed in what you were doing to hear me. May I come in?"

"Of course, of course," I said, getting up to walk toward the door.

"I'm just on my way to pick up some lunch. Can I bring you something?" He reached into his pocket and passed me a small brown envelope. "I don't know how I could have forgotten, but your mother asked me to give you this when you got here."

"What do you mean? That would have been over a year ago. I don't understand." I looked down at the envelope that looked a bit dog-eared around the edges. I wasn't at all sure I was ready for any more surprises.

"I know, Charlie. But you will." He put his hat on. "I'll pick you up a sandwich. Back in an hour or so." Then he left, closing the door behind him.

I squeezed the envelope to determine if it might be able to tell me something more. But I felt only a lump. I'd have to open it. But first, I'd put on some more music.

I walked back over to the record player and looked down at the Brothers Four album that was now sitting still and quiet on the turntable, then looked at more of the records on the shelf. I pulled a few out, examining them one at a time. The artists' names were familiar—Ian and Sylvia, Peter and Gordon, The Seekers—so many old folkies from the 1960s. I'd been completely unaware that my mother even liked this kind of music until after she died, and an old friend of hers told me about their mutual love of folk music. Now, I would never have a chance to ask Mom why she never played her music at home. Anyway, I finally came upon a more familiar name. Simon and Garfunkel. *Sounds of Silence. This one seems appropriate*, I thought. As the music filled the room, I walked back over to the desk, sat down and placed the brown envelope on the desk beside the white one. Which would I open first? And why was this so hard? I decided that the white one probably contained a letter.

I lifted the letter opener and carefully slid it under the flap, wondering where Mom had been and what she had been doing just before she wrote this letter—which I presumed was from her.

The letter was hand-written, and yes, it was from Mom. I smoothed out the folds and put it down on the desk in front of me. *Oh, Mom*, I thought, *what do you need to tell me?*

It was dated December 1, just over a year ago, three weeks before Mom died. I swallowed hard and started to read.

"My dear, sweet Charlie.

It sounds so cliché for me to write this, but by the time you read this letter, I will have died. There would be no other reason for you to receive it, and there would be no other reason for me to write it. But here we are.

I will have died, and you, without a doubt, will already know some things about me that will have come as a surprise. Perhaps even something of a shock. Brace yourself.

Charlie, darling, you are the artist of my heart. I have known that since the first time I laid eyes on you, just born, tousled, dreamy. I knew that you were nothing like Evelyn. Your lovely older sister was born competent. She came out with a kind of defiant look that said, "Don't mess with me, Mom." And I didn't, and she has been fine. She has always been that way, but I hardly need to tell you that. You, on the other hand, never could see your competence. Your strength. It has always been bundled up in your dreams and the efforts it takes for an artistic dream to take flight. But I know it will.

I also know that you will be reading your letter before Evelyn has hers in hand. I know this because I also know that you will have been the one who will have, by now, cleaned out my house. I know that you will have found some things that made very little sense. I hope you have been able to figure out a few things about me and the life I had before you and Evelyn became my heart. I hope I will have had time to tell you some of the details in this letter, but there are no guarantees. But, as I said, brace yourself. There are a few more things you need to know.

By now, you will have met Ed. I only wish you had met him long ago, but know that he is someone you should get to know. Know that he is special to me. I'm sure he has said very little to you about anything. But if he hasn't done so already, please ask him to give you a small brown envelope. If you haven't already opened it, please put this letter down, open it, then return..."

I was starting to feel very creeped-out. To say that it is unnerving to have your mother talk to you from beyond the grave would be an understatement. I briefly wondered why she hadn't made a video recording, but I was grateful—in the extreme—that she had not. I don't think I would have been able to stand it. So, I listened to my mother's instructions, put the letter down and picked up the brown envelope. Once again, I could smell a faint hint of that spicy perfume.

I'm not sure what I expected to see when I pulled out the contents, but this wasn't it. I was holding an old-fashioned-looking gold and silver-coloured key with what looked like a ruby embedded at the top of the shaft. About two inches in total length, it wasn't big, but it packed a wallop. If this was what Mom meant by bracing myself, she was right.

I placed it down on the desk beside the letter. After contemplating it for a moment longer, I went back to Mom's letter.

"…Charlie, now that you have opened the envelope, you know that it contains a key. It's a very special key to me, and I'll get to that eventually. But for now, you need to know that it opens a mahogany box that's in the cabinet where you've likely already found my record collection. I know that collection probably surprised you, too. I fear that there are many more surprises ahead. First, I know that you probably have questions about the atelier where you find yourself…"

I looked around. So, that's what Mom called this, is it? An atelier. A studio. A workshop. Questions? You bet I had questions.

"…but that will all become clear if you just stay on this path with me for a while. I want you to find that box, sit down at my desk and open it with this key."

I went over to the record player and crouched down on the floor in front of it. The door to the space beneath the turntable was stuck, but with a little effort, it finally yielded. I opened the door and couldn't see anything in the dark. I finally put my hand inside (hoping that there were no uninvited critters within) and found a wooden box, which I pulled out into the light.

As promised, it was mahogany, but more to the point, mahogany that was gleaming. Someone had been polishing it regularly if I guessed correctly, but I wondered who it could be. It certainly hadn't been Mom. She'd been dead for over a year.

I got up off the floor and took the box over to the desk, placing it beside the letter and the key. The box was about fifteen inches long, almost half that much wide and stood about eight inches high. It had brass fittings (again, shining), including a brass keyhole. Obviously, I was meant to open it, but I thought I'd better see if Mom had said anything more before I did. To tell you the truth, I was a bit afraid of what I might find inside. This was all too weird.

"...be careful with it, Charlie, it's actually quite an important antique. But go ahead and open the box and take out its contents..."

I did as the ghost of my mother told me to do. I placed the key in the lock and turned it. I'm not sure what I expected to happen—perhaps I thought that ghostly mists would begin to emerge. Of course, nothing happened except for the fact that the beautiful key opened the box. I lifted the lid carefully.

The box was full. At the very top was a red-leather-bound book. I lifted it out and began flipping pages. Hand-written. A diary. My mother's diary.

Under the diary were photos. Hundreds of them, or so it seemed. The picture at the top of the pile looked vaguely familiar, so I picked it up and peered at it. Yes, of course. Evelyn and I had found a similar photo in a box of old pictures in Mom's attic. It was Mom again, in a slightly different pose, but there was no doubt that it had been taken at the same time as the one we had already found. Then there was another and another. Someone had done a series of photos of my mother. And I knew from having seen one before that they were taken at Woodstock. Yes, Woodstock, in 1969, a place neither Evelyn nor I could ever imagine our buttoned-down mother setting foot. She was so not a hippie, that's for sure, but in this photo, you could have drawn a different conclusion. There she was, smiling, wearing a breezy, floral dress that fell almost to her ankles and a crown of flowers in her hair. She had never looked so lovely in all the thirty-two years I'd know her. To me, as I mentioned, Mom was a prim, polite, suburban mother of two. She wore Brooks Brothers shirts and cardigans, pencil skirts and even pearls on occasion. She was no flower child. Good god…here was evidence to the contrary.

"…Now, Charlie, you need to proceed carefully. Get yourself a glass of wine, put on that Petula Clark album in the stack of records (be sure to listen to the song 'Downtown'), and settle in. You have my permission to read my diary. And you're going to want to refer to the photos. When you're finished, there is a green file folder in the front of the top drawer in my filing cabinet. Read that file, then call Evelyn. You'll know what to do."

It was signed, *"From your loving Mother, Kat."*

I really could use a drink right now, I thought, *but where would I get a glass of wine?*

I heard a faint knocking at the door of the atelier. It was Ed again. He was holding a paper bag—my lunch presumably—and a bottle of wine.

"Your Mom kept wine glasses in that cupboard over the desk," he said. "You're going to want this." He passed me the bottle of wine and reached above me for a glass.

"How did you know—?"

"How did I know you'd be needing this? Trust me," he said. "I knew." Then he turned and left, closing me off from the world.

I opened the bottle, poured myself a glass of wine then walked over to the record player to search for an album by Petula Clark. The name rang a faint bell—I had heard of her, but I wasn't so sure I'd recognize her music. What did not ring a bell, however, was that my mother had liked this singer. As I looked through the album covers, again, I saw many names I would never have associated with Mom's taste in music—or in life. I finally found the one I was looking for.

19

Staring back at me was the face of the 1960s, or so it seemed to me. With her black eyeliner, short, almost shaggy blonde hair and enigmatic smile, Petula Clark seemed to be beckoning me forward. Or perhaps she was beckoning me back. I slid the record out of its jacket, replaced the Simon and Garfunkel, then checked the track list on the album cover. "Downtown" was the last track on side two. I took the record off the turntable, turned it over, switched it on and carefully placed the needle on the vinyl. As I walked back to the desk, the music began to fill the space. I sat down, took a sip of wine, took a deep breath and opened the diary to the first page.

"Sunday, September 12, 1965…

Kat
1965–1967

Toronto

Don't Think Twice

Peter, Paul and Mary, 1963

MY FATHER'S WORDS WERE STILL RINGING IN MY EARS three months after the fact. Three months after he had told me that I could not, under any circumstances, pursue the only thing I wanted to do: study art so I could eventually be a fashion designer. I had to study to become a teacher. I hated him. And I hated my mother more for standing there and not saying a word. The only person I could talk to about it was my grandmother, who was hugely sympathetic, but there wasn't anything she could do. And now, here I was, unpacking my things and settling into a residence room at a university I really didn't want to attend, in a city I didn't know. As someone who'd never spent much time in big cities, I had begun to feel just slightly uneasy as I'd found myself being spit out of Union Station propelled along with the throngs of people quickly departing the train platforms. And now, to top it all off, I evidently had a roommate. I wondered what fresh hell this would bring. It didn't take long to find out.

Her name was Darla Cuthbert. I knew this because both our names were publicly proclaimed on one-inch-by-three-inches

21

cardboard placards in brass holders on the wall outside our door. Since it seemed that I was the first to arrive, it behooved me to claim my space quickly. I chose the bed on the left side as you walked in and its corresponding desk farther along under the window. The beds were single (of course) and were made up with institutional-looking white linen topped with flat pillows that looked as if they'd seen better days. At least I'd listened to my mother, who had insisted that I bring my own linens. That was probably my first good decision of the academic year.

I was just folding up the institutional linen when a hurricane blew in through the door.

"Oh my! Isn't this small!" The blonde and sparklingly blue-eyed young woman noticed me standing there with a bundle of sheets in my hands. "In a darling sort of way!" She stuck out her hand that jangled with what appeared to be a bracelet dripping with solid gold charms. "And you must be?"

"I must be Katherine." Then I corrected myself. I wasn't going to be Katherine here. "Kat. Kat Wilson."

"Charmed!" And she shook the ends of my fingers.

"And you are?" I wasn't going to let her get away with thinking I already knew who she was since she didn't know who I was.

"Oh my!" Darla said, her hand clinking toward her mouth. "I plumb forgot! I'm Darla."

"Darla, do I detect a slight southern accent?"

"Oh my!" *Geezus*, I thought, *this is going to be a long year*. "I suppose you just might. I spent the entire summer—the entire summer!—visiting my American kissin' cousins. I must have picked something up!"

I fervently hoped it wasn't contagious, whatever it was she had picked up. Further, I had no idea whatsoever what a kissin' cousin could possibly have been. At that moment, I wasn't at all sure I wanted to know.

Darla dropped the overstuffed, overnight bag she had been holding. It thudded to the floor. "Oh my!" she said, yet again. "Do you mind if I take that bed? I don't think I can get up on that side. I always get up on the other side." She pointed to the bed on the right.

At that moment, I just wanted to shut her up, and since I hadn't actually begun to make up the bed yet or set up my desk, I acquiesced. I hadn't yet really identified with the bed on the left, anyway. And so, we began our forced companionship, each unpacking our lives into a space that would be home—at least for this year. Maybe only this semester?

Darla asked if she could put on a record so we could hum along as we worked. I nodded absently as I refolded cardigans and arranged them in one of the four drawers in the wooden dresser that had to hold so much. I was tapping my chin with my index finger, a habit I shared with my father oddly, considering how to arrange things, when I was jolted out of my reverie by the strains of The Beach Boys belting out that they were going to have "Fun, Fun, Fun." I wondered if that just might be Darla's personal anthem. I looked up to see her bopping along, head going back and forth as she mouthed the words, all the while folding clothing pieces and putting them in drawers. I wasn't a Beach Boys fan, but she made me smile a bit anyway. The truth was, I was more of a folk music fan.

My father had been adamant that I learn to appreciate classical music to the exclusion of all other kinds, sending me for piano lessons, at which I was hopeless, for seven excruciating years. I hated every piano teacher I had ever encountered, and hated even more, those music books from the Royal Conservatory of Music. Now that I thought about it, the Royal Conservatory was a part of the University of Toronto. It said so on those bland covers. *How ironic*, I thought. *And here I am now*. Then, as if I had been hit by a bolt of lightning, hearing Darla's apparently favourite music made me think that I was no longer under my father's thumb. I could buy any kind of music I wanted. I could have Pete Seeger, The Weavers and even Harry Belafonte. I'd just have to brave the big city to find someplace to buy them. And then, maybe, borrow Darla's turntable. All in good time.

I sat down at my little wooden desk and began to arrange pens, pencils, notebooks and paper clips.

"What's this?" Darla said, over the strains of four-part harmony.

I looked up at her. She was standing between the two beds wearing pink-flowered baby doll pyjamas she'd changed into because she said that she was too warm in the slacks and silk blouse she'd been wearing (she *had* been a tad over-dressed for this hot September day). She had one hand on her hip, and in her other hand, she was holding a notebook. My notebook. My sketchbook, to be exact. I was overtaken by a feeling of stark vulnerability, something that was wholly unfamiliar to me until that moment—except when confronting my father.

Before I had a chance to snatch it from her, she sat down on the side of her bed, opened the cover and started turning pages. As I watched, I wasn't sure whether I wanted her to stop so that I could maintain my secret life as an artist of sorts, or I wanted her to continue—and be impressed. I wasn't sure it would impress her, though. I'd seen some of the clothing pieces she'd been stashing in drawers and on hangers. I had seen cashmere cardigans, silk blouses, tweed skirts, numerous shift dresses and soft leather shoes—Mary Jane's with their ubiquitous little straps as well as kitten-heel pumps and a pair of Keds. The latter seemed to be more my style. There was even a suit. When I sneaked a look at the label, I almost swallowed my tongue. It said, "Yves St. Laurent." This was a young woman with some serious money behind her.

"Katherine," she said slowly, raising her head.

"Kat," I said automatically.

"Oh, I think you're a Katherine," she said. "Is this yours? Did you do these?" She pointed to a page with a series of sketches of mini-skirted shift dresses with what I thought were innovative neckline and waist details.

"Guilty as charged," I said.

"Katherine," she continued, paging through the sketches. "These are freakin' unreal! You're a genius!" She stopped at a page and pointed. "This one! I love this one!"

I hadn't realized that this was the sketchbook I devoted strictly to fashion sketches. I liked to sketch outfits I'd seen on the street, but I was particularly fond of rearranging them to develop my own interpretations. Mini-skirts were a personal favourite of mine, possibly because I was forbidden to wear them. *But now*, I thought, *I can!*

I looked at the sketch Darla seemed to love so much. It was a page of drawings I'd done more than a year before when everyone was planning prom dresses. Prom dresses weren't my personal focus, but at the time, it had been fun. Darla was pointing to a particularly sexy one, in my opinion, with its Grecian goddess vibe, swathes of glittering fabric and a single shoulder.

"Do you make them, too?" Darla had a slight, knowing smile playing across her pink-lipsticked lips. I could almost see the wheels in her brain turning around and around.

"Sadly, no," I said. "I could, but I don't have my sewing machine with me. My parents thought I'd spend too much time sewing and not enough time studying."

Darla sat back, still clutching the sketchbook. "Well," she said, "if you had one here, would you be able to make it?"

"I suppose, but it's moot, isn't it?"

Darla frowned.

I continued. "Irrelevant? I don't have one, and I can't see that I'm going to have one in the near future. Anyway, why would you want it?"

"Katherine!" She almost screeched. "Don't you know about the parties? The frat parties and sorority mixers? There will be at least four formals this year alone, and we'll need a different dress for each one!"

Geezus, I thought, *and here was I thinking that I was at university to study and get a degree.*

"Katherine, if I had a sewing machine and let you borrow it, would you consider making this one for me?" She held it out in front of me again.

My mind was racing because, although I'd been sketching my own designs for years—since I was about twelve years old, anyway—I had never made one. I had made clothing from commercial patterns for myself but had never dared to try my hand at making a pattern for a design I'd created myself—especially for someone else.

"Well," I said slowly, trying to think clearly about this prospect. "Again, since neither one of us actually has a sewing machine, I don't see how I could."

Darla's eyes were dancing now. "I'll be calling Daddy this evening to let him know I'm settling in well. And that I have a treasure for a roommate. I'll ask him to buy me a sewing machine and send it to me. Shouldn't take too long."

"And, just like that, he'll send you a sewing machine?"

She looked at me as if she might be eyeing up a small child—a rather daft small child at that. "Katherine, of course, Daddy will send me a sewing machine." She put the sketchbook down and went over to her desk. She picked up a pencil from among the mess of books and sweaters that were still perched there. "So, we have a deal?" she said, eyeing me closely.

I nodded. Darla's smile was so wide, and her teeth were so dazzling, I almost had to shield my eyes from their brilliance. She stood up quickly and was on me with a bear hug before I knew what was happening. She smelled faintly of a spicy, slightly wicked foreign fragrance.

Then she returned to her seat, put the pencil to paper and said, "Now, then, tell me what kind of sewing machine you want. I presume there are different brands?"

I knew in a flash that I could not, under any circumstances, think twice about this. My first year at university suddenly didn't seem to look quite so dreary.

Downtown

Petula Clark, 1963

IF I HAD HOPED TO EXPLORE THE CITY to find music stores and perhaps even fabric stores in those first days on campus, two things were holding me back. First, I had so much to do as the semester started—getting registered for courses, finding the library, the dining rooms, the washrooms, finding my way around the campus. The second thing holding me back was a bit more difficult for me to face. The truth was that I was just a bit frightened of the city. Despite my veneer of worldliness that I hoped Darla bought, I was a small-town girl with little experience of a city as big as this one. And I didn't like that feeling of vulnerability it summoned.

The first thing I had to get used to was the new living arrangement that I considered might be a bit of an adjustment for an only child. I was living in one of the many women's residences on campus. The building itself was designed to resemble a private home—a very large private home. Made entirely from grey stone, the "house" welcomed new students onto a large front porch with an overhead canopy held up by four fat columns reaching up the entire four stories to the roof. On either side of the massive double doors were large bay windows. As you entered the spacious central hall, the main common room with

28

an imposing fireplace and that large bay window was on the right. As you peered into the common room, staring at you from the wall above that fireplace was a massive oil painting of a woman who seemed to stare through you as you made eye contact. I had no idea who she was, but I was reasonably sure she had been "someone" in her day. On the left side of the front foyer was the dining room, where meals were served at four-or-six-person tables covered with snowy white tablecloths. Directly ahead of you was a central staircase that divided half-way up.

My room was on the fourth floor—as were all the freshmen rooms—meaning that we had to trudge up four flights to reach our little rooms. We were practically in the attic, but I didn't mind at all. I was away from home. On the first day, as I walked in, I could see young women running up and down the stairs excitedly chatting to one another as their pony-tails flew out behind them and their summer dresses billowed around them. It was clear to me that the British fashion invasion hadn't hit college co-eds yet. There wasn't a mini-skirt in sight. I vowed I would change that. I would buy one the minute I had the chance now that I wasn't living at home anymore.

As I sat in the dining room that evening—waiting to be served my dinner, yes, served—I began to feel as if I'd fallen down a rabbit hole. Until that moment, I had eaten practically every meal with my mother and father, and occasionally my grandmother, seated around their large, heavy dining room table, politely asking someone to pass this or that. My father would ask what I'd done that day. I'd tell him that I worked on a new sewing project and studied Latin. He'd say, "You'd have more time to study if you'd stop that trivial activity." My mother would hush him gently. My grandmother would say, "James, leave the girl alone. She's an artist." My father would look daggers at his mother, but he would never challenge her. This evening's dinner was so different.

I was assigned to sit at a table of six. We were required to take these places every evening for this semester, after which we would have a table change. At breakfast and lunch, we could sit wherever we wanted, with whomever we wanted. But we were expected to dress "properly" for dinner and be on time, at least that's what our housemother said as she greeted us all and asked us to join her in saying grace.

"Let us pray," she said, and the other five girls at my table immediately bowed their heads as if they had been taught to act on command, like trained seals. I had resisted my father's religious training vehemently, much to his chagrin. I held my hands together tightly in my lap and stared straight ahead as the housemother, in a toneless drone, implored us to thank God.

When she had finished, everyone immediately pulled their linen napkins onto their laps, and the chatter began. It occurred to me that I could put up with the nightly recitation of "grace" if table chatter followed, a most unaccustomed activity for me.

We each introduced ourselves then the conversation moved quickly to sorority pledging, an activity that was of little interest to me. I looked across the table at Nancy, who had just introduced herself, and watched her as she ate quietly, not engaging in the conversation at all.

Nancy had dark hair held back in a low ponytail, and she wore large, dark-rimmed glasses. I suppose she might have been someone unkindly described as mousy. "Nancy," I said, "what are you planning to study?"

She immediately brightened up, and I knew that my first impression of her had been correct. Like me, she had come to university to get an education, not a husband, which was clearly the objective of the other four girls at the table, Darla, chief among them.

"I plan to go to medical school," Nancy said. At that remark, our four table mates stopped their chatter.

"You want to be a doctor?" Darla said, now interested in the conversation.

Nancy nodded. "Both of my parents are doctors."

"Oh," Darla continued, "medical school and law school are the best places to meet boys. But you might need a makeover before then!"

Nancy looked horrified, but before she had a chance to say anything, Darla turned to the entire table and continued. "Ladies, I need to tell you a very important thing about Katherine here."

What in the world is she on about? Oh, no, I thought. *She's going to tell them about my sketches.*

"Katherine is a fashion designer!" she said loudly.

There was a hushed silence. Even the girls at the next table stopped chattering for a moment. I wanted to crawl into a hole. I certainly wasn't a designer. "It's really only a few sketches. I just like to draw," I said weakly.

"She is too modest," Darla said. "And I'm going to have a Katherine Wilson original for the first formal!" She clapped her hands in glee.

It was going to be a longer semester than I had planned.

~

The next day, Nancy and I left the house together to see if we could register for our courses. As soon as we arrived at the gym, where massive numbers of tables staffed by professors and their assistants were set up, we parted ways. She was off to find the tables representing the science departments. I went in search of something called "English Language and Literature." That was the program into which I'd been accepted. Now I just had to select my courses.

I looked around and spotted the hand-drawn sign. I sighed, observing that the line-up snaked almost the entire way around the auditorium. It seemed that the honours Bachelor of Arts program was a very popular choice. At least I'd have time to review the calendar and select the optional courses before I reached the desk and the point of no return for the year.

I had decided to register for French and Italian—both of these seemed to be languages I could benefit from. I already spoke rudimentary French from my high school classes, so this was an easy choice. I had to choose from among a group of courses that included Fine Art, Greek and Roman History and Philosophy. And, of course, I had to take an English course or two.

An hour later, I finally got to the front of the line. The professor who greeted me didn't bother introducing himself but got straight to the point, informing me that the Italian course was already full, and I'd have to take Slavic Studies, whatever that was. The Fine Art option was "Ancient and Medieval Art," something that didn't hold a lot of appeal for me, but it was better than the thought of having to take Latin again. It hadn't occurred to me that I wouldn't be able to get into all my preferred classes. I'd have to arrive earlier next year.

Thus, I began my academic career. It turned out that I actually liked studying ancient and medieval art, which, by the end of three classes, had already inspired some new sketches. I also discovered that Slavic Studies was interesting and that the French course was dull. We had to spend three hours a week in a language lab where we sat in little cubicles and listened through headphones to a tape of French conversations that we then had to repeat. It was a few weeks later before I had the time even to consider exploring off-campus. My first step would be to find out where I could buy records. The second, and more difficult step, would be to pluck up the courage to venture out on my own. The first step fell into my lap.

It was Friday afternoon, and I'd just come from a dull hour in the language lab. I decided to take a cup of tea into the common room to recover before mounting the stairs to my room to prepare for an evening of popcorn and reading. It would be the calm before the storm. Tomorrow evening, Darla had arranged (in fact, she had insisted) for me to attend a fraternity party with her. I was dreading all that forced conviviality.

I sat down at one of the couches whose peach-coloured chintz upholstery matched the peach-coloured chintz drapes. I put my cup on the table beside what looked like a newspaper. *The Varsity*, the student newspaper. *This looks interesting*, I thought, picking it up.

I took a sip of tea then started paging through it. There was an article about the bookstore offering discounts, a few pieces about how the national student union was going to fight to abolish tuition fees, a few ads for clothing stores, an article about how the engineering students were rejoicing that there were more girls registered this year and then I saw it. On page seven, just below an advertisement for "Kitten Sweaters, Skirts and Slims," there it was.

"Sam the Record Man," it said. "Canada's largest and best-known record store...bus stops at *Sam's* door." Then, "Super-special discounts for students." I had to find out where 347 Yonge Street was.

The next day was Saturday. After consulting a map of the city I found in the front hall, I discovered that it would take me only half an hour to walk from my residence to *Sam's*. So, after lunch, I tucked my largest handbag under my arm, put on my most comfortable walking shoes (the ones that didn't look too ugly with a pencil skirt) and headed out. I studiously avoided everyone so that I could maintain my courage. I was venturing downtown alone in a city I didn't know. I hoped I'd be safe—because I was determined to find some music.

Fifteen minutes later, as I walked along Yonge Street, I felt as if I had landed on another planet. There were crowds of people—all kinds of people. People who looked as if they hadn't a penny to their names. People who looked as if they had just stepped out of a Rolls Royce. But mostly, they seemed to be under thirty and so worldly—more worldly than I ever imagined I could be. Suddenly, I wanted to be like them. I wanted to strut along with all the confidence in the world, feeling as if I truly belonged. I looked down at my little sweater and pencil skirt and sensible shoes, and I felt prissy. Old-fashioned. I was an artist, damn it, and I was going to start behaving like one.

I suddenly found myself outside *Sam's*. I looked up at the vast, red marquee and smiled. I joined the throng of young people going in and quickly tried to get my bearings since everyone else seemed to know exactly where they were going. I saw a sign that said "Folk Music" and followed the arrow upstairs. As I reached the top, I knew I was in heaven. There were records as far as the eye could see. Where to begin?

I took a deep breath and realized that I was no longer nervous. I was downtown Toronto—about a million miles from where I'd started last month, in more ways than one. I began to concentrate on the records when it occurred to me that I'd probably have to get a job if I wanted to buy records and new clothes. My father would never agree to increasing my allowance for those purchases. But that could wait. Today I would buy two or three records and start a collection of music that I loved.

I was thumbing through albums by The Weavers when someone came up behind me.

"I think you might like this one."

I turned and looked at the album that was being held out in front of me. Bob Dylan was staring out at me.

"It came out last year. If you don't have it, you should."

Just One Look

The Hollies, 1964

I LOOKED UP FROM THE ALBUM COVER to find myself staring into a pair of penetrating dark eyes framed by a mop of dark hair flopping over a forehead.

"Yes," I said when I finally found my voice. "I think I would like that." The times they are a-changing, indeed.

"I haven't seen you in here before," he said as he flipped through the bin of records beside me.

"I, well, I've never...I mean, I..." What in the world was wrong with me? I'd talked to my share of "boys" in high school. But suddenly, this seemed so different. It seemed as if this young "man" might be expecting me to be an actual adult.

"Hey, this is cool," he said, seemingly oblivious to my lack of verbal coherence. "You should get this one."

I fixed my gaze on the face staring out from this cover. The face was unfamiliar, but the album name was not—*Eve of Destruction* by Barry McGuire. I remembered the name distinctly because the album was released just a few weeks before I'd left home, and the song quickly became a kind of touchstone for argument. Some radio stations in the U.S. had even banned it. My father read about it one evening in the newspaper, after

35

which he had taken great pains to lament the state of young people these days. Always protesting things they knew nothing about, he said. End of conversation.

"Um, yes," I said, finally finding my tongue—in a matter of speaking. On the bright side, things could only get better from here. "Yes, I think I'd like that one."

"Have you ever heard it?" Was he baiting me? Well, I could play that game.

"No," I said, turning to look at him. "I haven't heard it, but given the importance of the topics it raises, I think that it might be one of those records I should have in my collection." I felt as if I should bat my eyes now. I did not.

"Yeah," he said, "you dig it. Yeah." He kept thumbing through the bin. "You from around here?"

"I'm a student at the U. of T.," I said, realizing that this was the first time I'd identified myself that way. It felt good. It felt almost grown-up.

"Good school," he said. He lifted another album from the bin and held it out to me. I took it from him and looked at it. "Bet you haven't heard this one."

The picture on the cover was one of those quintessential, gritty, downtown scenes. A grimy alley, it was home to posters in various stages of peeling off the red brick walls with a graffiti peace sign as a kind of bullseye. The young man sitting on the ground propped up against the wall seemed to be defying anyone to argue with him. The young singer's name was Phil Ochs, and the album was called *I Ain't Marching Anymore*. I had never heard of Phil Ochs, and I certainly had not heard the song—but I was fascinated. I knew I had to hear it. When I looked up to thank him for the suggestion, the young man who had handed it to me had vanished. Fifteen minutes later, when I walked out of the store, I was in the company of Bob, Barry and my new man, Phil. I hoped Darla would lend me her record player.

When I arrived on the fourth floor of my residence, the girls were in full-on prep mode. I had been so focused on looking forward to hearing some new music that it had completely slipped my mind. Tonight was the first major fraternity party.

"There you are!" Darla stuck her head out of our room. She had huge, pink rollers in her hair and some kind of a gross-looking blue guck thing all over her face. "I thought you might have forgotten."

"Oh, no," I said, lying through my teeth. "Anyway, it's only five o'clock. There's lots of time."

"Lots of time! There is not lots of time. It's going to take you at least an hour to do your hair!"

"My hair?" I touched my hair. "What's wrong with my hair? It's clean."

"On my god, Katherine!" Darla still refused to call me Kat. "It's a party!"

As I placed the bag of records on my bed and swung my shoulder bag down beside it, I wished, with all my heart, that Darla would stop speaking with exclamation points. "Okay, Darla. I'll do something with my hair." I wasn't sure what was wrong with a headband that pulled my thick, dark-blonde locks off my face so that they could fall freely down my back. But, what harm could there be in doing something with my hair? Then, I looked over at the dress she had placed on a hanger outside her closet door. "Nice colour," I said, pointing to the dress.

"Do you think so?" Darla took it off the door and held it up in front of her. It was red, with a small collar and buttons down to the hem. It had short, cap sleeves and looked like it would probably fall somewhere south of her knees at a most unflattering (in my opinion) point. To tell you the truth, it looked suspiciously like a dress her mother was wearing in a family photo Darla kept on her desk—Mom, Dad, Darla and her younger brother on the steps of some sort of building with massive columns. I thought it best not to mention this resemblance at that moment.

The dress was pretty, and I did like it, but to my eye, it looked as if it might be too long for a young woman. Now that I thought about it, the dress I was planning to wear was also too long. I suddenly felt an idea pop into my head. I would take up the hems in both our dresses. Darla's father had evidently agreed immediately to procuring a sewing machine for his daughter—no questions asked—but it had not yet arrived. No matter. This job didn't require a machine. I could have both of the dresses hemmed in about half an hour.

"Darla, how would you feel about wearing your dress more like they're wearing them in London these days?"

"What do you mean?"

"Well," I said, pulling a magazine out from under my French textbook, "look at this." I opened the magazine to an article I'd marked. It was a short article on a British designer named Mary Quant. The two dresses shown on the page were both cut just above the knee. "What do you think of these hemlines?"

"Oh, Katherine! They look so sophisticated on those girls." She picked up the magazine and took a closer look. Then she looked up at me. "Do you really think I can pull this off?"

"We both can, Darla." I went over to my closet and pulled out the dress I was planning to wear. It was a black and white houndstooth check with a wide neckline framed by a white collar. It had long sleeves that ended in cuffs. Although I had loved the design when I bought the pattern (I had made it a month before I left home as part of my new university wardrobe), I felt just a tad like a nun whenever I put it on. It was a Mary Quant-designed pattern, so its lines were fabulous—straight up and down—but it bordered on dowdy, in my view. Now I realized what was wrong. It was too long. And just like that, I took out my sewing scissors, cut off the hems of two dresses and set about sewing them by hand as fast as I could. I even let Darla put rollers in my hair while I worked.

By the time I had finished them, and we tried them on, we concluded that they were perfect.

"Oh, Katherine," Darla said as she stood in front of the full-length mirror she'd had installed on the back of our door. "This is beyond cool! I look so… so…mature! But…" She turned toward me. I could see that a dark cloud was beginning to flit across her face. "Do you think they might be a bit too risqué?"

"Risqué? Because they're above our knees? Have you seen magazine pictures of some of the girls in London? I mean, those skirts are seriously short."

Darla nodded, and the smile returned to her face. "Do you think boys like these skirt lengths?"

"Really, Darla? What do you think?"

She giggled at that. "Anyway," she said as she sat down to put on her matching red kitten heel pumps, "we'll be the trendiest girls at the party!"

Oh, were we ever wrong! The thought that I wasn't in Kansas anymore, like Dorothy in the *Wizard of Oz*, popped into my head (like it had been doing a lot recently) the moment we reached the bottom of the porch steps at Delta Delta Kappa, the fraternity hosting the party that evening.

It was a chilly evening, so we were both wearing light coats, as were the other six or so girls from our residence who arrived with us. As I looked at the other young women hurrying up the steps—because, unlike us girls, they were, indeed, young women—grasping filmy shawls around their shoulders as they balanced clutch bags under their arms, I began to feel just a tad dowdy—again. This was getting to be a habit with me since I'd arrived in the big city. I felt as if I'd just fallen off the turnip truck. I was like a misshapen pearl that had somehow landed among a group of glittering diamonds and sapphires. And this wasn't even a formal event, far from it. This was a late-September,

Saturday evening mixer. I made my mind up there and then that neither wild horses nor Darla could drag me to a formal event later in the semester.

"Oh, Katherine," Darla said excitedly, evidently not feeling as dowdy as I did. "There's Imogen Chandler!" She was pointing to one of the glittering diamonds, who was standing on the porch at the top of the steps in the middle of a group of admiring young men. This particular diamond was sporting a slinky, navy-blue dress that shimmered as she moved. It had a hemline that skimmed the top of her calves, but length notwithstanding, it was smashing.

"Who's Imogen Chandler?" I said.

Darla then took a moment before we began our own ascent into the abyss (can you ascend into an abyss?) to tell me about Imogen. I began to wonder if this is what the Galactic Empire's Mad Mind felt like when it was pushed to the edge of the galaxy. You know the one. Arthur C. Clarke's first novel, *The City and the Stars,* had been popular when I was in high school. As it turned out, Imogen was the current president of the sorority Darla was hoping to join. The following week, the sorority would decide who would be invited to join, so tonight was very important.

We hadn't been there for more than twenty minutes when I remembered why I hadn't wanted to go. The greeters on the porch were clearly neither freshmen members of the fraternity nor were they seniors. I drew this conclusion from two facts. It was too early in the year for the pledges to be greeting anyone (I learned this word from Darla, who had been boning up on the Greek societies on campus). The second fact was that two, pipe-smoking, tweed-jacket-wearing gentlemen—I use the word loosely—whose behaviour suggested that they thought quite highly of themselves, were standing in the doorway telling the greeters what to do. As we reached the top of the steps, each of the greeters took our hands, looked us up and down and said, "Welcome. You may now enter Delta Delta Kappa." It was as if they might, at any moment, decide that one or more of the girls might be unworthy. When I asked Darla about this later, she shrugged me off.

We could hear music and laughter wafting out into the fall evening. As we made our way into the house, I began to feel claustrophobic with the masses of people jammed up against one another, the aroma of cigarette smoke and the faint pong of alcohol hanging in the air like a kind of miasma. There was also something else, but I couldn't identify its sweet scent. And there were so many people. I'm not sure what I had expected, but this wasn't it. My preconceptions were fuelled by my apparent misinterpretation of Darla's descriptions of the sorority girls who, according to her, were like some sainted apparitions of budding womanhood. As far as I could tell, they were a gyrating mass of pent-up female hormones that had the males of the species circling them before coming in for the kill.

"Let's go downstairs," Darla said, pulling me by the arm as she moved toward the staircase.

"What's downstairs?"

"The bar, of course," she said as I slowly followed her.

"How do you know that? Have you been here before?"

"No, silly, of course, I haven't been here before. But I certainly did do a bit of reconnaissance. I never go to a party without investigating the place and the people. My parents taught me that. You just have to ask the right people the right questions."

I wished that my parents had taught me something so concretely useful. Since the scene upstairs was just a tad scary, I figured that the basement couldn't be much worse. I was wrong.

As we reached the bottom of the staircase, I could hear the Beach Boys screaming that they wanted everyone to be a California Girl and the gyrating bodies singing along at the tops of their lungs. It was dark and cramped, with a low ceiling, but that didn't seem to bother anyone. It was clear to me that they had been drinking (I'm a sucker for understatement.).

"Darla," I said, hissing as loudly as I could directly into her ear, "there's probably alcohol here. We're under-age."

Darla rolled her eyes at me and continued to drag me toward the bar, dipping and dodging as necessary to make her way to the long, wooden bar that was clearly being operated by frat newbies. They were run off their feet.

"Two beers," she said as we finally found a space at the bar. She retrieved some money from her purse and put it on the bar, trying to avoid pools of beer that were already there.

"I don't actually like beer," I said. I had only ever had one beer in my life.

"God, Katherine. You're starting to sound like a drip. Would you rather have that hideous punch they're serving upstairs?" I said nothing. She took that as a no. "Good, then. Here's your beer," she said, handing me one of those brown, glass stubbies.

I sipped it a bit—it wasn't bad—and we turned toward the party.

"Isn't this fabulous?" she said, her eyes sparkling.

I grunted in response.

"Oh my god," she said, "he's looking at me. Don't look over. He might see us looking at him."

"Him?" I said, nodding toward a young man in the middle of a group of giggling girls. He was wearing a blue and gold-striped ascot with a white shirt and a navy-blue blazer. His trousers were grey flannel, and he was wearing what looked like expensive leather loafers without socks. I had never actually seen anyone in the flesh wearing an ascot. I was mesmerized.

"Stop looking at him!" Darla hissed.

He began to extricate himself from the group around him and made his way over to the bar. A few people moved aside. He must have been "someone."

"Hi there," he said to Darla when he finally reached us. "I like your style." He looked her up and down. "Great dress."

Darla smiled that dazzling smile of hers, and he seemed momentarily blinded. In a split second, he regained his poise and extended his hand—the one that wasn't holding a pipe that looked exactly like the one my father smoked out in the garage. "I'm Thomas Bevan-Rhyss II," he said, holding her hand for dear life.

Darla introduced herself then, "Oh, Thomas, this is my friend Katherine."

I held out my hand. "It's Kat."

He looked at me for a moment. "Kat. Hmm." Then he turned back to Darla.

The rest of the evening was something of a bore. Darla spent it cozying up to Thomas—or the other way around. I'm not sure who was leading the way. A skinny young man with a serious halitosis problem asked me to dance. I did, then excused myself to find the ladies' room. That was a mistake. The line was ten-deep, but since I had to use the facilities after finishing my very first beer, I figured I could use them back at residence. It was time to hit the road. Darla would never notice if I slipped out. And our residence was only two blocks away, so she'd be just as safe getting home as I would.

As I ran down the steps and out onto the sidewalk, I realized that this evening had given me as much of a taste of the fraternity/sorority life as I would ever need.

~

It was lunch-time on Monday, as I made my way across the lawn in front of Hart House, still thinking about my first university social event, when I found myself in a group of students gathered around a speaker holding a megaphone.

I was standing beside a young woman wearing a blue beret, rakishly poised at an angle on her dark curls. She was clutching two fat textbooks as she listened intently to the speaker. He was

43

saying something about principles and the right to higher education.

"This is not a protest," he said. "This is an expression of our concern for the next generation of students. It's our right to be here. It should be everyone's right!"

"Isn't he marvellous?" the young woman said as he took a breath.

I stood on my toes for a better view. The speaker somehow looked familiar. "Who is he?" I said. "Do you know who he is?"

"I'd love to *know* him if you know what I mean. Don't *you* know who he is?"

"I'm kind of new here," I said. "I hardly know anyone."

"That's Eddie Lancaster," she said.

And suddenly, I did know who he was. Eddie Lancaster was the mysterious young man whose taste in music was now affecting my taste in— well, just about everything. I had met Eddie at *Sam's*.

Catch the Wind

Donovan, 1965

THE YOUNG WOMAN TURNED TO LOOK AT ME. "By the way, I'm Liz," she said.

"I'm Kat," I said. "And I love your beret."

"Thanks! Nice to meet you, Kat."

Eddie had finished speaking, and the group was breaking up so that they could march to the legislature in support of access to higher education. I'd never followed protests or student rallies very much, but it seemed that there might be a bit more to them than I had thought. At home, the only student protests I'd ever seen had been on the television news at six p.m., where they showed Vietnam war protests in the U.S. almost every evening.

Liz and I started walking away together.

"So, Kat, what's your major?"

"English and history. First year. Yours?"

"English right now. I'm in second year, but what I really want to do is teach."

I laughed. Liz wanted to be a teacher. I didn't, but I probably would be anyway. "You want to be an English teacher?"

"Not English. I want to be a Home Economics teacher, but I may have to finish my degree back home."

45

"Really?" I thought this was fascinating. "Where's home for you?"

"Halifax," Liz said. "On the east coast."

"You won't believe this," I said, "but that's where I'm from?"

"For real? Why have we never met before?"

It turned out that we had gone to different high schools. Liz had gone to the Catholic high school; I had not. She was a year ahead of me and had been in Toronto a year longer, but seemed light years ahead of me in sophistication.

"Kat, do you like folk music?"

"Do I ever!"

"Next weekend, a few of us are going to *The Riverboat* coffeehouse in Yorkville to listen to some new musicians. Why don't you come with us? I think you'd like the group I hang out with."

I felt a little prickle of excitement when Liz mentioned Yorkville. It was a very different prickle than the shudder I'd felt when Darla had invited me to the frat party. I had overheard a few things about Yorkville. According to the latest gossip around the residence, it was something of a den of iniquity, full of artists, musicians and general-all-around Bohemian types.

"Sure. I'd love to."

We made arrangements to meet outside my residence on Saturday evening. The city's Yorkville area was only about a fifteen-minute walk, so we'd go as a group. I could hardly believe my luck. Now, all I wanted to do was spend a bit of quality time listening to the new albums I'd bought. But that was going to have to wait.

Later that afternoon, when I arrived back in my residence room, Darla was bending over a large cardboard box that she'd placed on the floor between our two beds.

"Katherine, it's here!" Darla was excited. But, so was I. The sewing machine had arrived. I would finally be able to create one of my own designs.

We managed to get it out of the box and put it in the middle of my desk. I wondered how I'd be able to use the desk for studying, but given that Darla liked to listen to music while she studied, and I needed complete quiet, I would be spending most of my study time in the library. I'd use my desk as my sewing station.

I retrieved the instruction booklet from the bottom of the cardboard box before we flattened it so that Darla could take it down to the basement, where we had to put large pieces of garbage. I sat on the edge of my bed, staring at this brand new, top-of-the-line machine. I wished that it was mine, but having use of it was the next best thing. When Darla returned, she began prattling on about the fabric for the dress.

"Take a breath, Darla," I said. "We have lots of time. I'll figure out the best place to find the fabric, and then we can get to work." By we, I meant me. I wondered if Liz, with her interest in home economics, would know the best places to shop for the city's fabrics. Anyone who wanted to be a home economics teacher was surely interested in sewing. I'd have to ask her on the weekend.

For the rest of the week, whenever I found myself in the library, ostensibly studying, my mind kept drifting back to Eddie up there with his megaphone, rallying the students to do something to make a difference in the future. It was commendable, to be sure. I had been mesmerized by his ability to capture their imaginations. He captured mine, and I wasn't even the slightest bit knowledgeable about their objective. I was sitting at one of the large tables in the library, with my books and notes scattered around me as if to protect my little space, thinking about Eddie. I was thinking about what it would be like to get to know him—and not just as a protest leader. I'd have to ask Liz if she knew anything more about him.

~

When Saturday evening rolled around, I was standing outside my residence in the chilly air, waiting for Liz as we'd arranged. Since I didn't smoke, I just stood there fiddling with my scarf when I heard Liz's voice and laughter approaching.

She was in the middle of a group of five, two other girls and two boys—or perhaps, young women and young men. They were arm-in-arm, laughing and talking as they came toward me. When Liz saw me, she broke away from the group and hurried along the sidewalk, waving.

She threw her cigarette butt down then stamped on it before taking me by the arm while the rest of the group caught up to her. "Kat, this is Marilyn, Debbie, Frank and Philip. Everyone, this is Kat."

I had been a bit nervous about being the odd man out in a group that knew each other well. I needn't have worried. Philip took my other arm, and it was as if we had all known one another forever. Fifteen minutes later, I felt as if I had walked onto a different planet.

Yorkville was a revelation to me. In addition to the gossip going around the residence, I had heard stories about Yorkville even before I arrived in the city. It was the kind of place that made the national news from time to time. There was nothing the national news reporters liked better, it seemed, than a salacious story about ne'er-do-well young adults, presumably drug-infested establishments and free-living bohemian artists. It was so not like mainstream society. And it was so not like me. But as we rounded the corner onto Yorkville Avenue, we came face-to-face with the Saturday night crowd. I was enthralled.

We walked past knots of people on the street smoking in front of funky, little boutiques that I longed to get inside (alas, they were all closed), edgy art galleries that looked as if they held the secrets of the soul and other venues where acoustic-guitar music wafted out onto the sidewalk to mingle with sounds of muffled laughter and the clouds of sickly, sweet-smelling smoke. Much to my embarrassment, I asked what that smell was. Judging from the incredulous looks on everyone's face when they turned to look at me, I was supposed to know. Frank held in his laughter as he whispered to my ear, "That's grass, Kat. Weed?" Of course, it was. I'd never have to be told again.

The line-up to get into *The Riverboat* coffeehouse, obviously one of *the* places to be on a Saturday night, snaked down the street. The would-be patrons seemed to be a mix of university students, older folkies and a few kids who looked like they'd just escaped from suburbia, with their fashionable clothes and slicked-down hair. They were all smoking. It looked so cool I figured I might have to give it a try.

We took our place in the line and hoped that we'd get in before the evening was over. We were in luck. We finally made it to the front of the line. We took the few steps down to below street level and were instantly inside yet another world. I looked around, trying to take in every detail of the place and the people. I didn't want to forget this.

Once my eyes had adjusted to the dim light, I could see that the walls were covered in a light panelling that looked as if it might be pine. All around, there were red booths and brass portholes on the walls. We squeezed ourselves between the people visiting other groups and found a spot close to the stage. We all crammed into a booth that was clearly designed for fewer people. I was in heaven.

We sipped the coffees we'd picked up at the bar on the way to our table and were settled just in time for the next act.

As I was settling back to enjoy the music, I saw him. Wearing a black leather jacket, jeans and a beret, Eddie Lancaster had just walked into *The Riverboat*.

Kat, I said to myself, *give it up. You're trying to catch the wind.*

You Were on My Mind

We Five, 1965

THE MOMENT I SET EYES ON EDDIE across the dim, crowded space, I stopped hearing the music. Everyone in the place seemed to know him. As I watched him effortlessly make his way across the room, nodding and shaking hands, I was reminded of a politician on the campaign trail. His expression, though, was more one of concentration, of genuinely caring about what people were saying. There was no false smile, no forced joviality. His demeanour was one of attentiveness as if whatever anyone said to him was important. I hoped he might make his way over to our table.

I looked around at the others at my table. Intensely focused on the stage, they all seemed to be listening intently to the three musicians who were doing a cover of a new song by the group We Five. Liz suddenly shook her head.

"Not as good as Ian and Sylvia's version," she said to no one in particular. The others nodded. I wasn't at all sure any of them were listening. "Come on, guys, you know what I mean. That's kind of a pop version. The folk version—the original version is what it's all about."

Ian and Sylvia were a kind of newish Canadian folk duo—they might even have been married to each other, although I wasn't sure. Anyway, Ian played a twelve-string guitar (the sound of which I loved—clearly, Liz did, too), and the two of them sang amazing harmonies. These ones on stage were channelling a pop version done by a popular quintet. It kind of lost something in the translation by three amateurs, but it was a version that I quite liked, to be honest. I wondered what Eddie thought. After all, he did seem to be a music lover. I turned back toward him.

He had taken a seat not far from our booth and was sipping a cup of coffee, his beret now on the table in front of him. I watched him run his fingers through his thick hair.

"What are you looking at?" Liz said, noticing my inattention to the music. Her eyes moved in the direction I was staring. "Oh, I see." Then she smiled. "Someone has a crush on Eddie."

I turned to her, pouting. "I wouldn't say that."

"I would." Liz was laughing quietly. "Why don't you go over and talk to him?"

"Me? Talk to Eddie Lancaster? Eddie Lancaster, who seems to practically own the place?" I whispered. "Tell me about him. Is he a student?"

The musicians had stopped and were now telling the crowd about having just come from playing a gig in Montreal on the McGill campus and that they were from Winnipeg.

"All I know about him is that he's a grad student in media studies. There's this thing called the Centre for Culture and Technology on campus. A kind of famous prof runs it. I think his name is McLuhan or something. Anyway, Eddie has become something of a culture critic and a bit of an activist, as you saw this week. I guess he's going to be a prof himself someday."

Eddie sounded more and more interesting to this east-coast girl with her prosaic life experiences. As the evening progressed, I looked over at him from time to time, perhaps hoping that he

51

might glance over and remember having met me. I was equally terrified that he might. And he might come over. Then, what would I do? What would I say?

I needn't have worried. It wasn't long before I could tell that Eddie was saying his good-bye's. He jammed the beret back on his head and made his way toward the door without a backward glance. I turned around toward the stage where another singer had taken over. She had kind of a high, shrill voice that vibrated on every other note, and I wished that I could leave with him.

Later that night, as I lay in bed, unable to sleep, my mind was racing. I was replaying the events of the evening over and over. I had a feeling that Liz and her friends, with their penchant for the folk music scene and their laid-back approach to life, were going to become good friends. I felt so much more comfortable with them than I had at the frat party. My problem was Darla. I had promised to make her a dress for the upcoming formal, and she expected that I would find a date and go, too. The idea of it was becoming less and less appealing as every week went by. In any case, I'd have to find somewhere to buy the fabric as soon as possible if I wanted to finish it in time—oh, and there was the little matter of exams looming in the not-too-distant future. My first university exams. It felt a bit daunting.

~

The next week, I met Liz for lunch in the commissary in the basement of the old humanities building. It was loud and crowded, but I had discovered I preferred to have lunch here than in the staid quiet of my residence dining room. It also had the benefit of being closer to where I went to class. I needed to pick Liz's brain.

"Liz," I said, taking a plate of macaroni and cheese from the server behind the glass of the servery, "if you're studying to be a home ec teacher, you must sew."

She looked at me as if I must have two heads. "Why do you think I have six berets, all different colours, and that green coat you always tell me you like?"

"You made those?" I was impressed.

"Of course. I can't afford to dress this way, you know!" She picked up a bowl of red Jello that reminded me of Mom's hateful tomato aspic and put it on her tray before moving to the end of the line. I was right behind.

We sat down at the only empty table and were soon joined by two other girls we'd never met before. It was just the way lunch in the here went. Sometimes I met people I wouldn't otherwise get to know—usually people studying things like science or philosophy. This day, the two girls were deep in conversation, which they continued—*sotto voce*—presumably so as not to disturb our *tête-à-tête*.

"Of course. I should have known," I said, taking a big spoonful of the gloppy mac and cheese.

"Do you sew?"

And, of course, she couldn't have known that I did since I'd never mentioned it.

"I do, but I haven't been doing much lately. My roommate, Darla—I'm not sure if you've actually met her—happened to see one of my sketchbooks —"

"Whoa! Wait a minute. Sketchbooks? Do you design?"

"I've always been kind of a sketching dabbler." Then I told her about my father's reaction to my acceptance into art school and how I ended up in Toronto studying to be a teacher.

"God, Kat, that's a bummer. If you're meant to be an artist, maybe you need to find a way."

"Liz," I said, wiping a bit of cheesy goo from my chin, "you would have to know my father to understand how impossible that would be."

"Impossible isn't an immovable object, Kat. It's only a problem whose solution you have yet to find."

I was unconvinced but decided to say nothing. Liz didn't know my father.

"So precisely what is it that's impossible?"

I jumped then turned toward the voice that had come up behind me.

"It's Kat, isn't it?" Eddie Lancaster was looming over Liz and me, smiling in that lop-sided kind of way he had. "I'm Eddie. I don't think we've been formally introduced."

"How do you know my name?" I said when I finally found my tongue. *Well, that sounded rude,* I thought.

"Oh, I have my ways," he said, his eyes twinkling mischievously.

"I'm Liz, by the way," she said, extending her hand to him.

Eddie shifted the two fat textbooks he was carrying to his left arm and shook her hand. The two other girls at the table looked up at Eddie, crammed their last bites of lunch into their mouths, picked up their trays and fled. He sat down.

"So, what is it that's impossible?"

As much as I'd been sort of fantasizing about getting to know Eddie for the past week or two, I wasn't sure I could immediately begin spilling my life story to a perfect stranger. Did I say perfect? Perhaps that might have been a Freudian slip. I needn't have worried. Liz had no such qualms.

"Kat is an artist. And here she is studying to be a teacher."

"A noble profession if ever there was one."

"Being an artist?" I said.

"Being a teacher." Eddie put his books on the table and unwound his long, striped scarf. "But an artist? That's beyond cool. Anyway, what's so impossible?"

Liz jumped right in and told him about how I had to give up my art school dreams and come to Toronto to study English and history. She then added that she didn't see it as an impossible dream, but I did.

"*The difficult is what takes a little time; the impossible is what takes a little longer.* Fridtjof Nansen."

"Fridtjof...?" I said, puzzled.

"Nansen. Norwegian North Pole explorer, among other things. Won the Nobel Peace Prize in 1922. He knew a bit about impossible."

I shrugged. My art school dreams were a bit of a sore point with me. This was not what I'd had in mind all those times that I'd daydreamed about getting to know Eddie Lancaster. But as far as those daydreams were concerned, that ship had sailed.

"Hey, you two. We're having a post-lecture coffeehouse thing at the grad house on Friday. It's a bit of a musical amateur-hour with a few throw-back beat poets in the mix for a hoot. Why don't you come?"

"We'll be there!" Liz said, a bit too enthusiastically if you ask me. "What time?"

Eddie gave us the particulars, threw his scarf over his shoulder, picked up his books and walked off into the sunset. Well, perhaps not the sunset, but he *was* swallowed up in the lunch crowd and vanished. And just like that, I (or at least we) had become at least a peripheral part of the Eddie Lancaster movement—or at least, that's how it looked to me.

As Liz and I finished lunch, she suddenly remembered that we'd been talking about sewing. "You said Darla had seen one of your sketchbooks."

"Yes. And she loved one of my designs. She loved it so much, it seems I somehow promised her I'd make it for her to wear to Delta Delta Kappa's pre-Christmas formal."

Darla had been seeing a lot of Thomas Bevan-Rhyss II, and he had invited her to attend the event with him. I didn't mention to Liz that she'd also been trying desperately to find me a date so that we could "double-date," an effort that I discouraged at every turn.

"Did you bring a sewing machine with you?"

"No," I said, "and that's the thing. Darla just called her father, asked him for a sewing machine, and a week later, one arrived."

"Just like that?

"Just like that. And now I need to find a fabric store to look for something I can use to make it for her. I have no clue where to go, and I hoped you might give me a few ideas."

"I'll do one better than that," Liz said as she buttoned her coat and picked up her bag of books. "I'll take you down to the garment district, and we can shop together. I need a few things myself. How's Thursday afternoon?"

Neither of us had any classes on Thursday afternoon, so that seemed to be a good time. I was excited, but I had two papers due and a mid-term to study for in the next two days, so I had no time to think about art school, sketchbooks, fabric—or Eddie Lancaster.

I Know a Place

Petula Clark, 1965

THE FIRST SNOW OF THE SEASON FELL HEAVILY on Thursday, and, to me, it suddenly seemed like it should be Christmas—although the 25th of December was still almost a month away.

As I headed out to meet Liz, my feet were already cold, but I was too excited about the prospect of finding myself in a fabric store that I hardly noticed.

I caught up with Liz at the corner of College and St. George Streets, and we made our way through the drifting snow along College toward Spadina, then south to Queen Street West, where we turned. I found myself gazing through the dancing snowflakes down a long street with few pedestrians (no doubt because of the snow) but full of grinding streetcars making their way through the snow in the middle of the street. The tallest of the buildings was probably eleven stories high with large windows, and, judging from the art deco touches I noticed, many seemed to date from the 1920s or '30s. Many looked to me to be warehouses and manufacturing outlets with street-level shop fronts. Liz confirmed this.

"As far as I know, the Jewish textile experts set up shop here a few years back, and this is what we have. And they even let us shop retail from some of their left-over fabrics. You're going to love it!" She hurried along, sure of her destination.

That was something of an understatement. We found Liz's favourite shop and brushed ourselves off as best we could before opening the door to go inside. We didn't want to melt all over the bolts of fabric.

"You'd love this street in the summer. Racks of clothes and bolts of fabrics on the sidewalks, loads of people. Well, at least we won't have to fight the crowds."

Liz wasn't kidding. Apart from the store's proprietor, we were alone among the thousands of bolts of colourful fabrics that filled the shelving from floor to ceiling.

"Good afternoon, ladies. You are the few who have braved the elements this snowy day. May I be of assistance?" The proprietor was an elderly gentleman with wispy white hair, silver-rimmed glasses and a smile that was as broad as he was tall. He looked as if a sudden gust of wind might blow him over.

"You may," Liz began. "My friend is looking for a piece of glittering silk or something to make a Grecian-style formal gown. I, on the other hand, would enjoy a browse." She smiled at him and nodded at me. "If you'll excuse me..." And she left me alone with him.

"I am Ezra," he said, holding out his hand in greeting. "So, you're looking for something special today."

"Yes. Hi, Ezra. I'm Kat." I shook his hand. The grip was surprisingly forceful. "I'm working on a dress for a friend. Here," I said, rummaging in my purse, "I have a sketch of it." I'd reworked the sketch so that it would flatter Darla's ample upper section—if you know what I mean—and highlight her narrow waist, all without looking tarty. I had torn it out of my sketchbook to make it easier to carry around.

Ezra took the sketch from me and whistled softly. "Kat, did you do this?" I nodded. "It's quite exquisite." He came out from behind the counter where he had been working and gestured for me to follow him. "Come with me, my dear."

He led me to a room off to the side. When I entered, I was dazzled by the colours and the glittering array of shiny fabrics. On the far-left side of the room, I also saw six mannequins, each of which was in some state of dishabille, by which I mean that each of them was wearing a half-or two-thirds finished gown in varying styles and colours. I was drawn to them immediately while Ezra stood in the door watching me.

"Ezra, these are wonderful!"

"Yes," he said. "My girls do beautiful work."

I turned to look at him. "You have people making custom formal gowns?"

"Yes," he said. "Formal gowns, suits, day dresses. Samples."

"Samples for what?" I couldn't help myself. I started to touch the various fabrics while I walked around to see the designs from every angle.

"Samples for...our factory. But our schtick is the day dresses for the factory and the gowns for the Rosedale ladies who come for custom formal wear."

"The Rosedale ladies?" I had no idea what he was talking about.

"How long you've been in Toronto, Kat?"

"A few months. I'm a student."

He nodded knowingly. "Then, of course, that's why I have not met you before. And why the Rosedale ladies are not familiar. You will learn. They like their custom-made clothing. Perhaps your friend you make the dress for, she is from Rosedale?"

I had no idea. I did know that Darla was from somewhere in the Toronto area, but she had insisted she wanted to live in residence and not at home, as many local students did. And it seemed that her father would support just about any whim his only daughter had. By now, I did know that she was the youngest in her family that consisted of her mother (whom I had met once—she favoured wool day dresses with matching jackets and pearls. Maybe she *was* one of these Rosedale ladies), her father (she said he was in the grocery business—clearly a successful enterprise) and two older brothers.

"She might be, Ezra. Anyway, she discovered my sketchbook and pounced on this design."

"I can understand why. '*Everyone is kneaded out of the same dough but not baked in the same oven.*'" I had no idea where he was going with this. "An old Yiddish proverb. In any case, if you execute it as well as you drew it, she will be the envy of every other girl at the dance. Mark my words." He reached up to the third shelf beside him and pulled four bolts of fabric down. He placed them on a small table near the door then turned back to me. "Kat, would you ever show me those other designs in your sketchbook? I always love to see what the young people are doing these days. At least when they're not screaming blue murder for some rock and roll group. Oy, those Beatles fans!"

I laughed and told him that I'd be happy to bring along my sketchbook the next time I came. And there would most assuredly be a next time.

When Liz and I left the store an hour later, the snow had abated, and there was a slice of moon just beginning to show in the dusk. I was carrying a bag that contained four yards of ivory silk charmeuse encrusted with scattered ivory sequins. I could hardly wait to get it wrapped around Darla. Liz had three lengths of fabric to make herself a jumper, a dress and a pair of cigarette pants.

I couldn't start the project until a few days later, though. I had that mid-term exam looming. And I had that coffeehouse "date" with Eddie—oh, yes, and Liz and anyone else he brought along.

~

Liz and I arrived at the grad house at 8:30, as Eddie had indicated. There were only a few people there when we made our way downstairs to the coffeehouse area. Like the frat house, the bar and general entertainment venue were in the basement, although the grad house seemed smokier and a bit seedier. I hadn't thought that possible.

Eddie had warned us that the grad house crowd generally didn't head out much before ten p.m. after finishing their studying on Friday nights. That, however, didn't stop the amateur musicians and poets from starting their sets. As a result, it was easy to find a table. Eddie greeted us at the door then disappeared, promising to return.

As I sat at the table with Liz, sipping my coffee, I tried to take in as much of everything around as I could. Liz had been here a few times before, so was just sitting back, listening to a young man who was sitting on a wooden stool up on the stage, reciting poetry about oppression and tyranny while plucking the strings on a twelve-string guitar he clearly had little skill at playing.

My first impression was that this was a very different collection of individuals than the crowd I'd encountered at the frat house party. The group was, naturally, somewhat older and more diverse. Its cool, mellow kind of vibe made me feel like I was something of a child. As a first-year undergrad, the fact that I was even here was something of a coup. These were students who had already completed their first degrees and were now back at school working on Masters degrees or even Ph.D.'s. I could feel a sense of inadequacy beginning to creep up my spine and into my neck. They all looked so serious and grown-up. When I compared them to the giddy, excited, possibly scatter-brained crowd at the frat house, it was a bit shocking that two groups of young people, students at the same university at the same point in time, could be so different. It suddenly occurred to me how odd it was that these coffee-drinkers seemed so mellow, while the alcohol imbibers seemed so animated. Perhaps as you study more, you see the world differently.

I turned to Liz, who was engrossed in the young woman with the blackest hair contrasted with the palest complexion I'd ever seen, now singing something to the effect of "Kum Ba Ya" with a warbly falsetto. I had to stop myself from plugging my ears. "Liz," I said, trying to get her attention.

Liz suddenly seemed to wake up. "Oh, Kat. Sorry, I'm just mesmerized." I must have frowned at her. "And not in a good way." She laughed. "This one's unbelievable."

"That's one way to put it," I said. "Liz, how is it possible that all these coffee drinkers are so mellow? Is there something in the coffee here?"

She laughed. "Not as far as I know. But there is something in all those cigarettes with that sweet smell they're passing around."

And suddenly, I felt just a little bit naïve. Again. I turned to look around and saw Eddie heading toward our table with two other people—a tall, young man with red curly hair and a compact young woman with very long, straight, jet-black hair who was wearing a leather jacket and smoking a cigarette. I wondered if she might be Eddie's girlfriend. I hoped not.

"Liz, Kat, Red, Izzie." He pointed to each of us as introductions. We all grunted hi, and they sat down, Eddie pulling up a fifth chair from the adjacent table. Izzy seemed to be sizing me up, and, judging from the sour expression on her face, she found me wanting.

"We were just talking about the Peter, Paul and Mary show at Massey Hall last week. Either of you go?" We shook our heads. "Yeah, well, we're having a disagreement about it. I thought it was great. For what it was."

"And what, precisely is that, Eddie?" Izzie seemed to have a different take.

"Well, they're not a serious folk group, but what they offer is entertaining." I was happy Eddie thought this since I did like their sound. But since I hadn't been at the concert and knew very little of real substance about music, apart from what I liked, I was definitely going to keep quiet. I figured I might learn something about music and other things.

Izzy stubbed out her cigarette in the tiny metal ashtray in the middle of the table. "Well, I agree with Volkmar's review in the *Varsity*. We both thought it was artificial, cluttered and over-stylized, I think was how he put it. I couldn't agree more. They're not a serious folk group. As he said, they're bowing to the suburbanite musical tastes to sell records." She lit another cigarette. Maybe it was true what they said about smoking. Perhaps it did keep you slim. Either that or it made you sour.

Eddie shook his head. "Volkmar's reviews aren't exactly objective."

"Are reviews supposed to be objective?" Oops. I had promised myself to keep quiet. I waited to be lambasted by Izzie.

"Well, the young one speaks," Izzie said, inhaling deeply. I hated her then and there. "Quite right, Kat, is it? No, not objective, but coming from a place of greater knowledge."

Eddie started to laugh. "Sure. If you say so. Anyway, if I could change the subject for a moment. Would that be fine with you, Izzie?" She nodded, reluctantly it seemed to me. "We're planning a human rights sit-in at the university president's office the first week in January, and we're looking for some undergrads to volunteer." He looked at me then at Liz.

"Sure," Liz said immediately. "I'm in." She turned to me. "Kat?"

I wasn't sure what to say. I suddenly realized that if my father ever found out that I was even considering taking part in any kind of protest, he'd probably pull my tuition money for next term, and I'd be stuck at home with my parents for the rest of my natural life. "I'll have to get back to you on that. I'm not sure about my course schedule for next term."

Liz made a face at me. "It's going to be identical to this term's schedule."

"Leave her alone." Red seemed to be scrutinizing me. "Not everyone is meant to be an activist."

I was grateful for the support, but I would have preferred it to have come from Eddie.

"Well, you'll let me know before you leave to go home for Christmas, won't you, Kat?" Eddie was actually smiling at me.

"Sure, Eddie. I'll do that." I wasn't at all sure I'd be able to do that unless my answer was still going to be, I can't.

We spent the rest of the evening talking and sipping coffee, and from time to time paying attention to the performer on stage. I felt kind of sorry for them since so few people seemed to be there to listen to the performances. Once or twice, someone passed a joint over to our table. Everyone, including Liz, appeared to enjoy a puff. I pretended. I wasn't sure I was ready for that. At the end of the evening, as we left the grad house, Red and Izzie were arm-in-arm (why did this make me so happy), and Eddie was between Liz and me, one arm draped over each of us as he escorted us back to our respective residences. We dropped Liz off first, and I was left with Eddie, his arm still firmly planted over my shoulder. I liked it.

When we reached my residence, he turned to me, pecked me on the cheek and said, "Good night, Kat. Talk soon?" I nodded, went up the steps, closed the door behind me, and the night seemed to swallow him whole.

I leaned my back against the closed door and thought, *What just happened?*

~

A week later, I was still in bed at 7:30 when Darla started shaking me awake. I was alarmed since Darla never got up before me. She always got up late, dressed and made up her face faster than anyone I knew, then flew out of residence to class without breakfast. Occasionally, she grabbed a piece of toast from the dining room on her way out. Why in the world was she up so early today?

"They posted grades, Katherine! You have to get up!"

Oh. My. God. Today was the day. The first marks were up. I still had one more exam to write, but the marks for our Fine Arts exam, which had been first on the list, were obviously ready. I wasn't sure I was ready, though.

It was the only class Darla and I took together, and it was clear she wanted company. She was probably worried about her mark. I wasn't so worried about mine, but this would be my first university grade, and the truth was, I didn't know what to expect. We weren't in high school anymore. So, I got myself up and ready, skipped breakfast (which I was loathe to do) and raced to the Arts building along with Darla and half our residence mates.

When we arrived, there was already a crowd of students scrambling to get close enough to the bulletin boards to find their names. And their marks.

Darla squealed. "There they are, Katherine. Over there!"

She managed to squeeze her way to the front of the mob and ran her finger down the page tacked to the overcrowded bulletin board. Her finger stopped. "Oh, dear." She clamped her hand over her mouth.

"What?" I said. "Darla?"

She just pointed. I squeezed through, and when I was close enough, scanned down the list. "Oh. Dear."

Have Yourself a Merry Little Christmas

Andy Williams, 1965

I STOOD THERE, STARING AT THE GRADES. Every single person in the class's name was there with their student numbers and semester grade for everyone to see. There was not even a nod to privacy. I found mine very quickly. I made a respectable 84% in my first-term Fine Arts course, which was just fine with me. What I was staring at, however, was Darla's mark. Darla had pulled off a 93%.

"Oh, dear," Darla said again. "Oh, dear." She looked as if she might cry.

"Darla," I said, "you don't seem happy. That's a terrific grade. What in the world is wrong?"

Darla started sniffling as she moved away from the bulletin board. "I didn't get the highest mark in the class. I'm second. Second best."

I didn't dare tell her that it was blowing my mind that she had made a higher grade than I had or that my opinion of her as a slightly dumb blonde was crumbling. At that moment in time, for the first time since I'd met her, it occurred to me that it might be all an act.

"I put my arm around her shoulder as we both moved down the hall. "Darla, the grade is terrific. You should be very proud. It's our first term at university."

"Yes," she said, her eyes streaming now, "I know that. But it's the first year for that Donald whatever-his-name-is who came first, too. I should have done better."

Given the fact that Darla was a bit of a party girl, and I had seen her studying only twice the whole semester, I thought she had done remarkably well. But all this angst over coming second? I didn't quite know how to console her—especially with my delight at having made over 80% myself.

As we walked down the steps of the old stone building, we both threw our scarves around our necks and took a deep breath of cold air. This seemed to revive her a bit. Darla wiped her mitten across her face to dry the last of her tears and stood up taller. "Well, Kat, at least I'll have the best dress at the formal this evening!"

I had all but forgotten that the dance was this evening, but I was even more shocked by the fact she had just called me Kat rather than Katherine, for the very first time. I wondered where that came from.

"I'm devastated that you're not going to the dance tonight, Kat. I hope you won't be too sad."

Sad? I was delighted. Elated. Thrilled. I was certainly not devastated. Anyway, I was more interested in getting Darla done up in the dress that had taken me the past three weeks to complete.

After bringing the fabric home from Ezra's shop, I'd spent some time draping it on Darla while she squealed in delight at the fabric and the possibilities. The sewing machine her father had sent was heavenly. It was far superior to the one I'd left behind at home. I found that my time at the machine helped me relax between study sessions, paper writing, and exams. At some point in the process, it had occurred to me that I would have to get myself a part-time job so that I'd have money to buy fabric for myself. My father wasn't likely to see that as a good place to spend his money, so it would do me no good to ask. I had missed the design and creation process. Although I'd been sketching whenever I had a chance, seeing a design on paper come to fruition was unmatched. And this evening, it would really come alive.

At eight o'clock that evening, those of us who were not attending the fraternity Christmas formal waited in the common room for the lovelies to sweep down the staircase and make their entrance. I had helped Darla get ready, but she had insisted on doing the finishing touches herself so that she could make an entrance, and I could experience it.

I had a little red Canon Demi camera that my parents had given to me as a present for starting university. They hoped I might use it to "make memories," as my mother said. I had used it only a few times since September, but this seemed like a good time to give it a work-out. I was reasonably sure I knew next to nothing about taking pictures, but I did have a bit of an artistic eye, so I thought I might be able to get a few good shots.

I looked up as Darla began to make her way down the staircase. I could barely breathe. Darla looked like a movie star with her flowing silk dress, her blonde hair done up in a beehive and her sparkly evening bag hanging from her wrist. She was wearing elbow-length, white, doe-skin gloves with a jewel-encrusted cuff bracelet over the glove on her left wrist. There was also a matching brooch of some kind in her hair—I wondered if she had borrowed them from her mother. Darla and I had kept the dress-making a secret up to this point, and now I could hear some murmuring around me. (They had clearly forgotten Darla's first-day-of-the-semester announcement to one and all in the dining room that I was a designer, thank goodness.)

"Look at that dress!" "Where did she get it?" "Do you think it's real silk?" "A bit risqué, don't you think?" Since several of the girls were wearing strapless gowns, that last remark must have been because this dress, unlike the wasp-waisted, ballgown-skirted, pastel concoctions with those wide skirts, Darla's dress (my dress) was an elegant, luscious, slinky, swathe of fabric that clung to Darla's body in all the right places. She looked like liquid sophistication.

I came to my senses and snapped a few pictures as she descended the staircase. After acknowledging her audience, Darla came over and embraced me tightly. "Thank-you," she whispered in my ear. Then she broke away and looked at her admirers. "Everyone, I want to let you in on a secret. Kat is a designer. She designed—and made—this dress for me. Applause, please."

Her wish was their command. They applauded me, and I felt like I had just hosted the first show of my first New York fashion collection. It was only one dress, but it was a start—even though I was now training to be a high school teacher. *Small detail*, I thought. All was right with the world. But, like everything, that was about to change. In two days, I would board a train and head east for Christmas. I would be returning to the warm bosom of my family for the holidays. There was nothing I was dreading more.

~

Liz and I had tried to coordinate our train trips back to Halifax for Christmas, but, as it turned out, she had finished exams before I did and had already left. I was going to be on my own for a couple of days on the train. I didn't mind, but it would have been fun to be with Liz. We vowed we'd return together the first week in January.

I expected that in the morning after the formal dance, Darla would have slept in. I was wrong. She was up earlier than usual, buzzing around the room, clearly trying to get me to wake up. I was burrowing deeper into the bed because I knew that when (if) I got up, I'd have to begin packing for my Christmas trip home, so I pretended to be sleeping. Eventually, I couldn't fool her any longer.

"Oh, Kat!" There it was again, calling me Kat. A new Darla. "The dress was more than I ever imagined it could be! The dance was a gas, and Thomas told me I looked like an angel. An angel!" She sat down on the side of my bed while I clutched my blankets around my neck to keep out the chill. Did I mention that as beautiful as Ardmore Hall was, the windows were old and draughty? "Kat, you must go into business. I can help."

One thing I knew for sure at that very moment was that I could not and would not go into business. At least not here and not now. As much as I loved the idea, I knew it was just another of Darla's whims. It would pass. But it did make me smile just a bit, although I tried hard not to let her see it. I sat up against the wooden headboard and quickly stuffed one of my pillows behind my neck.

"So, Darla, tell me all about the dance." And so, she did.

She started with the decorations—the theme was winter wonderland. According to Darla, the decorating committee had transformed the ballroom at the Royal York Hotel into a glittering, snow-covered valley with sparkling snowmen, myriad filigree snowflakes (someone had been busy with scissors and paper for the past few weeks) and Christmas trees. She said it was magical. Then she told me about the band and the music—rock and roll—then the dresses. According to Darla, the place overflowed with, as she put it, the remnants of an explosion in a multi-coloured tulle factory with every dress a concoction of layers and layers of tulle making the girls look like outrageous ballerinas who had escaped from a demented ballet. At least that's how Darla saw them. Then there she was, a vision of sophistication and refinement in her Kat Wilson original. I thought it might almost have been worth going just to see it.

70

Almost. I had turned down one of Thomas's pimply friends to avoid it.

When she finished telling me about it, she quickly packed her purse, grabbed her coat and headed out the door. "I'm having breakfast with Thomas!" She turned around with her hand on the doorknob. "Oh, Kat, by the way, don't leave without saying good-bye. I have something for you!"

I had written my last exam the morning before, and now all I had to do was clean up, pack and get ready to board my train at eight o'clock that evening. As I considered my Christmas gift for Darla, I thought I might have to do a bit better than a Christmas card and a box of chocolates, which is what I had planned. Shopping would have to be on my agenda for the day.

After a quick breakfast in the dining room with the housemother glaring at me for bolting my food, I grabbed my coat and other winter accoutrements and headed to *Sam the Record Man*. I hadn't had time to go back since I'd met Eddie there in September, so I was looking forward to it.

Grime coated the snow mounds lining Yonge Street. We hadn't had a new snowfall in a week or two. Those Christmas-card scenes of snowy, white Christmases were a fantasy in the world of a big city. But at least there wasn't any snow on the sidewalks, making the walking easier.

I had walked briskly, making it to *Sam's* in record time. I was surprised by the crowds, but perhaps I shouldn't have been. It was, after all, only a week before Christmas. Everyone in the store seemed to be searching frantically for gifts. I pushed my way through the crowd and found myself in front of a display of Beach Boys albums. Their wholesome, California, sun-kissed faces smiled out at me with perfect teeth. I knew Darla was a Beach Boys fan, but their music wasn't something I knew a lot about, so I didn't know which albums she already had. I started thumbing mindlessly through them when I suddenly felt a hand grab my upper arm.

"Step away from the bin, miss," the voice said.

I turned and looked up into Eddie's grinning face. "Eddie," I said, my panic subsiding, "here again!"

"Well," he said, "I do work here. Anyway, why are you standing in front of Beach Boys albums? Are you a closet rock and roll fan? Have you been holding out on me?"

I was astonished on several levels. First, I had no idea he worked there. Second, was the fact that he even commented on my perceived taste in music suggested to me that he had thought about me. I loved that. I told him I was looking for a present for a friend.

"May I make a suggestion?" When I nodded, he said, "Come with me." I followed Eddie over to the other side of the store. "Why don't you give your friend something that reflects your kind of music?" I started to interrupt, but he stopped me. "Hear me out. There's some new music that's kind of a cross-over between rock and folk. They call it folk-rock. Clever, eh?" He laughed at his little joke. I did, too—I couldn't stop myself.

I looked up at the poster above the table of albums. "The Byrds?"

He lifted one of the albums off the table. *"Turn! Turn! Turn!* You'll love it. I guarantee it. And so will your friend. Trust me on this."

I did. Then Eddie did something very unexpected. As he rang through my purchase, he leaned down under the counter and pulled out a little package. It was small, square and flat. Clearly, it was a record single. "Hope you like Donovan. It's his "Colours" single. Anyway, Merry Christmas, Kat. Let's get together in January."

I looked down at the package. It was in a small brown paper bag decorated with a red bow. Eddie had written my name on it in bold, dark letters. It was clear he had planned this: it wasn't just some spur-of-the-moment kind of thing. It was genuine. I was so shocked by this gesture that all I could do was nod my head. He seemed to understand, though, and besides, there was a long line forming behind me. I had to leave. I took the present and put it in the bag with Darla's record. "Thanks, Eddie. I don't have—"

He stopped me. "You know, presents don't require reciprocation. January?"

"Of course. Merry Christmas, Eddie."

~

I gave Darla the new Byrds album later that afternoon just as I was stuffing the last of my winter clothing into my suitcase. She seemed genuinely touched by the gesture and immediately put it on her record player. We sat side-by-side on the edge of her bed and listened to the sounds.

"It's almost rock and roll," she said after the first track. She turned and threw her arms around me. "Thank-you, Kat. Thank-you for everything." Then she reached over to her desk and retrieved a small, beautifully wrapped package. "Merry Christmas!"

I unwrapped the little package to find a pair of delicate two-toned gold and silver embroidery scissors in the shape of a stork.

"Do you like them?" Darla sounded like a small child hoping for approval. "They're real gold, you know."

"I love them, Darla. It's too much."

"No," she said. "It's not too much for my best friend."

Her best friend? I had no idea she thought of me that way. I expected her best friend was one of the sorority girls she was always talking about, although she had yet to be invited to join them. I guess there's more to friendship than the kind of frivolous interaction that passes for friendship in many circles these days. I knew I would cherish this gift all my life.

After dinner together in the residence dining room with the few girls who hadn't yet left for the holidays, Darla and I said good-bye on the front porch as her father alighted from a large car that was waiting at the curb. The car was black with a white roof and white-wall tires. It looked like the Cadillac that my doctor back home drove when he did house calls. Darla quickly kissed me on the cheek, grabbed her suitcase and ran down the stairs into her father's arms. He seemed very glad to see her, although it had only been a few weeks since she'd been home for a visit, home being only about a fifteen-minute drive away, as I'd learned. I had never met her father, but he turned and waved to me as if he knew me. He had, no doubt, heard all about me.

Then it was my turn to get ready to leave. I took a cab to Union Station then waited in that mass of Christmas travellers to board the train for home. I looked around at the crowd. They were all bundled up in winter coats and hats, trailing kids and suitcases and piles of Christmas presents. I wondered how there would be space on the train for all the paraphernalia everyone was toting. It's a funny thing about Christmas travel, isn't it? Everyone is excited to get home, and then when they get there, all the old family disputes raise their ugly heads. At least that's what I expected I'd face when I got home. I wasn't wrong.

~

Two days later, my train pulled into the station in Halifax, Nova Scotia. As usual, I was tired and grubby. I'm not one of those people who is lulled to sleep by the sounds of trains. I might have dozed off a few times since I'd left Toronto, but I was groggy from lack of a sound sleep.

When I emerged from the train station into the dull grey winter day, that distinct smell of salt air immediately assaulted me. I hadn't really missed it, but it did make me take a deep breath of appreciation. I could see my father's yellow station wagon with the fake wood panelling on the sides. He had stopped across the street in a no-parking zone, so it was clear to me from past experience that my father expected me to get over to the car as quickly as possible. Unlike Darla's father, my father could not be expected to get out of the car and help me, much less throw his arms around me. It just wasn't who he was. And I could only imagine the conversation in the car.

My mother would probably have said, "James, I'll just go over and help Katherine with her things."

My father would probably have said, "No need, Betty. She can manage." That's what he always said.

There was no point in standing there, waiting to see if one of them would emerge to help me. It was not going to happen, so I looked both ways before I crossed the street (if I had not been obvious in doing so, my father would undoubtedly mention it—he always did), then quickly made my way to the car and opened the door to the back seat. My mother turned and smiled at me. "Katherine, welcome home."

I smiled at my mother as I tried to heave my suitcase onto the seat before I heaved myself in.

"Katherine, go around and put the suitcase in the back. It looks as if it might dirty the upholstery." He turned back toward the steering wheel. "And be careful of your boots when you get in." *Well, hello to you, too, Daddy.*

How could I have forgotten how particular my father was about his upholstery? I did as I was told and vowed that I'd be as amenable as possible to keep the peace during this visit.

The drive home took about ten minutes. On the way, my mother, god love her, tried to keep up a conversation with me about the train trip, the weather and the neighbours. I smiled and nodded. My father said nothing, as usual.

We drove into the driveway, and Dad got out to open the garage door. He then pulled this big boat of a car into the garage and got out again. To his credit, he took my suitcase from the rear, closed the garage door and headed into the house through the side door into the kitchen. Mom and I followed him.

"Welcome home, Katherine," he finally said as he placed my suitcase on the kitchen floor. "We've… We've missed you."

Well, this was unexpected. "I've…missed home, too," I said. There was no family hugging, though. It just wasn't done in our family. My mother patted my shoulder and smiled.

That night at dinner, out of what appeared to me to be genuine curiosity, my father asked me about university. I told them about the residence and my room and Darla. I had to tread carefully about my adventures in city life. I knew they would never approve of their daughter wandering around the city, even if people did refer to it as "Toronto the Good" and especially alone. When I mentioned *Sam the Record Man*, my father frowned a bit but said nothing. I guess he thought I'd been buying classical music records or maybe jazz, which would be fine in his opinion. But he did ask, "What do you play the records on in your room?" I told him about Darla's generosity in sharing. Then, when I told them about my marks, all over 80% so far, he perked up a bit.

"It sounds like you've settled in well, Katherine," he said when I'd finished—or at least finished as much as I planned to say. I certainly didn't tell them about the coffeehouses, or Eddie, and nothing whatsoever about the sewing machine and the dress design, although I really wanted to. I might tell Mom or Nan. My grandmother, Fran, Dad's mother, was probably the most special person in my childhood. She would be joining us for Christmas dinner and would love to hear about my design adventures. She always did. I could never understand how Dad could have had a mother like her yet turn out as sour as he often appeared.

I'm not sure why I thought things might have changed since I'd left. I'd been gone less than four months. My room was the same. The house was the same. My parents were the same. Dad told us what he thought about current events and the neighbours, and Mom and I were expected to agree with him. I think the fact that he always considered himself to be right was the one thing about him that made him difficult to live with. It wasn't the first time I'd wondered how Mom could put up with him or how he'd become who he was. It wouldn't be the last.

Christmas morning was identical to every single Christmas morning I'd experienced since I could remember. Mom, Dad and I sat around the Christmas tree in our bathrobes, drinking orange juice and passing around the presents piled up under the tree. I sipped my orange juice and stared at each of the old ornaments on the tree between gifts. I saw the one Mom had bought for me when I was five years old and had fallen in love with it at Woolworth's department store. It was a pair of sparkling, pink ballet slippers. Mom had explained to me that it was probably reminiscent of the ballet *The Nutcracker*. She told me she had never seen it herself, but my grandmother, Dad's mother, Fran, was a big fan. Since Mom and Dad listened to classical music, she knew the music well.

"Here, dear. Take this one now," Mom said, passing me a large brightly-wrapped package that surprised me by how heavy it was.

I put it down in front of me, where I was sitting in front of the tree. I brushed off the strand of tinsel that clung to it and looked at the card. It said it was from "Santa." No matter how old I got, Mom and Dad always had presents under the tree for me from Santa. I carefully peeled back the tape so that I could avoid tearing the wrapping paper. Mom and Dad would want to re-fold it to re-use the next year. This, I knew. As I pulled back the flap of wrapping paper, I gasped. I couldn't believe it. Santa had brought me a record player! Dad looked at me and nodded without really smiling. It was his way.

"Do you like it?" Mom was beaming from ear to ear. "I know you like to listen to music sometimes." She hesitated for a moment. "But not while you study!"

"Of course not, Mom. And I love it." I got up from the floor and hugged Mom. Then I went over to Dad and saw an almost imperceptible stiffening of his arms down by his sides. *Too bad,*

Dad, I was thinking. *I'm going to hug you.* And I did. I felt him stiffen for a split second, then relax. "Thank-you, Dad," I whispered into his ear.

"You're welcome," came his gruff reply. It was enough for me.

I was still smiling as I got ready for dinner later that afternoon when I heard a car door slam out in front of the house. I looked out my bedroom window and saw Nan alight from a taxi. I could feel my smile widen even further and rummaged through the paraphernalia on my dressing table to find some lipstick. My father wouldn't say anything about lipstick in front of my grandmother. She loved the stuff, and I loved her.

I quickly finished dressing and flew down the stairs. Mom was hanging Nan's coat in the hall closet while Nan smacked her lips together in the mirror, checking her makeup as she always did. She turned when she heard me thump down the last step.

"Kat! My darling granddaughter! Come to Nan!" she said, flinging her arms wide open. If Mom and Dad were a bit reticent when it came to hugging and the like, Nan was utterly the opposite. She revelled in it. And I had loved her for it from the day I was born.

I flew into her arms and was at once enveloped by her presence—and the slightly exotic, woody fragrance of the perfume she always wore and refused to tell me what it was. That fragrance would forever be my grandmother. "Oh, Nan, it's so good to see you!"

I followed her into the living room, still holding her hand. She was carrying a large, pink and ivory floral carpet-bag-type tote in her other hand, out of which she would eventually pull presents for all of us. I remembered sitting in the Capitol Theatre on Barrington Street the year before watching the new movie *Mary Poppins.* When the scene of Mary's arrival at the Banks' residence came up, and Mary Poppins took all manner of unbelievable objects out of her carpetbag, I was astounded. Mary's bag was a dead ringer for Nan's bag. *Nan had hers first,* I remember thinking. I also remembered that Mary Poppins had said, "You should never judge things by their appearance." It was a lesson I was still trying to learn. Anyway, all throughout my childhood, Nan had come bearing gifts for all of us, and they all emerged from her own carpetbag.

When she had finished placing all but one of them under the tree, she turned to me and offered a small, beautifully wrapped package. "Kat, my dear, this is for you. Well, it is one of several, but I think it's the most important. You are now ready for it."

I was curious. What in the world was I now ready for? I sat on the sofa and pulled the paper off slowly.

"For heaven's sake, Kat, don't bother trying to save the paper." She sniffed and threw a slight frown in my father's direction by the fireplace where he was chewing on the end of his pipe. "James, for god's sake, stop smoking in the house. The smell is repulsive." For some reason, Nan, his mother, was the only person with whom my father did not argue. Then she turned back to me. "Throw caution to the wind, my dear. Just open it."

Just as my grandmother told me to do, I pulled the paper off a beautiful box with the word "Shalimar" emblazoned across it. I opened the box and took a moment to take in the beautiful crystal flask with its indescribable shape and black stopper. It was filled with rich, amber liquid.

"Do you know what it is?" Nan asked.

"It's perfume," I said as I removed the bottle from its nest in the box.

"Yes, of course, but do you *know* it?" When I didn't answer, she continued. "Ever since you were a little girl, you always asked me about my signature scent. This, my dear, is it. I have been wearing Shalimar since my twenty-fifth birthday." I looked at her, and she continued. "Yes, for forty years. I was privileged to have one of the very first bottles. You know, it was created by Jacques Guerlain, whom I had the pleasure of meeting in Paris. It was brand new, and it was the very first of the oriental fragrances." She then leaned over to me and whispered, "But it is too sexy for younger girls. You're ready for it now."

I knew my grandmother had spent a few years in Paris in her early years but never dreamed that she would have met someone like Jacques Guerlain.

Christmas dinner proceeded much as it had any other year. There was roast turkey, cranberry sauce, mashed potatoes, boiled carrots and canned peas. It was all smothered in Mom's delicious, fatty gravy. The dinner was finished off with flaming plum pudding, courtesy of my grandmother. Her English heritage always shone through at Christmas. As far as I was concerned, the only fly in the ointment was that disgusting tomato aspic my mother insisted she had to serve as an appetizer—the stuff I always thought about whenever Liz ate red Jello for lunch in the commissary.

As usual, I ate far too much dinner, followed by a round or two of the inevitable chocolates we passed to one another as we recovered in the living room. Before she left that evening, my grandmother took me aside.

"Katherine, Kat," she began, "I know that becoming a teacher is not your dream. Have you read that Aldous Huxley book I gave you?" I nodded. "Well, then, you'll know where he stands on so many issues. His advice for dreams? *'Dream in a pragmatic way.'* I took his advice. Now it's your turn."

Cast Your Fate to the Wind

We Five, 1965

I RANG IN 1966 WITH MY PARENTS AND NAN, who hugged me tightly as her taxi waited out front just after midnight and whispered in my ear, "Remember what I said. And don't let anyone tell you your dreams are fantasies." Then she kissed me on the cheek and carefully made her way across the icy walkway, holding her hat lest the wind should take it. I had offered to help her, but she was having none of that.

The next morning, I started the new year by meeting Liz at the CN train station down by the harbourfront. Winter semester classes began in four days, and we would be spending two of them on the train, me in an upper berth, Liz in a lower. I was more than ready to get back to school.

We arrived back on campus after an uneventful train journey, although, as usual, I was exhausted. It occurred to me that I ought to fly in the future, but I had never been on an airplane. Perhaps it was time I had that experience. Liz and I went our separate ways to our respective residences promising to meet for lunch at the basement commissary the next day.

When I opened the door to my room, Darla was sitting on the side of her bed, wringing her hands. In truth, she was twisting a pair of red leather gloves.

"Happy New Year, Darla!" I tossed my two suitcases on my bed then peeled off my coat and scarf, which landed in a heap on top of the cases. "You might want to be a bit kinder to your gloves." They looked expensive.

Darla looked down at her hands and stopped fidgeting. "Oh, dear, Kat. You're back!" It seemed as if she were surprised to see me.

"Did you have a nice Christmas?" I said as I pushed my coat and scarf aside and began to open my suitcases in an attempt to unpack and get myself organized for the months ahead. One of my suitcases was almost entirely filled with only my new record player. We probably didn't need two record players in our residence room, but I couldn't rely on Darla's kindness forever. Before I had a chance to take it out, she got up and threw her arms around me.

"Oh, Kat! I have bad news. Well, it's not really bad news. I suppose there's good news, and there's bad news."

"Give me the bad news first," I said, always wanting to save the best for last. It's a little how I still broke a piece of cake in two through the middle, leaving the part with the most icing on it for last.

"I think I'd rather give you the good news first."

I shrugged—whatever she preferred.

She continued. "You remember that sorority?"

How could I forget? I nodded.

"Well, they've finally accepted me. Me! I'm going to be a sorority sister!"

I was happy for Darla since this is what she had wanted. In fact, she told me about her desire to be a sorority sister almost daily from September until December. I was a bit surprised, though, since I thought they made these decisions only once a year in the fall. Oh well, what did I know about sororities? I'm sure the rules were a bit flexible. Perhaps someone had died or been expelled? Anyway, it wasn't important. What was important was that my friend had achieved an important goal—for her. "That's fantastic for you, Darla! It's what you've been wanting. So, what's the bad news?"

"Oh, Kat! I'm going to be moving into the sorority house, so you and I won't be able to be roommates anymore." She looked as if she might cry at any moment. "Kat, will you still consider making me dresses even if we're not roommates? We can still be friends, can't we?"

I sat down beside her on her bed and took her hands. "Darla, I pledge to you that we will always be friends." At that moment, I realized that I genuinely meant it.

I had come to appreciate Darla as a roommate, especially after hearing Liz's stories about her roommate from hell. That's when it occurred to me. Maybe it wasn't bad news, after all. And that's how Liz and I came to be roommates and best friends forever. At least that's how it looked in the fall of 1966.

~

On Sunday, January 23, it snowed. I mean, it really snowed heavily and for a long time. We found ourselves smack in the middle of what would come to be known as one of the epic Toronto snowstorms of the decade—maybe even the century, for all we knew then. We could hear the wind bashing against the windows, rattling them within an inch of their lives. And, as we sat in the common room moaning about how we were missing various social events today, we could see the snow as it blew and drifted along the sidewalk out front.

Liz and I had been invited to a poetry reading that evening at the grad house courtesy of Eddie and company, after which we were supposed to go to *The Riverboat*. As a prized employee at

Sam's (at least according to him), Eddie had acquired a copy of singer-songwriter Gordon Lightfoot's brand-new folk album. We had listened to it a few times before we all dispersed for Christmas. I hadn't seen Eddie since we'd returned to campus because he'd been on an extended holiday break from which he had just returned, but Gord was supposed to play tonight, and *Sam's* had given a few tickets to each of their employees as a kind of Christmas present. We were among the honoured few with whom Eddie had shared his. I had been looking forward to it.

I was in love with one particular track on the new album—"The First Time Ever I Saw Your Face" (I thought it was so dreamy)—and I'd been hoping to hear it in person. Eddie had told us all the song's background. A British singer had written it some nine years earlier for his lover while still married to his first wife. It was so romantic. So, it wasn't a new song, and I'd heard it before, but I was in love with this new Lightfoot version. However, I wouldn't be hearing it that night. Everything was cancelled. My only consolation was that Gord was booked in for winter carnival, so I'd have to make a point of getting a ticket to that—despite Eddie's clamouring about how bourgeois winter carnivals and all their trappings were. I think I rolled my eyes at that while Liz sat there nodding.

Anyway, that's what I was thinking about as we sat listlessly thumbing through magazines in the common room when the lights went out. After a few brief screeches from the more easily startled among the girls, we lit candles while another log landed on the fire that was already blazing in the fireplace. All in all, it was a bit cozy, our lost evening of music and general socializing notwithstanding.

"What're you looking at?" Liz said as she sat down beside me with her candle.

"I was reading *Vogue* magazine before the lights went out."

"Oh, let me see." Liz moved her candle closer to the page, so close that I feared it might catch fire. "Oh, that's gorgeous," she said, peering at the spread I had been studying.

As I thought about it, it did occur to me that I had, indeed, been studying it. And suddenly, I knew why. Staring up at me from the left-hand page was the smiling face of Audrey Hepburn. Her gorgeous, almond-shaped eyes ringed with dark kohl. She was wearing what looked like a headband matching the scarf wound around her neck. On the opposite page, she was sitting with her legs crossed, one elbow on her knee and her chin resting in the palm of her hand. The smile in both was mesmerizing, as was the haircut. And I suddenly knew why I was so riveted. I was suddenly overwhelmed by the notion that I had to get that haircut. With bangs swept to one side, the cut was short enough to show her ears with almost a kiss-curl in front. For the briefest second, I wondered what my parents would think. This fleeting thought was immediately replaced by wondering what Eddie would think. In any case, I made up my mind. As soon as I could get out of this house, I was getting my hair cut.

The next morning, the new week started clear, cold and very bright with the sun glistening off all that fresh snow. About a foot and a half of snow had fallen, but there had been so much drifting that there were mountains of snow (or so it seemed to me) up against most of the buildings, occasionally obscuring the doors. By noon, most of the entrances to the academic buildings were cleared, and classes resumed. Street and sidewalk clearing around the city would take a bit longer, so I had to wait until later in the week to accomplish my two non-academic goals—I wanted that new hair cut, and I wanted a job. Scratch that thought: I needed both.

My plan was to wander along Yonge Street trying to find a hair salon that looked promising, by which I mean a place where I didn't see lines of women sitting with curlers in their hair under hair dryers. I hadn't needed a hair salon my first semester since my hair was well below my shoulders and only needed me to trim it once in a while. Now, I wanted a mod cut. I planned to continue south to Queen Street to visit Ezra in his fabric shop after getting my new hairdo. I wanted to show him the photos of Darla's dress and look at fabric, of course, to make myself a new mod dress to go along with my new hair when I could figure out a way to regain access to a sewing machine. I also had my sketchbook in my purse since he'd asked me to bring it the next time I came. Oh, and I was looking for a job.

It didn't take me long to figure out that the blue-haired-curler ladies didn't frequent Yonge Street hair salons. All the shops seemed to be populated by cool, young, bohemian, chain-smoking hairdressers who appeared to be itching to do something new and modern. I was a prime candidate. So, when I left the salon an hour later, perhaps I didn't look exactly like Audrey Hepburn in *Vogue* magazine (I mean, who could, anyway?), but I didn't feel like the same Kat who had walked into the salon, either. And I felt ten pounds lighter with all that long hair gone. Despite the cold, I felt a lightness in my step as I headed toward Ezra's shop. At least I had as much lightness as one can have while climbing over a snowbank at every traffic light and sliding along the ice now forming in front of shops whose proprietors had neglected to clear their sidewalks before the pedestrian mob trampled it. The ice was likely to be there until June at this rate.

When I arrived at Ezra's shop, I could hear the buzz of sewing machines coming from the back. He popped out onto the shop floor the moment the bell on the door I'd just opened jangled. His face seemed to light up when he recognized me, and he gestured to me to come to the back. I followed him into the workroom where two seamstresses were busily sewing their way along seams on swathes of what looked like hot-pink silk lamé.

"Come, Kat, come in!" Ezra made his way to the far corner, where it looked as if he had been working on fitting a new design on a mannequin. It looked like a tweed suit in the making. It seemed to resemble recent jackets from the House of Chanel—the ones I'd seen in a current *Vogue* magazine spread. The multi-coloured braid he was pinning to the front of the jacket was the clue.

"Ruth! Edna! Stop for just a moment, if you please."

The two seamstresses stopped mid-seam and looked up from their work. Both wore wire-rimmed glasses and looked to be in their forties.

"Here is Kat. She is the young designer I told you both about."

I started to say something about not being a designer, but he held his hand up. Both Ruth and Edna smiled and nodded, then immediately returned studiously to their work.

"Kat, have you brought me sketches?"

I told him I had, but I first wanted him to see the pictures of Darla in the finished product that I'd made from his exquisite fabric. I knew that if I owned a fabric shop, I'd be interested in seeing what people made from my fabrics. When I handed them over, he pushed his glasses up on his nose then sat down on the small stool beside the mannequin. For a moment, he simply shuffled through them, then again. Then he looked up at me. "It is extraordinary, dear Kat. May I keep one of them to put up in the store?"

I was delighted that he'd asked. Then, in response to his repeated request, I handed over my sketchbook and nervously stepped back a bit as if to give him some air in which to examine them.

Ezra turned two or three pages slowly then looked up at me. "Kat, dear girl, why don't you browse the shop. This is going to take me a few minutes."

I had no idea what he meant. For a brief moment, it occurred to me that he might be planning to steal some of my designs. Maybe Ruth or Edna could sketch. Perhaps he wanted to copy one of my designs. Who was it that said, "Imitation is the highest form of flattery?" It was either Oscar Wilde or Coco Chanel quoting Oscar. Either way, it was a flattering thought, but a thought that upset me a bit. As fast as I thought about this, the thought evaporated when Ezra appeared at the door of the workroom and beckoned me.

When I walked back into the room, Ruth and Edna were now seated at a small table I hadn't noticed before, with my sketchbook open in front of them. They were having an animated conversation, pointing to this sketch then another one, after which a lively exchange seemed to follow.

"Kat, your designs are superb. I was right about you. I know about these things. You are going places."

"Right now, the only place I seem to be headed is for the front of a high school history classroom."

Ezra shook his head. "Dreams will have their way, my dear. And this talent is too good to waste."

Easy for him to say, I thought.

"Kat, I would like to buy two of your designs."

He wanted to buy my designs? Were they even for sale? Never in my wildest dreams had I considered this possibility. Well, maybe in the wildest ones.

"The secret to success, Kat, is to be ready when opportunity knocks. Or at least that's what Benjamin Disraeli said." He wiped his glasses. "Are you listening for the knock?"

I was now. I agreed to sell Ezra two of my designs. He had permitted Ruth and Edna to recommend which two he ought to consider, and they would make them for two of their Rosedale clients seeking new coats (I loved designing coats). Then they would consider selecting a less expensive fabric and putting them into production to sell to Creed's and Harridges, their retail clients in the city. I was so excited that I almost forgot to ask him what I came to ask. Now seemed like an opportune time.

"Ezra, would you happen to need any help in the store on Saturdays?"

"You are looking for a job? And you don't even ask me how much I will give you for the designs?"

I hadn't even considered that he would pay me. But, of course, he would. And that is how I became a "designer" and a fabric shop clerk.

The Carnival is Over

The Seekers, 1965

FOR THE NEXT MONTH, EVERY TIME I ENCOUNTERED someone I hadn't seen since early January, the response was the same. "What in the world have you done to your hair?" People couldn't have been any more confounded if I had shaved my head.

First, it was Liz, who, to her credit, seemed so excited about it, she considered chopping off her own hair. After sober reconsideration, she decided to keep her long, flipped bob that could occasionally find its way into a beehive. My beehive dreams were over—if I ever had them in the first place, which I didn't.

I was getting quite used to my new look. After a few weeks, whenever I caught my reflection in a passing window or mirror in the washroom, I no longer startled myself. I was finally beginning to recognize my reflection, and I liked what I saw. I wondered what Eddie would think of it.

I still hadn't seen Eddie since he'd returned to campus after his extended visit home in Winnipeg with his parents. I supposed that if you were a prized graduate student working with a famous professor, you could get away with a lot more than a lowly freshman coed who couldn't miss any classes or she might be kicked out of them permanently. I knew absolutely nothing about Eddie's family. I only knew that I would rather be here at school, working every Saturday in Ezra's shop, than I would be lolling around my parents' house.

I had missed seeing him the night of the snowstorm. Finally, he called me a few days later to say hi and invite me (and Liz) to attend a small protest march.

"It's only a small thing, but anything is better than nothing when it comes to protesting an illegal war." Eddie was referring, of course, to the Vietnam war.

"We're not in that war, though, Eddie. I'm not sure—"

"We're all in it," he said, "even if we're not *in* it."

I knew that Eddie was much more socially conscious than I was. Still, I cut myself a bit of slack since I'd been living in the insulated cocoon of obliviousness that wrapped itself around the Canadian Maritime provinces where I'd spent my life up until now. The war was a distant news story being played out on foreign soil by protagonists who had nothing to do with us. At least, that's what I'd always heard at home. Eddie thought differently.

I was twisting the payphone cord around my fingers peevishly as I listened to him. There were now two girls waiting for the phone in the basement where the other two were also in use. They were our lifeline to the outside world, and I was stalling for time. Any time I could be with Eddie was great as far as I was concerned, even if it was only on the phone. But a protest? It really wasn't me. *But maybe my consciousness could use a bit of raising*, I thought. So, I agreed to participate.

"Great!" He sounded genuinely delighted. "We can all go for a bite to eat in Yorkville after the protest," he said as if a protest were nothing more than going to the hairdresser.

Maybe it was for him, but I couldn't be quite that blasé. In fact, I felt a bit nauseous for a minute or two. He told me we'd meet at eleven a.m. on February first in front of the grad house (it was a

91

Tuesday and I had a class that ended only five minutes before then, so I'd have to rush), then we'd walk from there to the American consulate. That's where we could be most effective, according to Eddie. I didn't share his optimism on the effectiveness front. Oh, and he would have placards for us. I did feel sick at that thought.

Later that evening, I found Liz sprawled out on her bed, surrounded by textbooks, library books and writing paraphernalia. She seemed deep into the paper she was writing. I sat down on my bed and tried to get her attention.

"Liz, can we talk for a moment?"

Liz looked up and refocused on me. She pulled herself up and sat cross-legged on her bed. "No problem. Shoot."

"Eddie has invited us to take part in a protest against the Vietnam war on Tuesday. We'd have to meet him at 11 in the morning."

"Tuesday? No can do," she said. "I have a mid-term that afternoon. I guess you'll have Eddie all to yourself!" She smiled conspiratorially then immediately returned to her writing.

I can't lie—I was definitely conflicted by this turn of events. On the one hand, I was itching to get Eddie to myself (although to tell you the truth, I had been a bit puzzled about what interest he, an important grad student, could have in me, a first-year English and history major). I had come to terms with the fact that I had a mad crush on him. On the other hand, though, the very idea of me attending a war protest of any kind was terrifying, and I had thought that if Liz were there with me, I'd feel a bit less like a fish out of water. It seemed that I was on my own this time. For a fleeting second, I wondered what one wore to a war demonstration.

~

Tuesday dawned bright and very cold. It didn't matter what I wanted to wear to the protest; I would have to wear anything that could possibly keep me warm. I was wearing my warmest duffle coat, two sweaters under it, with a University of Toronto striped scarf—blue and red—wrapped twice around my neck.

Eddie and five of his friends—a motley group of fellow peace activists, who, as far as I could figure out, were all majoring in philosophy or political science—flew by as I waited in front of the grad house. I was sucked along as if in a slipstream. Eddie pushed a placard into my hand before I had a chance to read what it said. As we quickly made our way down the street toward the American consulate, I could see some of the slogans on the placards the other students were carrying. "Withdrawal, not negotiation," was the general theme. Eddie trotted along beside me, giving me crib notes on what we were protesting. It was kind of like instant Activism 101. It made me wonder how I could possibly have insulated myself from the issue for so long. In fact, from what I'd gleaned from the minimal news I read or saw on the television or heard from my father's comments at the dinner table for so many years, the war was an American thing with little to do with Canadians. Up until that moment, I had also wondered why they couldn't negotiate an end to the war. Eddie set me straight.

According to him and his peace activist friends, any attempt by the Americans to negotiate a peace treaty would suggest that they had a moral right to be fighting in Vietnam in the first place. Eddie's position was that they did not have this right. This was news to the ears of an uninvolved, naïve freshman like me. He also told me that Canada had been supplying goods to the Americans in support of the war. That opened my eyes. I think I held my sign up a bit higher, although I wasn't yet sure how this affected me or how I could affect the issue.

When we arrived at the consulate, a few people had already gathered in front of the unprepossessing grey, concrete building.

Waving placards that they, too, had hand-lettered, they were far more subdued than what I expected at a peace rally. In fact, by eleven o'clock, the hour we had all planned to gather, there were only about thirty people there by my quick count. It seemed a bit sad to me. As I glanced around, I noticed what appeared to be a camera being hoisted onto a shoulder. It was one of those ungainly television ones that the news people used, and it was pointing at the young man who had just picked up a megaphone. Then the camera began to scan the crowd. I could feel a mild panic rising in the back of my neck, and I looked around for a place to hide my face.

I moved slightly closer to Eddie, who was straining to hear the speaker now introducing himself as the university's communist club president. I pulled my scarf up over my nose and burrowed deeper into my coat. At that moment, I knew that if my parents sat down with their cups of after-dinner tea in front of the evening news that night, and my face appeared on the screen, there would be no going home. Literally or figuratively. I had the overwhelming feeling that I was in the wrong place.

The protest was, after all was said and done, a peaceful gathering, and I had managed to keep my face buried from sight. Afterwards, Eddie chatted animatedly to those of us in his entourage about the sit-in on Parliament Hill the next month. I sympathized with their cause, but I couldn't help but think they were spinning their wheels. I wasn't sure how productive a sit-in in Ottawa could be to the powers in Washington. I was also well aware, though, that I knew next to nothing about it. I would have to do something about my lack of current events knowledge, especially if I hoped to keep Eddie interested in me. And, for some reason, that was important.

~

Liz had been mildly interested in my description of the protest, but she was off on her own consciousness-raising journey.

About a week after my peace protest experience, I returned to residence from class to find Liz lying on her bed with her head in a book—as usual. Beside her on the floor was a small pile of books, and I noticed the top one was called *The Feminine Mystique.* When she saw me come in, she sat up. "Oh, Kat, a box came for you."

"A box?" I said as I arranged my books on my desk.

Liz pointed to a large box on the floor under the window. I'm not sure how I could have missed it. It was a large cardboard box with a white envelope affixed to the top. As I read my name on the envelope, I recognized the writing. It was from Darla. I opened the envelope and withdrew a one-page letter written on pink paper with Darla's name and address formally printed on the top.

"Dear Kat. I hope you will accept this as a token of my everlasting friendship. It was always intended to be yours. By the way, would you consider designing a dress for me for the end-of-semester fraternity formal dance?" It was signed *"Your best friend today and always...Darla."*

I suddenly realized what it was. When Darla moved out of the residence in January, her father sent movers who took away all her belongings, including the sewing machine. Of course, I had been disappointed to lose access to it, but it wasn't mine in the first place. Darla, god love her, must have realized that the machine was of no use to her without someone to operate it. My first thought was that I couldn't accept it. My second thought was that I'd have to run over to her sorority house and thank her the minute I had a chance. I decided that the second thought was the best thought. Liz wholeheartedly agreed. And, yes, I would design and make Darla another dress, and I'd make that mod one for myself.

Once I had the box open and the sewing machine on the floor, Liz got up to take a closer look. "Wow! It's gorgeous! Darla's a generous friend. I can't wait to see what fantastic things you'll make with it, Kat."

I organized the machine on my desk and then gathered up all the cardboard to take to the basement garbage room. Liz was sitting on her bed when I came back, leaning up against her headboard with her head bent over the book I'd seen earlier.

"What's that book?" I said.

Liz looked up and wagged the book at me. "This one? Oh, this one's that book by Betty Friedan, the feminist."

"Oh, yeah," I said, looking at the cover that Liz was showing me. "She's that women's liberation person, isn't she? I didn't know you were interested in that kind of thing."

"That kind of thing? Oh, Kat. We all need to be interested in what Betty and the other women in the movement have to say. We're the future."

I was looking through the pile of books on the floor beside her. "I've heard of this one," I said, holding up a copy of Simone de Beauvoir's *The Second Sex*, except this one was the original French: *Le Deuxième Sexe*.

"I love that one, but it's kind of old, now. I guess Simone de Beauvoir sort of started the movement, though, back in the late forties after the war. Anyway, I actually went to hear Betty Friedan speak last week."

"You did?" This was quite a surprise to me since she hadn't mentioned anything about it. "Why didn't you tell me about it? I might have gone."

Liz gave me a kind of raised-eyebrow look as if to say, *Really?* "It was at a synagogue. I didn't think you'd go based on what you've told me about your parents."

"My parents?"

"You know how you said they're kind of strait-laced white-Anglo-Saxon-Protestant, I think was how you put it."

"Well, there is that," I said, sitting down opposite her on my own bed. "But you're a Catholic, aren't you? I didn't think you were even allowed to go to a synagogue.'

"Technically, we're not," Liz said, putting her book down. "But my parents were never very strict, and that stuff never made any sense to me. Besides, I kind of had a date."

"A date to go to a synagogue to hear a women's' lib speaker?" Things were getting curiouser and curiouser, as Alice in Wonderland would have said. "Who with?"

"I've actually been seeing that T.A., Marcel Bertrand, for a while now."

She had never said a word about seeing someone. "You mean Dr. Sanderson's teaching assistant, Marcel?"

Liz nodded, smiling conspiratorially. Dr. Sanderson was my English professor. He taught first-year Greek and Latin literature, but he also taught several upper-level courses, one of which Liz was taking. We both had the benefit of Marcel's marking, not a happy fact from my perspective. I thought his marking was often too subjective, where his personal opinions seemed to shine through. Anyway, it seemed that my roommate was seeing him.

"So, how long have you two been dating?"

"Well, dating might be putting too fine a point on it," Liz said. I was confused, and she could tell. "We have, however, been sleeping together."

"Sleeping?"

"Yes, well, no, Kat. We don't really do much sleeping. Which brings me to my current dilemma."

Liz was sleeping with someone? This was almost too much for me. There was so much about her that it seemed I didn't know. I thought we were friends who told each other things. Well, to be fair, she was telling me now. Maybe I wasn't as shocked as I was jealous. My mind wandered to Eddie, but Liz brought me back to the present in a hurry.

"Do you know what the doctor I went to told me when I asked him for a prescription for birth control pills?" I shook my head. I was so shocked that I could not even imagine. "First, he went into a long tirade about the evils of 'sleeping around' as he put it. Sleeping around? I have one single person I sleep with. Then he had the nerve to suggest that good girls don't need birth control. I guess that's when I snapped and decided that I had to learn more about the women's movement."

"You said that was the first thing he told you. What was the second."

"Oh, yes. This doctor told me that he couldn't prescribe it anyway because it's still illegal in Canada. Illegal? Imagine all those old men up there in Ottawa deciding that I can't have the birth control pill that's been perfectly legal for six years in the U.S. He told me he could only give it to me if I had what he called 'menstrual irregularities.' Well, at that moment, I considered making up a few irregularities, but he didn't seem inclined to believe me. So, Marcel and I have to use condoms. Really? Condoms? I always thought only prostitutes used condoms."

"Why didn't you go to Student Health on campus? You can probably get the birth control pill there," I said quietly. I'd heard some gossip suggesting that this was the case and was surprised she hadn't gone there in the first place.

"You're probably right. I should have gone there first. Marcel suggested this guy."

Hardly a week went by these days when I didn't feel that I had lived a very sheltered life up to this point. The truth was that I'd never in my life had a single conversation with anyone about condoms or sex or anything remotely related to the requirement for birth control. I don't even know how I figured out that sex existed. My mother had certainly never told me. As I thought about it, it occurred to me that Nan Fran might have slipped me a brochure when I turned thirteen or so. I wondered what I'd done with it? I'd probably hidden it from my parents, that's for sure. I desperately needed to change the subject.

"So, what did this Betty Friedan say at her lecture?"

"Oh, Kat, she was so great. She said that a woman is never really defined as a real person. She's always a daughter, a wife, a mother. Think about it." I was thinking about it, that's for sure. "She said that a woman is told she is nothing until she's Mrs. Somebody. Isn't that awful?"

It did sound really awful. I had always thought that I'd be able to be an artist and maybe, someday in the future, a wife and mother. Even now that I faced a life as a high school teacher instead of an artist, second-best no matter how I looked at it, I guess I just thought that I'd always be myself. Maybe I was wrong.

~

Just before the end of the semester, when I was deep into final papers and studying for exams, Eddie asked me to have dinner with him. We went to a restaurant in Chinatown—the kind of place where you entered through a bead curtain, and the waitresses were all wearing those beautiful, slim Chinese dresses. They seemed to be run off their feet, although those dresses didn't allow for much running. Anyway, I was over the moon. This would be the first time that I'd had Eddie to myself. The protest we'd attended didn't count. Here, there wouldn't be that entourage of bohemian misfits that seemed to trail around with him everywhere he went. Tonight, it was just me.

He ordered for us. It seemed as if the staff knew him, and he seemed to know all about Chinese food. I had never had Chinese food before, and the aromas around us as we sat there sipping Chinese tea seemed exotic to me. The lights were dim, and I was feeling more grown-up than I ever had in my life. Here I was, alone with a man—not a boy—in a restaurant that served exotic food in a big city where everything seemed just a bit more intense and a whole lot grittier than my entire life before.

When the food arrived, Eddie explained it all to me then tried to show me how to use chopsticks. I figured out that I'd probably not be able to eat very much given how much food I was dropping. And eating rice grain by grain? This was going to take a long time, and that was just fine with me. I could have sat there forever. I was on a date with Eddie Lancaster.

We talked about the fact that I was coming to the end of my first year, and Eddie asked me what I planned to do with my life. "When we talked before, you told me that you wanted to be an artist. How's that going?"

I told him about my artistic pursuits and the finer details of my parents' response. I'd only briefly mentioned it before when Liz spilled the beans to him about my artistic passion.

"Man, that's a real bummer," he said after I'd finished my tale of woe. "You really should reconsider that artistic stuff. We only go through life once," he said, wiping his mouth with a large, paper napkin. "At least as far as we know." He grinned.

Then I told him that my artistic dreams were focused specifically on my design and sewing interests. As I spoke, a cloud seemed to drift across his face, his icy blue eyes becoming more piercing. "Fashion design? That's the kind of art you're interested in?" I nodded. "Geez, Kat. That's a bit bourgeois, don't you think?"

I thought I knew what bourgeois meant, but I didn't want to get tripped up. "How so?" I said, hoping that he'd clarify what he meant. I didn't know where he was going with this.

"Well, fashion is so materialistic, so middle class."

I was puzzled by this line of thought. "But we all have to wear clothes," I said. I sounded like a petulant child.

"True, but we could all wear uniforms like they do in communist China."

I was horrified. I'd seen pictures of those uniforms in the newspaper a few times and felt so sorry for the poor peasants who were forced to dress alike all the time. I didn't know how to respond, but I didn't have to. He continued.

"Great artists lead unconventional lives, Kat. You want to be a great artist, don't you?"

I was thinking about Coco Chanel and realized that I did consider her to be a great artist. I also remembered when my grandmother had told me about a French designer named Paul Poiret and showed me a picture of his sketches. He was a great artist, too. But Eddie was off on a tangent about art and conventional living, then suddenly, he said, "You know, I've been accepted to Berkley to do my doctorate. Dr. McLuhan recommended me, and I've got a full scholarship, so I can afford to go. U.S. schools are brutally expensive."

"When are you going?" I could hardly squeak it out. Suddenly, my throat had gone dry.

"I start in August."

So, Eddie was leaving for California. And I wasn't. The carnival was over.

Can't Help but Wonder Where I'm Bound

Tom Paxton, 1964

IT WAS FINALLY OVER—MY FIRST YEAR OF UNIVERSITY, that is. I was pleased with how well I'd done academically, although my final mark in English lagged behind the rest of them, not a promising start for someone who was supposed to be on the path to a career as an English teacher. So, from an academic perspective, I seemed to have been a success as a university student. But what about socially? Emotionally? Every time I heard the group the Happenings' rendition of "See You in September," my eyes kind of misted over. I wouldn't be seeing anyone in September—or at least anyone who really mattered. These were the things on my mind as I made my way home to the east coast for the summer, which promised to be a long one.

To tell you the truth, I didn't know how I felt. When I walked back into my family home, where I was to spend the entire four months of the summer break, I felt I was not even the same person. I no longer seemed to know who I was or where I belonged. After Eddie dropped his bomb on me, I spent an entire week walking around in a kind of fog. By the time I arrived back on the east coast, I wasn't at all sure that fog had lifted, and the Atlantic coast's misty weather didn't help. I only knew that I'd have to get a hold of myself. I'd have to face the fact that I'd probably read more into Eddie's interest in me than had been there. After the evening when he told me he was going to California, I didn't see him again. There was no good-bye. Nothing. So, I'd have no choice but to bury myself in my summer job.

The summer seemed endless. To most people in the northern hemisphere who suffer through long winters, this is usually a good thing. All it meant to me, though, was that I had to forget about how grown-up I'd been feeling in Toronto and regress into my former immature, high-school self. It was what seemed to make my parents comfortable. My father's approach to life hadn't changed at all, but then, why should I have expected anything different? I was the one who had left home to start a new life. I realized this the moment my father laid eyes on me and immediately launched into, "What have you done to your hair, Katherine?" And it just went downhill from there—although, surprisingly, my mother liked my hair. She just didn't express this opinion in front of my father. I adamantly refused to let it grow, though.

I was beginning to consider the world outside myself and my life as a small-city girl. I was starting to question things that I had never considered challenging before.

One night as Mom, Dad and I settled into Mom's spaghetti and meatballs, the newest addition to my mother's menus, my father stopped cutting up his spaghetti (yes, he cut up spaghetti) and turned to me. "Katherine, what was that I heard coming from your room last evening?"

I had no idea what he was talking about. I'd been alone and quiet all evening.

"I suppose you might refer to it as music. What was it?"

Then it clicked. "Oh, I think I was listening to Phil Ochs."

"Well, I think you should stop," Dad said, shaking grated parmesan cheese out of the cardboard tube it came in.

"Why?"

"I heard something about draft dodging and not marching anymore. And there was something about old people leading us into war. I don't like the perspective, and I'm quite sure you don't either."

My fork with its compactly twirled spaghetti was halfway to my mouth. I had to catch myself so as not to drop it in my lap—or alternatively, throw it at my father. I dropped it onto my plate instead. My father must have been standing outside my closed bedroom door for some time to have heard that much of the album. I thought for a moment before speaking, a tactic that had stood me in good stead with my father for all of my teenage years.

"Well, Dad, I think that his lyrics have a sentiment we should consider these days. It's like contemporary poetry, don't you think?"

"Music can be like that," Mom said, joining the conversation as she topped up our lemonade.

"Betty, modern music isn't poetry." My father lifted a fork-full of spaghetti and carefully placed it in his mouth. I knew that his fastidious nature must be chafing at this newfangled menu item. He chewed and swallowed, patted his mouth with his linen napkin leaving a large red, tomato stain on it—I saw my mother flinch ever so slightly—then turned to me.

"Tell me, then, young lady, what it is about that particular sentiment that attracts you. What do you know about war? What do you, or does anyone your age, know about why we go to war?"

Whenever Dad called me "young lady," I knew I was in for an earful. I would have to choose my words very carefully, partly because I didn't want to set him off on a political tirade, but also

104

because I knew there was a grain of truth in what he was saying. What, in fact, did I know about war?

"Dad, it's folk music. And some folk music makes me think about things I've never thought about before, like how Canada is supporting the Vietnam war. Now that I know about it, I think I have to, at least, have an opinion."

He started randomly chopping away at his spaghetti with the edge of his fork. "An opinion, eh?"

I sat up straighter and put my napkin on the table beside my plate. "Yes, Dad, an opinion. I have opinions, and I'm starting to see that I may need to learn more about a lot of things in life."

"Well, Betty," he said, addressing my mother rather than me, "I think young women's opinions are highly over-rated, don't you?"

"May I please be excused?" I said, getting up from my chair. Mom nodded, and I left the table, furious. It was going to be a long summer.

~

By mid-August, I had convinced my parents that I should fly back to Toronto rather than take the train to save time. They finally agreed, so on Labour Day weekend, I found myself standing in the middle of the Halifax airport with both my parents, trying to swallow down the apprehension that was crawling its way into my throat. I noticed that my mother was clutching and twisting the strap of her leather handbag so vigorously, I thought it might break. She seemed as nervous as I felt.

I had never been on an airplane before, and neither had my mother, although my father had flown once before, years ago. Even so, I wasn't at all sure that he trusted that a heavy, metal tube could get off the ground, much less get his daughter or anyone else safely to Toronto. I wasn't sure that I did, either, but

I knew I'd have to face my fear sooner or later. It had been my choice anyway.

"Ladies and Gentlemen," the booming voice over the loudspeaker began, "Air Canada flight..." And all I could hear was a loud rushing in my ears. My father started poking my arm.

"Katherine, they're calling your flight."

I said hurried good-bye's to Mom and Dad and joined the queue of people making their way toward to exit door leading to the tarmac. Most of the rest of the passengers seemed to be men in suits with fedoras and briefcases, punctuated with the odd well-dressed woman in a suit and matching hat.

I don't think I started to relax until we were well up into the air, and I was watching with the fascination of a child, the trees and tiny houses disappear from view beneath the clouds. By the time the pretty stewardess with her blue suit and tiny hat approached me to ask if I'd like something to drink, I was beginning to think I liked this air travel thing. I vowed then and there to do more of it as I got older.

When I arrived back on campus, I felt so grown up. I'd managed to get myself in from the airport on the bus and was exploring the second floor of the residence. Now that I wasn't a frosh any longer, I wasn't relegated to the attic floor and the four flights of stairs. Liz and I would once again be roommates, although she wasn't arriving for a few days. Her grandmother had died suddenly two weeks earlier, and she had to stay to help her mother organize the funeral and all her grandmother's affairs.

As I sat in my new residence room, looking around at the bare walls and the empty drawers, all I could see was potential. I could see possibilities for new beginnings, new ideas, even new people. I had gotten over Eddie's departure, although it still stung that he hadn't taken the time to say good-bye before leaving for good. I wondered what it was like on this day at the University of California, Berkeley. I wondered how many peace protests Eddie would attend this year and how they would be different from those here in Canada, where we were much more insulated from the war. At least our young men weren't getting draft notices and dying (apparently needlessly) on foreign soil. Then I wondered which young woman would be his companion this year. Enough of that. It was time to unpack, fill those drawers and hang a few posters.

I'd left my sewing machine in storage in the residence basement, so once I had my suitcases ready to store, I took them down and exchanged them for my machine. I set it up on my desk—I planned to study in the library again this year. I sat on my bed and looked at it for a few moments, then I took my sketchbook out of my bookbag and started making a few sketches of coats that were reminiscent of styles I'd seen in the September issue of *Vogue* magazine I'd read on the plane. The coats were calf-length A-lines with wide leather belts. I liked them, but I thought I could do better. I wanted to make the collars more interesting and design them so that the buttons didn't go up the middle of the front. I thought they should be off-centre and that they should have more eye-catching buttons.

I was immersed in my drawing when there was a knock on my open door. "Excuse me," came a timid voice.

I looked up to see what was very likely one of the new girls, first-year girls. It felt so odd not to be one of them anymore.

"There's a phone call for you...Katherine. They told me this was your room."

"Thanks," I said, getting up from the bed and putting away my sketchbook. "And it's Kat." She looked puzzled. "My name. It's Katherine, but everyone calls me Kat."

"Nice to meet you, Kat. I'm Abigail. People call me Abbie!" Her smile was so wide it practically split her face. She glanced over my shoulder. "Is that a sewing machine?"

I nodded.

"Oh my god," she said as her hands flew to her mouth. "I love sewing. My dad taught me when I was five years old."

Her dad? Five years old? *Well, that is unexpected*, I thought. "Let's talk about it sometime, Abbie, but right now I think I should go answer the phone."

She nodded and disappeared down the hall. Odd girl.

The call was from Ezra. He wanted to know if he could count on me for Saturdays again this year. I was so happy to hear that he wanted me back that I'd have run over that very moment if he needed me. He laughed and assured me that Saturday would be fine. He did say something peculiar, though.

"Katherine, my dear. You and I, we need to talk." He sounded so serious that it made me wonder if he might not be ill. I hoped not. I'd have to wait for Saturday to find out.

~

There was something about being a second-year student. It wasn't so much that I felt like I owned the place or anything, but it was a feeling of no longer being so naïve and inexperienced. It was a feeling of knowing my way around. And yet, in the midst of this, I had an ever-increasing feeling that I didn't quite belong yet. Would I ever get there? I wasn't so sure.

When I talked to Liz about it, she shrugged it off. "Once you really settle into your major, you'll feel like you belong. I know I did."

That, however, was the problem. I thought I had settled on a double major—English and history—but I didn't find either the classes or the professors inspiring. In fact, they were stultifying. My English professor droned on down in front of the classroom staring at his copious notes. My history professor was in love with the overhead projector and spent the entire class standing with his back to the class, reading illegible hand-written notes off the screen while we sat in the dark so the screen would be brighter. I thought the overhead projector had been designed so that it projected over the lecturer's head while the lecturer faced his audience. Then again, what did I know? The bottom line was that I was unimpressed with my classes this semester, and we were only halfway through the first week.

"By the way," Liz said, "Marcel and I are going to *The Riverboat* Saturday night. Want to come?" Liz and Marcel had picked up right where they had been when they parted for the summer four months earlier.

"I'm not sure," I said. "I have to work at Ezra's store on Saturday, and I don't know yet what kind of hours he wants."

"And besides which, you don't really want to go out, do you?"

Liz was so right. I preferred to stay home, sketching and sewing.

Then, desperately needing to change the subject, I told Liz that Ezra sounded very serious when he said he needed to talk to me. After I'd finished, she said, "You don't suppose he's closing the store or the tailoring business?"

"I sure hope not."

On Saturday morning, at nine a.m., I presented myself at Ezra's shop on Queen Street West. It wasn't yet open, so I knocked and waited for him to answer. He wanted to chat before he opened the shop for the day.

"Come in, come in!" he said as he smilingly gestured for me to enter while he locked the door behind me. "You had a good summer? I suppose you did back there on the coast. All that sea air must have been invigorating." He bustled down toward the office at the back of the store. "Sit! Sit!" he said, gesturing toward one of the two metal chairs across the desk where he now sat.

"So, Katherine. I have a proposition for you. This summer, my wife and I had visitors from New York. Her cousins!" He waved his hand in front of his face. "Oy, they are so American. You know what I mean." I was reasonably sure that I did not, but I chose not to make this observation. "They stayed with us for three weeks. Three weeks! Can you imagine putting up with 'America this,' and 'America that' for three whole weeks? But you don't need to hear about my family matters." He lifted a pipe from the saucer on the desk in front of him and put it between his teeth, but he didn't light it. "Those pieces we made from your sketches last year—the customers were very happy with them. I had a few photos. My wife's cousin Vinnie has a store in New York. He said he could sell them there. How would you feel about sketching some more for me? Of course, if you have the time."

Did I have the time? This was the first inspirational thing that had come my way since last spring. And so, Ezra and I began a kind of business relationship. I did a few design sketches for him every month and his seamstresses, Ruth and Edna, made up the samples. Then he sent them to New York, where someone (or many someones, I suspect) created the final products that Vinnie began selling in his shop somewhere in the garment district. I hoped that someday I could visit the shop and actually see a few of the pieces. Or even better, I looked forward to the day when I might see someone on the street wearing one of them.

Late in November, I finally saw one of the creations. Ezra's wife had just returned from New York, where she attended a family funeral, and she brought home two samples of the pieces made from my designs that were now being sold in Vinnie's store. When Ezra called to tell me about them, I was so excited that I could hardly wait for Saturday to come.

Finally, the moment had arrived. Ezra brought a bag out from under the cash register and placed it on the counter. "You and I see them for the first time together," he said, his eyes twinkling.

Then, with grand ceremony, he pulled them out of the bag. It was a dress and a jacket. He lifted them out one at a time and placed them on the counter, full-length, to get the full effect. Then, we both stared silently. I don't know how long we stood there like that, but I think it's safe to say that we were both speechless. They were hideous.

The dress, only marginally based on the design I'd sketched and the sample Ruth had created, was fabricated from a flimsy, vomit-green coloured fabric that hung like a pair of wet curtains.

"Dear god," he said before I could even begin to get my thoughts together. "They are not quite what you designed, no?"

"No." I shook my head in disbelief. I was so disappointed I thought I might cry.

Ezra began stuffing them back in the bag. "I will tell him to stop production immediately. I am so sorry, Katherine. I had no idea." When he had finished stuffing them out of sight, he stood up as tall as his five-foot-six-inch frame permitted and looked at me so earnestly. "I will make this right, Katherine. I promise you that."

I had no idea how he might accomplish that, and I was beginning to think there was no point in pursuing it, anyway. After all, I was destined to be a high school teacher, and that's all there was.

~

We were well into November of that fall semester when first-year student, Abbie, arrived back at my door one evening and tapped timidly. I looked up to see the light from the hallway glinting off her incredibly straight, black hair. But I couldn't quite see her eyes since her fringe almost covered them.

"Katherine, Kat," she began quietly, "some of the girls told me that you design dresses."

Oh, dear. Was she going to ask me to make dresses for the first-years in addition to the ones I was making for Darla and her friends? I told her that I had done so from time to time in the past, although I wasn't sure how much I'd be doing this year.

"Well, it's just that my dad does that, too."

Her dad? Well, that would explain her remark about her dad teaching her to sew, although it seemed strange to me. Wasn't everyone's father an accountant or something like that? I sat up from where I'd been lying on my bed with textbooks scattered around me and invited her in. She sat on the edge of my desk chair, glancing at the sewing machine.

"I told him about you," she said, holding her hands tightly in her lap. "I saw that photo of the dress you made for...who was it? Oh, yes, someone told me her name was Darla."

"Where did you see it?"

"Oh, it's on the bulletin board downstairs beside the payphones." Her eye caught three pages of sketches that I'd ripped out of my sketchbook. "Are those yours?" I nodded. "May I look at them?" I shrugged. Abbie picked them up and stared at each one for a long time. I was starting to get a bit uncomfortable, or perhaps a bit impatient. "These are wonderful," she said finally. "Anyone would love to wear them."

"Um-hm. Tell me about your dad. Did you say that he designs things?" I said, trying not to roll my eyes.

Abbie put the sketches back on the desk and sat up straighter. She smiled, and her eyes lit up. "Oh, yes. My dad. He's been a designer for as long as I can remember. Mom told me he used to sketch everything—trees, flowers, people—before deciding what he liked to do best was draw clothes. Strange, isn't it? A man like my dad, with three children, a fashion designer."

I could not imagine where he was a designer. "So, where did your father study?"

"Well, he was born in Hong Kong, but his parents didn't want him to be an artist, so he went to medical school for a few years then dropped out. He went to Paris to study at the *Chambre Syndicale de la Couture Parisienne*. Do you know it?"

I did but only slightly. I'd heard of it, but I had never heard of someone actually going there to study. Was she serious?

"Anyway, that's where he met my mother. She's born and bred Parisienne. You know, it's kind of hard to be the daughter of a French model." She laughed. "Anyway, she wanted to go to America, so Dad followed her and ended up at the Parsons School in New York. He eventually graduated."

Good lord, I thought, *she does know what she's talking about.* Unaccountably, my heart started thumping. I could hear it in my ears. "What's your father's name?"

"Oh, I forgot that." She giggled nervously. "His name is Alfred Chang."

I almost swallowed my tongue.

"Have you heard of him?" Abbie said.

"Hasn't everyone?" Alfred Chang's story was well known to any young woman in North America who followed fashion, as I had. The truth is that I had often coveted his designs. Although he designed mostly sportswear—sweaters and slacks—his real genius was suits, and, unlike the boxy, fussy suits that women seemed to favour these days, his designs were sleek and just a bit off-beat. I would have killed for one of his suits, but they were so far out of my budget that it wasn't even funny.

"Anyway," Abbie said, "after I saw that photo of the dress, I told my father about it. He asked me to ask you if I could bring him a few of your sketches."

Alfred Chang wanted to see my sketches? This was too unbelievable. I had to try to be calm. "Well, Abbie, that would be very nice." *Very nice? Dear god, is that the best I can do?* Although, in truth, showing my sketches to someone like Alfred Chang was daunting. But if I ever wanted to get anywhere with my designs, I'd have to swallow my trepidation. "In fact, I'd love to share some of my sketches with your dad. I'll have to get a few ready."

She beamed. "That would be terrific, Kat!"

Later, when I told Liz about the odd interaction I'd had with Abbie Chang, she was a bit more cautious. "Kat, that's terrific, but what do you think will come of it?"

"What do you mean?"

"Well, do you really believe she'll take your sketches to Alfred Chang? I mean, do you even know if she's telling the truth?"

This perspective seemed so odd coming from Liz, the free spirit who often threw caution to the wind. Was this caution I heard now? The truth was that I didn't know for sure that Abbie was telling the truth. I didn't know that Abbie was who she said she was. But why in the world would she tell me such a ridiculous story? It was too outlandish even to be a lie, as far as I was concerned. Then I remembered something Ezra had said after the debacle of his cousin's execution of my designs.

A man is not old until his regrets take the place of his dreams. According to Ezra, it was an old Yiddish proverb, and he said it applied equally to a woman. I was too young for regrets. What did I have to lose, anyway?

Both Sides Now

Joni Mitchell, 1964

TRUE TO HER WORD, ABBIE TOOK MY CAREFULLY prepared sketches and delivered them to her father. I knew she had taken them to him because she told me she had, and I chose to believe her. Then I waited. Whenever my mind wasn't otherwise occupied for the next few weeks, I wondered what Alfred Chang was thinking.

Does he think they show promise? Does he think they're any good? Does he love them? Does he hate them? Has he even seen them? Has he forgotten all about them? My mind would not stop. There were so many reasons why none of this should have made a bit of difference to me, but, somehow, it did. I mean, it was getting late in the semester, and I had mid-terms looming, papers due, tutorial classes to attend, and all I could think about was my fantasy of being a designer someday. How that could possibly happen now was beyond me. Even if he did like them, then what? I would get a momentary feeling of triumph that would then die and shrivel as I slogged to yet one more class on sixteenth-century English prose and poetry, or pre-Confederation Canadian History. My studies seemed so immersed in the past that I wondered if I could ever get back to the present—and the future.

115

I'd slid my sewing machine to the back of my desk to make some room for reading and writing. It turned out that I didn't favour doing all my studying in the library. I was sitting at my desk, my head in my hands, slumped over the textbook open in front of me when Liz bounced in one Thursday afternoon.

"Your head in a book again?" she said as she reached for a Pop Tart from the open box on her desk. I almost gagged. I despised them so much. But she loved the cardboard pastry and the glue-like "strawberry" filling, even without the benefit of a toaster. It was her go-to snack after class every single day of the week. At least she needn't ever worry that I would steal her stash. "Hello, Kat? Are you with me?" I looked up. "Marcel and I are going to *The Riverboat* again this weekend, and I think you should come this time."

The idea of going to a coffeehouse without Eddie made me feel kind of empty, perhaps even a bit queasy after all these months. He had been my music mentor. I hoped I'd hear from him, but he was obviously too busy working on that doctorate to think of his old friends back in Toronto. I started to say no when Liz put up her hand to silence me.

She shook her head. "Not this time, Kat girl. You're coming. You haven't been out in weeks, and it's time. Anyway, there's this young singer who's been doing the coffeehouse circuit in the northern U.S. who's going to be performing. I've heard good things about her. And she writes her own songs. I think we should go just to support other women following their dreams, don't you?"

I couldn't think of a thing that would deflate Liz's argument on that premise. If anything, I should be applauding her for thinking that we girls had dreams at all.

Liz chewed on her tart. "I've heard that she's had kind of a hard time."

I turned my chair toward Liz. "What kind of a hard time? Trouble with the old boys' network of musicians?"

116

"Not sure." She popped the last piece in her mouth and chewed for a moment—as one must with those disgusting tarts. "Anyway, even if she stinks, I think we should go to support her."

"What's her name?" I said, wondering if I'd seen anything about her in the *Varsity News*.

Liz shrugged. "I can't remember. I guess we'll just have to go to find out, won't we?" And she smiled.

~

Saturday evening was upon me, and I couldn't get out of my "date" with Liz and Marcel. I only hoped they hadn't thought to bring along an extra male. Liz had broached the subject of my lack of dating more than once, and I knew she was itching to play matchmaker. So far, I'd managed to deflect any advances she might have begun to make.

I had spent the day in Ezra's shop, where I could always immerse myself in the world of fabrics and creation. My time there passed so quickly and so agreeably that I often thought it was robbery to take his money. Ezra was paying me to have fun. But I needed the money.

Ezra didn't usually spend much time in the shop on Saturdays anymore. He left it to me. But he usually stopped by to say hello, deliver my paycheque and continue to rail against the New York debacle, vowing to make it right somehow. This day was no different.

"Katherine, my dear," he said as he was leaving, "*The smoothest way is full of stones.*"

"Yiddish Proverb?" I said.

He smiled broadly, tipped his hat and left. I thought about the proverb. The *only* thing I felt I felt right now was stones, or so it seemed. Was this as smooth as life got?

Later that evening, I was sitting in the common room leafing through *Varsity News* while I waited for Liz, who was still fixing her hair. Since I'd had my hair cut, it took me far less time than it took Liz to get ready to go anywhere. I looked up to see the housemother escorting Marcel into the common room, the only place in the residence where men were permitted to visit. I caught his attention and gestured to him.

"*Bon soir*, Kat," he said as he slid his toque off, revealing a tumble of thick, straight, dark-blonde hair. Marcel favoured what I referred to as the Beatnik look, making him either a throwback to the 1950s or a new wave Beatles fan. "How does it go this evening?"

Marcel's English was very good, but he still had a few difficulties with his verbs. However, his English far outpaced my own high school French, much to my grandmother's chagrin. She was fluent. Marcel had kind of grown on me since Liz met him last year, but he and I didn't seem to have much in common. A very sophisticated urbanite, Marcel was from Montreal, the son of two doctors who was, himself, headed to medical school. It was the family business, as he put it. His interests ran to Quebec politics and sports cars, neither of which I knew anything about nor had the slightest interest in anyway—thus, our lack of common ground, except for Liz, of course. Before we had a chance to get caught up, Liz arrived to put us out of our misery.

By the time we got there, the line to get into *The Riverboat*, as usual, was already meandering down the block. We would simply have to wait. As we neared the door, a pang of sadness seemed to engulf me, and I felt lightheaded. I did miss Eddie, no matter what I'd told myself. Maybe I'd have to write him a letter—and I would if only I knew his address in Berkeley.

A few minutes later, we were ensconced at a table with three other people we didn't know, and I was settling into my coffee. Despite the bustling all around me, I just wanted to lose myself in the music and stop my mind from pinging from one thought to another. They bounced from my non-existent artistic career to missing Eddie to the term paper due Monday morning—the one I should be working on right this moment. Then the announcer (one of the waiters that evening, I think) made his way to a microphone on a stand in the middle of the small, smoky stage.

"Hey, everyone," he said as the microphone squeaked alarmingly, "we've got a new singing, song-writing girl for you this evening. She wowed the crowds earlier in the week, and she's back. Let's welcome to the stage Miss Joni Mitchell."

And with the spotty applause all around the small room, a young woman, not much more than a year or two older than I was, took a seat on the wooden stool. She had long, lank blonde hair with a fringe that almost covered her large, dark eyes, and a guitar that looked too big for her. She pulled the microphone toward her, adjusted it and started strumming.

Accompanied only by her six-string guitar, she began singing in a voice that quietly coaxed me back from my mind mess into the present moment, a feeling I hadn't had for a long time. She began her set with a song she said was called "Just like Me." As I looked around, it seemed as if some of the people here had heard it before, at least judging by the number who were silently mouthing the words while they gazed intently at this young performer. Perhaps they had been here for her two performances earlier in the week since it didn't seem to me to be a song that had ever been recorded, at least not officially. Sometimes, when Eddie was here last year, he'd have tapes of new songs that no one had ever heard before, and then, we'd hear them at one of the coffeehouses. Overall, the audience this evening seemed genuinely absorbed by the talent, but, as usual, there was the predictable group of boors crowding a specific table in the back, laughing and smoking—cigarettes and grass as far as I could tell—paying the performer not the slightest bit of attention. I felt a sudden urge to go over to their table, slap each one of them up the side of the head, and tell them to listen. But I resisted the urge, making a conscious decision to ignore them and concentrate on the stage.

I turned my attention fully to Miss Mitchell. She had just finished her first two songs. "I have a new song I just wrote," she said. "No one's heard it before. I hope you like it. Here goes." She looked down at her guitar and seemed to will it to begin. Then it did.

As I listened to her words, I felt the haunting melody overwhelm me, and I realized that I was crying. Softly and quietly, but tears were running down my cheeks. And, for a moment, I didn't care. Her words were more poetic, more graceful, more profound than any of those recited by my English professors quoting long-dead poets.

"Wow, that was great!" Liz said when the song was over, and Joni left the stage to take a break. Marcel was off to find more coffee and a snack, and the other patrons at our table seemed to be packing up to call it a night. "What do you suppose the words mean? I mean, 'Both Sides Now' seems a bit deep."

I was so lost in my reaction to the poetry that I could hardly concentrate on Liz enough to engage in conversation. To me, the meaning had been crystal clear and resonated down into my soul, presuming I even had one. I was beginning to think I might.

"Reality versus fantasy," I said when I finally got my thoughts together.

"What? What about reality and fantasy?" Marcel, who had returned with three cups of coffee and three bags of chips, joined the conversation. "She is hot, no?"

I rolled my eyes at Marcel and caught Liz doing the same. Marcel might have excellent marks in chemistry and biology, but he'd never win any awards for his depth of character. Liz and I both ignored him.

"Okay," Liz said, "if it's about reality versus fantasy, what's that got to do with everyday life? There must be some connection. When it comes to folk music, there usually is."

I took a sip of the hot coffee then mindlessly picked a chip from the bag open on the table in front of me.

"It's like a meditation on the way we see the important things in our lives—or at least the things that seem important at the time—until we hit a rough patch and let ourselves be overwhelmed by what looks like reality. It's like when you're young and passionate about something, and you see its dark side, then you let that colour how you view it for the rest of your life."

"I see where you're going with this," Liz said. "When Ezra's plan to have your designs created in New York didn't work out, that was the rough patch, and you now see the reality of the world of design. Is that kind of it?"

It was only "kind of" it. My youthful passion for design might be just that—a youthful passion whose reality I could now perceive. But that wasn't what I was thinking about. I was thinking about two sides to love. Love looks like a place you want to take refuge, a place where you can seek shelter from everything bad in the world. But you win a few, you lose a few in life—and love. And I never told him I loved him. At least now, I know I did.

~

It was the first week in December, the last week of fall semester classes, and the beginning of exam week was almost upon me. I had two more papers still due and three exams to write. I would write two of those exams in one of the enormous auditoriums where several hundred students would sit with spaces between them so that no one could see anyone else's paper and cheat by copying. Five or six professors and teaching assistants would sit at the front of the room—the invigilators. It would be their job to make sure we all followed the rules, including accompanying anyone who had the urge to go to the bathroom within the three hours allotted to the exam. When I sat down, the exam question paper would be in front of me. Beside it, there would be two or three booklets containing lined pages—blank until I began filling them as quickly and accurately as I could with all the wisdom I had acquired since September. Like everyone else, I would line up several pens and pencils on the desk—no one likes to have to raise a hand to ask for another pen since this would result in getting the stink-eye from both the proctors and other students whose train of thought has just been broken. Oh yes, and I would have removed my watch (again, like everyone else) so that it could sit on the desk, staring at me for the next three hours, either willing me along or mocking me for how little I've done and how little time is left. And the exam question paper on the desk stays face down until that fateful moment when the head proctor—invigilator—looks at the clock on the back wall and says, in a loud voice that can be heard across the street, "You may turn over your exam papers and begin. Now!"

Anyway, that's what I had to look forward to when Abbie knocked timidly on my door just before dinner one evening.

"I have a letter for you," she said, still standing in the doorway. "It's from my dad."

I looked up at her. She was quite stunningly beautiful. Since the last time she'd stuck her head in the door, I'd learned that her mother had been a French model in her youth who had married her Asian boyfriend, Alfred Chang, much to her parents' chagrin, which had been one of the reasons she had wanted to pursue her career in New York. That's when Abbie's father attended Parsons. I don't know what she had meant when she said it was difficult to keep up with a mother who'd been a Parisian model. Abbie looked like someone who could have a top-notch modelling career herself if the university gig didn't work out. She was fairly tall, had beautiful, straight, jet-black hair that hung to her waist, dazzling white teeth and seemed to have inherited the best of her Caucasian mother and her Asian father. She was a knock-out, and unless I missed my guess, today she was wearing one of the jackets from her father's fall collection. I had seen it in *Co-Ed Magazine*. I was speechless.

Abbie came over to me where I was sitting at my desk and placed a cream-coloured envelope down in front of me. "I hope you have a Merry Christmas, Kat! Don't you just love Christmas?"

I wasn't at all sure I did love Christmas anymore. I used to love Christmas, but in recent years, Christmas had become as much about getting through it and out the other end without doing too much damage to family relationships as it was about celebrating—well, anything. Maybe coming through unscathed was celebration enough. However, I was looking forward to seeing my grandmother, Fran, who always made any visit home to the east coast bearable. I didn't share any of this with the perpetually sunny Abbie.

I put my pencil down and closed the three-ring binder that held my history notes as Abbie bounced away down the hall and clunked up the stairs to her attic-floor room. I picked up the envelope and looked at it. In the return address area was "Alfred Chang," in a clean, modern script beneath a stylized A-C logo design. Very crisp and very cool. My name had been written in the centre of the envelope in calligraphy. I wondered if that was some kind of a hobby of Abbie's multi-talented dad. I looked around and picked up a pair of scissors, which I used to open the envelope. There was no point in waiting any longer. I opened out the single page of cream-coloured, linen-finished paper and looked at the exquisite handwriting.

"Dear Miss Wilson:

I am very grateful to my daughter for bringing your work to my attention. I am more grateful to you for sharing some of it with me. I must say that it is not often that I've seen such raw talent in a young, self-taught designer. I have had the privilege of being a mentor to several students at the Parsons School of Design in New York for the past few years, and even after three years of training, many of them cannot produce what I've seen in your sketches.

I have taken the liberty of sharing some of your sketches with a friend of mine, Simon Carmichael, who happens to be, among other things, on the admissions committee of the fashion design program at Parsons. Of course, if you are interested in pursuing this further, you must apply and produce the portfolio demanded. There would likely be an interview in New York, which you would have to attend in person. There are no guarantees, but I can pave the way for you to at least get to the portfolio review.

Please let me know if you would like me to pursue this for you. Once you have completed the application procedures, however, you would be on your own.

Most sincerely, Alfred S. Chang."

When I arrived at the end of the letter, I immediately began to reread it. I must have been dreaming. Things like this don't happen. And Simon Carmichael? Where had I heard that name before? After a second read-through, I sat down on my bed and stared at it where I'd smoothed it out on my desk. Of course, these things happen. All that had really happened was that someone thought I had potential. I already knew that. Potential. Raw potential. I began to fantasize about being a fashion student in New York City, a place I'd dreamed of visiting someday. But like the song that Joni Mitchell had sung at *The Riverboat*, there is fantasy, and then there is most assuredly reality. The reality had many layers.

The first layer was preparing a suitable portfolio. Then there was the matter of getting to New York for an interview. And what happened if I got in? My parents would never agree—and they had a point. I knew that it was absurdly expensive. It couldn't be done, so I might as well not even try. I was just about to ball the letter up and toss it in the wastebasket when I heard a voice calling loudly from down the hall. "Kat Wilson!? Telephone!"

I folded the letter and hurriedly put it back in the envelope, then slid it in a drawer and headed downstairs to the telephones. It was probably my mother wondering when I was arriving home. I was wrong.

"Hey, cool Kat!"

I hadn't heard that voice in a very long time. And what was that "cool Kat" thing all about?

"Eddie!" I was delighted to hear from him although I should have been angry that he left without saying good-bye. "How are things in California?"

"California's a blast, but Berkeley's a bummer. My thesis supervisor's a real drag, but I'm loving some of my classes, and there's a real sense of righteousness for free speech. You'd love it here!"

I didn't think I would. I thought I'd probably feel even more out of step with Californian students than I did with Toronto students.

Eddie then began apologizing profusely for leaving without a backward glance, or so it might have seemed. He meant nothing by it. He just didn't like saying good-bye to anyone. But now he wanted to know how I was and whether or not I'd been to any student protests this term. I had not. I did, however, hesitantly begin to tell him about the letter I'd just received. I was hesitant because last year we'd had more than one disagreement about the value of the whole fashion and design thing. He thought I should pursue art, just not fashion. So, I was a bit circumspect in my explanation.

When I had finished, I had told him everything. He whistled. "Geez, Kat, you have to go."

"Well, Eddie, it's not a simple matter of just going."

"It is if you think it is. Did you ever finish reading that Simone DeBeauvoir book Liz kept toting around?"

"You mean *The Second Sex*?"

"Yeah, that one. Old Simone had a lot of great things to say, you know, Kat."

"Sure. Like what?"

" *'Change your life today. Don't gamble on the future, act now.'*" He stopped for a moment. "Kat, I mean it. I've been thinking about you, and I think I've been unfair to you. Fashion design *is* your art —real art. Don't let this go without a fight."

At that moment, I realized that Eddie, himself, would be the last thing in my life I'd let go without a fight.

The Way I Feel

Gordon Lightfoot, 1967

I SPENT MOST OF MY CHRISTMAS VACATION working on my portfolio and trying to avoid my parents. Whenever I retreated to my room to work, inevitably, one of them would wonder what I was up to. I told them I was just trying to get ahead of the winter semester work. Well, it wasn't really a lie, was it? My grandmother, as usual, though, seemed to know. At least she seemed to know that something was exciting me and that it had nothing to do with ancient history or dead poets.

By the time I returned to school in January, winter had set in once again. The campus was a winter wonderland of snow-coated trees and stone buildings that seemed to rise out of snowdrifts like fairy castles. I must admit that I truly loved the campus and what campus life represented. It was just that I found the classes I was taking so stultifying. I sometimes felt as if I were choking when I sat there, one of some two-hundred undergrads high up in the back of a stuffy auditorium while a professor down in front droned on about dead white guys. But there was still music on the weekends.

Gordon Lightfoot, who had gained quite a following over the last year, was playing a month-long engagement at *The Riverboat* all through January, and Liz and Marcel must have tried to get there every single night. I went twice because I liked his voice. His music made me think about the way I felt about so many things in my life at that moment—my school work (mind-numbing), my love life (non-existent), my future (murky, to say the least). However, there was one thing that kept me going. That was the possibility, as remote as it might have been, that I would be able to get an interview at Parsons at least.

I sent off my application before the end of January, then waited. When I wasn't writing papers or studying for mid-term exams, I studied the fashion magazines the library had subscriptions to, as well as the ones other residents left in the common room when they were finished with them. It was the only way I had to keep up with the industry I was so far removed from. By mid-March, I was starting to lose hope of ever having a chance to get an interview when Abbie walked into the common room where I was leafing through an old edition of *Vogue* magazine that I'd found under a pile of the latest edition of *Varsity News*.

"Hi, Kat," she said, plopping down on the couch beside me. "You must be excited!"

"Hi, Abbie. Umm…excited about what?"

"Your interview at Parsons, of course! I'd be dying!"

"Oh, yes, my interview. Well, to be honest, I haven't actually heard back from them yet." I closed the magazine and put it back on the coffee table.

"Oh, well, Dad said you were sure to be interviewed. I think he talked to his friend Simon in New York. I just thought…and since there's a letter for you out on the table in the hall with a Parsons School return address, I assumed—"

"Sorry," I said to Abbie as I got up and raced out into the hall.

Just as she had said, there was an envelope on the round table in the middle of the foyer where our mail was left for pick-up. I must have missed it in the pile when I came in earlier—there had been such a lot, but most of the girls had been through by now, and there was only this piece of mail left on the table. For a moment, I considered racing to my room and opening it by myself just in case the news was bad. But I couldn't wait and found myself, almost without conscious thought, tearing it open right then and there while Abbie, who had followed me, stood in the archway leading to the common room.

I snatched the letter out of the envelope, unfolded it and began reading.

"Dear Miss Wilson. We have reviewed your application and portfolio. Please be advised that we wish to interview you as the next step in the application process. Please present yourself at the school at 410 East 54th Street, New York, on Wednesday, April 19 at 2 p.m. Please confirm this by return post..."

I stood there staring at the letter, expecting it to explode or disappear. I read it again. They wanted to interview me—the trouble was that I had an exam that day. What could I do? Could I really go? How would I get there? So many questions and so few answers. But for that one moment, I wanted to simply savour the delicious feeling that my work was acceptable—at least acceptable enough for the Parsons School to want to interview me. The rest I'd worry about—and soon.

"I was right, wasn't I?" Abbie said.

~

I should have known that Liz would have a plan or would at least be able to come up with something plausible on short notice. The first step in her plan required me to tell a lie. She told me that on April 17, I was to inform the registrar's office that my grandmother had died and that I had to go home for the rest of the week. That would give us an extra day in case anything went awry with the travel plans. My exam would have to be postponed. In other words, I'd have to do it "out of sequence," as

129

they called it. Once I got over being appalled by the very thought of such an incredible lie, she assailed me with step two of her plan— hitchhiking to the border in Niagara Falls and taking a bus to Manhattan. I think I almost passed out when she suggested hitchhiking without even the hint of a tongue in her cheek. My first thought was that my parents would be nothing short of apoplectic. Of course, as Liz pointed out, there was absolutely no point in even mentioning the interview to them, nor how I planned to get there. She, of course, was entirely correct.

Naturally, she didn't expect that I'd execute this crack-pot plan alone. She was coming, and there was no arguing with her about that. And why would I? I agreed that I had little alternative. So, we set the wheels in motion.

A week before we were set to leave, as I strolled past the Yorkville coffeehouses, I spied the cover of *Vogue* magazine's new issue on a newsstand near *The Riverboat*. The model was wearing a very short, pixie haircut, even shorter than my Audrey Hepburnesque cut, and immediately I knew I needed it for my interview. I had seen pictures of Twiggy's hair, and this style resembled it. When I pointed it out to Liz, even she was shocked. At that moment, I knew it was right.

On April 17, at nine a.m. on the dot, I presented myself at the Registrar's office, clutching the required form in hand. I had to put the lie in writing. There was no way around it.

When confronted by the Registrar's secretary, I almost backed out, although I had already informed the Parsons School that I would attend the interview. The severe-looking woman looked at me over the top of her reading glasses while I stared at the light twinkling off the gold chain hanging from them. I couldn't look her in the eye, so I pretended to be overcome with grief for my grandmother's death (god, I hoped I'd be able to tell Nan about this someday).

"So sorry for your loss," she said as she took the paper from me and read the details. She didn't sound the least bit sorry. She sounded tired, which made me wonder how many of these forms she'd seen in the past week or two.

Anyway, she told me that they'd reschedule the exam and that there would be a notice in my mail when I returned from the funeral. I fled as fast as I could.

Liz and I took a city bus down to the lakefront to access the highway that headed toward Niagara Falls. A light rain began to fall just as we stuck out our thumbs. I should have been overcome with anxiety, but as we stood there, arms outstretched toward every passing vehicle, with Liz holding a cardboard sign that said "Niagara Falls," I felt a kind of freedom that I'd never experienced before. I was doing something so not like me. Or maybe, I was doing something that wasn't like the me before today. Perhaps this was something today's me would do. Whatever it was, I felt light. Then a blue Volkswagen van pulled over. The driver leaned over and cranked the passenger-side window down. "Niagara Falls, eh?" he said. "Hop in the back."

Somewhere between thirty and fifty by my reckoning, he had shoulder-length hair and a beard. He was wearing overalls, and there was some odd-looking equipment in the back behind the passenger seat. I hoped it wasn't the kind of stuff people used to murder unsuspecting girls hitchhiking against all common sense.

My fears were completely unwarranted. His name was Jeff, and he was heading to Niagara Falls to do some kind of plumbing job. He said he would drop us off at the Canadian side of the Rainbow Bridge. We could walk over the bridge, go through U.S. immigration and catch a bus about half a mile beyond that.

Surprisingly, at least to me, all went exactly as he had suggested. We were damp and tired by the time we reached the bus terminal in Niagara Falls, New York, but we were on our way. The bus trip would take us almost twelve hours, but it hardly seemed to be a problem since it was overnight. Liz and I both slept most of the way (I sleep better in a bus than on a train, it turned out), and when we arrived at the Greyhound terminal in Manhattan, the sun was shining brightly. It was April 18, and I was in the Big Apple. I had twenty-four hours before the interview.

The First Time Ever I Saw Your Face

Peter, Paul & Mary, 1965

NEW YORK CITY. THE CITY OF LEGENDS. We had only two days, so, despite being tired from the overnight on the bus, Liz and I walked the streets for hours that first day, mesmerized by the sheer size of the skyscrapers and the number of people crowding every intersection. They hurried along, briefcases in hand, checking their watches as if they had somewhere very important to be. We, on the other hand, were the ultimate tourists, gawking and pointing at every corner. I had my trusty little red Canon camera on a strap around my wrist, and we made good use of it that day. I found myself humming the only song I could remember about New York.

"What is that tuneless thing you're humming, Kat?" Liz finally said to me as we sat on a bench enjoying a hot dog for lunch in Central Park.

" 'Autumn in New York,' " I said, wiping mustard off my chin with a flimsy paper napkin.

"Could have fooled me," she said, laughing.

133

"Hey," I said. "It's Ella and Louis. So New York, don't you think?"

"What I think," Liz said, "is that you should stick to the designing and avoid singing at all costs."

All I could do was laugh. The humming was really to cover up the mounting apprehension I felt as the hours ticked away, and my interview grew ever closer. But Liz kept me sane. She had done the research. Liz had dropped in to see one of her food science professors she knew had studied at Columbia University in New York before we left Toronto. From her professor, she'd gotten the address and telephone number of a women's hostel—a hotel for women only—where we could stay. I hadn't been very enthusiastic about the idea. It reminded me of the hotel where the girls stayed in Sylvia Plath's book *The Bell Jar*, which had been all the rage a few years earlier. I had read it, but I hadn't been very keen on either the main character Esther or her experience in New York. She had been so riddled with angst that it was impossible for her to experience what I knew in my heart New York had to offer. And the fact that the author had committed suicide a month after the book was published had always left me cold. Anyway, we stayed at the hotel on West 39th Street, a few blocks from the New York Public Library, less than a ten-minute walk to Times Square and fifty minutes to Central Park. Liz had gone to the library to check the maps and had plotted our route for the day. She was determined that we'd both get as much out of this brief sojourn in New York as possible.

She also figured out that it would take me not much more than half an hour to walk from the hotel to E. 54th Street, the Parsons School.

By the end of the first day, we had walked for miles and were both exhausted when we tucked into a plate of spaghetti and meatballs at a small Italian restaurant around the corner from the hotel. It was late, and I was famished.

"Shall we try to get rush tickets for a show?" Liz seemed to have stamina galore.

"Sorry," I said, "but I'm beat, and I still have a few details I'd like to review in my portfolio. In case you'd forgotten, we're here for my interview. You know? The one that's at ten tomorrow morning?"

She laughed and spun a forkful of spaghetti, then stuffed it into her mouth. "Okay," she said after chewing and swallowing, "but I'm going with you. I'll just wander around outside or wait in the hall."

We'd had this conversation already about five times. I told her that she didn't have to come with me to hold my hand. I'd be fine. But the more often we discussed it, the more I realized that for all her bravado, she was a bit uneasy about being alone in the city. Strangely, I didn't have that same anxiety. The city invigorated me (miles of walking notwithstanding!), and I would have happily walked the half-hour by myself. In the end, of course, she came with me.

The next morning, I was up at the crack of dawn—well, probably not quite that early, but it was early for me. It was hard not to wake Liz up since the room was so small. I kept bumping into her bed as I surveyed my interview outfit for the millionth time. She finally got up and headed out to take a shower while I dressed.

I had designed the outfit myself. Ezra had insisted on giving me the fabric as a gift and had even let me work on it at his shop, where I would have access to threads and trims galore. Now, as I got dressed, I realized that there was no full-length mirror in the room, so I couldn't really know exactly how it looked. It was a black mini-skirted jumper over a black turtleneck. On top, I created a mini-skirt-length fire-engine red coat with a stand collar and a belt. I and also made a black beret. I finished off the outfit with black tights and shoes. Now, as I looked down at it, I wondered if the red might be a bit much. I was starting to panic, but it was too late to change my mind. The next thing I knew, Liz and I were flying out of the hotel's front entrance on our way to the rest of my life. Or so I hoped.

~

As we approached the imposing building, I could see what appeared to be groups of students milling around outside on the sidewalk. They all looked so sure of themselves, talking, laughing and smoking. *Could I ever be that self-confident and composed?* I wondered as I watched them.

When we reached the door, Liz squeezed my hand and told me she'd be right back here in this very spot in an hour. I squeezed back, turned, looked up at the sign, took a deep breath and plunged forward.

The building was a rabbit warren of corridors, doorways without signs and people hurrying around. Looking down at the piece of paper I had clutched in my hand, I realized that I had no idea where to find the interview room specified. There didn't seem to be anyone I could ask for directions, so I started to wander. It was fascinating. I peeked into a couple of studios and classrooms and passed a library. Before I knew it, I was confronted with a large clock on the wall outside the library, which told me, in no uncertain terms, that I'd be late for my interview if I didn't find someone to give me directions. It was 9:55.

I stopped the first young woman I could flag down. She gestured in the direction of the stairwell and told me the room was at the top of the stairs, three doors down, three flights up. I thanked her and started to run. By the time I'd made it up the three flights of stairs, I was almost out of breath. I quickly opened the fire door at the top of the stairs and turned abruptly. Where he appeared from, I'll never know, but the next thing I knew, I was crashing into a young man with a camera slung around his neck and another one, which was now flying out of his hand and skidding across the floor.

"Oh my god," I said. "I am so sorry."

"Geezus!" he said, scrambling for the camera that had landed with a thud up against the far wall. He picked it up and looked over at me, where I was trying to set my beret back on my head. "Can't you look where you're…"

I looked over to him to apologize again when I locked onto the deepest brown eyes I'd ever seen. "I…I'm…" I looked at my watch. "I'm late," I said, grabbing my portfolio and escaping.

~

"So, Miss Wilson, tell us why, precisely, you believe you belong here. Tell us why you are not simply another young woman crazy about clothes who thinks it would be quite a lark to be a designer."

The woman speaking had introduced herself as the head of the fashion design program. She was seated in the centre of a long, wooden table facing me. Two men sat on her left and two women to her right. All of them were what I would have considered quite old—probably all over fifty, with one exception. And they were all smoking. Little streams of exhaled smoke rose over their heads. They had all introduced themselves, but I could recall none of their names except for the man on the far left of the speaker—the one who was nowhere near fifty. He was Simon Xavier Carmichael. He was Alfred Chang's friend in New York and very likely why I was even being considered for admission.

When the head of the program asked me the question, I thought I could see a slight smile begin to play around Mr. Carmichael's mouth. I knew him to be something shy of thirty since I'd seen him celebrated on the pages of one fashion magazine or another recently. They had described him as a boy wonder, the American Christian Dior. He seemed to nod slightly to me as if to say, "Well, go ahead. Tell us," he said. So, I did.

I sat in the single chair that faced them, looking down at my hands in my lap. I had removed my red coat and was sitting primly with my ankles crossed. I was still wearing the black beret. I took a deep breath and looked up. "I suppose I *am* another young woman who's crazy about clothes. But I'm also much more. I believe that clothing goes beyond what we see in the glossy photographs on the pages of fashion magazines. It's much more than young college co-eds scrambling to decide what to wear on Saturday night to impress a man. And I believe that those in the front lines of the women's movement who profess to believe that only repressed housewives and vain socialites care about what they wear are completely overlooking the reality of what clothing means. I believe that they are doing women a disservice by disregarding one of the most powerful weapons women have in their fight for equality. I believe this because I believe that clothing is our armour and our weapon—for both men and women. Our appearance is the first thing anyone notices about us. You see me here in an outfit of my own design and creation, and you draw conclusions about me. Some of those conclusions may be accurate, while others may be wrong. But If I get it right, you draw the conclusions *I* want you to draw. The rest comes later." I stopped and looked up and down the row of interviewers. A couple of them were jotting notes while the others sat with their arms folded across their chests. Mr. Carmichael was stubbing out a cigarette and lighting another one.

I figured that since no one had said anything, I should continue. "I also think that, in my soul, I'm an artist. The feeling I get when I'm sketching a new design is a kind of crackling energy. It's like a power that I need to find a way to harness. Studying here would train me to harness and develop that electricity."

"Do you think that fashion design is an art form?" Mr. Carmichael had put down his cigarette. He placed his hands with fingers laced in front of him on the table and leaned forward.

I looked straight at him. "I do, Mr. Carmichael. Harmony, balance, proportion, pattern—even rhythm and movement—all of the artistic elements are part of fashion design. And I want to design clothing for women in the new world order that's coming."

Good lord, I thought, *that might have gone a tad too far.*

"Well, Miss Wilson, I think we've heard enough," the program director said as she shuffled the papers in front of her on the table. ". Thank-you so much for coming. We'll be in touch."

I got up, took my coat off the back of the chair and picked up my portfolio. I walked over to the table, thanked and shook hands with each one of them in turn. When I got to Mr. Carmichael, who was seated closest to the door, he pulled me slightly closer and whispered, "Call me Simon...Kat."

I nodded and fled. When I got outside in the corridor and was sure the door was closed tightly behind me, I sagged back into it and just breathed. I looked up and was startled to see someone leaning against the wall across the corridor staring at me. It was him.

"Well, how'd it go?" said the owner of both the camera I'd knocked to the ground earlier and the deep brown eyes. "Oh, by the way, I'm Chuck."

Kat
1967–1970

New York

See You In September

The Happenings, 1966

"I'D LOVE TO TAKE SOME PHOTOGRAPHS OF YOU," Chuck said. He ran a hand through the dark curls flopping onto his deep-set, deep brown eyes, then gave me a lop-sided grin as he continued to lean against the opposite wall. He raised his camera.

I clutched my coat and looked at him, not at all sure what to say. "You don't even know me."

"But I'd like to," he said, moving toward me, his hand outstretched. "Charles Cohen, but like I said, you can call me Chuck. And you are?"

"Kat," I said, involuntarily reaching for his outstretched hand. I couldn't keep my eyes off him. What was going on? "Kat Wilson."

"Well, Kat, Kat Wilson, I do hope the interview went well because I'd like to get to know you better."

I should have felt uncomfortable, but oddly, I didn't. That being said, I hadn't completely taken leave of my senses. Of course, he couldn't take pictures of me, and I told him so. He pouted.

"Anyway, I'm leaving tomorrow." I didn't know what else to say. But Chuck wasn't having any of it.

Before I knew it, Charles Cohen had set himself up to take photographs of both me and of Liz (I had insisted on a friend coming along) in Central Park at dusk. Then the three of us would have dinner at his favourite Italian restaurant right around the corner from the school. He was very persuasive. I was beginning to think that the only restaurants in New York were Italian, but I didn't mind.

He insisted on accompanying me out of the building where Liz was waiting. When she caught sight of us, her eyes were immediately on Chuck. I couldn't blame her. There was something about him.

"Kat," she said as we approached her, "how'd the interview go?" I could tell that focusing on me was taking as much concentration as she could muster.

I was still trying to process the interview, as well as my encounter with Chuck. I didn't know what to say.

"Okay, I guess. It was hard to tell." I introduced her to Chuck.

"It's always hard with that crew," Chuck said. It turned out he was a photography student and native New Yorker. He had two years to go before he graduated. "Anyway, don't worry about it. I have a good feeling." Then he gave me that smile again. Who could argue with that smile?

After setting up a time and place to meet this evening, Chuck snapped a quick picture of the two of us in front of the school. Then he turned and headed off in the opposite direction.

"What just happened?" Liz said as she took my arm. We threaded our way through the pedestrians.

"I'm not sure," I said. "He was just there when I came out of the interview room." I also told her about crashing into him before the interview.

"Well, as far as I can see, it's kismet." Liz was an incurable romantic who believed in destiny. On the other hand, I was far less sure about the notion of fate when it came to romance. *However, I might make an exception for Chuck,* I thought.

The evening was extraordinary. For an hour in Central Park, Chuck had us laughing and moving from one place to another, all the while snapping pictures. I thought I'd feel self-conscious about posing outdoors in full public view, but I didn't. For the briefest of moments, I wondered what my father would think. But of course, I knew what he would think. He'd take a very dim view of his daughter cavorting in public. Not very lady-like, I'm sure. I realized that I didn't care. Of course, one of the reasons I couldn't really care was because this was a small matter compared to what I'd have to face if I actually did get into the Parsons School, and I did manage somehow to find a way to pay for it. It wouldn't be pretty. So, I put it out of my mind.

After the photography session, the three of us walked the twenty-five minutes to the restaurant. Chuck seemed to know every nook and cranny of this part of Manhattan. Like a tour guide, he pointed out various attractions as we made our way down Fifth Avenue and turned into East 55th Street. Born and raised in Brooklyn, Chuck told us he'd been finding his way around New York by himself since he was thirteen. His parents had given him his first camera for his birthday that year, and he'd made the city his subject. When I asked him about his photographs, he pulled half a dozen black and white cityscapes and a few pictures of people from his jacket's inside pocket. I had always prided myself in my artistic eye, and as I looked at Chuck's photographs, I knew in a minute that this talented young photographer was going places. I briefly wondered what my designs would look like if they were photographed on a model by a gifted photographer.

When we finally reached the restaurant, there was a short line. We had to wait fifteen minutes before we could be seated, but it was worth the wait. A small space holding about ten tables, it was as if the room had been plucked up out of a small Tuscan village and plopped onto the island of Manhattan. The tablecloths were red and white checks, and the candles in the middle of every table were in wine bottles coated with many layers of wax that had dripped over multiple dinners for a very long time. But more than how it looked was how it smelled. The aromas of garlic and tomato wafted from the kitchen, making me hungrier by the minute.

Over the next three hours, Chuck regaled us with stories of growing up in Brooklyn and being the only boy in his high school graduating class who didn't want to be a doctor or lawyer or football player for a living. Ever since that birthday when he'd received the camera, his passion for photography had grown. It had taken on such a large role in his life that there was never again any doubt in his mind what he had to do with his life.

"I just couldn't ignore it," he said, lounging back against the red vinyl of the booth, which squeaked softly. "There's something about the way art sucks you right in. I've met so many people, though, who just ignore that siren call. I guess they just grow up and away from it." He leaned in and picked up his wine glass. "I have a framed picture of Pablo Picasso on the wall of my darkroom." *He has a dark room? Of his own?* I thought. He continued. "It also has a quote of his. *'Every child is an artist. The problem is how to remain an artist once we grow up.'* I guess you two have probably already figured out that I've never really grown up. And I'll never grow away from my art."

I nodded—perhaps a bit sadly since, at that moment in my life, I had no idea if or when I'd be forced to grow up. As I sipped my second (or fourth) glass of Chianti, I said, "How did your parents take the news that their son wanted to be a photographer?"

He smiled. "Dad asked me where I planned to go to school. And Mom said she hoped it would be close enough to still come home on the odd Sabbath."

"They didn't try to talk you out of it?" Liz asked, perhaps voicing the question that I seemed not to be able to ask.

"Not for a second," he said. "You know, I remember it clearly, the day my father finally asked me what I planned to do with the rest of my life. I was seventeen and cocky as hell. When I told him, he stood in front of me, placed one hand on each arm,

144

looked me in the eye, and told me the only way to live my life was to know what I was living for and to make my living with that knowledge."

"A wise man," I said, a tear forming behind my eye. I chugged another bit of wine and contemplated my future. Then Chuck told us a joke, and all I could do was laugh.

The three hours we sat in that restaurant seemed to race by. I couldn't seem to make them slow down, although I wanted to. I wanted to so badly. By the time we left, I felt as if I'd known Chuck all my life, and the prospect of leaving New York in the morning and possibly never seeing him again was almost too painful to bear.

When he left us in front of our hotel, which he insisted on doing even though it wasn't on his way home, he stood in front of me and placed one hand on each of my shoulders, just as I imagined his father had done to him. "Kat Wilson," he said, "I think you already know what you're living for. Now just make sure you make your living with that knowledge." He dropped his hands, kissed me on the cheek, turned and pecked Liz, then started to move down the street waving. He stopped half-way down the block and turned around. "See you in September, Kat."

I hoped so. I really hoped so.

~

The two letters came in the mail three days apart. I had spent the past six weeks in a whirlwind of final papers, exams and clearing out of residence for the summer once again, not knowing where I'd even be in September. Then I had arrived home to find my parents in the throes of planning a road trip to Maine, a "family" vacation that I could not have wanted any less. Given that I was twenty years old, I thought I'd earned the right to stay home alone while they went. That was the first argument. Then there was the second—the one that was far more important.

Every morning, before my mother could get to the mailbox hanging on the wall outside the front door, I scrambled to retrieve the letters. Each day, nothing. Until, finally, on June 1, the first one arrived. I stared at the return address. The Parsons School. New York City. I ran upstairs and locked myself in the bathroom—the only door in the house with a lock—and ripped open the letter.

"Dear Miss Wilson: We are pleased to inform you..."

That was all I needed to see. They were pleased to inform me. I had been accepted. Now, I had no idea how I'd broach the subject to my parents or how in the world I'd ever pay for it. But I decided to savour the moment and called Liz, who was still in Toronto working for the summer before her last year.

"When are you going to tell your parents you're dropping out of U. of T. and going to New York?"

I hadn't actually considered that I'd have to "drop out" of one school to go to another. It sounded horrible. "God, Liz, I'm not even sure I *will* be going."

"What do you mean?" She was now yelling at me through the phone. "Of course, you're going! Who else will I have to visit in the Big Apple? And I'm going back. You can be sure of that!"

I laughed a bit nervously because, as much as I loved Liz, I did have to face some realities of my situation. Being a Canadian headed to an American school would mean that I'd have to provide them with some kind of proof that I could pay my tuition—and it wasn't insignificant. Then, I'd have to live there. There was so much to consider that I thought my head would explode. On top of everything, the thought of having to turn them down made me feel physically ill. I told Liz I'd let her know when I told my parents. What I didn't tell her was that it was not a foregone conclusion that I'd ever tell them. Then I thought about Chuck and what he'd said to me. And about his parents. What I wouldn't have given at that exact moment for parents who would accept my dream. Then letter number two arrived.

Since I'd received my acceptance letter, I'd stopped rushing to the mailbox. But it was the fourth of June, three days after letter number one, when my mother came into the kitchen where I was eating breakfast and placed an envelope beside my plate. "Mail for you, Katherine." She stood beside me for a moment, looking at the envelope. "What would you be getting from New York City?"

A frisson of excitement—or perhaps terror—ran up the back of my neck. I put down the piece of toast I was about to bite into and picked it up. It was another letter from Parsons. Were they having second thoughts about me? Would I be spared having to tell my parents? Would my dream be pulverized at this very moment? There was only one way to find out. I picked up the envelope, muttered "excuse me" as I passed by my mother and fled once again to the bathroom.

I sat down on the floor beside the bathtub and looked at it. I didn't rip it open this time; I needed time to prepare myself for...for what? I had no idea. I slid a finger under the flap and slowly inched it open.

"*Dear Miss Wilson,*" it began—just like the last one. "*We are pleased to inform you...*" They were pleased again? What? "*You have been awarded...*"

I had won a scholarship. Full ride, as they say. I was going to New York.

~

"Absolutely not!"

My father was furious. Furious that I'd "gone behind his back," as he said, and applied to an "art school." If he was angry about that, he was livid when I told him that I'd gone to an interview in New York City. He was nothing short of apoplectic, just as I had predicted, when I told him that Liz and I had hitchhiked. I suppose I could have left out the details, but I was on a roll, and I figured he needed to have the complete picture.

"Dad, it's what I'm supposed to do with my life. I'm absolutely sure of that."

"What you're supposed to do with your life is get married and have my grandchildren. You're supposed to learn to keep house and be happy doing it!" he turned to my mother. "I told you we should never have let her spend so much time with my mother." *What is that supposed to mean?* I thought.

I took a deep breath and tried to step back for a moment to put myself in his place. As far as I knew, this was the only life he had ever known. But times had changed, although there was little doubt that there was nothing I could say that would change his way of thinking. The only thing I could do was hold my ground. Now was the moment to pull out the scholarship offer.

He looked at it and stopped his tirade for a moment. My mother was sitting on the sofa, her hands in her lap. "Well, James, if money isn't an issue—"

"Betty, don't take her side. The scholarship is moot since she's not going." But his voice was a bit subdued now.

"Mom. Dad. I love you both. But this is my life, and I have to live it. I know you don't understand my passion for an artistic life—for fashion design. Dad, I know you think it's frivolous. But it's who I am, and I can't turn my back on this opportunity. They think I have promise. Talent. They're opening a door for me, and I have to walk through."

I left them sitting in the living room, looking at my back as I retreated to my bedroom. I had to write a letter to Chuck.

"See you in September," I began.

America

Simon and Garfunkel, 1967

WHENEVER I TRY, I CAN'T EVER GET IT RIGHT. I try to tell people about the feeling I had as I walked down the steps off an airplane and onto the tarmac in New York. I was here! And this time, I was staying.

I remember how fast and hard my heart was beating in my ears as I walked through the airport juggling cases, trying to follow the signs to the taxi stand. I felt as if everyone around could probably hear it and, by extension, know how nervous—and excited—I really was. I felt like a small-town girl all agog with the big city—which I was but sorely wanted to get over. I wanted to be a real city girl. Even my two years in Toronto hadn't yet turned me into an urban sophisticate.

My parents had driven me to the airport somewhat grudgingly. Two months had gone by since I broke the news, and things had been tense for a while. I think that Dad just got tired of being angry all the time and gave up. He wasn't exactly supportive, but he didn't throw me out of the house, and I was grateful for that. I sucked up the tension until it sort of dissipated.

Mom quietly told me that she had always dreamed of visiting New York and that perhaps now she might have a reason. I loved

149

her all the more for that. When they dropped me off at the airport, Dad nervously pushed an envelope into my hand. "You might need some of those American greenbacks."

Once I had settled into my seat on the plane, I opened the envelope to find three-hundred American dollars. What? I silently thanked my father and reminded myself to say it out loud the next time I spoke with him. Maybe I'd even write him a letter. A telephone call would be expensive, and he wouldn't be in favour of that! But three-hundred dollars! It was a small fortune, and at least I now knew I could pay my rent for the first month or two and eat. After that, I'd have to find a part-time job to supplement my scholarship.

Speaking of rent, Chuck had magically arranged for me to have a room in the flat he shared with three other people. We had been corresponding all summer, and I had discovered that he was just as charming and funny in letters as he was in person. (I had continued to run to the mailbox before Mom got there every day—no point in letting her ask more questions about letters from New York!) He had told me stories about all of his room-mates whose names I'd made a point of memorizing in advance. They included Virginia, an opera student and her sometime boyfriend, Carl, who was part-owner of a small bar in Greenwich Village, and a dancer named Louise who was trying to make her living on Broadway. Evidently, that wasn't going so well. They all sounded so "New York," and I wasn't sure how I'd fit in with them, but I was certainly going to give it my best. As I sat in the taxi, it occurred to me that I had only one chance to make a good impression—both with my new roommates and next week, with my teachers when classes started. I stared out the window, trying to take in as much of the passing street life as I could when I started thinking about my new home.

I realized that I had begun categorizing things as either "New York" or "not New York." Home was not New York. Being a high school teacher was not New York (although I'm sure NYC high school teachers would argue that one). Not caring about artistic pursuits was not New York. Which one was I? I was hoping to become "New York" as soon as I possibly could.

The taxi disgorged me and all my worldly belongings (except my sewing machine, which was still in the basement in my old residence in Toronto until I could get it shipped) in front of a three-story brownstone in the heart of Greenwich Village. I stood on the sidewalk with my belongings piled around me. Then, holding onto my beret so that the stiff September breeze couldn't whisk it away, I looked up at my new home.

Its three stories made it exactly the same number of floors as all the houses lining the street, although the rooflines weren't the same, giving the street a kind of jagged appearance against the blue sky. My new home was red brick with white trim and a white door, while the ones on either side—attached together—were painted white brick on one side and orange-hued brick on the other. There were four concrete steps with a black, metal railing leading up to the front door, exactly like the ones leading up to the two neighbours. Like all the houses lining the street, I could see metal fire escapes leading from the third floor and ending abruptly at the first floor's ceiling level. I also noted an air conditioner unit was hanging out of one of the two ground-floor windows. I took a deep breath, gathered together my belongings and slowly climbed the four steps.

By the time I reached the door, I'd obviously been spotted since before I had a chance to knock, the door swung open. Instead of Chuck as I might have expected, I was face to face—or more accurately face to the top of a head—with a portly middle-aged woman wearing a pink and green floral housedress with a white apron around her ample middle. She was also wearing a broad smile.

"Come in, come in," she said, gesturing me toward the foyer and trying to grab suitcases from my hands.

151

I was immediately unsure if I was even at the correct address. Who was this woman who seemed to be treating me as if I might be her long-lost daughter?

"Katherine, Kat, my dear. I am so happy to be meeting you!" Well, at least I seemed to be in the right place. "Please, come. You must be hungry. Leave your things, leave your things. You should not have to carry them any longer after your long plane ride from so far north." Did she think I lived in the Arctic? Well, I guess Canada did seem to be a far north kind of place to an older woman from New York even though my home wasn't that far north of New York itself.

I started to pick up my suitcases. "Leave them, child. Charles will take them up for you when he gets home." By Charles, I presumed she meant Chuck. I still had no idea who she was. The housekeeper, perhaps? What a concept!

She took my hand and led me to the back of the house in the direction of wonderful aromas. When we reached the kitchen, she practically pushed me down into a chair then immediately poured two cups of tea. After placing a few cookies on a plate, she sat down opposite me at the large wooden table. "Now, then," she said, brushing a tendril of hair from her face, "we get to know one another. I am Rose. Rose Cohen. I am Charles's mother."

~

After I had recovered from my surprise—and, admittedly, a moment of terror at the thought that she lived here, Rose plied me with food—chicken soup, home-made challah bread, bagels with smoked salmon and jelly donuts. While I ate, she practically told me Chuck's life story. At least, by the time he arrived an hour later, I knew that his father had immigrated from Germany, and Rose, the American-born daughter of Polish immigrants, had gone to nursing school. Chuck had weighed almost ten pounds at birth. He had a sister named Sally, who lived in California, and they grew up in Brooklyn. Most importantly, however, I learned that his mother was inordinately proud of her son.

When Chuck walked into the kitchen, his mother started. "Charles, you did not tell me that Kat was so beautiful. And so smart."

Beautiful I had never been, but if she thought so, maybe it was time I started believing it. And speaking of beautiful…

Chuck stood in the doorway, shining that lop-sided smile I remembered so well from the spring. We had written countless letters in the months since I learned of my scholarship, and I felt like I knew him. Now, as he stood there with his hand on the doorframe, gazing directly into my eyes, I had a moment of clear knowing. I simply could not let him leave my life. Ever. It seemed to me that his eyes held the same knowing. I hoped I wasn't wrong this time.

"Well, she's that and a whole lot more," he said. He came over to the table, sat down opposite me and took my hands in his. "Welcome to New York, Kat. It suits you already."

It seemed that Chuck had prevailed upon his mother to be here when I arrived since neither he nor any of his three roommates could get here on time. It also turned out that Mrs. Cohen, Rose, was more than welcome in the house since she cooked for them whenever she came for a visit. It seemed to me that she loved doing it, and she was exceptionally good at it, as I had just discovered.

"Charles," Rose said as she fixed her hat and coat and picked up her handbag a half an hour later, "mind you treat this young lady well." Then she smiled a little conspiratorial smile in my direction. "And Kat, my dear, I know you will treat my boy well." Then she winked.

"You've won her over already. Not that I ever doubted you would," Chuck said, waving good-bye to his mother as she hailed a cab in that way only New Yorkers can. I was going to have to learn the fine art of aggressively hailing a taxi while standing on the edge of the curb.

Chuck showed me my room on the third floor, which would be my home for the next few years—I hoped. I was delighted that it looked out onto the street and almost squealed with glee when I saw the view from the window.

"You might regret that, Kat, when you hear the noise from the street in the middle of the night. You know we're in the city that never sleeps!"

I didn't care one bit. I wanted to experience everything New York had to offer.

Later that evening, after I'd had a chance to settle into my room, Chuck came upstairs from his room on the second floor and tapped on my door. He wanted to show me something. I followed him down the stairs and past the door he'd pointed out earlier as the door to his room. Tucked away in the corner was a narrow door. I noticed that there was an odd bulb hanging above a door. He saw me looking at it.

"Whenever that's on, everyone knows that they can't come inside."

"What're you doing in there, making a bomb?'

He laughed, opened the door, reached inside to turn on the light and gestured for me to go in ahead of him. I immediately knew where I was. It was his darkroom, and hanging on the wall directly in front of me were four large black and white photographs. I was looking at an extraordinary portrait of myself, laughing at something he'd said, no doubt. I gasped.

"Pretty great, huh?" he said as he reached up and took it off the wall. "You are remarkably photogenic, Kat Wilson. We have to do more. But first, it's time to meet the roomies."

By the time I fell into bed on that first night, I realized I was starting to feel just a tiny bit more "New York." Virginia and her boyfriend Carl, who shared the largest room in the house on the third floor, had invited me to Carl's bar *Urban Underground*, which sounded like a place only cool kids went. I was going to try my best to fit in while still being me. I didn't think that would be so difficult, though. And the other roommate Louise, a petite blonde dancer who had just landed a background role in an off-off-Broadway show, had invited me to opening night—which was a month away, but I was delighted. They all treated me as if I'd always been a part of Chuck's life. I had three days before my tiny bit of "New York" would be put to the test. Classes were starting at nine o'clock on Monday morning.

Autumn in New York

Louis Armstrong and Elle Fitzgerald, 1957

THERE WAS NO DOUBT ABOUT IT. I was in a whole different world. The moment I stepped a foot over the threshold of that building where I'd run head-long into Chuck five months earlier, I knew that I'd never experienced anything like it before. There was a kind of electricity running down each corridor, and it was contagious. I found myself walking a bit faster, breathing a bit faster, living a bit faster. The first day of classes at the University of Toronto had never been like this.

Everyone seemed to know everyone else—another thing that was different from my past two years at a massive university. Of course, that wasn't true of us first-year students. As we gathered together that first morning for our orientation of sorts, we all seemed to be eyeing one another warily.

"Ladies and gentlemen," began the woman who had conducted my interview this past spring. She glanced around the room, catching an eye here and there. She missed mine. "Ladies and gentlemen, welcome to Parsons. As you look around at your colleagues in this room today, know that your particular interest in fashion design might have made you special in your hometowns. You are not so special here. You are all here because you are talented. At least you are talented enough for us to wish to give you a chance, a chance that you squander at your peril. Whether you are talented enough to thrive in this business or even survive in it remains to be seen." She took a breath and looked around again. This time, I caught *her* eye. "Look at the person on each side of you. Say hello if you wish, but know this. Only one of you will be given the opportunity to show your designs in public from our stage. The other two will be long gone. Which one of you will that be?" We timidly looked at one another. Well, we all looked timid except for the girl to my right. She glared at me as if daring me to be the one who succeeded while she failed. I had only two choices, ignore her or smile and nod. I smiled. She glowered. Okay, not such an auspicious start with that one.

I was propelled from class to class on that first day by sheer adrenaline and the crush of other students carrying me along. They all seemed so much more sophisticated and worldly than I did. By the time I reached my final class of the day, I was a bit punch-drunk. I slipped into the studio, where the instructor was lounging on a stool at the front. He looked familiar.

I took a seat, bent down to stash my belongings under it and when I raised my head, he was standing directly in front of me, his hands clasped behind his back, smiling. At least it looked as if he were smiling—sort of.

"Miss Wilson, Kat," he said. *How in the world does this man know my name?* "I see you have ventured into the unknown here in New York. I hope you'll find it to your liking." Then he winked, and I remembered him.

My instructor for this draping course (where I guess I'd learn to drape fabrics over mannequins and maybe even models to create designs) was Simon Xavier Carmichael, known (as I may have noted when I first met him) as the bad boy of American designers. A recent article I'd read in *Vogue* said that he was a predator—in the nicest sense of the word (was there a nice way to be a predator?)—and a bit of a shark who was taking the American design scene by storm. They also said he'd probably burn out quickly. He was also Alfred Chang's friend and might well have been involved in me getting admitted to this prestigious school in the first place. Oh, and I didn't think I'd call him Simon any time soon although he had asked me to. At least to his face.

Simon was what the school referred to as an adjunct. He was a part of their "Critic Design Program." I had heard that he, among other working designers in New York, was a mentor, an active designer rather than merely a teacher, who would select a few students each year to advise. These chosen few would then spend time in his workshop in the garment district, learning from the master—if you could be considered a master at an age somewhere shy of thirty. I knew all this from reading the materials the school had sent over the summer. I understood that new students would be slotted to work with specific adjuncts at some point during the semester. I had no idea how they made their decisions.

The entire class with Simon flew by in a kind of a blur. He was charming and witty (were there any men in New York who weren't?) and got a sort of faraway look in his eyes when he talked about his design vision. I watched him closely while he demonstrated the kind of draping we'd be learning to do. He was mesmerizing.

As I watched his hands lift the swath of shimmering green fabric and begin to drape it around his live model—over one shoulder, down across the front, wound around the middle, pins flying every which way—I thought I was watching an old movie that the projector had sped up. It was a wonder to me that he didn't stab either the model or the young woman standing beside him in her white lab coat holding a large, red velvet pin cushion from which he pulled the many pins he needed. I briefly wondered if holding things such as pincushions was the kind of work he expected of students. I suppose you could learn a great deal from that simple service if you paid attention, but I was thinking that I'd be spending more time trying to get out of the way of a pin stab than I would be observing a master at work. When he finished, and we all began to file out, I could almost feel his eyes on me. It was a peculiar feeling.

Along with my classes, I was also beginning my journey toward learning what it was like to be a student in New York City—the Big Apple, home to the centre of the universe, namely Times Square. Chuck decided that it was his job to ensure that I quickly assimilated, something that I longed to be able to do. I wanted to be a New Yorker, or at least not stick out like a tourist. The evening Chuck introduced me to Times Square's finer details, with the help of Virginia, Carl and Louise, was the moment I started to feel as if I belonged here. It was as if I were finally home.

It was just about eleven p.m., and most of the theatres had already disgorged their patrons. They were all making their way through the square, talking and laughing and looking for someplace to eat or drink or both. Of course, this being New York, the city that never sleeps, there was no shortage of dining and drinking establishments. The cacophony of voices, traffic and honking horns, along with the almost hypnotic flashes of lights and colour, should have made me anxious that I not lose my friends in the bustling crowd. But it didn't. I knew I'd be all right.

I stood in the middle of Times Square and looked up at the massive Coca-Cola sign, flashing its neon red from dizzying heights. Then I slowly turned, taking in every billboard, every sign, every light while Chuck snapped my photo at every turn. I made myself a promise: I was never leaving this place. The city had begun to find me.

Well, that's what I thought at the time, anyway.

By the time the end of October rolled around, I realized that the first two months at my new school had already taught me a couple of important things. First, art and design students weren't at all like students at a regular university. Their focus was palpable in almost every class they took, every assignment they worked on, every conversation over a wax-paper-wrapped tuna sandwich. The second thing was that, even though most of them seemed pleasant and personable on a superficial level, whether passing in the hallway or having a drink at a bar in Greenwich Village, competitiveness lurked just beneath that surface. And they held that competitiveness with a resolute embrace. It was every man—or woman—for herself. I learned that I, and I alone, would be responsible for my fate over the next few years. And then they assigned us to work with a partner.

Back on the first day of classes, I had noticed that one young woman with the don't-mess-with-me kind of determination. She was the one sitting beside me, glaring at me when the director said only one of us would make it. Clearly, she expected it to be her. After my first decision to smile at her, I determined that the best course of action was just to steer clear of her. That worked until the Friday I walked into Simon's class, and his assistant in the lab coat was handing out mimeographed sheets of paper.

I took the page from her and immediately wondered why they couldn't have arranged for the purple ink to have dried before handing them out. It was going to be everywhere. Then I looked down at it. On that paper was the description of the next assignment. Everyone had to work with a partner. We were not, however, permitted to choose our own partners. They had assigned them. *Dear god*, I thought as I looked at the list of designated partners, *it's her. Suzanne.* I have to work with her.

Suzanne was beautiful. I mean, she was knock-out beautiful. She had smooth, almost perfect chocolate-brown skin, deep brown eyes and an extraordinary Afro hair-style. She was probably five-feet-ten inches tall and had long legs. She carried herself like a dancer and could undoubtedly have been a model. She looked extraordinary in everything she wore. I would have asked her if she'd designed her wardrobe herself, but, as I said, I'd decided it was better to steer clear. I wouldn't be able to do that anymore.

"I suppose you're Kat," she said by way of introduction when we found our assigned seats for the day. "I see we're working together." Was that a sneer I saw? Well, it wasn't a promising start, but on the bright side, there was nowhere to go but up from here.

I told her that I was, indeed, Kat, and I was looking forward to working with her. She rolled her eyes at me and began rummaging through her tote bag. Without looking up, she said, "I suppose you think you're a sister." I had no earthly idea what she was talking about.

The Times They are A-Changing

Bob Dylan, 1964

"MOM AND DAD HAVE INVITED YOU TO DINNER this Sunday," Chuck called out to me from the living room when I arrived home later that day.

Rose, his mom, had been over a few times to cook for us, but I had yet to meet his father. All I knew about him was that he was a physics professor at Columbia University and that he had fled the Nazis in Europe years ago near the beginning of World War II. I also knew that Rose had been a nurse, but I had no idea when or where they had met. That was the extent of the family history known to me.

"What should I wear?" I said after I had hung my coat on one of the hooks in the vestibule. "And should I take anything?" I walked into the living room, where he was stretched out on the sofa, eating a bowl of popcorn, his favourite snack. There was a half-finished beer on the coffee table. "And you're going to have to tell me how to talk to a physicist. I don't think I've ever met one."

"Stop worrying. Dad's going to love you," Chuck said.

I wasn't convinced, but I was looking forward to meeting him and would put my best foot forward. Two days later, we were making our way to Brooklyn on the subway.

Chuck's parents lived on a lovely, leafy street lined with immaculate brownstones. It seemed as if every single one of them had two pots of late-autumn chrysanthemums still in bloom—or just past their best-by dates—flanking their doorways. As we approached number fourteen, I could see the door opening. Out popped Rose wearing a robin's blue dress under a frilly white apron. She was wearing matching pumps and a broad smile.

"Welcome to our home," she said, embracing me warmly as we came into the house. Rose took our coats and said, "I'll send Harry right down."

Chuck led me into the living room. It was one of those warm, family spaces with over-stuffed furniture and scads of family photos scattered around. I was just about to pick up one that looked like Chuck at about age ten when I heard a booming voice behind me.

"Well, I'm delighted to meet the famous Kat finally."

I put the photo frame down and turned toward the voice. I couldn't help myself. "You're black," I blurted, regretting it to the core of my being the moment it was out of my mouth.

"And you're white," he said sternly. Then a broad smile broke across his face. "I love doing that." He turned to Chuck. "You could have warned me that you didn't warn her. "

"Wicked boy," Rose, who had come into the room, said to Chuck. She, too, smiled.

"Hey," Chuck said to me, "where did you think I got this gorgeous head of black curls and this beautiful tan?"

Good lord, how could I not have seen it? I guess it made him so gorgeous that it didn't matter. And it didn't. I just wished that I could have been a bit more sophisticated in my introduction to

Harry. But now, what I really wanted to know was how a short, stout white Jewish girl had met a tall, black (Jewish?) physicist.

As I looked at Rose and Harry together, I knew what Suzanne had meant about supposing I was a "sister."

~

Dinner was marvellous. As I had already discovered, Rose was an incredible cook, and now I realized that she was an incredible hostess as well. I had only to place an almost-empty glass on the table and, before I knew it, the drink was topped up. Sometime between the prime rib and the apple cake with vanilla whipped cream, I lost count of the number of glasses of wine I'd had. Perhaps that's why I felt so at home and comfortable with the Cohen's. And maybe that's why I felt I could say, "Harry, tell me about how you came to America and met Rose."

"You sure you want to know the details?" he said.

I nodded, and he topped up everyone's glasses before settling back in his chair at the head of the table and told me his story.

Chuck's paternal grandfather—Harry's dad—had been a white, German businessman, a Jew, who'd met the woman who would be Chuck's paternal grandmother while on a business trip in London.

I barely had time to digest the news that Harry's dad—Chuck's grandfather—had been white when Harry continued with his story.

"My mother, who, as you've probably already figured out, was black, was a maid to the family in whose house he was staying." Harry took a sip of wine then continued, his slight German accent becoming more pronounced. "My father always told me how they'd fallen head-over-heels in love and, despite the problems they knew would lie ahead of them in Germany, they married in England and returned home to Munich as a married couple."

His mother, a Baptist by background, converted to Judaism and became what Harry described as over-zealous. "You know what converts are like," he said, laughing. "They're more pious than the rest of us."

As Harry told it, he never had a single day of his childhood when he didn't hear some kind of racial slur. He looked exactly like his mother. Everything in his life changed when he was fourteen.

It was 1933. As Harry related his story, I realized how little I knew about history, especially about war. As Harry told it, that was the year that of the notorious Nuremberg Laws. "It was outrageous. It stripped us—Jews, that is—of our citizenship, our right to run a business, our right to live."

Despite the bigotry Harry had faced in school, he was a brilliant student headed for university at an early age, but these new laws forbade Jews from entering university. At fourteen, a black Jew, he already knew he'd never go to university in Germany. That's when Harry's parents decided to flee to America. They were among those thousands of immigrants who came by the shiploads from Europe, landing at Ellis Island.

"And Mom and Pop only got as far as Brooklyn before settling down," Harry said. "I went to Columbia, met Rose when I had my appendix out, and the rest is history, as they say."

I suspected that there was much more to the story, but I didn't dare press for more details. I'd ask Chuck about his father's work some other time. I did know for sure that I would have to open up my mind and learn more about people whose experiences are different from mine. It occurred to me that knowing more about the people I would be designing for in the future would make me a better designer.

~

"Your parents are amazing," I said to Chuck just after we'd left the house following dinner and dessert. We were laden down with bags of food that Rose had insisted we had to take home to share with our roommates.

"Yeah, they are. I guess I'm pretty lucky," Chuck said as he shifted the bags to one hand so he could get out his money for the subway. "But yours must be pretty amazing, too. After all, you turned out amazing."

I followed him down the steps into the underground. I wasn't sure exactly what to say. If he had asked me that three years earlier, I'd probably have agreed. That was because I didn't really pay that much attention to my parents, which is perhaps the reason I didn't really know them—or at least I didn't seem to know my father. Then again, how many adults really know their parents? After my father's visceral reaction to my life choices and his insistence that what I really should do was be a good girl, a.k.a. housewife and mother with pearls and a cashmere twinset, my feelings about him and my mother had taken a turn. I decided to ignore Chuck's comment for the moment. I changed the subject to the big elephant in the room or, in this case, the elephant on the subway train.

"Why didn't you tell me?"

"Why didn't I tell you what?" he said as he looked down into one of the bags he'd placed on the floor. He withdrew one of his mother's mouth-watering jelly doughnuts. How could he possibly still be hungry?

"Don't be coy," I said. "You know exactly what I mean. I was blindsided."

"Kat, honey, you couldn't possibly have been completely blindsided. I have to believe that you must have pondered my ethnic background." He ran his fingers through his curls. "I mean, come on."

"Yes, I pondered. But only to the extent of wondering about your Jewish heritage."

166

"So, do you have a problem with my dad?"

"You're joking, right?" I was feeling defensive, although I knew that I had no reason to feel that way. I had never judged people by the colour of their skin, but I also had to be honest with myself. I had never had anyone close to me who didn't look just like I did.

"Anyway, like Dad said, he's only half black." He smirked just a bit.

~

The following Tuesday morning, Suzanne and I had set up a meeting to discuss our project. As I walked into the room we'd booked, she was already there. She had her sketchbook out in front of her and was absorbed in her work.

"Good morning, Suzanne," I said as I put my armload of books on the table across from her.

"If you say so," she said. Oh, this was going to be fun.

I wanted to get to know her better, but I realized that any attempt I made to broach the subject of race could go horribly wrong. However, I did want to be sure I had understood her meaning when she had chastised me—because that's what it sounded like—for pretending to be a "sister."

"Suzanne, what exactly did you mean when you said you supposed I thought I was a sister?"

She closed her sketchbook and sat back, staring at me. I could almost feel two holes being bored into me. "Maybe you're denser than I thought you were. White chicks who date black guys always feel this sense of moral superiority. Hey, look at me, they seem to be saying. Skin colour doesn't matter to me."

"It doesn't," I said.

"No, maybe it doesn't until you take him home to meet mom and dad. Then it will matter. It will matter a lot." She opened her sketchbook and started doodling. She looked up. "You know,

I've been dealing with girls like you for my whole life. You think you understand, but you don't. You have no idea what it's like. I have to fight harder than anyone around me to get where I want to go. But I'll get there."

"I think you probably will, Suzanne. But the truth is, white girls like me will never understand you if you don't let us. Could we start over?"

Suzanne put her pencil down again and cocked her head to one side. "Precisely how do you plan to do that?"

I held out my hand to her. "Hi there," I said. "My name is Kat Wilson. I'm looking forward to working with you."

She stared at me for a moment then took my hand, her fingers firmly curling around mine. "I'm Suzanne, Suzanne Smith. Let's get started."

A Hazy Shade of Winter

Simon and Garfunkel, 1968

THE PROJECT SUZANNE AND I HAD TO WORK ON together was on the topic of colour theory. The irony was not lost on either of us. And it was precisely this irony that we decided to harness as we moved through the work—together. Oddly, I learned more about her from listening to her talk about colours in design than I did through general conversation. I learned that she was drawn to the hot, fiery energy of red that we learned is also associated with violence and warfare, a fact that did not make Suzanne happy. But she was also drawn to yellow's warmth and energy, which, we discovered, can also be the colour of hope. I liked knowing that about her. As for me, it seems that I'm the polar opposite— polar being the operative visual.

Despite my recent foray into red, as in the coat I designed and made for my interview, my personality was always cooler. I love blue. When I told Suzanne that, she looked at my black bell-bottoms and the blue sweater I was wearing and said, "Calmness and responsibility? Or sadness? Which is it, Kat?"

She had me there. I didn't know. The thought of being calm and responsible was appealing, but it seemed to lack the artistic sense I hoped to cultivate. But sadness? I had never thought of

169

myself as someone prone to wallowing in the blues. Anyway, although Suzanne and I explored many facets of colour theory together, we knew that, in the end, we would focus on only two: black and white. That's what our project was about: what each one represents, how design portrays each colour and how one could not exist without the other. That was the key.

The final part of the assignment was a presentation. Although it had been a hard slog at first, Suzanne and I had finally settled into a kind of grudgingly accepting working relationship. At least she was grudging. However, the one thing that did bug me about her was her constant assumption that everything and everyone would be against her. Since I had little idea about her life and could only imagine what barriers she had faced, I tried very hard to be accommodating. It was this big chip on her shoulder that I really thought might get in her way.

As we stood outside the room before our turn in front of the faculty and our first-year classmates, she said, "They're going to hate it. They're going to think I'm trying to make a political point."

I clutched my portfolio tighter to my chest and sighed. "Suzanne, we *are* trying to make a political point of sorts. It's the theme of our presentation. I thought you said that design was going to be your way of making a difference."

I suspected that she felt a bit guilty about being here in this cushy school, as she put it, while so many others were on the front lines of the protest movement. I have to admit, being here in New York had made me much more aware of the issues. It was hard to miss the news every day—protests mostly centred on race and the war, juxtaposed against the daily serving of images emerging from Vietnam, and they weren't pretty. But here we were, studying something that most of the activists would likely have called frivolous.

Suzanne shared one piece of information about her that helped me understand her a bit better: her brother had been killed in Vietnam three months before she started at Parsons. It looked to me like she saw the world through a veil of rage simmering just beneath her carefully cultivated veneer. I had been tiptoeing around her for the past month, always hoping to avoid an unintentional minefield. Today I was tired of it.

"For the love of god, Suzanne, brush that chip off your shoulder just for a few minutes. It's a good presentation, and you know it. It might well be the best one in the class. At least, I hope it is." Suzanne stared daggers at me, but she didn't say anything. "And you know as well as I do that we're both solid students—maybe the best first-years here. Anyway, it's the last day of classes for the semester. Let's go out with a bang."

And we did. The presentation went well. As it progressed, I could see her warming to her topic as the faces around the room looked transfixed. We knew it had gone well when, as he left the room, Simon Carmichael handed us each a slip of paper that he tore out of a small notebook. On it was an address.

"I'll see you both in my atelier on January 12 at 9 a.m. don't be late." And, just like that, we became SXC interns. (SXC was, of course, his fashion line.)

~

Christmas at home was surprisingly calm. For the most part, my father kept his opinions about New York, the den of iniquity, to himself, although he did find it necessary to mention it while we had eggnog on Christmas Eve. My grandmother, Fran, was unimpressed. "Keep quiet, James. Leave the girl alone. It's Christmas." She was the only one who could get away with talking to him like that. He was her son, but I'd often wondered why she still held such sway over him after all these years.

I missed Chuck, but we had made plans to be together for New Year's Eve, and I was looking forward to spending it with him in Times Square, followed by a party back at our house. New

York had been dropping the ball for decades—six now if what Chuck had told me was correct—and I was going to see it for myself this year.

Nan came to the house to say good-bye to me before I headed to the airport on December 28. As I buttoned up my coat in the hallway, Mom and Dad had gone ahead to put my suitcases in the trunk and warm up the car. She wasn't coming to the airport. She had things to do, she said. But before I left, she pulled me into a hug.

"Kat, my darling girl, follow your dreams." I closed my eyes and breathed in the subtle scent of her Shalimar, wondering how this wonderful woman could have spawned a child as sour as my father. "I have a surprise for you," she said, breaking away. "I'm coming to New York to celebrate my sixty-eighth birthday."

My eyes widened. "Nan, New York! Are you sure you want to come to the big city?"

"Don't you want me to come?"

"Of course, I do, but…"

"I'm only joking, darling, but I'm not joking about coming. I have already booked a room at the Plaza for three nights starting on January 31. If you and your young man are amenable, we'll all have dinner on the Friday evening, the second,"

"Of course, Nan, and we'll celebrate your birthday in style." I knew that she, at least, would love Chuck. At least I hoped she would.

"By the way, Kat, in case you're worried about your old grandmother, it won't be my first visit to New York." Before I could pick my jaw up off the floor, she looked out the door and said, "You better get going. They seem to be ready." Just then, my father honked the horn, and I dashed down the front steps.

~

New Year's Eve in New York City was everything I hoped it would be and more. As we headed out on foot toward Times Square, the usual rising cacophony of noises was a kind of siren call—it was as if we were being lured to the centre of the universe. Then, when we arrived, the neon lights were flashing as if they could hardly wait for the ball to drop. And the people—the masses of people not minding the cold and the snow that had begun to fall. As I stood amid the crowd, I looked up and watched the snowflakes dancing in the alternating red and blue lights and was momentarily dazed. I didn't want any of this to end. Ever.

Then, in the middle of all this noise and commotion, Chuck grabbed my hand, drew me toward him and shouted in my ear. "I have something for you." He looked around, then, holding my hand tightly, dragged me through the crowd. We headed toward the edge of the street, where there was a bit of an opening, then pulled a box from his pocket. What in the world?

We had already lost the others but had agreed to meet back at the house after midnight. I looked down at the small, flat box he had pressed into my hand. It was wrapped in red tissue paper. "Open it."

I did the best I could, given the jostling that was going on around me. When I had removed the paper and opened the box, I pulled back a layer of white tissue paper. Lying inside the box were two bangle bracelets. They were both made of some kind of translucent amber with carved surfaces. "They're beautiful!"

"Do you know what they are?" I shook my head as he took them out of the box and tried to put them on my wrist over my mitten. I laughed and took off a mitten so that they could glide over my hand and onto my wrist. "They're made of Bakelite." That didn't illuminate me at all. "It's a real New York thing. It was patented here about sixty years ago. My mom's been collecting them for years, and she wanted you to have these—actually, she asked me if I'd like you to have them."

I shook my wrist a bit and listened to them as they jangled. At that moment, the count-down began. By the time the chanting had reached 'one,' I was kissing the man I fervently hoped to spend New Year's Eve with for decades to come. And then it was 1968.

~

Suzanne and I showed up at exactly the same moment, at precisely six minutes to nine on the morning of January 12 as directed by Simon. Wordlessly, we stood together in the biting cold wind, clutching our scarves around us, waiting for someone to answer the buzzer. Eventually, a disembodied female voice intoned, "Ye-es?" We told her who we were, and the door buzzed open.

The voice directed us to take the stairs to the fourth floor. The stairway was dark and poorly lit, which seemed to me to be the antithesis of what I'd seen in Simon's designs—and perhaps in him, the man. I judged too soon. Breathing hard, we finally made it to the fourth floor. The minute we opened the door, we were in another realm entirely. Stepping across the threshold, I got a little frisson of excitement as we moved from one world into another utterly different one.

It was as if we had emerged into the light out of the darkness and mundaneness of our lives, and it struck me that this was exactly the kind of image Simon liked to create. The door opened into a bright space, almost blinding in its intensity. Wrapped in blonde wood, the vast atelier seemed to take up this small building's entire top floor. There were skylights above and a wall of windows extending into the ceiling on the opposite side of the room, reminiscent of a greenhouse. Scattered throughout were large, blonde-wood worktables upon which there were bolts of brightly-coloured fabrics, as well as fabrics spread out, dripping off the edges. Between each table were two or three mannequins, many partially draped, others wearing what looked like finished samples. Buried in the deepest reaches of the studio were two rows of sewing machines. Several young women, all clad in white lab coats, motored along seams, presumably producing the samples we saw on the dummies. Several other young people—I counted three women and two men— all sporting identical white lab coats, sat at various tables, deeply engaged in their work. No one even looked up.

And there, in the centre of the room was Simon, the peacock in his lavender turtleneck and grey bellbottoms, sitting on a stool, a cigarette between his lips, pinning a swath of jewelled pink fabric on a live mannequin. His turtleneck was so tight that we could see his biceps rippling as he draped the material from one place to another, muttering, "Turn." Her bored expression never changed. I wondered what models thought about while people pawed all over them. I'd have to make a note to ask one day.

He finally placed what seemed to be his last pin, stood back and looked at his creation. "Well, ladies, what do you think?" He had noticed us standing there, gawking. He was wearing a pair of large, aviator-style glasses with lenses that had a hint of a lavender-blue hue that matched his sweater, and I wondered if they were just for show. He stubbed out his cigarette in an ashtray that had miraculously appeared at his elbow in the hand of one of his assistants. "Well, don't just stand there. Come in. Clarissa will find you lockers and lab coats, then you can meet me back here, and I'll get you started."

And so began my internship with the famous (infamous, perhaps? *L'enfant terrible*?) Simon X. Carmichael.

~

For weeks, the work Simon had us doing was mundane in the extreme. He assigned us to the pattern-makers. Although I did love the geometry of creating flat patterns that would someday be made into beautiful three-dimensional garments, our work was tedious. Suzanne and I were, after all, not the designers. We were merely assistants to the assistants, drawing dotted lines as directed or taping new design lines on pieces of semi-transparent paper. Sometimes, we even got to cut the patterns out of the paper. Okay, it was all part of the learning process, but I longed to be involved in the finished products. Just imagine how excited I was when, during the last week in January, Simon asked me to hold pins for him while he adjusted a sample on one of the models—one of the many who paraded through the atelier. Only two weeks into my internship with him, I had already heard rumours of his many indiscretions with these models—which was, reportedly, the reason they never stayed around for very long. The gossip was that if one appeared for several weeks, she must be one of his favourites. Simon was known in the industry for having a short attention span when it came to designs, and perhaps it spilled over into his other inclinations. That's why I was probably just a bit taken aback when, that day, while I was holding his pins, his hand brushed over mine, lingering for just a moment too long. When I looked up at him, he just smiled.

I didn't have a chance to give it much thought, though, because Nan was arriving, I was supposed to meet her at the Plaza at three p.m., and I didn't have much time to get ready.

~

"I had forgotten how cold it is here in the middle of the winter," Nan said as she hurried toward me when I met her later in the lobby of the Plaza Hotel. I had never been here before, so I was torn between wanting to throw myself into my grandmother's arms on the one hand or stop and stare at the magnificent décor on the other. Of course, lingering in the back of my mind were a few notable questions. First among them was the question of when my grandmother had been to New York

City before, and why. And perhaps more important, why had she never shared this with me? *I suppose she'll tell me when she's ready,* I thought.

"Where did you get that lovely dress?" she said as I handed the coat check girl my black overcoat.

I smiled and did a little twirl. "Like it?" I said. "I made it."

"Of course, you did, darling. I should have known," Nan said, placing her arm around my shoulder and leading us on toward tea. "You've always been so talented."

We were "taking tea" at the Palm Court. I had heard about the Plaza's famed Palm Court, but all descriptions about its grandeur had been incredibly understated. As we approached the *maître d's* desk, I remembered seeing photographs of the dining room in a magazine—one of those fashion magazines that had littered the coffee table in the common room at Ardmore Hall where I'd been in residence in Toronto. Now, seeing the magnificent glass ceiling with its myriad panes and central design, I realized that Chuck might not be entirely correct in his contention that a photograph can capture the essence of a thing. The picture didn't do it justice at all. The *maître d'* picked up two menus from under the desk and beckoned us to follow him. He was a tall, grey-haired man and walked with a regal posture, one arm holding the menus, the other stiffly behind his back. Oh, and he was impeccable.

Arm-in-arm, Nan and I followed him in past the white marble pillars that stood as sentries guarding the grandness just inside. Every table was covered with a snowy white cloth and topped with a gleaming array of silver and crystal. As we passed other patrons, I noticed the china cups and saucers and the three-tiered cake plates laden with what looked to me to be delicious morsels. My mouth was watering already. Oh, and the serenity—I didn't think it was possible for a group of people to be together in such a place, and all one could hear were murmurings and the occasional tinkle of sterling silver on bone china.

We finally settled into our table for two half-way into the space, giving me an excellent view of everyone and everything around me. And, much to my delight, the Palm Court actually did have palms. They weren't the kind of palm trees I had seen in posters about Florida vacations in shop windows every winter. They were huge indoor palms, elegantly placed around the room in just the perfect spots to keep one set of diners from having a direct view of another group. Despite my lovely dress, as Nan had put it, I felt slightly underdressed. It was 1968, and it had never occurred to me that women still wore hats to take tea. And there were so many strands of pearls around, including on my grandmother who had just flung her fur stole on the back of her chair.

"So, now, my darling, Kat," Nan began as she settled into her chair and placed the snowy white linen napkin on her lap, "I want to hear every detail about what you've been doing at school and in this wonderful city since you got here in September."

And so, I launched into a play-by-play of classes, assignments, what I'd been learning in class, and what I'd been learning outside the classroom. Then I told her about Suzanne and our budding friendship. Nan was a good listener.

"I'm never quite sure how to respond to some of her comments," I said. "I often find myself saying the wrong thing."

"We all find ourselves in those situations from time to time," Nan said, lifting her china cup to sip her tea.

"Well, Suzanne is different. She comes from a different world than I do."

Nan put her cup down and leaned in intently. "We are all different, darling. In what specific way is Suzanne different?"

"Well, actually, Suzanne is...black."

Did Nan raise her eyebrows slightly? "Well, then, Kat, you are quite right. Suzanne does come from a different world, and it is high time you learned something about it. You have no idea whatsoever what she has had to endure through her life in this country. And, make no mistake, it's no better in ours. It's just that we dole out our prejudice more politely than Americans do. Your hometown is a cesspool of ignorance and bigotry, in case you hadn't noticed."

Was she right? If my hometown was all that, then I had been very blind. "Nan, I really do like her and want to be her friend. I think that, beneath the surface, we have a lot in common."

"I'm going to give you a single piece of advice, my dear. But I can't take credit for it. It's something that Dr. King said recently—you do know Martin Luther King, don't you?"

I think that may have been the first time I'd ever felt insulted by my grandmother. "Of course, I know who he is, Nan. What did he say?"

"He said, '*Shallow understanding from people of good will is more frustrating than absolute misunderstanding from people of ill will.*' Suzanne will feel the shallowness of your understanding. It will come off as superficial." She sipped her tea and looked me in the eye. "And if you think I don't know what I'm talking about, rest assured, I do."

Something about her tone didn't invite a question as to the source of her knowledge, so I didn't pursue it. Then her face softened.

"Kat, darling, I only tell you this to help you to deal with this problem that may become a festering sore for your generation if nothing is done about it."

The only thing we hadn't yet talked about was Chuck. She didn't ask, and I didn't volunteer anything. We were supposed to have dinner together the next evening. I took a deep breath. "I want to tell you something about Chuck before you meet him."

Nan smiled and put her hand on mine across the table. "Do not tell me a thing, Kat darling. Let me see him for myself." She patted my hand. "Now, let's go shopping."

~

There were two things I knew for sure about my grandmother: she had a mind of her own, and she did not wax sentimental about anything. How she had developed either of these had always been a mystery to me. I also had no idea how she managed to combine those two characteristics with the love I felt from her every moment I was in her presence. So, when I introduced Chuck to her the next evening, I was ready.

At first, she took his outstretched hand and shook it firmly—I could see that. Then, she let it go and stood back, looking at him as he stood there smiling. She nodded just slightly, then, before he could say a word, she moved in and threw her arms around him.

"Now, Charles, tell me about your family." And he did. And the two of them seemed to find some kind of common bond, the sort of bond that defies generational divides and seems to be based on some kind of mutual respect and understanding. She may have been unsentimental, but she was not hard-edged. She seemed to get him, and she hung on every word he said about his passion for visual images.

Before she left the next day, I shared my trepidation with my grandmother about introducing Chuck to Mom and especially to Dad. I wanted to take him home for a visit in the summer.

She looked at me thoughtfully. "Do you love him, Kat?"

"I do, Nan. I really do."

"Then, when you introduce him to your parents, remember something that the Chinese philosopher Lao Tzu wrote. '*Being deeply loved gives you strength. Loving deeply gives you courage.*' If it's authentic, you'll find the courage."

We never did talk about when she'd been in New York before this visit. It just never came up.

Too Many Martyrs

Phil Ochs, 1964

THE LONG NEW YORK CITY WINTER was finally coming to an end. It was nearing the end of March, and the days were getting longer so that I no longer shuffled off to class in the dark, only to arrive home also under cover of darkness. And were those buds I saw on the trees? Chuck said no. Then he took some amazing close-up photos of them just to prove it to me.

"Guess what I have?" Chuck said one Friday afternoon as I walked into the kitchen after a long week. It was getting close to evaluation time, and I had a lot riding on my developing portfolio. I had also received a letter from Liz, who was about to graduate with her teaching degree and had just landed a job back home in Halifax on the east coast. I was thinking about her spending the rest of her life in a small city.

"Hello, Kat? Are you somewhere else? Guess what I have," he said again and shook what appeared to be some kind of tickets in front of my face. He then passed them to me as I dropped myself into a kitchen chair.

I looked at them, and they didn't register at first. Then it dawned on me: Broadway tickets. To the musical *Hair*. "Where did you get these?"

They were for opening night, which was still five weeks away. We'd been hearing a lot of buzz about it since it debuted off-Broadway in October just past.

I looked them over. The tickets said they were for *Hair* at the Biltmore Theatre, West 47th Street, April 29, 1968. "They finally found a theatre that would agree to show it?" There had been a lot of controversy about the production. According to reports, several theatres had already passed on it, citing concerns about the anti-Vietnam-draft-dodging plotline as well as, or perhaps mainly because of the nudity. How it included nudity was beyond me.

"I know one of the cast members."

"What did you have to do to get him to give you two of his comps?" I just assumed they were comps —complimentary tickets that cast members were entitled to in their contracts. And the fact that they were for opening night suggested the friend must have near-top billing.

"I offered to do headshots for anyone in the company who wants them—and I get to photograph a rehearsal. My friend worked it out with the director." Chuck picked an apple up from the basket on the table the crunched down on it as if getting tickets to a Broadway opening was just another day at the office. It assuredly was not.

I was excited at the thought of my first Broadway musical, but I had to accomplish a lot of things between then and now, and at that moment, I didn't know the half of it.

~

"Dr. Martin Luther King, the apostle of non-violence in the civil rights movement, has been shot to death in Memphis, Tennessee." Those were the words I heard from Walter Cronkite on the CBS evening news as I walked past the living room on the evening of April 4. Chuck always watched the news. He said it was research for his future as a photographer. He was especially drawn to the images of the Vietnam war that crowded the screen every night, but tonight the news had veered off into an unexpected direction. At least, it was unexpected in my world. "The police have issued an all-points bulletin for a well-dressed young white man seen running from the scene…"

Chuck listened to the report for another moment as I sank into a chair, staring at the television screen, my hand over my mouth. I could feel the prickle of tears behind my eyes. Then he got up quickly and moved toward the television, leaning down to turn the dial to ABC. Of course, they were also broadcasting about the tragedy, but they were showing footage from Memphis, interviewing one of Dr. King's associates who was, as far as I could see, in a deep state of shock. It was horrendous. I was thinking about Suzanne and how she'd told me Dr. King would be the difference between the civil rights movement really gaining ground or stalling. Now he was gone. I wondered if I should call her but then thought my intrusion probably wouldn't be welcome at this point.

Chuck stood up quickly. "I'm going," he said.

"Going? Going where?"

Chuck headed toward the door where the telephone stood on a small table. He lifted the receiver and started dialling. "I'm going to Memphis. I'm going to call Danny and see if he can come with me." Danny was Chuck's friend and a classmate in the photography department. But Danny was more interested in film than still photography. They'd worked together before.

"You can't just leave and go to Memphis. You have school. And…" I didn't know where else to go with this. "…and it'll be dangerous. There could be riots." I was suddenly terrified for him. Chuck had never been the kind of activist that Eddie was, but I knew he harboured a deep desire to be the one chronicling events that were shaping the world. I realized that he probably saw this as his chance to be a part of it.

As soon as he had hung up from talking to Danny, who apparently was keen to join him, he made a second call to book two train tickets. He was leaving from Grand Central Station at midnight. There was nothing I could say that would change his mind.

Chuck was gone for five days, during which I heard from him only once. We had a brief telephone conversation in the middle of the trip. All he said was that it was an incredible experience and that he was fine.

When he finally arrived home, I sensed something just a bit different about him.

"Kat, I don't think I really knew what the situation in this country is like for anyone who isn't white. We're so privileged."

"What about the Holocaust? And your own family history?"

"Yeah, I know. There's that. But this is here and now. This is in our faces unless we choose to ignore it. I guess I've always known that I wanted to be in the middle of things, but now it's real. Before, it was all theoretical."

"So, you're going to give it up and be a wedding and portrait photographer?"

He turned to look at me intensely. "No, Kat. You don't get it. I *want* to be in the middle of real things more than ever. I *need* to be. It's what I'm supposed to do with my life. I've never been more certain."

In a way, I was happy for him. But I was also terrified.

~

On April 29, Chuck and I walked to the Biltmore Theatre. I had submitted my first-year portfolio the day before and was feeling both nervous and excited. I was nearing the end of my first year. If all went well, I'd start designing my own pieces in my second year. It would only be children's, juniors and sportswear, but the idea of it was exciting. If I made it through.

But, that evening, I was thinking that that there was nothing better than a first-time Broadway experience to get my mind off myself.

We stood in a line outside the theatre, waiting for them to open the doors. As I stood there looking around at the crowd, I noticed that it was a curious assortment of different styles. Some people had really dressed up for opening night, but interspersed among them were young men and women with long, flowing hair, headbands, colourful beads, and lots of bellbottoms. I felt downright conservative. I *was* conservative, but I longed to be able to carry off a bit of the bohemian style that seemed to be making itself felt in design. I regretted not having my small sketchbook with me. I'd try to keep them in my mind's eye until I got home.

I glanced at the posters plastered on the walls outside the theatre. The posters were all silhouettes of what could have been the face of either a young man or a young woman with a wide Afro on a green background with a reflected shadow of the same image upside down in red beneath. The tag line was "The American Tribal Love-Rock Musical." I was prepared to have my mind blown.

We finally arrived at the door and gave our tickets. As we walked into the lobby, Chuck told me to stay put. He'd go in search of a glass of wine and a beer. As I stood on the periphery of the crowd, holding onto my jacket, I was trying to take it all in and hoping that I'd never forget this evening. I turned back toward the door just in time to see two hairy young men pass their tickets to an usher. Just as I was about to turn to see if Chuck was returning, something caught my eye. One of the young men with all the hair was coming toward me while the other veered off in the direction of the bar. I stared as the young man came closer.

"Oh my god!" he exclaimed from behind the hair that was flopping over his eyes. "Kat! It *is* you! What the hell are you doing here?"

"What the hell are *you* doing here?" I said, peering behind the flop of hair into those eyes I knew so well. It was Eddie.

Society's Child

Janis Ian, 1963

EDDIE THREW HIS ARMS AROUND ME then stood back, holding me at arm's length. "You look fantastic, Kat! I mean, I knew you were in New York, but you've changed somehow. It's great!"

"You never said good-bye." The words were out of my mouth before I had a chance to think about it. For the past two years, I'd heard from him only twice, and not at all in the past six months, but I thought I was over it.

A cloud of confusion seemed to crawl over his face. "I thought you understood."

I saw Chuck winding his way through the crowd, a glass of beer in one hand and wine in the other. I mentally shook myself. I knew I'd have to pull myself together.

"Yes, of course." I forced a smile as Chuck approached. I seemed to understand nothing.

Chuck passed me the glass of wine, waited a beat (as I look back, I think he was waiting for me to introduce him) and turned to Eddie. "Chuck Cohen," he said, extending his hand.

Eddie shook his hand.

"Sorry," I said. "Chuck, this is Eddie Lancaster, an old friend from my Toronto days."

"What am I missing?" The young man I'd seen Eddie arrive with materialized at his side carrying drinks. The young man had auburn hair in exactly the same style I'd seen on photographs of the Beatles. He was a dead-ringer for Paul McCartney. Maybe that's why he looked familiar to me. He passed a glass of beer to Eddie and casually draped his arm over Eddie's shoulder.

"Buzz, this is Kat," Eddie said, then turning to Chuck, "and this is Chuck."

"Kat? *The* Kat I've heard Eddie talk about so much over the past year?" He removed his arm from Eddie's shoulder and shook my hand. "Thanks for looking after him for me."

I had no idea what he was talking about. "So, how do you two know each other?" I said.

"We're both grad students at Berkeley," Eddie said. "Buzz is doing his doctorate in chemistry."

"We've been together since we met at an anti-Vietnam rally our first month at Berkeley." Buzz again draped his arm around Eddie's shoulder. *Together?*

"And you and Buzz have something in common," Eddie said. "He grew up in Halifax, too. You might have even gone to the same high school."

I peered at Buzz and realized that he'd been a few years ahead of me in high school. He probably didn't even know I existed then, but I knew him because he had played football, and football had been a big thing at my school back then. I also remembered something else about Buzz. The rumours. That's when the penny dropped. "You and Eddie…?"

Eddie leaned in toward me and said quietly, "I always thought you knew, Kat."

"How long are you guys in town?" Chuck said. "I'd love to do some photographs of you together while you're here."

I explained to Eddie that Chuck was a photographer, or rather a photography student at Parsons. Eddie said they'd be around for a few days before they headed north to visit Buzz's family and that we should all get together. We agreed just as the bells sounded. Five minutes to curtain time. I don't remember a single part of the first act of *Hair*. I was too stunned. By the end of intermission, I realized that I should be delighted. It meant that Eddie and I could never have been a thing. But I knew that we would always be friends. That made me smile.

~

When I arrived back in Halifax for my summer vacation in 1968, it appeared to me that Mom and Dad had come to terms with their daughter's artistic plans. My father seemed to go out of his way to try to avoid confrontations with me, which meant that we didn't really spend a lot of time in quality father-daughter bonding, but we both managed to get along through July without any angst. My mother made occasional references to style and design, which I thought was kind of sweet. I spent part of the summer working part-time in a downtown fabric store while Liz and I spent our weekends together as often as we could. She had a new boyfriend named Alan Davies, someone she'd gone to high school with years before and had lost touch with when she was in Toronto. But now she had graduated and had a new job lined up for September at the local Catholic high school where Alan was the school guidance counsellor while he studied for his Master's degree part-time. He was planning to go on to become a psychologist. Liz and I had the same conversation at least twice a week throughout June and July.

"Alan and I are going out for drinks with a few friends this weekend. You should come," she'd say.

"I think I'll pass," I'd say.

"Geezus, Kat, you need to get out," Liz would respond.

"I'll probably write a letter to Chuck." End of conversation.

Then, one weekend in the middle of July, my grandmother and I were sitting on my parents' back deck having a pre-dinner glass of wine when she suddenly said, "When is Chuck coming to visit?"

My grandmother, who had been coming to dinner at least once a week since I'd been home, had become something of a confidante to me. Liz was a great listener, but she was so caught up in her newly emerging life that I often felt a bit sidelined. Not so with Nan. And you had to admire her directness. She had recently taken to reminding us that she had to be direct since she had no idea how much longer she'd live. A fair point, I suppose, but she wasn't even seventy yet.

"We haven't made any concrete plans, Nan," I said.

"Well, Kat, darling girl, it's time you did. And if you must know, I'd like to see him again. I liked him a lot, and I know that he really likes you. Unless you've decided not to introduce him to your parents?" She took a dainty sip of her wine. "Don't mind me. It's none of my business."

"You know, he actually called last week to ask when he could come," I said. Nan's eyes widened. "I guess the real problem is that I don't know where he should stay. I know Dad would disapprove of putting up a stranger in his house."

Nan took a big gulp of wine and firmly placed her glass down on the arm of the Adirondack chair she was sitting in. "First, I have something to tell you about your father's house. It is not his house; it is my house." She put a hand up in front of me to silence me. I closed my mouth and tried to take in that piece of information. What could possibly be second? "And second, Chuck can stay with me."

Nan lived in a large three-story Victorian house on a leafy street, a ten-minute drive from my parents' post-war two-story. She had plenty of room in her completely renovated interior with five bedrooms and four bathrooms. She lived almost entirely on the main floor, where she had her bedroom with an ensuite bathroom and a large walk-in closet. I had always been envious of that closet where she kept current and vintage clothes. I never knew my grandfather, and I had always just assumed he must have left her well-off, but the idea that she owned my parents' house? That was not something that made any sense to me.

"What do you mean this is your house?"

"I believe that's quite clear." She leaned forward, picked up the half-empty bottle from the table in front of both of us and poured herself another glass of wine. She offered me some more, which I gladly accepted. "I think it's time you knew some of the details of your parents' life that they probably would prefer you didn't know. One of those things is that I own this house." She looked around at the garden that was my mother's delight. "I must say that your mother has taken good care of the yard."

"Dinner in ten minutes," my mother called from inside the house.

Nan stood up and picked up her glass. "Then it's settled. Chuck is coming, and he is staying with me. Any other questions before I go powder my nose for dinner?"

I had nothing else.

Chuck arrived two weeks later.

~

I was way past nervous. I hoped Chuck would like Halifax, but he was a big-city boy and an American. I was a bit worried that he'd find it (and, by extension, me) a bit too pedestrian. Of course, the thing that panicked me most was the fact that I would have to introduce him to my parents—my father, in particular. All this was whirling around in my mind as I stood in the dappled sunshine under a tree on the sidewalk in front of the Lord Nelson Hotel. I was mere yards from the spot where the airport bus deposited weary air travellers every few hours.

I checked my outfit several times before leaving the house. I had just put the finishing touches on this baby-blue sleeveless mini-dress and hoped that he'd like my latest creation. I'd been buying dozens of commercial patterns this summer from the single place in town that carried them—the fabric store where I worked that summer. I'd made this dress using one of them. It had occurred to me that if I didn't end up being a successful fashion designer, at least I could get a job developing and drawing sewing patterns. So, this was my research for the future. At least that's what I told my father when he asked about this new shopping habit.

I pushed my large, round sunglasses up from where they had slid down in the humidity and patted my hair. My hair was still as short as Twiggy's, and I'd taken to adding an extra coating of mascara to emulate the latest trend in the magazines. I was gazing across the street at the public gardens where the trees were swaying in the afternoon breeze when, out of the corner of my eye, I spotted the bus coming up the street. I involuntarily smoothed my dress and took a deep breath. Showtime!

When Chuck stepped down from the bus and swung his large camera bag over his shoulder, my heart melted. His hair was a little longer than it had been when I'd left New York, now curling down around the Nehru collar of his white shirt. He was wearing round, wire-rimmed glasses with lightly tinted lenses, more for fashion than for sun, I thought. I loved it. Suddenly he spotted me, and his smile was so wide it nearly cracked his face in two.

When we reached one another, he dropped his camera bag and the suitcase he'd picked up on the sidewalk on his way over from the bus and threw his arms around me. "I've missed you so much!"

In a split second, I stopped caring about what my father would think of Chuck. It only mattered what I thought of him. And what he thought of me.

I had parked a block away. My mother had lent me her little Ford Cortina, navy blue with a white top. Whenever I drove it, I felt as if it wasn't even as sturdy as my Pfaff sewing machine. It rattled so much, but it got me where I needed to go. I dropped

Chuck off at Nan's so he could get settled in and told him I'd return in a couple of hours to pick up both of them for dinner at Mom and Dad's. Chuck and Nan greeted one another as if they had been friends for their entire lives. She just seemed to understand him.

"You know, Kat," he said later when I had returned, and we were waiting for Nan in her living room, "your grandmother is a blast. I mean, do you know how lucky you are to have such a cool grandmother? She even let me take a few photographs of her, and we're planning an outdoor photo session tomorrow. You're coming, of course. I'm hoping to do a grandmother-granddaughter series."

When we pulled up in Mom and Dad's driveway, I took a deep breath before getting out of the car. Chuck was already out and holding the back door for Nan to alight. I looked at the house and could see the front door opening. They were planning to greet us on the front porch.

My heart was thudding as I introduced Chuck to my parents.

"I'm so happy to finally meet you, Mr. Wilson," Chuck said, shaking Dad's outstretched hand. "And, Mrs. Wilson, thank-you so much for inviting me to dinner this evening. If there's anything I can do to help you, I'm pretty good in the kitchen." He looked around at the front yard. "This is an extraordinary garden. Not much like this in Brooklyn." My mother beamed. He continued. "If you have time, I'd love for you to show me around so I can take a few photos." My mother was smitten. My father was looking at Chuck with a peculiar look on his face—one that I didn't recall having seen before.

Chuck was a master at this winning-friends-and-influencing-people stuff. He was a Dale Carnegie fan and had quoted him to me more than once. No doubt, he was using Dale's contention that "flattery is telling the other person precisely what he thinks about himself." Or, in this case, herself. I had seen him in action before. And, so, the evening began.

Mom served roast chicken and gravy with mashed potatoes and boiled carrots. Chuck's mother, Rose, seemed to have a wider variety of items on her menus, but my mother did a mean roast chicken. Then she served blueberry buckle for dessert. Blueberry buckle, basically hot blueberry sauce topped with sweet, steamed dumplings further topped with ice-cream, was clearly a dish that a Brooklynite had never had before. I was pleased that Mom had chosen to serve a traditional east-coast dish—and one that she did remarkably well. Chuck swooned, and Mom revelled in the praise.

Dinner was going well. Mom finally shooed us out of the dining room, telling us that she didn't need any help. So, the four of us, Dad, Chuck, Nan and I, went outside to the back deck to enjoy the summer evening. Dad poured each of us a glass of port before settling into his Adirondack chair.

"Well, boy," he began, "tell me about your intentions."

Boy? Intentions? Where is this going?

Chuck wasn't taking the bait. He began to tell Dad about his intention to be a photographer, how he wanted to be a stringer for a news organization and travel the world taking photographs. These plans made me a bit nervous to think that he intended to travel so much. Perhaps I'd be a famous designer and travel the world, too. Anyway, I was thinking ahead too far.

"So," Dad said when Chuck had finished, "your name's Cohen? I suppose your father's in the rag trade in New York?"

What in the world was he getting at? I didn't know, but both Nan and Chuck seemed as if they did.

"James, must you be so boorish? I believe it's highly inappropriate to make any kind of assumptions about anything, much less something you know nothing about." Nan was clearly peeved. "It smacks of prejudice."

"It's okay, Fran," Chuck said to my grandmother. "I think James [*he called him James!*] has a right to ask anything he wants in his own home. As a matter of fact, James," he said, turning to my father, "my dad is a nuclear physicist. He teaches at Columbia."

My father was undeterred. "What does he think of Katherine here?"

Chuck looked at me and smiled. "Both my parents love her."

"Even though she'd not their kind?"

I think I gasped.

"And what precisely, James, is not their kind?" My grandmother's eyes bored into her son. "Proceed with caution."

My father hesitated for a split second, then said, "Well, you're Jews, aren't you?"

And that was the end of the conversation. My mortification didn't fade at all between that scene and the moment when Nan and Chuck got into a taxi to head back to her house half an hour later. My mother had been oblivious to all of this. She seemed flustered when the three of us stood in the living room watching the cab move down the street, and I said to my father, "What the hell was that all about?"

"Watch your language, young lady," my father said angrily. "First, you bring him here, and then you swear at your father. New York hasn't been at all good for you."

"James," my mother began, "what's going on?"

"He's not our kind, Katherine, and you know it."

I said nothing.

"But, James, he's just Jewish," Mom said pleadingly.

"Sure, he is," Dad said, stomping out of the room.

That was the last time I ever brought Chuck home.

Reach out of the Darkness

Friend and Lover, 1968

AFTER CHUCK'S VISIT, I REALIZED THAT THE ZEITGEIST of the year had somehow shifted unalterably some time ago on that day back in June when Bobby Kennedy was assassinated—long before the upsetting visit to Halifax. An era was over as far as I could tell. When I returned to New York in September for my second year at Parsons, things felt different. Public sentiment toward the Vietnam War had grown increasingly hostile since even before Bobby Kennedy became a martyr to democracy. It's true I had never been very political, notwithstanding Eddie's attempts to raise my consciousness by dragging me to protests. Still, it was hard to miss the constant references to the war that were all around us in New York that fall—student protests, increasingly gory news stories, personal profiles of soldiers returning home with every manner of life-altering injury. Even students at a design school were not immune. There were increasing calls for the Americans to leave Vietnam, and the student protests were the loudest voices.

With an end to the war nowhere in sight, I was becoming increasingly concerned about Chuck. He was about to graduate, and his protection from the draft would be coming to an end. He didn't share my pessimism, though. He believed that his government would do the right thing and "get them the hell out of a war that was never theirs," as he put it on numerous occasions. His focus that fall was on developing his final portfolio, and his subject matter would be anti-war protests. He was especially excited about this since there was a presidential vote looming in early November. Candidate Richard Nixon was running on a law-and-order platform—the law and order he referred to were not about ending the war, though. Instead, it focused on ending anti-war protests. Chuck saw this as a chance to capture the visual side of anti-war versus anti-protest. For my part, I was excited to be designing a sportswear collection. The seeming superficiality of what I was engaged in was not lost on me.

The new year brought all kinds of new things I had to learn. My course on production techniques was interesting, but I was much more interested in the textiles class. I had always loved fabrics. And I was still a junior intern for Simon Carmichael.

There were four of us now. Suzanne and I were still working in his atelier along with a senior student named Kyo, a young man of indeterminate age who said he was from Japan but spoke flawless English, and first-year student Emmeline, a blonde Californian. In early October, Simon called us all to a meeting in his office at the atelier. We had no idea what it was about, but there were rumours he was planning something big. I hoped it would be some kind of fantastic fashion show and that he'd let us take part.

"Take a seat, everyone," he said as we filed into his large, airy office. There were two white sofas facing one another with a white marble-topped coffee table between them. We sat on the sofas, two of us each one. He stood at one end.

"I have exciting news," he began. He then turned to an easel that I hadn't noticed when we came in. It was draped with snowy white fabric. With a flourish, he whipped the cover off the easel to reveal a large poster.

I stared at its psychedelic splashes of colour. It was as if I were looking into a kaleidoscope. If I moved my head even the slightest bit, the reds would suddenly begin moving into the purples and the yellows into the reds on the opposite side. Amid the hallucinogenic experience, a face peered out. It looked slightly familiar.

"I give you Mary Quant," Simon said with obvious satisfaction.

Indeed, I could see it now. Or rather, I could see *her* now. It was a likeness of British fashion designer Mary Quant, who, these days, was at the top of her game. And whose styles, I grudgingly admitted, I often seemed to emulate despite my attempt to find my own aesthetic. Even the dress I was wearing at that moment was a take-off on a Quant dress I'd seen in a magazine sometime over the past few months, even down to the colour.

"Ladies and gentleman," he said, looking in Kyo's direction, "welcome to the SXC magical fashion tour. I have arranged a field trip for the four of you."

I was baffled. Surely if Mary Quant planned to have a show or some kind of exhibit in New York, I'd have heard about it. I turned to Suzanne, who was sitting beside me, resting her chin on her hand with a bemused look on her face. I whispered, "Have you seen anything about a show here in New York?" She shook her head and shrugged. I turned back toward Simon, who was now handing out what looked like brochures.

"We leave in just over a month. Make sure you all have up-to-date passports."

They were not brochures he was passing around. They were airline tickets and itineraries. I looked at mine. It clearly said that it was a return ticket from New York to London, Thursday, November 14, 1968, for me, Katherine Wilson. We were going to meet Mary Quant. In London. The feeling I had at that moment was one that I'd experienced only once before: the day I received my acceptance to Parsons. I felt as if my life might be about to take a turn in the right direction, and I couldn't wait to tell Chuck.

Then Simon began to provide us with a few more details about the upcoming trip. We would be in London for five days, during which we would visit the Victoria and Albert Museum's costume collection, Mary Quant's store on Carnaby Street and have a final meeting with her in one of her studios. We were to be indoctrinated into the British sensibility.

"I'm sure you're all excited at the prospect of meeting Mary Quant," he said, peering at me, "but there needs to be some kind of counter-point. As much as I admire Quant's many contributions to youth culture, there is another designer whose work, in my view, is far more important both today and for the future. In addition to Carnaby Street and all that it has to offer to you as budding designers, we will also have an audience with Jean Muir."

There was an audible intake of breath all around (although I think Suzanne may have tut-tutted). If Mary Quant was that singular, in-your-face and of-the-moment designer so many of us seemed to emulate, Jean Muir was that hope-I-can-come-close-someday kind of fashion influencer whose fluid and highly tailored designs were like the sophisticated aunt to Mary Quant's cheeky little girls. I was in heaven. I don't think I had ever been more excited in my entire life. I couldn't wait to tell Nan and Liz.

~

When I arrived home that evening, I was quivering with excitement. I had to share my news with Chuck and whoever else might be around, or I thought I might burst. Virginia was the only one home.

I knew this the moment I walked in the door. The only time loud opera music wafted through our house was when Virginia was home alone. None of the rest of us could stand it, not even Carl, who had only recently asked her to marry him. I sometimes wondered about what their household would be like in the future. But that's not what I had in mind at that point.

I walked into the living room, where I could hear the grating (to my ears) voice of Maria Callas emanating from the record player. I knew that the only way to get Virginia's attention was to turn off the music, to which she was silently lip-syncing while stretched out on the sofa with her eyes closed. I walked over to the record player and lifted the needle. She shot up to a seated position immediately.

"Hey! What the...?" She swung her legs off the sofa onto the floor and sat up. "Kat, I didn't hear you come in." *Of course, you didn't hear me come in*, I thought. "You turned off my music." Clearly another statement of the obvious.

"Sorry about that." I wasn't really sorry at all, but it seemed like the polite thing to say under the circumstances. Then I told her about my news.

"Oh my god, Kat. London! I've been dreaming of a trip to London for so many years. Will you get to see the Royal Opera House in Covent Garden? I've seen photographs. Oh, I'm so jealous."

I told her that I did hope to see the opera house since I, too, had seen pictures and it looked like the kind of place someone should see when visiting London. (I didn't mention to her that I would only be interested in seeing it minus the actual opera singing.)

"And going with Simon Carmichael! My friend Eleanor is a year ahead of you and talks about him all the time." I knew Eleanor in passing. Virginia had mentioned her many times before. "She says he's dreamy." I had sat down on the other end of the sofa. Virginia now moved toward me in a kind of conspiratorial gesture. "Are you worried about the rumours?" Before I had a chance to answer, she continued. "You know, I wouldn't be. If something happened—well, let's just say that there's something to be said for slightly older men in my experience, if you know what I mean."

I sincerely did not know what she meant on that last point. On her first point about the rumours, I had heard about them, but I figured two things. First, I didn't think Simon would make any kind of unwelcome advances toward a simple, small-town girl like me when there were so many other more sophisticated ones around, and second, I was sure I could handle him if he did. As it turned out, I may have been slightly naïve.

~

Chuck finally made it home from his latest photoshoot after dinner had been long over. Before I had a chance to say anything, he started throwing things into his overnight bag and checking lenses excitedly.

"Are you going somewhere?' I said when I finally had him alone.

He turned to me, the exhilaration on his face blatantly obvious. "I am, Kat. I'm going to California for a few days. I wish you could come. I'm going to Berkley to photograph the protests."

"How do you know there'll be protests?"

"That's the great thing," he said. "Your friend, Eddie, has been feeding me information about west-coast student activism since I met him back in the spring. I thought I told you about that."

He assuredly had not told me. *I guess that's all right*, I thought. *After all, it really has nothing to do with me.*

"I'm going to stay with Eddie and Buzz on campus."

"Are you sure that's a good idea?"

"What? Going to Berkeley student protests or staying with a couple of gay guys? A good idea on both counts, in my view." He came over to me and gave me a bear hug. "Don't worry. Nothing will happen. On either front." He let me go, and I didn't really know how to respond. "What was it you wanted to tell me?"

"Oh, it's just about a trip to London that Simon Carmichael has arranged for the four of us students who work in his atelier. It's next month."

"That's really terrific, Kat. I loved London that one time I was there." He continued with his packing and zipped up the bags.

I was a bit deflated by his reaction, but I was also curious about what he'd been doing in London. I had no idea he'd ever been outside the country except for that recent foray across the border into Canada. But it was clear I wasn't going to get anything more out of him about it that evening. He was focused on getting ready to get to the airport. He was on the red-eye. His self-imposed assignments always seemed to be spur-of-the-moment things. I figured I'd just have to get used to his jaunts if I planned to spend my life with a photographer—especially one who seemed to be bound for news and art photography instead of that nice wedding and portrait photography I thought he might consider.

So off he went to California. He took his photographs and returned a few days later unharmed and none the worse for wear. I didn't see his photographs until four weeks later at an exhibition he'd been working on with a Greenwich Village gallery owner. As you know, Carl, Virginia's other half, was part-owner of a bar called *Urban Underground*. His business partner was also co-owner of a gallery that specialized in art photography. He'd agreed to give Chuck's work a chance, and his exhibit opened the week before I was scheduled to fly to London.

As I walked through the dimly lit gallery that evening, holding a half-full glass of champagne whose bubbles had ebbed away ages ago, I was dumb-struck. I knew that Chuck was a talented photographer, but these were extraordinary.

The exhibition was called *Disobedience*. The pictures were less about the anti-war sentiment that the subjects expressed and more about the people. He seemed to be able to get below the superficiality of the veneer we all carry with us. He was able to lay bare their souls. I couldn't put my finger on what it was, but I was trying to figure this out as I stood in front of a particularly striking photograph of a young woman, presumably a Berkeley student. She was off to the right at the very front of the frame. Her dark hair looked like it was in motion as the wind seemed to be rippling through it. A single strand of hair caught in the corner of her mouth as she seemed to be pleading with onlookers to listen. Just slightly out of focus behind her were masses of students, mostly young men, who appeared to be yelling while she wordlessly pleaded. I was mesmerized.

I didn't hear anyone come up behind me until I felt a slight nudge. I presumed it was Chuck, but, when I turned around, standing there holding two fresh coupes of champagne, was Simon. "Remarkable, isn't it? I think I'm going to buy it."

Those Were the Days

Mary Hopkin, 1968

THE LAST PERSON I EVER EXPECTED TO SEE at Chuck's exhibition was Simon. It was as if my two worlds had just collided, and I hadn't even been aware that they were so separate for me. As I thought about it, though, I'd always had to separate my little fashion bubble from what I'd begun to think of as real life.

"Yes," I said, "quite remarkable." I had no choice but to take the fresh glass of champagne he was offering. He then put my dead one on a nearby ledge. "What are you doing here?" Until recently, I wasn't generally someone who blurted before thinking, but perhaps this was a new skill and not a good one.

Simon laughed. "Charles Cohen is one of our star seniors at the school. Just because he's not in my department doesn't mean I'm not interested in his work. And besides," he said, sipping his champagne, "perhaps he'll photograph one of my collections someday. He has a good eye." He looked at me with a kind of half-smile playing around his lips. "And what are you doing here?"

"I'm here because Charles—Chuck—is…" What exactly was it I should call him when speaking with one of my mentors? A friend? A boyfriend?

"I know he's your boyfriend, Kat." Simon looked around at the nearby photographs. "Do you ever find he's somewhat melancholy?"

"I'm not sure I know what you mean."

"Well, look around. There's so much anguish in the eyes of almost every subject he's taken."

I looked around, and although I had to admit Simon might have had a point, I felt a tad defensive. "He's taken a lot of happy pictures," I said, thinking about the photographs of me and of Liz and even the photographs he'd taken of Eddie and Buzz. He had captured a lot of happiness in those.

"I suppose," Simon said thoughtfully, "but you have to admit that the ones he's chosen to exhibit all show a sort of despondency in the eyes. In fact, I see a lot more anguish than disobedience in these photos." He was referring to the exhibit's name. He turned back to me from scanning the room. "Don't get me wrong, though. They're all captivating, although I have to admit that I rarely see that being disobedient results in despondency."

He almost winked. What in the world was he getting at? Before I had a chance to ask, Chuck arrived at my elbow. "Well, the famous Simon Carmichael. I am honoured, sir."

Simon smiled and then shook Chuck's hand. "Congratulations, Charles. By the way, I'm buying this one." He gestured toward the photograph in front of us. "I think I just might have found the inspiration for next year's collection," he said as he nodded and walked away. Waving, he disappeared into the crowd.

"Well, that was bizarre," Chuck said when Simon was out of earshot. "I never expected to see him here."

"You should take it as a compliment, Chuck," I said, squeezing his arm.

He took my hand. "I think I'm going to have to keep an eye on him." I frowned as he continued. "I think he has a thing for my girl."

I rolled my eyes.

~

Our flight from New York landed at London's Heathrow airport just after six a.m. on Friday, November 15. The overnight flight had been long, but I was so excited, it seemed to fly by. I was sitting in the window seat beside Suzanne, who was on the aisle, as we descended toward the airport. It was still dark, but I could see so many lights.

"Oh my god, Suzanne, it's London. It's England. We're in England!"

"What?" she said, sounding as if she were in a daze. Suzanne had slept almost the entire flight, much to my chagrin. I'd had no one to chatter with for hours. It was high time she woke up. I'd had to prod her a few minutes earlier when the stewardess told us to put on our seatbelts as we prepared to land.

"Suzanne! We're here!" And suddenly, she was awake, and I was delighted.

Simon had travelled in first class (of course) but was gentleman enough to wait for us on the tarmac at the bottom of the stairs leading out of the plane so that we could all go through immigration and customs together.

We were all staying at a small hotel, *The Exeter Inn*, a grand Edwardian mansion near Carnaby Street. Simon evidently always stayed there when in London, and when we checked in, it was clear they knew him well.

"Yes, Mr. Carmichael." "Of course, Mr. Carmichael." "As you wish, Mr. Carmichael." And one, "No problem at all, Simon." The last one from a tall, blonde woman wearing what looked to me like an SXC creation from two years ago. It was a mod-style, pink wool crepe shift dress with a matching cropped jacket. What made it distinctive were the sleeve and shoulder details in leather. I wondered if it had been a gift from the designer.

Simon had given us all detailed schedules for the five days we would be in the city. Or should I say his assistant gave them to us two days before we left so that we'd know what to bring with us. There were only two slots of free time left open during the entire visit—one afternoon and one evening. I intended to make good use of those times.

The first day, jetlag notwithstanding, we embarked on an afternoon of exploring the *Victoria and Albert Museum's* costume collection. I have to admit that I was as mesmerized by the sheer beauty of the building itself as I was by the collection we were supposed to be visiting. While everyone was listening intently to the docent Simon had arranged to guide us through the exhibit, I scanned my surroundings. There was something I had to find.

Before we left, Nan had sent me a letter. I had told her we were going to London, her birthplace, and she provided me with a list of places I might consider visiting, one of which was her family home. That was on my list for that free afternoon. But she also told me to look for three specific pieces that she was sure the *V and A* had in their collection. She didn't tell me why I should see these three dresses, but I would always oblige if Nan asked, and it did seem important to her that I see them.

The dresses were creations of the early twentieth-century French designer Paul Poiret. As I shuffled along with my little group past glass cases full of fantastic garments by famous designers from years gone by, I was desperately trying to figure out where the Poiret dresses might be without having to ask. If I had to ask, someone would likely want to know why I was asking, and I didn't want to explain myself.

We entered another salon. Simon gestured toward the mannequins lining the aisle. "I give you the father of haute couture." He seemed very pleased with himself as if he had personally discovered *The House of Worth* and its founder, Charles Frederick Worth.

We had arrived in the salon housing early French designers. Worth, however, had initially been an English designer who had eventually spent his career in Paris. We studied these designers, and I remembered we had seen pictures of his late nineteenth-century designs. In front of me as I stood there, were a dozen magnificent ball gowns for which he had been famous. But there was something else about him that I was trying to remember. I turned to look down one of the aisles, and it suddenly came to me. Paul Poiret had worked for him. Surely his work must be around here somewhere. I thought if I could just slip away, I might be able to find him.

The lights were low, and everyone was focused intently on the mannequins wearing various silks and satins from the *House of Worth*. I turned silently down the next aisle and began scanning the tiny placards that identified each piece's designer. When I came to a peculiar-looking gown that looked like a lampshade over a pair of harem pants, I knew I had found him. This was one of the pieces Nan had described in her letter.

According to Nan, it was called "Sorbet," and Poiret had designed it for his wife to wear to a fancy-dress ball in 1911. I quickly took out my small sketchbook and began sketching as fast as I could. I had not brought my camera since the museum didn't permit photography, but we were all expected to sketch pieces we saw.

As I moved along the aisle, there was another Paul Poiret, but it wasn't one of the ones Nan had described. I could hear voices, but it seemed that no one had missed me yet. I tapped my pencil on my sketchbook and looked around. Then I spotted another one Nan had described.

The little placard said it was part of Poiret's 1925 collection. The dress had a wide, bateau-shaped neckline and long sleeves. It hugged the body until just below the waist, then flared out, ending just below the knee. It was a deep-chocolate velvet with panels of lace. It was exquisite. I quickly sketched it, then turned to the one next to it, also from the 1925 collection. I was sure this was the third one.

This one could only be described as a flapper dress—something a 1920s flapper might have worn to an evening out at a nightclub. I could picture the wearer sitting with a cocktail and a long cigarette holder at a table with equally sparkling people while enjoying a band. It was layers of shimmering silk that must have caught the light as the wearer danced the Charleston or perhaps the tango. How in the world did my grandmother know about these dresses? I was determined to find out the minute I had a chance to talk to her. I sketched quickly and started to make my way back to the group when Simon popped out from one of the aisles.

"Enjoying your private tour of the collection?"

I stuffed my sketchbook in my bag, but not before he had glanced at the last sketch.

"A good sketch." He plunged his hands into his pockets and stared at me. "Why the interest in Poiret? Are you planning to make him your inspiration for your senior collection next year?"

"Just interested in his work," I said. He was blocking the aisle.

Suddenly, he reached toward me and placed a hand on each of my shoulders, his face coming within inches of mine. "I can help you, you know."

I could feel his breath on my face. Just as quickly as he had moved in, he dropped his hands and once again put them in his pockets. "I think it's time to join the others." And he smiled at me.

That evening at dinner, I took a place as far away from Simon as I could. I didn't know what to say to him.

~

I wondered if my grandmother's childhood home might not have been razed during the city's post-war reconstruction. Perhaps I wouldn't be able to find it at all, but I was going to try. I set out from the hotel clutching my umbrella as the November drizzle coated the streets in a thin sheen that reflected the lights from the passing black cabs in a kind of shimmer. It wasn't exactly pleasant, but I wanted to walk.

Although I knew little about my grandmother's early years, I did know that she was born in London, had spent some time in Paris and then evidently met a Canadian somewhere along the line, and the rest was history—at least as much as I knew it. Now that I thought about it, I didn't know that much. Perhaps this little excursion would help me to know her better.

The house where my grandmother had lived as a child was on a quiet, leafy street in Belgravia about three blocks from Hyde Park. I had the address written on a small piece of paper that I clutched in my gloved hand as I walked alone down the street. *This can't possibly be the right place*, I thought as I passed by one after another beautifully restored Georgian mansion—at least they were mansions in the downtown London way. Nan's family would have had to be rich to have lived here. Why had she never talked about her life in England? The only thing I could figure out from her request that I take this little walk down her memory lane was that this was her way of sharing it with me. But I had a lot of questions for her.

I finally arrived in front of the house with the number she had given me. It was still there—and it was impressive. I stood on the sidewalk under my umbrella in the rain staring at the remarkable double doors with their gleaming brass hardware. Three stories high, it was light-coloured brick with multiple rows of windows, all of which were covered by sheer white draperies. It had three steps up to a small porch with its two-story roof held up by four massive pillars.

I don't know how long I had been standing there when a well-dressed man wearing a black overcoat and carrying a large black leather briefcase came up behind me.

"Excuse me, madame," he said in what sounded to me like an aristocratic British accent. "May I be of assistance?"

The rain was dripping off both our umbrellas, drenching our feet. I could see the rain sliding off my black patent-leather Mary-Janes. His expensive-looking black leather shoes, on the other hand, seemed to be soaking it in.

"Oh, I'm so sorry, "I said. "I was just looking at this house."

"You're an American." It was a statement, not a question.

"Actually, I'm a Canadian," I said.

"I do apologize," he said. "But I really must get past. I'm running frightfully late. Was there anything I could help you with?" he said when it was clear that I was not moving.

"No need to apologize. It's just that my grandmother gave me this address and told me that I should try to find it while I'm here. She says she lived here when she was young. But I'm not sure this is the right address." I looked up at the house in all its grandeur.

His interest seemed to perk up just slightly. He cocked his head slightly to the left as if he were trying to remember something. "Did she? Well, I'm certainly interested in the history of this house and would love to chat more, but, as I said, I'm running very late." He rummaged in his breast pocket and pulled out a business card that he then offered to me. "Perhaps we could chat another time?"

I took the card from him, nodded and moved out of his way. He hurried up the steps and disappeared in through the door. I stood in the rain, dripping wet and looked down at the card in my hand. *Oliver Lowther-Russell II, Barrister.* I fervently wished that I had some time to chat with him, but we were meeting both Mary Quant and Jean Muir the next day. We were flying home the day after that. Anyway, I had an interesting story to tell Nan when I got a chance.

~

Carnaby Street. The very thought of it made me shiver with delight. I forgot all about my encounter with Oliver Lowther-Russell II the next morning as we set out first to visit Mary Quant's boutique and then meet briefly with the queen of mod herself.

After the rain of the day before, this one turned out to be unseasonably warm and dry for London, or so the woman at the hotel's front desk had told us as we left. As we approached Carnaby Street, I felt as if this weather was a bit of a gift since the throngs of mostly young people strolling along the street, carrier bags in hand presumably from shopping, weren't wearing drab, dull rainwear. They were like a moving rainbow of colours. I was thrilled, and I could feel the excitement of my colleagues. Even Simon seemed to come alive as we marched along, joining the rainbow.

What I had always loved about the Mary Quant look, and the reason why it seemed to seep into my own designs (I'd have to do something about that before next year's senior project), was the fact that the lines were simple—simple shift dresses like the ones I was now seeing in shop windows—but the colours, and how she placed the colours into the designs were what made them fun and young. I couldn't see my mother wearing anything like these!

It turned out that our visit to the Mary Quant atelier was more of a visit to the back room of the boutique where M.Q. herself made a brief but memorable appearance. I stared at her sleek dark hair, blunt cut with those long bangs, wearing one of her own pantsuit designs instead of the mini-skirt I had expected. She was gracious, briefly eloquent as she gave us encouragement for our own careers, and ultimately in a hurry to be somewhere else. And that was that.

Simon then led us to a shop a few blocks from Carnaby Street, where the ambiance was totally different. The mannequins in the window were the first clue that we had walked out of one world and into another. The clothes were sophisticated and flowing, with a richness that seemed to emanate from the folds of high-quality fabrics that draped deliciously. As we walked into the shop, a woman closer to my mother's age than mine greeted us. She was wearing a beautifully tailored yet fluid suit that looked as if it might be silk crepe. I wanted to reach out and touch it, but I realized that this would probably look gauche. She wore a double strand of pearls around her neck beneath the open neckline, with a pair of reading glasses hanging from a sparkly chain around her neck.

Simon greeted her with a double kiss. She then moved to the back of the shop from where she retrieved a rail of clothing that she now wheeled into the middle of the shop. It was clear that she had pulled these pieces as representative of the designs they sold. Every one of them was a Jean Muir design. She pulled each one from the rail in turn, and Simon provided commentary on design, style lines, details and fabrics. As I took them all in, I realized that it wasn't my mother who would suit these; rather, it was Nan. They looked exactly like the kinds of pieces she might wear. I wished I could have afforded to buy her a gift, but each of them cost a sum of money that might keep a small family in groceries for a year or more.

There was something about being in London that made me think about Nan. What was it? Answers would have to wait.

~

Our final evening was upon us. Simon had planned a group dinner to finish off the field trip and to tell us about the

213

assignment he wanted us to complete upon our return. When I heard about the kind of illustrated paper he was looking for, I was glad I had sketched my way through London.

We had just finished a dessert—or pudding as the British called it—of something called bread pudding, which was delicious when Suzanne got up and said she still had to pack, and she'd see me in our room later. Kyo and Emmeline wanted one last walk down a London street in the rain (yes, it was raining again). That left me, with my final few forkfuls of pudding and Simon, who sat back and lit a cigarette.

"Tell me, Kat," he said, inhaling deeply then slowly blowing smoke out through pursed lips, "are you planning to wed this photographer friend of yours?"

I think I choked on my last mouthful of dessert. As I took a sip of water, I looked across at him, thinking, *what business is that of yours?* But I couldn't say that to someone who held such sway over whether I actually graduated in another year and a half. Besides, it wasn't a question I'd given much thought to. Yet. Chuck and I hadn't talked about it specifically, although we did discuss what we'd both be doing after graduation. My other thought was, *why are you even asking?*

"Well, Simon," I began when I finally had a moment to gather my wits about me, "I'm not sure I've thought that far in advance."

"Hmm. Are you familiar with the German philosopher Friedrich Nietzsche?

I was only dimly aware of him, but I nodded as if I knew where he was going.

"Apart from the fact that his work has influenced much of the way we think today in the Western world, he once said, '*The future influences the present.*'" He stubbed out his cigarette. "Something to think about, Katherine Wilson." He stood up, nodded and left.

214

Bad Moon Rising

Creedence Clearwater Revival, 1969

IT WAS ONLY A MATTER OF TIME before the subject reared its ugly head. And it had to be New Year's Eve, didn't it? Let me back up.

After the London trip, I had been so busy completing end-of-semester projects and trying to find some Christmas presents to mail home to Mom, Dad, Nan and Liz, I didn't have a moment to think about Nan's connection to London. That would have to wait. I stayed in New York this year and spent Christmas—actually, we celebrated Hannukah—with Chuck and his parents.

We were planning a New Year's Eve party at our place. The new year, 1969, was promising to be a momentous one for our little group of roommates, and it wasn't at all clear that, this time next year, we would even be living in the same city together. Chuck was graduating and had big plans for his career as a news photographer. Virginia had just graduated with her opera degree, or whatever opera singers had, and hoped to be offered a job back home in Minneapolis where they had a fairly new opera company (six years old, I think she said). Carl was considering selling his share in the *Urban Underground* to open his own bar in Minneapolis if Virginia got the job. And Louise

215

had a call-back in a couple of weeks for the national tour of *Cabaret* that was set to open in August. We were about to scatter.

It was just after five, and it was already dark. I was in the kitchen putting the finishing touches on what would pass for hors d'oeuvres, our finger food—pigs in blankets, three kinds of dips, cheese fondue. Louise was fussing over perfect little bread cubes for the fondue. Virginia was festooning the living room with Happy New Year banners and getting noise-makers ready. Chuck was in the dining room, laying out the ingredients for his signature cocktails for the evening—champagne cocktails and Manhattan's. We weren't expecting Carl until much later—when you run a bar, New Year's Eve is kind of a big working day. I heard the front door open and slam shut, then heard Virginia's voice from the living room, which had a clear view of the front hall.

"Carl! What a terrific surprise. Come and help me." There was a brief silence, then sobbing.

I dropped what I was doing and headed toward the living room. Chuck was already there. Carl was sitting on the sofa, his head in his hands. Virginia was beside him with her arm flung across his back. Tears were streaming down her face. Chuck was standing up, reading what appeared to be a letter.

"What happened?" I went to Virginia and knelt on the floor in front of her. She sobbed again.

"Kat, here," Chuck said, thrusting the letter at me. I got up and took it from him. I didn't even need to read it. It wasn't really a letter; it was more of a form. When I saw the logo on the left-hand side of the page, I knew exactly what it was. It was that thing we all feared.

The words "Selective Service System" were centred at the very top of the page. Directly under it, in all-caps as if it were shouting at the reader, it said, "ORDER TO REPORT FOR INDUCTION." It was Carl's draft notice. He was ordered to report to the induction centre on Whitehall Street in Lower Manhattan at 6:45 a.m. on Monday, February 10, 1969.

Carl looked up. "Hey, man, it was only a matter of time. I guess I kind of hoped the war would be over before it happened."

"You can't go! You can't go!" Virginia was hysterical.

I sat down beside her on the sofa and wrapped my arms around her. It seemed that she was having a harder time with this than Carl was. I looked up at Carl. "What about going to Canada? I could help."

He shook his head. "Can't do that, Kat. But thanks for offering."

Virginia sat up. "Of course, you can! I'll go with you. We'll be draft dodgers together!"

Carl took Virginia's hand gently and began stroking it. "Ginny, we've talked about this. You know I can't do that. I might think the war is a bad one. I might think that it's a war we shouldn't be fighting, but you know I come from a long line of American warriors. I have to answer the call to duty."

I wondered what Eddie would think of this line of reasoning. And then I immediately began thinking about Chuck. It was a conversation that Virginia and Carl may have had, but we had not. And Chuck was graduating this year, so he'd lose his student deferment the moment he picked up that diploma. I started to shiver. "We'll have to cancel the party tonight," I said finally.

Carl looked at me. "We'll do nothing of the kind. There's nothing I'd like more at this moment than to celebrate life with my friends."

I had the distinct impression that what was unspoken was that he wanted to celebrate life with his friends who he might never see again. I couldn't swallow the lump that was beginning to form in my throat. Real-life and the horrors that might lie ahead of him were starting to float in front of my eyes. I had to push them away.

"Then, it's a party we shall have!" Chuck said, putting the letter down on the coffee table. "Drink, buddy?"

Carl smiled in a kind of lop-sided way. "Yeah, but not one of those wussy champagne cocktails you're planning. Bourbon. And make it a double."

~

Despite it all, the party was a good one. People started arriving just after nine and didn't start leaving until almost two a.m. The festivities began a bit low-key since Carl had decided he had to get the elephant in the room out of the way as quickly as possible. He showed everyone his draft notice and asked everyone to raise a glass to a safe return for him—and everyone else over there in the jungles of southeast Asia.

Carl wasn't the first among the group of friends we had invited to be touched by the draft, and he wouldn't be the last. It seemed everyone had a brother, a cousin, a boyfriend or a friend who had been called up. And some of them had never come home. Suzanne, who had arrived with her new boyfriend, was one of them. I had worried that talk of the war would dominate the conversation. After we all listened to Barry McGuire sing "Eve of Destruction" and Bob Dylan sing "Blowin' in the Wind," though, Carl declared that the war was over for the evening, then someone dropped a Steppenwolf record on the turntable, and we all moved on to fondue.

The next morning, we awoke to a house that looked as if a cyclone had blown through. I was groggy and hung-over and had to listen to Chuck tell me why I should have smoked the weed that had been passed around last evening instead of that third—or fourth if you must know—champagne cocktail, sticking to my good-girl position that alcohol was somehow better. He wasn't nearly as hungover as I was. I'd have to remember that at the next party.

218

The new year brought what seemed to me to be an unprecedented number of anti-war protests around the country and around the world. But maybe I was just more sensitive to them since the day for Carl to leave for his army induction was fast approaching as February began. In preparation, he had gone ahead and sold his share in the *Urban Underground,* and he had encouraged Virginia to proceed with her audition in Minneapolis. At least she could be closer to her family. And they planned to get married the moment he returned.

"So, what do you think of Carl and Virginia planning to get married when he returns?" Chuck casually slid this into a conversation about grocery shopping one Saturday afternoon in early February.

"I think it's wonderful for them to be thinking ahead to after he gets back."

"Have you ever thought that marriage might be part of your future?"

I had no idea where he was going with this. "Well, I suppose we all do at some point in our lives," I said carefully.

That was it—end of conversation. We went back to completing the grocery list.

~

After his induction, Carl had to go to an army base somewhere in Georgia for eight weeks of basic training. He told us that more training would follow this and that he might not even be shipped overseas for upwards of six months. He was still hoping the war would be over by then, but we all had our doubts.

"Hey," Carl said, chugging a beer the night before he was up for induction, "this Nixon guy knows he has to get us out of there if he wants his presidency to survive."

Only weeks earlier, Richard Nixon had been sworn in as president. Although we knew Carl was right, it seemed like a dim hope, at least in the short term, which was really all that counted for him. But for Chuck, I knew it might count for a lot as the year wore on.

"I'm with you, buddy," Chuck said.

We were having a small, low-key farewell party for Carl while Virginia sat quietly in a corner, sipping a glass of wine. I had already tried to draw her out, but it was no use. She said she was saving her voice for her upcoming auditions.

Carl left the next morning.

Within six weeks, the President had escalated the war. Carl was the first person I personally knew who was facing this horrendous future, and I was suddenly terrified. I knew I should probably stop watching the gruesome nightly television coverage of the bloody battles in far-away Cambodia, but it all seemed to be creeping closer and closer to my doorstep like tiny drops of water that threaten to drown you in a tsunami if no one can stop them.

Virginia left three weeks after Carl to audition for an opera chorus position in Minneapolis. She took all her belongings with her. Louise had a successful call-back, was cast as a chorus member in *Cabaret* and started making plans to move back in with her family for a few months before the national tour started later in the summer. She would use that time to save some money, all of which left Chuck and me with an almost-empty brownstone. We couldn't really afford to live there on our own, and the thought of finding new roommates left us both cold. So, we started to look for an apartment—to share. We had never shared a room in the house, at least not officially. This would be a big step for the "good girl" from the small town.

In early April, Chuck poked his head into the studio at school, where I was working on a large drafting table among a dozen other classmates doing the same thing. I was trying to figure out where I was going with a design challenge. It was supposed to be some kind of far-out use of unexpected materials. Some of the students worked with toilet paper, which had a facility for draping around a figure. I had chosen cling wrap, and it was driving me crazy. I was more of a straight-shooter, classic kind of designer, but I was trying to branch out. It was a hard slog. Anyway, when I looked up and saw him in the doorway, it was a welcome distraction.

As I started to get up, he gestured for me to stay where I was as he whipped out his camera and began taking pictures one after the other. Click-click-click. Other students looked up.

"A few photographs for posterity," he said as I greeted him at the door. "And maybe the yearbook. But that's not why I'm here." He gestured for me to follow him out into the corridor.

"So, I think I've found us an apartment," he said as we tried to plaster ourselves against the wall to avoid being trampled by a group of first-year students who seemed to be late for whatever class they had next.

"That's great! Where is it?"

"That's the great thing. It's in the village on West 4th Street."

"Gosh," I said, calculating distances. "That's an hour's walk from here."

"Yeah, but half that on the subway, and we'll be close to all the clubs we like. So much more to photograph around there, you know? What do you say, babe? Come with me to see it this afternoon? I had a look at the building yesterday when I went down to my favourite camera store. I talked to the landlord, and it sounds perfect for us."

I told him I was excited, too, and that, of course, we should see it. According to the landlord, there were several other interested parties, so we'd have to act fast.

When Chuck met me at the school's main door at four p.m., I was mentally steeling myself for the rush-hour subway ride. It would be armpit-to-armpit crowded—something I had yet to get used to, but I figured I might as well start now.

We arrived in front of a four-story, red brick building with a French restaurant on the main floor. I gave it points for being so close to food. I looked up at the small windows toward the fourth floor.

"Okay, *monsieur*," I said. "Let's see this perfect abode."

We rang the bell, and the landlord's wife, Monique, appeared at the door. It seemed that not only was her husband Bertrand the landlord, but he was also the chef. They owned the entire building, the restaurant included.

"*Bonjour, bonjour*," she said, gesturing us inside. "Welcome to our little *château*." Then she giggled, causing her ample midsection to quiver with delight. "Bertrand told me to expect you." She shuffled us toward the stairs. "I believe you will like it. Let me know when you come back down."

"You aren't coming with us?" I said.

"*Non, non, ma petite.*" She laughed again. "I live on this floor and never venture upward. Bertrand and our son look after the rest of the building. But you will love the skylight, I am told!"

And the penny dropped. I suddenly realized that what she was really saying was that she didn't climb stairs. There was no elevator. I gazed up the first flight to where it turned in the distance. Then Chuck was off, grabbing my hand and pulling me along.

Did I mention that the apartment was on the fourth floor? That's why it had a skylight. It was on the top floor that could be reached only after walking up four flights of stairs. By the time we arrived at the top, I seriously wondered if it was humanly possible to do this every day. That's when a petite, white-haired woman who had to be at least eighty-five, popped her head out of the apartment across the hall and smiled in that grandmotherly way. I think she was smirking at our breathlessness. It was clear even to the dimmest among us that she did these stairs whenever she left her apartment.

Chuck took the key Monique had pressed into his hand when we started toward the staircase and turned it in the lock. He opened the door slowly. I'm not sure what I was expecting, but I wasn't expecting to be dropped into a movie set. There before me was, I swear to god, the apartment that Robert Redford and that young actress called Jane Fonda had rented just after their hasty marriage in *Barefoot in the Park*, a movie we'd seen only a year before.

The apartment was, in a word, small. It had plank floors like in the movie and even had a step up to a raised platform that housed the tiny kitchen and the master bedroom. There was even a wood-burning stove in the far corner of the living room. The two of us simultaneously, as if we had choreographed it, looked up toward the skylight and started to laugh.

"Remember the skylight?" Chuck said, hardly able to get the word out.

"I wonder if it will snow here in the living room?" I was practically doubled over with laughter, remembering the scene in the movie. "You know we have to take it, don't you?" I said when I got control of my mirth.

"You haven't even seen the bedroom yet," he said, pointing to a door that, no doubt, housed a tiny bedroom and minuscule bathroom.

"I think we can safely assume that it will be microscopic," I said. "And who cares?"

Neither of us did. We rented the apartment on the spot, and I vowed to improve my aerobic capacity. It was do or die, anyway.

~

Once settled into the apartment, I got used to taking the subway. In fact, by the middle of June, I was starting to feel like a real New Yorker. Chuck had just graduated and was doing some freelance work for a couple of underground newspapers in addition to one assignment so far as an assistant to a staff photographer at the *New York Times*. He was always on the look-out for that one picture that would rocket him into a plum position. That's why, in the early morning hours of June 28, when we began to hear an extraordinary number of sirens, Chuck said to me, "You stay here. I'm going to find out what's happening." He threw his clothes on, slung his camera bag over his shoulder, another camera around his neck and left.

It was after seven the next morning before the door opened, and Chuck walked in. There was dried blood on his forehead and spattered on his T-shirt that was soaked with sweat. It had been a scorching night. I was terrified, but he seemed to be electrified. Manic, even.

"What in the world happened?" I said, rushing for the alcohol to clean what turned out to be a two-inch gash in his forehead.

"It was unbelievable, Kat. I mean, there were police everywhere. They were loading guys into a police wagon when I got there. That's when all hell broke loose."

"Where were they?"

"At *The Stonewall*."

I gasped. He was referring to *The Stonewall Inn*, a bar not two blocks from where we lived, ostensibly Mafia-owned, but more to the point, a well-known gay bar. According to Chuck, just as he arrived, the police were roughing up one of the patrons—a cross-dressing man—when the crowds decided they'd had enough. A riot broke out. I wasn't sure what astonished me most—the fact that there had been a police riot mere blocks from where I was sleeping, or that Chuck seemed so unruffled as if this were some kind of balm for him. Of course, he believed he had captured the photograph of the month. He immediately went downstairs to lock himself in the broom-closet he had coerced Monique into giving up to him so he could turn it into a darkroom. He was too excited even to have coffee—and was on a natural high.

I was frightened as I left the apartment that day and for several days that followed. Our neighbourhood was inundated with protesters, all of them demanding improvements to gay rights. It had never occurred to me before that Eddie himself violated the law. I just thought that people could be who they were. I was so wrong. The whole thing made me want to cry every time I thought about it. How could I have been so dense? So parochial? So ignorant? I promised myself that I'd make my work count for something. My life count for something.

~

Two of Chuck's photographs ended up in the *Village Voice*, but even more exciting for him, one of them ended up in the *New York Times*. He had finally sold a picture to a major player in the business.

"You're not going home this summer, are you?" he said one evening as we made dinner in our tiny kitchen.

"I was thinking that I might go home for a couple of weeks at the end of July. I'd love to catch up with Nan," I said, throwing sliced carrots into a pot on the stove.

Chuck picked a carrot coin out of the pot and crunched down on it as he passed me what looked like a small poster. "Have a look at this."

I wiped my hands on a nearby towel and took it from him. I stepped down from the kitchen and picked up my glass of wine from our small dining table. I wasn't sure what I was looking at.

It was a crude drawing of a white bird sitting on what appeared to be the neck of a guitar, all on a solid red background. It looked as if it had been drawn by a three-year-old. In large letters on the right-hand side, it said, "Three days of peace and music." It seemed to be some kind of advertisement. "An Aquarian Exposition in White Lake, New York," it said.

"I've got four tickets," Chuck said. "Want to go with me to the Woodstock Music and Art Fair? Whatever that is…"

Piece of my Heart

Janis Joplin, 1969

IT TOOK A MONTH OF BACK-AND-FORTH LETTERS and phone calls, but finally, Liz said she and Alan would love to meet us in Manhattan so we could all drive north to upstate New York to go to a music festival in August. When she read the line-up of acts, she insisted that we educate ourselves a bit.

"You and I are old folkies," she had said during one organizational phone call. "There might be a bit of that, but it looks like there are going to be lots of rockers. We can't go in cold. Why don't we each buy a copy of that new album *Cheap Thrills* so we can get up to speed?"

"Who's the artist?"

"Something called Big Brother and the Holding Company."

"I don't see them on the line-up," I said. As we talked, I was perusing the sheets Chuck had brought home detailing who would be performing and when over the three days of the concert.

"No, but their lead singer is Janis Joplin. Or I should say was. I think they broke up. Anyway, she's a headliner, and I think we should get to know her."

So, I agreed and dutifully took myself to *Record Mart* in the Times Square subway station and found a copy. When I sat down at home later that evening looking at the brightly coloured cartoons festooning the album jacket, I was skeptical. I was just putting the needle onto the first track when Chuck walked in through the door.

The track started with voices that sounded like they had a live audience for the recording session. Then the sound of the electric guitar chords and vague screams began. Chuck walked over to the record player in the corner of the tiny living room, lifted the needle and said, "I think you should start with this one." He dropped the needle, and the room immediately came alive. It took less than ten seconds for me to feel as if I were in the room with the band.

The electric guitar begins slowly then—the voice. It was an unmistakable one to even the rock-challenged among us—that would have been me. It was Janis Joplin, at her raspy, rough best belting out "Piece of My Heart."

Chuck and I sat together on the small sofa and just listened. I had always thought of her voice as too harsh, too rough. But as we sat there, eyes closed, listening to the voice surrounded as it was by electric guitar, drums and a bit of background singing, all I could think about was that the music had a kind of feeling about it that I couldn't quite grasp. It was emotional in a kind of grab-you-by-the-balls, in-your-face way. And it dared you to ignore it. I suddenly realized that I couldn't ignore it. I was no hippie, but this raw emotion was something that I needed to experience. And I could be a weekend hippie, couldn't I?

~

Liz and Alan arrived on Tuesday, August 12. Our plan was to get everything we needed together on Wednesday and drive north to Bethel in upstate New York on Thursday. The festival didn't start until Friday evening, so I had questioned why we had to go up on Thursday. The drive was only a few hours long. Surely, we could be there on time if we left on Friday morning. But Chuck and his friend Jeff who was driving, insisted we had to get there a day early. Perhaps they were a tiny bit psychic.

Jeff was a newly minted journalist, having recently graduated from Columbia. He was trying to make his mark as a freelance writer, looking for that big break like Chuck. They both thought a piece on the '60s counterculture might be the charm for them if they worked together, so they were planning a photojournalistic piece. Jeff had gotten the tickets for all of us and claimed that he knew a couple of the musicians. That would give them access to backstage—or so they hoped. Anyway, Jeff and Chuck won the day, and we had to be ready to leave by Thursday morning.

The August weather was stifling—hot, humid, sticky and stinky in the city. We were looking forward to getting out for a few days. Liz had arrived with a new hairstyle—down below her shoulders and wrapped with a headband, hippie style. She had concerns about me.

"Jeezus, Kat, when you said you had let your hair grow, I thought it would be longer than this by now." She lifted a piece.

I had stopped cutting my hair sometime before Christmas, and now it reached my shoulders, but I wasn't sure what this had to do with anything. It seemed, however, that Liz had specific plans. She had taken it on as her duty to select our wardrobe for the festival.

Liz and I had never been hippies. We liked the mod style, mini-skirts and Mary Janes. We loved Twiggy, Jean Shrimpton and glossy fashion magazines. But for a few days, we were going to become something else. As far as Liz was concerned, going to the festival with our usual buttoned-down style would make us stick out like sore thumbs. We wanted to blend in a bit, didn't we? I hadn't given it much thought, save that fleeting thought about weekend hippies.

"Kat, you won't get the full-on music festival experience if you don't look the part." We were rummaging through a flea market in the Village. Liz was muttering something as she combed through the junk jewellery on offer.

"What are you mumbling about, Liz?" I said as I gazed at the rack of colourful, filmy skirts in front of me. As I touched them, I was thinking about how poorly made they were.

"I said we're going to need love beads to go with our outfits."

I started laughing. "Love beads? What in the world are love beads?"

She stood up straight and put her hands on her hips. "For god's sake, Kat, get with the program here. We're going to a hippie peace and love festival, and damn it, we're going to look the part."

And so it was that we became fashion hippies that weekend. And I hate to admit it, but it was fun.

Early Thursday morning, Liz, Alan, Chuck and I were standing in front of our apartment building (of course, Liz and Alan had stayed at a hotel nearby given our space limitations), waiting for Jeff to appear with his van. I was wearing a filmy, white caftan-type dress that ended mid-calf. Wound around my neck was a brightly-coloured scarf with fringes so long they reached the hem of my dress. Liz had found me a pair of fringed boots that she said I absolutely had to have, and I had a headband to go around my forehead that I'd wear later. It was a bridge too far for so early in the morning. I had an armful of Bakelite bracelets—the original one Chuck had given me, three more plain bangles he'd given me for Christmas and one I'd found at the flea market. I loved how they jangled together.

Liz wore a blue and teal floral dress she'd made herself. It was only slightly longer than mine and flowed around her legs. She was wearing cowboy boots and on her head a circle of flowers she'd picked up at the flower shop down the street. When I said I thought the point of the hippie flower crowns was that they were wildflowers picked from a meadow, she just made a face at me.

The boys had been less concerned about their attire. They were sporting two-days growth of beards, T-shirts and jeans. We were already sweating in the morning heat when a cream-coloured VW van pulled around the corner and stopped in front of us. I had expected to see peace signs on the sides, but the van belonged to Jeff's father. Beside Jeff in the front seat was a young woman who looked as if she were the real deal—hippie, I mean. He introduced her as Tina. She was wearing a midriff-baring peasant blouse and low-slung jeans with a wide, multi-coloured leather belt. She looked hot—in the warm and sticky sense. I was glad we were wearing dresses that at least might let the breeze in.

Chuck threw his camera equipment in the back next to our small duffel bags and climbed into the seat behind Tina. Liz and I clambered in beside him, and Alan got in the back. It was stifling already, even with the windows open. And we were off.

We stopped once on the drive north to pick up a few supplies—bottles of water and soda, potato chips, some sandwiches—but we expected to be able to buy anything else we needed at the festival. As we approached the exit from Highway 17 at Monticello, where we'd have to get off and make our way on a smaller highway toward Bethel, we noticed that traffic was slowing down. It was lined up all the way to the exit. We were still ten or more miles from the festival grounds. We all thought there must have been an accident up ahead.

When we finally got off the exit, we were bumper-to-bumper. We could see people in the cars, vans and pick-up trucks up ahead leaning out their windows flashing peace signs at the highway patrol car parked on the side of the road. Two highway patrolmen were standing on the side of the road, urging people to turn around and go home. That was when it dawned on us: there was no accident. We had become part of some kind of pilgrimage. Chuck and Jeff were as excited as a couple of little kids.

"This is going to be a blast!" Jeff said as he stopped to let two half-naked hippies run across the road.

"Epic!" Chuck said. "It's going to be epic!" With that, he grabbed a camera and jumped out of the van. "I'm going to walk on ahead and shoot some pictures. I'll catch up to you."

As the traffic ground to a standstill, people started driving off the side of the road and abandoning their cars and vans. We needed the camera equipment and our supplies, so that wasn't an option for us. We had to plunge onward. But it was so hot in the van that finally, Liz and I decided to walk ahead, too.

The moment we got out of the van, we began to smell the gentle aroma of weed. As we walked along, surrounded by jubilant festival-goers, the faint bouquet became an overpowering envelope that gave us a kind of contact high. We laughed and decided just to embrace it.

We caught up with Chuck, who was beside himself with joy at all the photo ops. Everyone was so happy to pose for him, and he was eating it up. I also thought he'd already had a hit or two of a joint that someone was passing around the crowd. Maybe I'd have to loosen up a bit. The three of us joined the group of revellers proceeding on foot to the festival, the distance be damned. It was like being in a slipstream of some grubby, well-used jet plane being dragged happily along.

~

Our two-and-a-half-hour trip took seven hours. When we finally arrived at the festival grounds, it was well past dinner time. The place was already swarming with people, although it was still twenty-four hours before the start time. As we looked around, we could see that the workers were nowhere near finished setting up yet. There were only a few fences around the grounds, and even the massive stage they were working on wasn't even close to completion. Yet festival-goers seemed to be arriving in droves.

We managed to find a place to park in a clearing in the woods not far from where the stage was under construction. If we had arrived even two hours later, I'm not sure where we would have parked within a mile or more of the site. If we had done as I had wanted to—left on Friday morning—we would still have been on the highway when the music began, which it did almost at its promised time of five p.m. on Friday.

We had found a spot not too far from the stage and were all sitting comfortably on a blanket in a sea of excited and brightly coloured (and well-lit) humanity when Richie Havens took over the stage. I wasn't a huge Richie Havens fan, but sitting there amid such extraordinary enthusiasm, Liz and I were trembling with excitement. Neither of us had ever done anything so deliciously counterculture—at least that's the way I saw it. It was exhilarating.

After the first set, someone called Swami Satchidananda climbed up onto the stage and was helped to a kind of rectangular meditation platform where he sat down, cross-legged and arranged his flowing robe around him. His acolytes sat on either side of him.

"Hey, Kat," Chuck said, leaning over to me while he held his large camera. "Take a look through this lens."

I looked into the lens he had trained on the swami. It was a telephoto lens, and I could see his full, white beard and even the hairs in his nose. I began to feel embarrassed at how intimate it seemed to be. I realized that this is just what photographers are searching for—that intimacy with a subject that is so fleeting it has to be caught like a butterfly in a net.

Swami Satchidananda began speaking. He was happy to be here to open the festival and talked about us being "gathered in the name of the fine art of music." *A nice turn of phrase*, I thought.

Although heavily accented, his English was surprisingly good. He then talked about how America helped the world so much, but that it was time for America to help the world with spirituality, and he lost me. I didn't know what he meant, given the country's situation at that moment in time. But the idea of peace and love seemed to be one that there was no argument against.

"And through the sacred heart of music, let us find peace."

Not being especially religious, I gazed around at the crowd as he spoke and was astonished by the intensity of the concentration on so many faces for just a moment in time. And I wished that praying for something could make it so.

It seemed fitting that the first evening's lineup was folk music, which felt most comfortable for me. After a couple of hours, though, I dozed off for what seemed to me like mere minutes but turned out to be almost two hours, waking in the wee hours just pre-dawn. I had missed, among other performers, Arlo Guthrie. Then Joan Baez walked onto the stage. When I heard the first strains of her pure voice, I was back in Toronto at the *Purple Onion* coffeehouse where I'd seen her once before. Now I was sharing her with hundreds of thousands of other people.

Sometime during the evening, though, it had started to rain. It was a gentle shower, refreshing at first and then just annoying, soaking everything in sight. And there was nowhere to take shelter except for the van. But I had to stay and hear her last song. Accompanied only by her acoustic guitar, she encouraged the crowd to join her in singing "We Shall Overcome." I didn't sing along, but I did feel the trill of her voice as it washed over me and the rest of the crowd, most of whom were now slightly subdued by the rain. The moment the last strains of her song rang out, I ran for the cover of the van and took a nap while the rest of the group kept dry under a tarp or searched for breakfast. I needed a more substantially dry space.

By that afternoon, when the rock line-up began, it was hot and humid with the occasional shower of rain and thunderstorm that brought short-lived bursts of sheer misery. Then the sun came out, and the steam began to rise. The line-ups at the portable toilets wound around for what seemed like miles, and it wasn't as easy as we had thought to find something reasonable to eat. But Chuck was still taking photos one after the other—of me, of Liz, of anyone around.

By Saturday night, the thunderstorms had thrown the schedule off by hours. Helicopters began swooping in like crazy birds, dropping the headliners in like soldiers behind enemy lines, except that we were all friendlies. I was desperately in need of a shower and a decent meal, but there was something about the whole experience that didn't make me want to leave. At one point, Chuck asked if I wanted to go to a hotel, but I knew that we'd never get back this close to the stage again. And it wasn't even clear we could get the van out even if we wanted to. I also knew that he didn't want to leave. He was prepared to stay through anything to get those all-important photographs.

It was three a.m. or so on Sunday morning when I felt as if my life began to shift. That's when Janis Joplin, in the flesh, took over the stage and the universe. The rain had stopped, and no one in the crowd seemed to have noticed that it was the middle of the night. When Janis threw her head back and started singing, there wasn't a single person among the hundreds of thousands who wasn't mesmerized—even people like me who hadn't thought much of this young woman. But now, it seemed as if she carried the angst of a generation—a generation that, up until now, I hadn't been an authentic part of. Deep down, though, I was who I was. I couldn't take my eyes off her outfit, trying to memorize every detail of her multi-coloured, panne velvet pants and the blue velvet caftan. The minute I got back to the van where I had left my sketchbook, I'd have to draw madly. In the meantime, I'd rely on Chuck's photos.

I could see him down near the front with his camera trained on Janis one minute, a band member the next, then the next minute, he was shooting the crowd. I looked in the direction where he was pointed now and noticed a group of girls, none of whom could have been much over sixteen. They were swaying and singing along with Janis, with their eyes closed in a kind of rapture. As I looked more closely at them in the dim light, a thought struck me. They were all part of a tribe, and that tribe had a uniform. It may not have looked like the one that Carl had donned as he shipped overseas to Vietnam, but it was, nonetheless, a uniform. And I had the inspiration for my senior-year fashion collection.

I would have thought that Janis might be the final act for the night, but I would have been wrong. Shortly after she left the stage, Sly and the Family Stone took over, and Chuck came running back toward where Liz, Alan and I huddled under a blanket against the pre-dawn chill.

"Guys! Guys!" he yelled as he picked his way around sleeping bags and bodies doing what some people thought was a great way to spend togetherness inside a sleeping bag (at least they were warm). Chuck started gesturing wildly. "Come on!"

It seemed like he wanted us to follow him. Reluctantly, we got up and made our way toward where he was standing. When we got there, he put his arm around me and squeezed me. "We can go!"

"Go where?" I said.

"Home?" Alan was the least enthusiastic among us. He didn't like to go more than twenty-four hours without a hot shower. I didn't either, but as I had looked around at the crowds throughout the day, I knew that we were somehow making history.

"No. Backstage! Jeff's waiting for us." He started to move us in the direction of stage left. "What Jeff didn't tell me was that his friend Doogie is one of the Kozmic Blues Band's guitarists."

236

I thought for a moment and realized that Janis had mentioned near the beginning of her set that her new band was called the Kozmic Blues Band. Now, this was exciting.

"Will we get to meet her?" I wasn't sure why this was important to me, but suddenly it was.

"That's the plan."

We had reached the side of the stage and made our way toward the back where Jeff was waiting.

"Hey, buddy, what'd she say?"

"Yeah, she said if she likes you, she'll let you take a couple of photos." Jeff lowered his voice. "But just be warned. The whole crew of them partied their way through the delay. I think they're all stoned." He snickered. "Nothing new there."

Jeff led us backstage, where at least it was sheltered from the drizzle and introduced us to Doogie. Musicians, roadies and all manner of hangers-on were milling around. There was a table in the corner littered with half-empty bottles of every imaginable kind of liquor. There were plastic glasses strewn about, and I noticed what looked like bowls of candy, but I knew better. I didn't know exactly what they were, but I would have bet my education on them all being one sort of speed or LSD or another, and the pong of marijuana was almost overpowering. The air was blue. Sitting beside the table by herself was the woman in the blue caftan.

Doogie went ahead and whispered something in her ear. She put on her big, round, rose-tinted glasses and got up, bracelets clinking as she pushed a stray hair (and there were lots of them) off her face. Doogie introduced us, and then Chuck made a bit of small talk. I just looked at her.

The contrast between this Janis and the one I'd just seen on stage was beyond words. On stage, she was larger than life, the flag-bearer of a generation. Here, down to earth, she was just a young woman, stoned clearly, but just like the rest of us—yet not.

Doogie introduced us.

"Was I okay?" she asked. No one said anything. I think we were all quite surprised that Janis Joplin would even ask that. "Come on, guys? Was the set good? Did I sound okay?" She really wanted to know.

"God, Janis, you were terrific." I had found my voice.

She turned and beamed at me. "Really? I worry sometimes." She took me by the hand. "Let's sit down." And so we did.

The two of us sat on a bench, and Doogie came over, asked her something, pointed to Chuck, and Janis nodded. Chuck took up the position—of photographer.

"You're..."

"Kat," I said, sparing her the embarrassment of having forgotten my name already.

"Hey, Kat, where you from?"

I told her I was originally from Canada, and she seemed to be tickled by that. She wanted me to tell her about it. I did.

"What's your sign, Kat?"

I thought for a moment. "Capricorn, I think."

Her face lit up. "Wow. Me too! When's your birthday?"

"January 19," I said.

"Far out! Mine too! We're, like, soul sisters." She put her arm around me, and I could see Chuck out of the corner of my eye. He wasn't letting this photo-op get away. "Kat, I want to tell you something I've learned." She pushed another stray hair out of her eyes. "You're only as much as you settle for." She looked at me through those rose-coloured lenses. "You get it?"

I got it.

~

Sunday was the last day of the festival, and the torrential rain showed no signs of letting up. We had all crammed into the van in a vain attempt to keep dry. At one point late in the afternoon, Liz sat up and said to me, "Kat, I really have to go to the bathroom, and I don't want to go alone." She looked at me pleadingly. "Please?"

Since I had to go, too, I agreed. Jeff had two tarps in the van, so we each took one and wrapped them around ourselves, then we picked our way through the oozing mud toward the toilets. We thought the rain might keep people from attempting the trek through the mud, but we were wrong. When nature calls, neither rain, nor drizzle, nor mud, nor excruciatingly long line-ups will keep you away—but the absolute reek emanating from them just might.

I covered my mouth and nose as best I could with one hand while holding onto the tarp and grabbed Liz's hand with the other. "Are you sure about this?" I said, my feet sinking ever further into the mud.

Liz slid toward me. "Oh my god, Kat. This is too awful!"

We both ducked back into the woods. I am sad to have to admit this, but we were among the people despoiling the grounds simply because we couldn't wait. As we stood up simultaneously, I looked at Liz, her hair plastered against her head, her dress dirty and sticking to her body. She looked at me—I know I looked even worse—then down to my feet.

"You'll never get those boots out of that mud, Kat!"

I looked down at my feet and started to laugh. She joined me, and our tarps dropped away. At least the rain was making us clean. I tried to pull my feet out of the mud, but it was no use. I slid my foot out of the fringed boots and was going to leave them there when it occurred to me that I needed to keep them. I leaned down, and by using two hands on each one, I was able to pull them out of the mud. There was a great sucking sound as each one came free. I lifted them high in the air.

"Liz, here is my souvenir!"

"Let's blow this popsicle stand, Kat!" Liz grabbed my hand, tarps forgotten in the mud, and we ran back to the van as quickly as it was possible as we slipped and sloshed and picked our way over sodden people. The next act was scheduled for five p.m., and we intended to be driving south by then.

Back at the van, Chuck was mumbling as he tried to clean his equipment. Jeff was making notes on a steno pad, and Tina was filing her nails in the front seat.

"Let's go, guys," I said as we climbed in through the back door.

"As in go home?" Jeff said, looking up from his notebook. "We'll miss C.C.R."

Liz and I looked at each other and laughed.

"Thought you'd never ask," Chuck said. "We'll see Creedance in the movie they make about this. 'Cause they will make a movie!"

As the weekend came to an end for us and we found a route out of the festival grounds, I looked around at the still somewhat happy but subdued crowd and considered the fact that thousands of people had just spent the weekend in less-than-ideal conditions and no riot broke out. I was thinking that this was something. As we pulled out of the grounds and back onto the highway, we once again joined a line of pilgrims now heading home, and I thought about the past few days of love, peace and music.

My mind wandered to Eddie and his peacenik ways that I'd never understood—at least not until now. Eddie, for all his tweedy, buttoned-down, academic persona, was a closet hippie (not the only thing he'd kept closeted from the world for so long). My own life up until that moment began to roll across my visual field in a kind of slow-motion movie—not like that flash I always imagined I'd get just before I die. I once again thought of Dorothy in *The Wizard of Oz* as she stepped into the technicolour land of Oz from her black-and-white life. Woodstock was my technicolour moment. I realized that the music was the soundtrack, and mine had just shifted. Among other things, it was the music that separated me and my generation from Mom and Dad, and there was no going back. I knew that Janis's advice was well-placed for me: *I knew that I could only ever be what I was willing to settle for*. And one other thing—I'd left a piece of my heart back there in that muddy, smelly cow pasture, and life might never be the same again.

Eve of Destruction

Barry McGuire, 1965

I HAD NEVER BEFORE EXPERIENCED such a rush of inspiration. My final year at Parsons was beginning, and I found myself physically breathless at least once a day as the ideas for my senior collection rushed at me so fast I thought I might not be able to catch them all. At the end of the year, there would be a major presentation of senior student collections. This year's showcase would take place at the Plaza Hotel in late April, and I fully expected to have at least one of my designs showcased. I also hoped that Nan might be able to make it to the show. However, my ultimate goal was to win Simon's personal award, one of several offered annually by the designers who would act as critics and judges. We would see.

Suzanne and I were still working for Simon two days a week. This year, we'd graduated from holding pins for him while he draped new designs to helping him with the final tweaks on samples of the designs that had been in the works for months. And this year, he had finally invited us to help backstage with his spring and summer collection scheduled for presentation during New York Fashion Week at the end of September. We were beyond excited.

242

The week before the show, Suzanne found me in the senior students' common room sketching madly in my new, red-covered sketchbook I was devoting entirely to this project. I had decided that it was important enough to warrant its own sketchbook rather than merely being a part of the one I carried around with me everywhere I went.

"Hey, Kat, we're going to be late," she said from the doorway. "Kat!"

I looked up at Suzanne then at the clock on the wall above the door. She was right. We were probably going to be late.

"We have to be at Simon's studio in twenty minutes, and you know what the subway will be like at this hour." She walked over to the table where I was sitting, pencils scattered around me and looked over my shoulder at the drawing.

"What're you working on?" She untwisted the thin, silk scarf she had wound around her neck even today when the temperature hovered around seventy-five degrees outside. She picked up one of the pages I'd torn out, thinking that I'd discard that idea. "Kat, these are incredible!" She leaned over to see what was on the page directly in front of me. It was a half-finished design for a caftan-style tunic with luscious gold embellishments. I was doing this one with coloured pencils. "These are for your senior portfolio, aren't they?"

"They are. I'm having an inspirational tsunami, it seems."

"Have you shown any of the work in progress to Simon yet?"

"Uh-uh. Not yet. I want the collection to be a bit more cohesive before I show him anything."

"Would you like Theo to have a quick peek? He's so in-synch with Simon's opinions I'm sure he'd give great feedback."

Theo was Suzanne's new boyfriend. More to the point, however, he was one of Simon's senior assistants. I had thought it a bad idea when she told me they'd started seeing one another—dating a colleague is never a good idea in my books—but I could see now that the relationship might have

243

advantages the two of us could exploit this year. After all, Simon was our mentor and ultimately would be the critic for our final portfolio collections.

"Yeah, maybe. But I don't think any of it's ready yet for anyone else to see." I closed the book and smiled at her. "Even you."

We knew each other well enough at this stage for her to make a face at me. "Let's go!"

~

Liz and I talked on the telephone twice in the month after Woodstock. Calls were expensive, but we liked a bit of real conversation along with our letter-writing. It seemed that the experience had affected her, as well. I just didn't know how much until early October.

It was Monday, and I had rushed up the steps to the apartment in anticipation of an evening in front of the television watching *Laugh-In* with a glass of wine in my hand and Chuck by my side laughing along with me at Goldie Hawn's wide-eyed innocent hilarity. I was breathless by the time I reached the top. I unlocked the door and walked in to find Chuck in the living room packing his camera equipment in a bag.

"Hey, babe," he said as I stood there panting. "Gotta go to a meeting with Jeff." He and Jeff had continued their photographer-journalist relationship after the weekend of peace and love that was Woodstock, and I knew that this would be important to Chuck's career aspirations. Still, I was disappointed that my Monday evening wouldn't go as planned. He stuffed his camera bag behind the sofa. "Won't be needing this tonight. Oh, and by the way, I nearly forgot. Liz called. She wants you to call her." He kissed me on his way to the door. "She sounded odd." And he was off.

244

I poured myself a glass of wine and studied the contents of the refrigerator for potential food before deciding that dinner could wait. It was an hour later where Liz was, so I thought I'd call her before eating.

"Hello?" it was Liz's voice on the other end of the line, but it did sound odd as Chuck had observed.

"Liz, it's me. What's up? You sound funny."

There was a slight pause during which I could hear shuffling. "Are you alone, Kat?"

Now I was starting to worry. "Yes. Chuck just went out for the evening, so I'm all yours. What's going on?"

"Kat, you have to promise me that this will stay between the two of us."

"Of course," I said, increasingly alarmed by the second.

"No, I mean it. You can't tell anyone, not even Chuck. I know you two don't have secrets, but this isn't your secret. It's mine." She stopped for a moment. "Promise."

"I promise," I said. "Whatever it is, your secret is safe with me. Now spill."

"I'm pregnant."

For the briefest moment, I was excited. A baby! Then reality struck me. This wasn't necessarily good news, so I knew I'd have to be careful here. "Are you sure?" Isn't that what everyone says in answer to this news?

"Kat, I wouldn't be telling you this if I wasn't absolutely certain."

"How could this happen? What about the birth control pills?"

"They gave me migraine headaches, so I stopped taking them. Kat, I need your help."

"Liz, you know I'd do anything to help you. Anything at all. Just name it."

"I need you to help me get an abortion."

I felt as if someone had slapped me. That wasn't exactly what I had in mind when I said I'd help in any way I could. An abortion? It was such a foreign concept to me. I wasn't exactly against the idea—it was more that I had never really thought much about it beyond hearing snippets of conversation at school over the past two years.

"But Liz, what does Alan think about all this?"

There was a moment of silence. "We broke up."

"When?!"

"Last week."

"So, Alan doesn't know?"

"Let's leave Alan out of this," Liz said, sounding more desperate by the moment. "You know as well as I do that nothing matters except that I make it go away. If this gets out, I'll lose my job."

Liz was the Home Economics teacher at a Catholic High School, and she was entirely correct: if news of this pregnancy got out, she would certainly lose her job. And if news of an abortion got out in the city where she lived, it would change her life forever—and not in a good way. I finally realized why she was calling me to help even though I lived far away and in a different country. She would have to leave town to have it.

"Kat, can you find someone?"

"It's still illegal here, Liz." Although abortion and contraception had been legalized north of the border earlier this year, abortion had yet to find the same support here in the U.S. I was well aware of the fact, though, that finding a doctor to perform an abortion wasn't that difficult in a city like New York. I could probably even set it up for her.

The whole thing made me seriously uncomfortable. My best friend was pregnant, her boyfriend didn't know, she needed an abortion, and I was supposed to organize the whole thing. Uncomfortable or not, I knew I had to help her.

~

Liz arrived in New York ten days later. It had been more difficult than I thought it would be to arrange the procedure. When I'd asked Suzanne if she knew anyone I could approach, she had been immediately suspicious of me (I was asking for a friend, I said), and then she was insulted. Did I think people like her might know more about these things? By people like her, she meant black women, the very idea of which had never once crossed my mind. In the end, I was able to allay her annoyance, and she ended up helping me to search for a suitable clinic. It had been more difficult, however, to do all this under Chuck's radar.

More than once over the past week, he'd asked me what I was up to. I'd been non-committal. It was a blessing that he was working on something with Jeff, something he said he'd tell me about when things were "firmed up." I hated that I felt as if I were lying to him when I simply omitted the news that Liz was in town, staying at a hotel.

The plan was for her to be in the city for four days. She had called in sick to her job and arrived here on a Thursday. On Friday morning, I picked her up at her small hotel not far from Central Park. We then took a taxi to a clinic run by a group of female doctors who ostensibly did screening and treatment for venereal diseases, among other things. Safe but illegal abortions were "among other things."

The nurse at the front desk told me to come back to pick Liz up in four hours, so I left her and went to school for an hour but couldn't concentrate. I was back on the street outside the clinic three hours later, walking around and around the block, hoping Liz would be all right both physically and especially emotionally. This had to be painful in so many ways.

I walked back into the clinic at the appointed time, where the receptionist at the front desk told me that Liz was in the back waiting room. We would then depart from the back entrance. When I walked into the room, it was silent except for the hum of a radio in the distance and the ticking of the clock on the wall. Liz was sitting alone in a plastic chair clutching a box of tissues and a kidney-shaped basin presumably to vomit in, on her lap. She looked up and smiled wanly at me.

"In my entire life, I will never be able to make it up to you for helping me with this and for keeping my secret," she said. "I know what it's cost you."

I helped her to her feet, and we hugged with one of those bear hugs that you need when you're feeling vulnerable.

I stayed with her for an hour at the hotel, then went home. The next day was Saturday, so I spent a few hours at Simon's atelier then visited Liz for a few hours. I was surprised at how quickly she seemed to be recovering, so I stopped worrying about her flying home by herself the next day.

By Sunday, I was exhausted and, to tell you the truth, happy that she had left. All the worries of the past two weeks were finally over, and I could relax. At least that's what I thought.

~

Jeff and Chuck were sitting in the living room sharing a few beers with the television tuned to a football game with the sound turned off when I arrived back at the apartment. It was early November, and I had been looking forward to an evening alone with Chuck, but at least Jeff wasn't needy in any way. He was a good friend and fun to be with. What you saw was what you got with Jeff—all the time. I opened myself a beer and sat down with them in the one remaining empty chair. They both put their beers down on the table, and I got the feeling that they had something to say.

When Chuck picked up his bottle again and started peeling off the label, I knew he was stalling. I'd seen this behaviour before when he had something on his mind. I took a sip from my own bottle and set it on the coffee table. "So, what are you two up to this evening?" Both of them remained silent. "Okay, what's going on?"

Chuck put his beer down again and sat back. He took a deep breath. "Kat, you know how much I love you." *Oh-oh, where is this going? I thought. It can't be good.* "And I would never want to do anything that would cause something to come between us." *Dear god, is he about to tell me he's gay?* "But the thing is…" He trailed off, looking at Jeff as if to ask him for help. Jeff just shrugged.

"Chuck, what is it you're trying to tell me?"

And he started. He began a long diatribe about the war in Vietnam, how he wasn't really supportive of its aims, and that he had lost his student deferral. That was the moment I could feel my heart start to race and the hairs on the back of my neck to stand up. *Oh my god!* I thought, *he's received his draft notice!* Fear crawled over me like a heavy blanket enclosing me in the dark, and my mind started racing so much so that I caught only a word here and there after that.

"Opportunity…don't want…Jeff and I…" What was he talking about? I had to get a grip on myself.

"So, that's what we've decided."

"What? What have you decided?"

"Kat, were you listening to me?"

"You lost me way back at loss of student deferment."

Chuck got up from where he was sitting beside Jeff on the sofa and came over to sit on the floor beside my chair. He leaned onto my lap. "Kat, I know this is going to be hard, but I think it's the best way."

When I finally got a hold of myself sufficiently to listen, Chuck, assisted by Jeff, who seemed to be here for moral support (Chuck's, not mine), recapped the "meeting" he and Jeff had on Monday night they left me to watch *Laugh-In* by myself. They had set up an informal meeting with an Army recruiter who had been recommended to them by the art director at one of the major newspapers—I didn't catch which one. It was the art director's opinion that both of them could take a major step forward if they were to enlist voluntarily and go to Vietnam as photographers. It seemed Jeff's journalism degree also gave him some kind of photography credential, although, as he mentioned, he really wanted to write about the experience.

I shook my head. "Does the army even have photographers?"

"Yeah, military combat photographers," Chuck said.

"Combat? Enlist? Why enlist? You might not even get drafted." I could feel the tears streaming down my face.

He looked up at me with those angelic eyes. "Babe, if I enlist, I get to choose what I want to do in the army. If I get drafted, I'll probably just get sent to the infantry or something."

"But you don't have to go at all. I'm a Canadian, remember? I can take you home. You can avoid the draft completely."

"It wouldn't feel right, Kat." He squeezed my knee. "And even if I wanted to go with you to Canada, I couldn't, knowing that you'd have to give up your final year at Parsons and probably any chance of a career in New York. I can't let that happen."

I begged him, but as I spoke, it was clear he had already made up his mind. I didn't have a say in the matter.

So, there it was. Chuck had decided that the Vietnam War was his ticket to fame and fortune as a photographer. Had he even thought about the danger? That he might never come home? He had, but he assured me that the danger was minimal.

"I don't believe that," I said. "I've seen those pictures and films on the news every night. Anyone who takes those pictures has to be in danger." My anxieties fell on deaf ears. But I wasn't the last to know. Chuck hadn't told his parents yet because he wanted my support when he did. I shook my head. "That's for you to do. Alone."

It was clear that the arrangements were already complete. This wasn't a decision we would make as a couple. When they told me that they were enlisting in one week, I got up and picked up my coat with as much dignity as I could muster, threw a scarf around my neck and ran out the door. I slammed it as hard as I could, dislodging a piece of plaster from the ceiling in the hallway in the process. I didn't care. I ran down the four flights of stairs and out onto the sidewalk, gulping for air. I realized that all the air had been knocked out of me in one blow.

Universal Soldier

Buffy St. Marie, 1964

ON NOVEMBER 12, 1969, CHUCK AND JEFF presented themselves at the enlistment centre in Midtown Manhattan. As predicted, the meeting between Chuck and his parents had not gone well. I knew this because Rose called me the minute Chuck had left their house, imploring me to talk him out of it. I tried but to no avail.

Chuck would undergo basic training for eight weeks just as Carl had done, but he figured that it was unlikely he'd have to do more training before being shuffled overseas. After all, he told me, he wouldn't be fighting, just taking pictures, and he didn't need occupational training—he already had it. I knew he was placating me. By now, I knew that combat photographers had to know how to handle a gun and all the rest of it, just like regular soldiers—because they were, in fact, regular soldiers. They would be in the middle of combat missions. They would live as soldiers. And they would point a gun at anyone who pointed a gun at them, and presumably some who didn't.

We didn't talk a lot that week, but we clung to one another like drowning sailors hanging onto a life raft each night. The day before he left, I decided that I would stop all this hanging on to him and be the kind of home support that I figured soldiers in combat longed to know was there. There would be no more imploring him to stay. No more snide remarks about the futility of war in general and the immorality of this one in particular. If the man I loved needed to do this, I would be there (or here, to be clear) to support him so that he could know that I'd be here waiting at the end of his deployment.

Chuck left the apartment at eight a.m. that morning. He told me he'd call when he had a chance. Like an automaton, I went through the motions of getting ready to go to class and getting myself on the subway. That morning, as I stood in the middle of the subway car holding onto an overhead strap, surrounded by throngs of New Yorkers heading for their comfortable offices, I had never felt more alone. I didn't know how I'd get through the day, but I was damn well going to try.

I was far enough along in my senior-year design project that I was at the point of searching for fabrics. I'd been gone from Toronto for more than two years now, but every time I went in search of fabrics, I felt as if Ezra were right here with me. I had missed spending time working in his little fabric shop, although many in the garment district here in Manhattan resembled Ezra's organized chaos, and they made me feel as if he might poke his head around one of the bolts of fabric at any moment. In any case, wandering through fabric stores always made me feel, if not happy, then at least more peaceful. I hoped it would work today.

I stepped inside what had become my favourite shop of all among many to choose from here, apart from the one where I had a part-time job. Like Ezra's shop, it was piled high with colourful bolts of fabric of every imaginable type. There was a section for shirting fabrics, one for corduroy, one for the new synthetics that were beginning to be popular, and the silk section? It was my favourite of all. Bolt after bolt of smooth, dreamy silk in every colour of the rainbow and any print you could imagine was there for the taking. I was in love with the silk velvets, and when I ran my hand over a bolt of electric-blue silk velvet, I knew that this would be the centrepiece of my collection. It would be the caftan embellished with gold cording that I wanted to be elegantly bohemian. I wanted it to be elevated hippie. And I remembered something Ezra had once said to me.

"The smoothest way is full of stones."

I could feel those stones along my path as I stood there, but I realized that, despite it all, I was going to find my smoothest way forward. When I left the store, fabric in hand, I felt lighter.

~

After his enlistment, Chuck was home for several days before heading off for basic training. We made the most of it, spending every available minute we could together doing things we loved to do. We ate at our favourite restaurants, and we made love under the skylight in the living room. We listened to jazz at our favourite jazz club, and Chuck had one last martini crafted by his favourite bartender. He acted as if he might never have these experiences again. And I knew he was right. Then he was gone.

Every week of his eight weeks of basic training, I received a letter from him. He told me funny stories about getting up at five a.m. and marching through the bush carrying massive amounts of gear. He seemed to be eating it up. This was so not like the Chuck I knew, the New Yorker, the city boy, the good Jewish son. I didn't go home for Christmas that year, either, and spent Hannukah with Rose and Harry, who were as surprised as I was by Chuck taking it all in stride.

Rose and Harry asked me to spend New Year's Eve with them, but I declined. Suzanne and Theo invited me to a party, and I declined that as well. I had a feeling that I needed to spend the end of the decade by myself. I'd watch the ball drop in Times Square on our little television set and drink a toast to Chuck and the life we'd have together when he returned. I had a lot to think about.

254

In the middle of January, at the end of the eight weeks, he wrote about "graduation."

"I looked around at all these kids—and they are kids, Kat—I'm one of the oldest here. The rest of them are eighteen or so. Most of them seem excited to be going overseas. But I've talked to a few who are frightened. No, not frightened. They are petrified. You can see it in their eyes. I've been trying to capture their souls. Here are a few pictures I developed today. Please keep them in a file somewhere for when I return. I have an idea about a book."

He had enclosed half a dozen black and white photographs. I put the letter down and laid all the pictures out on the coffee table. It startled me for a moment when I realized that he seemed to have succeeded. If you could lay bare someone's soul in a picture, he had done it. Then I went back and read the rest of the letter.

"I want us to get married the moment I return to New York after this is all over. Could you go out and get a dress to wear to our wedding? If you could do that, I'd be able to think about it there, waiting for my return along with you, and the time won't seem so long."

The next day, I bought a box—a mahogany one that someone had left in a pawnshop. It was the size of a shoebox, and it locked with an extraordinary key that looked as if the jewels embellishing it might be real. The pawnshop owner seemed not to have noticed, so I didn't bother mentioning my observation. I intended to store Chuck's photographs in the box. These were the ones he was taking with his own camera —the ones not assigned by the army. I would polish that mahogany until it shone, and I would place Chuck's photos in it so that I would have them here for him when he returned. I also thought about his request.

Of course, I wanted to be able to tell him that I'd have a dress waiting so that we could be married the moment he returned. But I was a fashion design student. I would make my wedding dress.

Liz called me later that evening with a bit of news.

"Alan and I are back together," she said.

I was a bit taken aback by this. She seemed so upbeat. I had expected a period of, I don't know, depression maybe, after the abortion. But she seemed to have weathered it well. "Does Alan know?" I said.

"Know what?" Was she being coy?

"You know, Liz, about why you were here in New York in October."

"Everyone has secrets, Kat. We're really happy together."

I was happy for my friend, who seemed to be moving forward in her life and career, but I wasn't convinced that Liz's story would have sat that well with Alan. Perhaps I didn't really know him very well (which was true). I also thought that keeping secrets like that might be too much in a relationship. I decided to change the subject and asked her opinion about designing and making a wedding dress. I told her about the collection I was developing and the fact that I hoped I could create a wedding dress that might resemble that aesthetic.

"You remember the day before we left for Woodstock?" Liz said. Of course, I remembered the day, but I didn't know where she was going with this. She continued. "Do you remember that I tripped over a cardboard box in the corner of your living room?" I was beginning to remember. "It was full of patterns you've never used."

"I love collecting them. You know that."

"Yeah, yeah. I know. But there was a pattern in there that resembles exactly the design you're talking about. If you were to use that one, you wouldn't have to design a pattern. You could focus on the fabric and the construction of it."

Liz was right, and I knew exactly which pattern she was talking about. Three days later, on a bitterly cold day, I went back to my favourite fabric store and found the perfect white silk lace as well as the perfect silk charmeuse for the underlining. It would be a bohemian-style, empire-waisted gown with a low-cut ruffled neckline and long, wide sleeves gathered into cuffs. It would reach the ground, and the silk would swish deliciously as I walked down the aisle. I would start working on it as soon as possible.

The next day Chuck called. I was thrilled.

"I'm going, Kat. I leave for the west coast tomorrow, and we fly to 'Nam a few days after that."

I felt as if he had punched me in the stomach. He was really going.

~

By the end of January, I still hadn't shown Simon my work-in-progress. Both Suzanne and Theo had been prodding me to get his feedback before I went further. I demurred. I wanted to be almost finished before he saw it. I was making good progress.

I was also making progress on my wedding gown. I borrowed one of the studios at school to lay out the yards and yards of silk on a proper cutting table. It had taken me hours to accomplish, but the pieces were all cut out, and I had begun attaching individual pieces of silk underlining to each of the pieces of the lace. Once I had that done, I folded each of them carefully and put them into a large, flat cardboard box so that I could take them home and work on the sewing at my own sewing machine—the one Darla's father had bought.

Chuck had been in Vietnam for two weeks when I received my first letter from him. He told me about spending two days in California before getting on a chartered flight full of new recruits for the twenty-three-hour flight to Tan Son Nhut Airbase in Saigon. I shivered as I pictured what he was experiencing.

"As we approached the airbase, the pilot, which was, incidentally, a chartered Continental Airlines flight, warned us that we would be going

in at a steep incline. I thought it was probably because of mountains in the area. I was wrong. After he told us that, he added that it was so that we could avoid ground fire. It was at that moment when the war started to become real for me. It was the first time that I would be trying to avoid being shot at, but I was fairly sure it wouldn't be the last."

I stopped reading for a moment and tried to catch my breath. I started to feel nauseous.

"We lined up to get off the plane, and the minute my foot stepped outside the door, I could see the heat rising in shimmering waves from the tarmac and the hills beyond. But it wasn't until it hit me in the face and I walked down the steps and into the soup of humidity that I really knew I wasn't in Kansas anymore.

We were assigned to our barrack—just Quonset huts all in lines in what passes for a community of soldiers—and our bunks. Yes, I'm sleeping in a bunk. I have the upper one in case you want to picture me here. It's a funny thought. I hope it makes you smile."

I wasn't at all sure it made me smile. I read on.

"I've enclosed more photographs I was able to develop after they gave me access to a darkroom. I have to use the new 35mm Pentax Spotmatic camera they issue to all photographers for official military business. That probably doesn't mean anything to you, but to me, it means that I have to use an inferior camera when on official business. It's okay, but not great. But I can use my own equipment when I'm on my own time. I can't send you official ones, but these are the first I've been able to take of my own. Again, please keep them for me. As you can see, I've been trying to capture something more than the superficial in these young soldiers. I can see the apprehension in most of their eyes, but there's a whole lot more. I've met a few who have just come back from up-country, and they have a kind of little-lost-boy look about them. I can see their loneliness. And they're tired, so very tired."

I took the new stack of photos and began to leaf through them. I was stopped in my tracks by one specific image of a young soldier smoking a cigarette, leaning against what looks like one of those huts Chuck mentioned. Smoke curled around his head like a mist of fog, but it was his eyes. I could feel his bone-deep exhaustion. And it made me frightened—for him and for Chuck. And maybe even for me. I came to the end of the letter.

"My darling, Kat. I love you more than anything in the world—more than I ever thought I could love anyone. I always thought that my life would be a solitary one, travelling the world searching for that next great image. But now that you are a part of my life, I can't imagine you not being there. By the way, I just received my orders. I'm to be shipped north for my first combat mission. I can't give you any details, but I'll write to you again the minute I can."

And that's when I laid my head down on the table and began to weep.

~

I wrote to Chuck every week. I had no idea if he received any of my letters, but I did it as much for me as I did for him. I desperately wanted to talk to him, but there was now no way for that to happen. Knowing that he was in some combat zone somewhere, I had to stop watching the nightly news. The images relentlessly marching across the tiny screen every night were gruesome. I could not understand why every single American citizen hadn't yet risen up in protest of the carnage.

It was only two weeks later when I received another letter from him. I marvelled at how the military could get a letter out of a combat zone and here on U.S. soil in under two weeks.

"...*we've been here for only three days, and every minute that passes makes me more anti-war than I ever was. You cannot imagine the horrors. These soldiers around me are so young. Most of them have never been anywhere except their hometowns, and here they are in a swamp, the monsoon rains pelting down on us, the heat unbearable, the silence of the jungle. I think that's the worst part. I can feel the VC looking at us, but I don't know where. I can hear gunfire off in the distance sometimes, but I don't know how far. I haven't had to fire my gun, but I know the time will come. You have to know that it's making me appreciate life and you even more, if that's possible. I see your face in front of me every time I close my eyes, pushing the horror away, at least to the edges of consciousness. I'm ageing fast, that's for sure, but I've never felt more alive.*"

He was alive, and that was all that mattered as I went about my business. I carried on and even managed to push the horror out of my mind for a while as I worked.

A week later, I was in Simon's studio. We were deep into preparations for the spring shows, and I was in the large, open part of the atelier, helping with the final touches on one of Simon's new creations when his receptionist came to the door and looked as if she were beckoning to me. I shook my head—I was busy. She came over and whispered in my ear. "There's a phone call for you. You need to come."

It was February 13, Friday the thirteenth, at two o'clock in the afternoon. Rose was on the phone. They had just been informed. Chuck was killed in action.

I dropped to the floor in the reception area just as Theo walked by. He caught me. "Kat, what's wrong?"

I blubbered something about Chuck, and he knew immediately. I told him I had to leave. I wanted to leave without even my coat, but he insisted on getting it for me and calling me a cab.

"I'll gather up all your stuff," he said as he helped me with my coat. "Don't worry about it. Suzanne and I will get it to you. Do you have any money for the taxi?"

I always had cash in my pocket in case my purse was snatched, so I didn't need anything but my coat. I didn't want to wait for another second to be by myself.

I ran down the stairs and out the school's front door just as the taxi cab was pulling up. I threw myself into the back seat, gave the driver my address and sat there rigidly as silent tears flowed down my cheeks.

Chuck was gone. And he'd never even know that he was going to be a father.

Where Have All the Flowers Gone?

Peter, Paul and Mary, 1962

FOR A FULL WEEK, I WAS PARALYZED BY INDECISION. I didn't know what to do. Rose and Harry tried to get me to visit them, but I couldn't do that—not until I decided what I would say to them. I couldn't go to school and didn't want to see anyone. When Suzanne and Theo arrived to drop off my bookbag, I couldn't even bring myself to let them in. I threw it in a corner and wondered if I'd ever feel the same about fashion design again. It seemed so inconsequential now.

After four days of wallowing in self-pity, I called Nan and told her everything. When I had finished, I was crying again.

"Nan, I can't go back to school. I don't know what I'm going to do."

"Darling Kat, you could go back to school, but it would be difficult. You are so close to finishing. Are you sure about this?"

"Nan, I'm not sure of anything right now. I only know that I feel lost and alone, and I'm pregnant. And I don't know how I'm ever going to tell Mom and Dad about this."

"Yes, they will probably be difficult, but they do love you, Kat, no matter what. You might be surprised. Leave them to me. Did the doctor say when your due date is likely to be?"

"Around August 23."

~

The call from my parents came the next day. My father was on the main phone I could picture hanging on the wall outside the kitchen with Mom on the extension in their bedroom. I could tell that Mom had been crying.

"Katherine, your grandmother has just left. She has told us very distressing news. I will not go over old territory here related to living in New York..." (by which he meant the den of iniquity), "...because I know that you are hurting very badly at this point. Of course, you are coming home immediately. I will make all the necessary arrangements."

I began to protest, but my mother cut in. "Katherine, you need us. You need to be at home among people who love you. You can stay here until you're ready to be on your own again."

Any further argument fell on deaf ears. I was to arrange to have my belongings packed and shipped to Halifax, and I was to pick up my airplane ticket at a travel agency near my apartment within the week.

"Mom and Dad," I said finally, "could we keep this a secret? I don't even want Liz to know about this yet."

"Have no fear, Katherine. We are the soul of discretion, as you well know."

So, it seemed I was going home—or at least back to my hometown roots. And I still had not told Rose and Harry.

Kat
1970-2019

Halifax, Nova Scotia Canada

Reason to Believe

The Carpenters, 1970

HOME. I SUPPOSE WE ALL THINK OF HOME AS A PLACE. Maybe it's the place we grew up. Perhaps it's the house where we lived. Or maybe it's wherever those we love are. When I walked in through the door of my parents' home in the middle of March in 1970, I didn't truly feel as if I were home. As I sat down on the edge of the bed in my childhood room, I looked around and realized that I couldn't even cry. It seemed as if every last tear I had in me, I had already shed. Chuck was gone. My career was gone. My life would never be the same—but what it would be, was still a mystery to me. But did I feel as if I had arrived home? Not even close.

From that moment on in my life, I knew that being home was a feeling, a sensation, a perception that defied location for sure, and logic. In so many ways, I felt disconnected from everything. I had told no one that I was heading back to my parents' home—not even Liz. I knew I just couldn't face her yet. I was ashamed because when I found out I was pregnant, I realized with sickening clarity that I'd held some disapproving opinions about Liz last fall. Even as I had not hesitated to help her, a friend in need, I had suppressed my immediate reaction at the time, which had been judgmental. I wondered how she could have been so foolish as to get herself in that situation, and now, here I was. I didn't know how long it would be before I could face her, and I knew I ran the risk of running into her, although I wasn't planning on showing my face outside the house for some time.

It was clear from the moment my father and mother picked me up at the airport that they were uncomfortable being around me. But I was their daughter, after all, and they had always taken their responsibilities very seriously. Even as I walked toward them at the airport, I could see the wariness in their eyes. I could see both of them furtively glancing at my mid-section as if trying to see if I might be "showing" already. Well, it wouldn't be long.

As the first few weeks went by, the three of us settled into a kind of cold détente. Nan and I talked almost daily, and she became my lifeline. My parents weren't the kind of people who spoke about their feelings or anyone else's. Ever. In fact, they studiously avoided any topics that might result in emotional outbursts. It had always been that way. That's why, when my father broached the subject of my pregnancy at the dinner table one evening about a month after I arrived, it took me by surprise. I suppose it shouldn't have. It wasn't exactly something we could ignore forever.

"Katherine," he began between mouthfuls of mashed potatoes and gravy, "you are having a baby." My father was nothing if not the master of the obvious. "Plans have to be made."

He was also a master of passive voice. Plans had to be made, not we have to make some plans. Nothing so active as that. What could I say to that except agree? Yes, plans had to be made.

"Your mother and I have looked into a few things." He looked at my mother, who had just patted her lips with her paper napkin and placed it back on her lap. I wondered what kind of "things" they might contemplate considering further. "There is a very nice place that we think you should stay for a few months."

My head shot up so fast I thought I might end up with whiplash. Stay? For a few months? Were they kicking me out?

"It's called Bethany House," my mother offered. "We visited it last week. It's quite lovely." She nodded to my father, her co-conspirator.

And I understood. My parents wanted me to go to a home for unwed mothers. They wanted to hide me—and my mistake—from the world. Their world. I knew they couldn't ignore this forever. No one in their circle of friends had ever had a daughter who had given birth "out-of-wedlock." I started to laugh—one of those snorting kinds of grim laughs. It was so predictable of them. They had a reputation in the community, and I was besmirching it.

"So, we can hide my love child," I said, quoting the Supremes.

My father's face began to redden from the neckline up. "Do you think this is funny, Katherine? Do you think it's a joke to have a child out-of-wedlock?" There it was—the out-of-wedlock thing. The next thing I knew, he was going to be referring to his soon-to-be grandchild as a bastard. I wondered what Rose and Harry would say, and yet I couldn't bring myself to tell them. I knew it was wrong to keep it from them, but I wasn't ready.

"Dad," I said, getting up from the table, "what I think is a joke is that it's 1970, and you still have to be concerned about what your friends will think." He started to interrupt me, and I silenced him. "I appreciate all you're doing for me at this point in my life, but I have to make my own decisions."

"Katherine, we are just trying to help." My mother looked at me pleadingly.

"Mom, I know you are, and I appreciate all you've done—taking me in and all. But this is about more than just hiding me away out of sight as if I were some kind of pariah." I started to get up from the table.

"Katherine, sit down. Please. We need to talk," my father said.

I sat down and looked down at my half-finished dinner of roast beef and mashed potatoes. I could see the gravy congealing on the plate and felt slightly nauseous for a moment.

"Katherine, this is not just about you. And it's not about us. It's about that child. All we're asking you to do is consider the possibility of spending time in a place where you will have people in similar situations to you and counsellors to help you make decisions about your future." He stopped for a moment. "Because you know that your mother and I are not the best at dealing with emotional issues."

It seemed my father had more self-awareness than I had given him credit for.

"Katherine, please think about it. Please come with us so that you can at least see the place." My mother pushed a brochure toward me. On the front was a photograph of a nice-looking, three-story red-brick building that resembled an old mansion—or if you squinted, which I did – a mental institution. She pushed it closer to me. I picked it up and immediately left the dining room.

When I reached my room, I spread the brochure open on my desk then crumpled it up into a ball that I flung across the room. It bounced off the window and landed on the floor at my feet. I picked up the telephone my parents had added to my room for my return and dialled Nan's number.

"My darling girl, how are you?" Nan said when she picked up after three rings.

I told her about the conversation at the dinner table.

"Dear god!" She sounded alarmed. "Have you told them you'd go to see the place?"

I told her I had not.

"Good. It's decided then. It seems to me that you can't stay there any longer, which means you'll have to come to stay with me. I'm sure you can imagine that the place they're suggesting is full of religious do-gooders who will brow-beat you into giving the baby up for adoption—which isn't the worst idea, by the way." I started to protest, but she silenced me. "You have to think about all the implications of all possible decisions, darling. But I think you'd be better served by avoiding those self-righteous religious types."

I started to feel a bit lighter, as I didn't have to shoulder this all alone. But Nan had one condition.

"Darling girl, you are one of the brightest young women I know. And very talented. At least you need to finish your education."

"I'm not going back to Parsons," I said. "I can't."

"I am disappointed but not surprised. Well, then, make your application to go to one of the local universities and finish your teaching degree. The baby is due in August, so in any case, you'll be ready to start classes in September. You need to have a real future. That's my condition."

Nan was right—I did need to consider the long-term. I rationalized my decision not to tell Rose and Harry because I knew that they would have an opinion on the best course of events, and I didn't think I needed anyone else's input. The time would come. So, I agreed and made my application, which was accepted. It would take me two years to get my teaching credential. It wasn't the worst thing I could do with my life. Then Nan broke the news to Mom and Dad that I was moving in with her for the duration.

~

Nan was a formidable roommate. She was up early every morning to exercise in the home gym she had set up in her basement. At age seventy, she was the fittest woman I knew. Her looks and her health had always been important to her—in that order. But I had never lived with her before, so I hadn't been privy to some of her rituals. I had no idea she was a yoga devotee. The truth was that I knew very little about what yoga even was. It was evidently something new to her. She had discovered a brand-new television show called "Kareen's Yoga" hosted by a young woman who had also recently published *The ABC of Yoga*, a small, spiral-bound book with the smiling Kareen sitting cross-legged on the front. Nan devoured it. She would don a black leotard and tights, sit on the floor in her den in front of her television, and move along to Kareem's calming voice. She encouraged me to join her, and I did try, though not very successfully.

Nan was also a gourmet cook, but she also had a housekeeper who came in three times a week to clean, do the laundry and a bit of baking, which Nan didn't enjoy. I had spent many happy times visiting Nan but had only ever stayed overnight once when I was about ten when Mom accompanied Dad to a business meeting somewhere. It felt odd to be here now. Sometimes I felt as if I were intruding, although, to be fair, it was a feeling that came from inside me; it was not something I ever felt from Nan. Nan also spent several hours every day in a lovely room at the back of the house overlooking the garden. She called it her office, but I had no idea what she did in there.

One evening in June, while we were flipping through *TV Guide* to find out what to watch for an hour or so, Nan said, "Kat, darling girl, I think it's time we talked about the baby."

I was sitting on the sofa across from her. I picked up the closest cushion and wrapped my arms around it, protecting myself from the outside world. I knew she was right—and it wasn't as if that very thought hadn't invaded my every waking moment—and a good many of my sleeping ones.

"I know, Nan. I now have to think about this, and I know that time is getting short."

"Katherine," she said, using my full name, "there are only two choices here. Either you become a single mother, or you give the baby up for adoption."

"I know what Mom and Dad would prefer," I said into the cushion.

"I heard that," Nan said. I could hear a bit of testiness coming into her voice. It wasn't something I often heard from my beloved grandmother. "Be careful, my darling girl. Do not avoid a particular path simply because your parents, whom you do not hold in a positive light at this moment in time, think it the best path."

I knew she was right. Something inside me didn't want to do what they would have preferred, just to stick it to them. But I was also responsible enough to know that it wasn't just me I needed to consider. But even if it were only me, I realized that my life would be very different depending on which path I chose.

My uncertainty was deeply rooted. I wanted what was best for this child, and I wondered what Chuck would think was the best thing. At night I would sometimes lie in bed and talk to him as if he could provide the answer from beyond. Nothing came.

I also knew that being a single woman with a child and pursuing an education and a career would not be easy—either for my child or for me. But could I really give him (or her) up?

Nan and I talked a bit more, and I agreed to think a bit more and discuss it further the following week.

"Why don't you call Liz?" she said. "You two have been such good friends. I'm sure you'd benefit from her support as well."

I still couldn't bring myself to call Liz, but I couldn't tell Nan why. Instead, I just said, "Sure. I'll give her a call sometime." But I didn't.

~

On a hot day in early August, my water broke. Labour started with a vengeance, even though I wasn't supposed to be due for another two weeks. I was alone in the house when it happened. Nan was out getting her hair done, so I was forced to call my parents, who rushed over to get me.

I was in such pain with each contraction by the time we arrived at the hospital that I couldn't keep up with the medical conversation going on around me. They gave me an injection for the pain, which made me feel a bit calmer, but equally made me dopey. I wasn't following what seemed to be something of a fracas around my bed in the labour ward. I caught snips of conversation only, but one word I did hear: breech. And I knew that things were not going to go well. Within an hour of my arrival at the hospital, I could hear the nurse at my ear saying, "We're going to have to put you out, dear." Then she said something about forceps or a Caesarean section before the world went black.

When I woke up in what seemed like only seconds later, but according to Nan, who was sitting beside my bed holding my hand, it had been several hours, and I was disoriented. But there was no baby anywhere. I was lying in a hospital bed, covered by a thin white sheet in a room by myself. On the bedside table, there was a flower arrangement that was clearly from Nan. My parents were nowhere in sight.

"Where…?"

"The baby?" Nan said, her face a mask of anguish. She stroked my hand gently. "He…didn't make it."

It was impossible. This couldn't be happening to me. I swallowed and tried to raise myself up. It was clear to me by now that there had been no Caesarean section, but I was sore everywhere. "Tell me." And she did.

Nan had arrived just after the birth. My parents were very distraught, she said. They told her that the baby had been stillborn and that he was gone. She did say, "he." It was a boy.

She had asked them if she could see the baby, but they told her the doctors had taken him away already. I wasn't to be permitted to see him, either. And that was the end of that. I had been pregnant for nine months, given birth, and now it was as if none of that had ever happened.

"Darling girl, you have to find a reason to get on with your life—a reason to believe that the world isn't as cold and uncaring a place as it seems right now."

When I walked out of that maternity hospital a few days later, I looked at the blue sky and listened to the wind rustling the leaves in the trees lining the boulevard. I took a deep breath of sunshine. I knew I needed it—in fact, I deserved it. Suddenly I could hear Janis Joplin in my head. *"You're only as much as you settle for." Kat, don't settle for less than you can be*, I said to myself. *No matter how long it takes.* That was a promise.

Three weeks later, I walked onto the campus at Dalhousie University and took on the role of a student once again. This time, I would finish what I started.

Bridge Over Troubled Water

Simon and Garfunkel, 1970

THE FIRST TIME I WALKED INTO THE "GREEN ROOM" at the brand-new student union building, I felt like a fish out of water. I was twenty-four years old, not so very much older than these nineteen and twenty-year-olds milling around, but a world apart. Searching for a place to sit and have lunch on that bright September day, I pulled open the large glass door leading from the building's lobby to this lounge and noticed the paper poster taped to the door at eye level. It was advertising what appeared to be a weekly event. The Green Room, so clearly named for the green shag carpeting that covered every imaginable surface, including the sunken "conversation pit" in front of a massive fireplace, hosted something called "Jazz 'n' Suds" every Friday. I didn't recognize the name of the local musicians scheduled to play this week. My first thought was that I was far too old (and perhaps weary) for this kind of thing.

On the other hand, I did like jazz. I had spent the past few weeks recovering physically. Now it was time to move on psychologically. Perhaps I'd rejoin the world.

My first strategy in rejoining the world was to call Liz and apologize for having disappeared for the better part of a year. It was clear that I had fences to mend—big ones.

"Where have you been, Kat? I've called and written…" I couldn't be sure if what I heard in her voice was simmering anger or hysterical concern. Probably a bit of both, and I didn't blame her. I'd been a shitty friend.

"Written? Where did you send the letters?"

"To your apartment in New York. Where else would I have sent them?"

I hadn't ever done anything about forwarding my mail. No wonder I hadn't received her letters, but even if I had, I wasn't sure I'd have responded. When I told Liz I was back in Halifax, she was stunned. When I told her I'd dropped out of Parsons, I thought she'd have a stroke. What I didn't tell her was anything about the baby. I told her I'd been ill. Her demeanour immediately softened.

"Kat, you should have told me. We're friends. I could have helped. But dropping out of Parsons? Are you sure you want to do this? What're you going to do now?"

I told her I was back at school, finishing off my teaching degree.

"What's that like? I mean, the kids, they must seem so young."

"You're not kidding," I said, laughing. I was beginning to feel as if we might be reviving something of the friendship I'd so carelessly discarded. Then I told her about the Friday night event as an example of the kinds of things undergrads these days did for fun.

"Kat, let's go on Friday!"

It seemed that this event was well-known to Liz, who had made it her weekly entertainment when she'd returned to school to finish her own degree in the city. She'd been at one of the other universities, but it seemed that the girls from her school went there every week. And she was convinced that we wouldn't feel so old there.

"Lots of grad students go, too," she said. "They're the only ones old enough to drink—legally, anyway!" She was laughing now. The legal drinking age was still twenty-one. A student could make it to graduation without ever being old enough to order a beer at the student union these days.

So, we arranged it. Liz and Alan would pick me up at Nan's (Alan had a car now) at nine-thirty on Friday evening, and we'd go together. When I asked her why so late, she said it really didn't get going until ten or so. I almost felt like it was old times with Liz, planning for an evening at a Yorkville coffeehouse. I hadn't been looking forward to something this much for over a year. It felt good.

~

The semester—and the year, for that matter—progressed quickly. Liz and I fell back into our old camaraderie—she came up with ideas for where we should go, and I went along with her. One weekend it would be to hear the Doris Saunders Duo at the *Jury Room*, the next Stu Loseby and the Rockers at the *Lobster Trap*. Liz was a dedicated, buttoned-down home economics teacher during the week, but on the weekends, she dressed up in her bellbottoms and satin shirts, sometimes with a feather vest on top, and her chunky platforms, and off we went. She took me shopping after the second week.

Nan was delighted with my seemingly new lease on life. One evening when I came downstairs after finishing up an essay that was due the next day, I found her sitting in the living room with a glass of wine.

"Come sit with me, Kat. We haven't had much time to chat over the past month." I sat down, and she poured me a glass of wine. She always took out two glasses when she opened a bottle of wine. After I settled on the couch beside her, she continued. "Darling girl, as much as I love having you here, I think it's time for you to get your own place."

This took me completely by surprise coming from her, but truthfully, it had crossed my mind. And so, with Nan's blessing (and an allowance from her that I agreed to only after promising to get a part-time job), I found a little flat a few blocks from the university. After a month or so by myself there, I realized that I relished my own space, despite its small size. And I did manage to find myself a part-time job in the fabric store where I had worked a few summers ago. After all, I was experienced!

I made straight A's that first term back at school, and I did enjoy my classes. At the same time, I missed my creative outlets, so I started sketching again. I began by getting myself a new sketch set, and then I set about drawing flowers, trees, buildings, then people. Nan even sat for me. At Christmas, Nan gave me a new sketchbook, specially for design, so I began filling it with a year's worth of ideas that I had bottled up in my head. It felt good to get them out.

New Year's Eve rolled around, and Liz and Alan had arranged for me to join them and one of Alan's buddies (whose name now escapes me) from work at the New Year's bash at the *Jury Room* downtown. I knew they were trying to set me up with someone (this wasn't the first time), but I didn't mind. It might be good fun.

Everyone dressed up that evening. In fact, everyone looked dazzling. I felt a bit dowdy in my black dress and heels. At least Liz had convinced me to borrow a pair of elbow-length gloves from Nan for the occasion. We ordered our drinks from the bar and started making our way toward a table near the stage. As we sat down, I leaned over to Liz and whispered, "There seem to be so many more men here than women."

She looked at me with a puzzled look on her face. "We've been here before. It's always like this. Hadn't you noticed?"

I had not, but as I looked around now, I realized that there were lots of couples. A man and a woman. A few women with women and a lot of men with men. "Is this a gay bar?"

"Not exactly," she said. "It's just the gayest bar in the city. That's what makes it so fun." She daintily sipped her martini.

That's when I spied him. Sitting at a table directly across the room drinking a beer and wearing a familiar-looking tweed blazer was someone I didn't know if I'd ever see again. At that very moment, he looked up, and we locked eyes. In a flash, the beer crashed onto the table, and he was standing above me, glaring down.

"Katherine Wilson," he said, "where the fuck have you been?"

I looked up. "Hi, Eddie. Nice to see you, too."

~

It was only really a matter of time. It seems I would have run into him sooner or later. Eddie was, as it turned out, a philosophy professor at my own university. He had been there for a year and had spent a good deal of time trying to get in touch with me. I had forgotten that this was Buzz's hometown, and it should have come as no surprise to me that he had chosen this city to settle down. They had settled down together. Although I never could bring myself to tell Liz the whole truth about what I had been doing since Chuck died, Eddie was a different story.

One evening in February, with Buzz (also a prof at Dalhousie) away at a conference in Ottawa, Eddie invited me over for dinner. I would have invited him to my place, but there was no room in my flat to entertain. There, over a bottle of excellent French wine, I told him the whole story.

When I had finished, he drew me into a hug, and we sat there for some time, as tears streamed down my face. I finally felt as if I had come home.

Eddie, Liz and I were a threesome again. Of course, both Alan and Buzz trailed along with us from time to time, but mainly, that spring, the three of us led the way. It was different but familiar. We had all evolved, but our friendship was intact. The three of us were having dinner at a new Mexican restaurant called *Zapatas* on a Wednesday evening in September when Liz piped up.

"Kat, did you happen to see any of the pictures of Simon Carmichael's new collection in *Vogue* magazine this month? It's his fall and winter 1970-71 collection that I guess he showed in New York in the spring."

I hadn't had time yet to see it. "Is it interesting?"

"You could say that," she said. "Do you remember showing me some sketches of your senior project designs when I was in New York for that ...special...visit?"

I did remember showing Liz the preliminary sketches. At the time, I thought it might get her mind off the reason she was making this whirlwind visit to the Big Apple.

"Kat, did you ever show those sketches to Simon?"

"No," I said, wondering where she was going with this. "I never showed them to Simon, not even once. I wanted the collection to be more or less complete before he saw it. It was supposed to be my ticket to fame and fortune." I almost laughed—almost.

"Well," Liz continued, "I think you'll want to see this fall and winter collection Simon's SXC brand has just launched." She leaned down to where she had stashed her purse under the table and retrieved three glossy magazine pages that she had torn out. She smoothed out the folds and spread them on the table in front of me.

Eddie leaned over to get a better look. "I don't know much about fashion, but these designs look amazing to me. They look like pieces real women could wear. Bravo to Simon."

"That's just the thing," Liz said. "They are amazing, and if I didn't know better," she looked at me, "I'd say that they were lifted from Kat's sketchbook." She watched me as I examined each photograph one at a time. "What are you muttering, Kat?"

I was, indeed, muttering. "This isn't possible. It's not possible." I lifted the photograph of one of the new super-models whose name escaped me and stared at the dress. It was a blue, silk velvet caftan-style dress with gold embroidery and braid embellishing the neckline and sleeves. It was, without a doubt, the dress I had designed—it was the dress that had been the centrepiece of my collection. *My* collection. And the rest of them? Every single one could have been lifted from my sketchbook. "How can this be?" I was speechless.

"So, you agree with me. Simon and company stole your designs."

I looked at Liz. I was so bewildered. "But how? I have no idea how this could have happened. It must be some kind of a coincidence."

Liz looked at me as if I had two heads.

"Who else knew that you were working on this project?" Eddie had moved on into his professorial, interrogatory persona. "Who did you show it to?"

I thought for a moment. "I showed it to Suzanne, but not all of it. But why would a student give another student's work to a mentor? And he would have known it wasn't her style. It doesn't make sense. And anyway, she only saw a fraction of the sketches, and they were early on at that." I picked up a second page. "And these are so detailed that it's as if whoever made the patterns had my complete sketchbook." My heart was thumping in my chest. There was no doubt in my mind whatsoever—this was my Woodstock collection.

"Where is your sketchbook?" Eddie was trying to get to the heart of the matter as he always did.

"I guess it's with the things I had sent from New York. I haven't seen it for almost a year."

"Here's what we're going to do." I loved it when Eddie took charge and told us what "we" were going to do. "You are going to find that sketchbook, and while you're doing that, I'm going to ask Buzz to contact a friend of his who works for one of the big law firms on Bay Street in Toronto. I remember him mentioning once that one of their particular specialties is the protection of intellectual property. You know how academics are always concerned about losing the rights to their original work. He has some experience with consulting with them once or twice."

I sighed and dropped the pages onto the table. "It's too late. This is Simon's collection now."

"*Never give up on something that you can't go a day without thinking about.* I'd wager that you'll never stop thinking about this," Eddie said. "By the way, that's not original to me. Winston Churchill said it."

You've Got a Friend

Carole King, 1971

TRUE TO HIS WORD, EDDIE GOT RIGHT ON THIS. He was in high dudgeon anyway, given his passion for equity and fairness. Over the next few weeks, what I witnessed was nothing short of a reignition of his former activist fervour. The thought of someone daring to steal another person's intellectual property was too despicable in his mind to not make it right.

Through Buzz's connections, he contacted the law firm of Rhyss Evans and Sturgeon and managed to get a law clerk assigned to the case. When I told Nan about it, she immediately offered to pay all legal expenses: she assumed we'd win the case anyway, and she wouldn't be on the hook after SXC paid damages. It took a few months to pull it all together.

As the fall semester flew by, I was busier than ever with both school and working at the fabric store. Now there was a potential lawsuit to take even more of my attention. The first thing the law clerk assigned to the case did was to send a letter to Eddie with a list of all the documents they'd require. Before I even had a chance to read the letter, Eddie was on it, and I trusted him implicitly. Naturally, the most important document was the sketchbook. The problem was that I couldn't find it.

I had looked everywhere but to no avail. It was just gone. I had no idea if it had even made its way north across the border or if I'd left it in my apartment in New York, stuck in the corner of a bookcase. Finally, I had to call the law firm myself.

I waited on hold, listening to canned music, when a voice finally broke through. "Rhyss Evans & Sturgeon, Ms. Bevan-Rhyss speaking. How may I help you?"

I was momentarily startled by the use of the term Ms. I had read an article about it in a newspaper in recent months, but this was the first time I ever heard a woman use it. I liked the sound of it.

"Hello? Anyone there?"

"Yes, sorry," I said. I was trying to figure out where I'd heard the voice before. "This is Kat...Katherine Wilson..."

"Kat?" There was a pause. "Kat, is that you?" The voice sounded excited.

"Darla?" I said tentatively, confused by the possibility that an old friend was on the other end of the line.

"Kat, it *is* you!" She was really excited now. "Yes, it's me, Darla. Oh my god, so you're the designer suing Simon Carmichael. This is so exciting!"

"I'm not actually a designer. Anyway, what in the world are you doing there answering the phone at a law firm?"

She giggled just a bit, and I could almost see her smiling face in front of me. "Well, you know I told you I would likely go to law school?" I did remember, but I also remembered being skeptical. "I graduated from law school at Osgoode Hall last spring and started doing my articling here right after. Thank goodness I married the senior partner's son! You know what they're like about women in law. But I'm planning to change that. Anyway, I'll be called to the bar next year if all goes well. I plan to be a partner someday."

I did not doubt that. Darla and her old boyfriend Thomas Bevan-Rhyss II had gotten married after her second year in law school. And it turned out her senior thesis was on intellectual property law, which was why they felt they could assign an articling law clerk to my case. I was happy to have her, but there was still the small matter of the sketchbook. I told her it was missing.

"Okay. I'm sure you've looked everywhere," Darla said in her most lawyerly voice. "Now, think carefully. Did you ever make other sketches of this collection outside of the sketchbook in question?"

I had made a few sketches both initially when I first started thinking about the collection and later on when I'd find myself with a new idea and without the red sketchbook close at hand. These were all in my main design book.

"Are they dated?"

What do you mean?" I said, confused by the idea of sketches dating.

"I mean, did you put dates on the sketches? Will we be able to see that you created them while you were in the employ of Simon Carmichael long before the creation of this collection?"

"Yes. I suppose. I date all my sketches," I said, realizing only at that moment that I did keep this kind of record. "But even if I give you those, they're not of all the pieces in the collection."

"That might not matter," she said. "Anyway, I plan to nail him for you."

And so, Ms. Darla Bevan-Rhyss, almost-barrister and feminist icon, became my champion in the fight to "nail" Simon. I was all for that.

~

I finally graduated. I was going to be a high school English and history teacher. If I wasn't deeply excited, at least I was relieved that I could get on with adulthood. The good news was that there was no problem finding a job. The local high schools were desperate for teachers, so it was a simple matter of applying, showing up for a cursory interview and receiving a letter offering me a job. I took the first one that came up. As it turned out, Liz and I would be at competing high schools, so I looked forward to going to football games with her to cheer on opposing sides. My career path seemed set out for me, but there was still the matter of the nagging need to create my art.

I had filled the sketchbook Nan had given me for Christmas and was itching for more. I noticed that my design direction seemed to be different now. I felt my ideas moving toward the kinds of pieces that the fashion world was calling sportswear these days. But I had yet to see any of them mocked up in actual fabric.

Even after graduation in May, I continued to work at the fabric store all through the summer. I didn't have to appear at the school until late August, after all. Being around all this fabric allowed me to think about what the finished garments in my sketchbook might look like, but I wasn't yet ready to start creating patterns and sewing them up—even for myself. The world of fashion design was a bit of a sore point for me because, as yet, I had not heard from Darla about any settlement on the little matter of the stolen designs. The whole process was so much more complicated than I had first thought, especially since SXC was headquartered in another country. I figured I had to put it out of my mind when I realized that one of the best ways to do this would be to sew some designs created by someone else. I would buy a bunch of commercial patterns and sew a fall work wardrobe. I was excited at the prospect.

I knew that I'd need dresses, something that I had rarely worn for the past few years while studying for my teaching degree. Whenever I was working in the store, all the fabrics were in their arranged places, and there were no customers about, I would page through the gigantic, hard-covered pattern catalogues. I loved them. They contained page after page of pattern design illustrations for clothes I could make. There were hundreds of designs from each of the three main pattern catalogues called *Simplicity*, *Butterick* and *McCall's*. Then there were the *Vogue* patterns. They were the ones I loved the most because many of them were creations of well-known designers, and I loved that they were more complicated.

I sat on a stool, thumbing through the *Vogue* pattern catalogue one Saturday afternoon in July, savouring the designs by Emilio Pucci, Pierre Cardin, Galitizine, Lanvin. These designers' names and so many others conjured in my mind elegant ateliers in Paris and New York. I sighed, feeling a bit nostalgic for what might have been when I flipped a page and there, in full colour, was a sketch that I swear was lifted from my Woodstock collection. And there beside the sketch were the words "Simon Carmichael original." I was furious.

I slammed the book shut and frantically started pulling dress patterns from the drawers packed with little pattern envelopes. I deliberately avoided the *Vogue* cabinet. As I stacked the five or six patterns that I planned to make for my fall wardrobe for the classroom, I couldn't stop myself. I scanned the draws that held the *Vogue* patterns, found the one containing Simon's pattern number and pulled it out. I had to have it. If nothing else, it was evidence, I thought. I would not, under any circumstances, make it, but at least I had it.

~

My first year as a high school teacher went well—or at least as well as expected. I liked some of my students. Others I could have slapped each time they walked into class. I didn't do that. I wasn't sure my students liked me, but to be fair, having them like me wasn't my main goal. I wanted them to learn something, and I knew I was developing a reputation as a hard marker. That was fine with me. Students who got an 'A' from Miss Wilson (every time I thought about Darla, I considered using Ms., but I never really got there) knew that they truly deserved it. As for the rest of my life, it was pretty quiet.

As time went on, I got frightened that I'd forget Chuck's face. I had photos, for sure, but it wasn't the same thing. Those two-dimensional representations each caught a brief moment in time only, but they didn't capture who he was. I didn't have the kind of photographic skills that Chuck had to capture someone's soul. I'd have to rely on my memories for that, which is why I was so sad when I began to realize that I was forgetting details about him. Then again, if I held too tightly to them, I could never move on. And I wanted to move on.

Then there was the lawsuit. It dragged on. Finally, one Wednesday in the fall of 1973, late in the afternoon, just as I was arriving home from work, Darla called.

"It's all done," she said. "They've settled."

"Did Simon admit to stealing my designs?" I said, not caring how much the settlement was.

"Not exactly," Darla said. "They've settled without admission of guilt. To tell you the truth, we had a hard time arguing in front of the judge with only the sketches you provided, but in the end, SXC decided to make you an offer on the condition that you never talk about this."

"A confidentiality agreement?" I said, realizing that I could never claim this as one of my creative accomplishments if I signed.

"Yes."

"Did Simon make this offer?"

"Actually, Kat, we never met him. He did all of this through his lawyers. For all I know, he might not even know that you're the one who made the claim."

"How is that possible?" I knew little about how lawyers worked.

Darla explained how these big companies had legal counsel who just took care of these kinds of things, often without the input from the company's principals. In the end, I simply stood down, realizing that it was time to move on. When she told me about the settlement amount, I was stunned. It was significant. That would have to be my solace. I put the matter behind me, and that was the end of it. At least I thought it was the end.

Killing Me Softly

Roberta Flack, 1973

I MET DAVID HUDSON IN LATE NOVEMBER of 1973. Nan had arranged for me to see a financial counsellor for help in investing the money from the settlement. It was hundreds of thousands of dollars, even after the legal fees had been paid. Although I was frightened about the prospect of investing, I agreed to meet with someone. Nan had been working with a "wealth manager" for years, she told me. I had no idea that she had enough money to warrant someone with this lofty title, but even as I looked around at her house and remembered what she'd said about owning my parents' house, it dawned on me that she might very well be "wealthy." Anyway, her wealth manager had recently taken on a young partner—an accountant who was also a qualified financial counsellor. And his name was David Hudson.

After Chuck died, I felt as if I would never again find someone with whom I wanted to spend my time. The past couple of years of dates arranged by Liz and Alan had cemented that idea even more firmly. So, when I met David, I was taken completely off-guard by my reaction to this handsome man who, on first impression, was the exact opposite of Chuck.

Chuck had been dark and brooding whenever he wasn't busy being funny and charming. David was blonde, blue-eyed, with a sunny, calming aura that seemed to shine into the room. As he rose from his desk to greet me at his office door, I tried to be nonchalant as I took him in. He was wearing a grey suit with tiny pinstripes, a crisp white shirt and a narrow yellow tie. His shoes were black and polished to perfection. He was, in a word, dazzling. At least I was dazzled. As I sat there looking at the charts he had prepared for me, I could barely concentrate. I wanted to look at him. No, I wanted to stare at him.

I agreed that he could go ahead and create an investment portfolio for me—whatever that meant—and we arranged to meet again the following week. He suggested lunch. I told him I couldn't leave school at lunchtime. He suggested dinner. I agreed.

David had lived here on the east coast his entire life, so I must have seemed a bit exotic to him, given that I'd "been around." It was hard for me to believe that *I* was the glamorous creature after all those years of feeling as if I were the drab, small-town girl among the sophisticates. As we began to see each other for dinner, a movie, or a concert, I found myself relying more and more on having him in my life. I was getting a bit anxious, though, about telling him my whole story, but I knew that if this were to become something more, I would have no choice. My stories about living in Toronto and New York fascinated him, though.

"Tell me about the coffeehouses in Toronto," he'd say. Or perhaps, "Tell me what Times Square is really like at night." And his eyes would widen, and he'd tell me that he'd visit those places someday when he wasn't so busy—and when he had someone to accompany him. And he looked at me.

I decided that when the time was right, I'd know. And I did.

~

Liz and Alan announced their engagement on New Year's Eve, three weeks after I met David. Although it had only been three weeks, I already hated the thought of not having David Hudson in my life. I got the impression that he felt the same. So, I invited him to the New Year's Eve party that Liz was hosting. At midnight, the moment after we had all shouted "Happy New Year," Alan stood on Liz's coffee table, blew his noisemaker as loudly as he could and told us he had an announcement to make. He and Liz were to be married in June. And Liz wanted me to be her maid of honour—I was honoured!

David and I continued to see each other regularly, two or three times a week through the winter and into the spring. Late in May, three weeks before Liz and Alan's wedding, I had to beg off from his invitation to attend the symphony with him—classical music was the only kind of music he listened to, a peculiarity I found charming (although I had found it obnoxious in my parents). Liz and I were going out on the town to celebrate her upcoming nuptials, and this was to be girls-night-out. Our night out turned into a downtown pub crawl.

By midnight on Saturday night, Liz and I were both plastered. I didn't often drink enough to make me feel any more than slightly tipsy. This evening was going to be an exception. On the other hand, Liz could usually hold her liquor, but even people with a large capacity for alcohol had their limits. We were sitting in the *Jury Room* just after midnight when she began to get maudlin. She began to talk about her abortion.

"So," I said, slurring only slightly, "does Alan know about it yet?" I sipped my Singapore Sling, savouring the silky-sweet gin-flavoured taste, knowing I should stop. Tomorrow was, after all, another day.

Liz gulped what remained of her third Tequila Sunrise (that was after a Pina Colada at each of the three bars we'd graced with our presence before this one) and shook her head.

"So, the man you're marrying doesn't know you were pregnant and aborted his baby?" I sniffed. "Liz, it's bound to come up someday. You can't keep this secret forever. It'll kill you. Or your relationship." I was proud of myself that I could still think straight enough to give out advice.

That's when Liz started to cry. I mean, really cry, loud sobbing gulps with tears streaming down her face carrying black mascara rivulets with it. I looked around, hoping there wasn't anyone around who knew us. I started to worry that she was having second thoughts about the wedding. *Well, better now than after the wedding*, I thought.

"Liz, it's going to be fine," I said, draping my arm around her shoulder. She tried to pick up her glass again, but I pushed it away from her. Perhaps it was time for us to start the sobering-up process. "You can keep your secret, but if there's something else…"

"That's just it, Kat," she said, sobbing, "I can't keep the secret. Not from you." She rubbed her face with the back of her hand. It came away smudged with makeup. "I lied to you. I did tell Alan about the baby. I told him the whole truth. But I lied to you."

I sat up straight as a coldness started creeping down my spine. I was suddenly sober. "What did you lie to me about, Liz?"

"It was about the baby." She stopped and reached across the table for her drink. I let her take it this time.

"What about the baby, Liz?"

"It wasn't Alan's." I stiffened as she continued. "It was Chuck's."

"You're lying," I said as tears began to well up behind my eyes. "You're lying. That's impossible."

Then she told me that it wasn't impossible. Remember Woodstock, she said to me. Remember the time I spent alone in the van sleeping and keeping dry after Joan Baez sang. Remember that the rest of them stayed under tarps. Actually, she said, only she and Chuck stayed—the rest went in search of breakfast. Remember the weed. Remember the red pills. Remember the sleeping bags. It didn't mean anything. We were just trying to keep dry. Together. One thing led to another.

I had heard enough. "You can't be sure," I said, trying to keep my voice down. I was grateful for the cacophony of voices and music around us.

She was sure, she said. She was sure because she and Alan had not slept together by that time. And anyway, it didn't mean anything.

To me, it meant everything. My mind was flooded with thoughts of Chuck's babies. One tossed away like it was nothing more than a mistake. The other dying inexplicably—the baby that, at that moment, I knew I could never have given up. And she threw hers away. She had a choice—I didn't.

I gathered my things and quickly stumbled through the bar and out onto the street. I was still sobbing when I got into the taxi that pulled up. As I sat there in the back seat, I knew two things: Liz was no longer a part of my life, and I had to tell David my whole story if there was to be any future at all with him. I just didn't know if I could.

~

It has long been my belief that our lives result from our decisions, but my faith in this philosophy is tested every once in a while. I didn't decide that Chuck should go to Vietnam. He did, and it affected my life. I didn't decide that he should never return. The fates did, and it affected my life. I didn't decide that Simon would steal my designs. He did, and it affected my life. As I sat alone in my apartment the day after Liz's stunning revelation, these were the thoughts that I was wallowing in. But, buried deep in the back of my mind, somewhere in my subconscious I suppose, was a nagging feeling like a tiny stone in my shoe. And like that tiny stone, if I ignored it and concentrated on something else—like my powerlessness to control the events in my life—I wouldn't notice it. A stone in your shoe, though, as we all know, doesn't just disappear. It stays, and it irritates, and it often results in a tiny blister that can turn into a festering sore. It will always irritate, annoy and chafe. The only way to avoid this is to face it and get rid of it.

Facing the truth hidden in the back of my life wasn't something I wanted to do. It was so much easier to sit alone and feel sorry for myself. I knew, though, that my life isn't really just a series of choices that I make. It's also the story I tell myself that connects the things that happen to me because there will always be things that occur outside of myself. That's life.

Chuck's decision to go to Vietnam was his choice to make. It wasn't my life. The way I would come to see that in relation to my own path was totally my choice. The fact that he died was also part of my story. The story I told myself about his death and my subsequent decisions was my life, and that story is, was and always will be my choice. So, now I had another choice to make. I could wallow alone for the rest of my life, or I could share my story with a man I was beginning to see as an important part of my future. I considered sharing my dilemma with Nan, but I didn't have to. I knew what she'd say. She'd tell me that often (usually?) the hardest thing to do is also the right thing to do and that there is no easy way out of life. I knew she would say this because she had said it to me before. She would also tell me that when the choice looks hard, it means the stakes are high. I could make only one choice.

~

I decided to invite David to dinner in my tiny studio apartment, which I was still living in despite the recent windfall from the lawsuit. I wanted to have some control, at least over my surroundings when I told him my whole story since I had no control over what he might say or do after I had finished. I also wanted to be somewhere comfortable if he walked out and never returned to my life.

I set up my tiny table with a white tablecloth and a candle. I would have liked to have two candles, but the table was too small. I put two other candles on the windowsill. I set the table carefully and prepared the only thing I was really good at making: lasagna. I poured two glasses of chianti and waited for him to arrive.

Looking into the candlelit space as he came through the door fifteen minutes later, David whistled softly. "Katherine, it's marvellous." He always called me Katherine because he told me he loved the name. He also said that since all my friends called me Kat, he wanted to be special. I loved that. I didn't have the heart to tell him that my parents also called me Katherine—if all went well, he would find that out soon enough. He hadn't met them yet. He took off his sweater (you always need a sweater in the evening here on the east coast regardless of the season) and stood there in front of me. "What's going on?"

I loved that he seemed to know me well enough already to sense that there was something on my mind. I didn't want to launch into my story before dinner, though, so I handed him a glass of wine. "What shall we toast to?"

He smiled slightly and tilted his head as if to look at me from another angle. "To secrets—and sharing them."

"What...?"

He put his glass down on the table and put his arms around me. "Katherine, you are the loveliest woman I know. And, if I'm honest, the best thing that's ever happened to me." He kissed the top of my head, which was an easy reach for his six-foot-one-inch frame. "I love the fact that you've lived in Toronto and New York. I know you wanted to be a designer, but again, in all honesty, that would have meant that I'd never have met you. I don't know why you dropped out of design school before you finished, but I know you must have had a good reason. I know that you have chosen not to tell me everything about your life, but I hope someday that you'll trust me enough that you will."

I broke free from him, sat down at the table and started talking. I told him about Eddie, whom he had yet to meet, and Darla and her dresses. I told him about meeting Chuck and our plans for the future. I told him about Woodstock. I told him about Vietnam and why I had returned home. I told him about the pregnancy. And the baby. I told him about Liz. And I finally told him where I'd gotten all that money I'd needed to invest. And when I finished. I just sat there silent, looking at the man I thought I might love.

David was sitting directly opposite me, looking at me straight in the face throughout my story. Now, he just sat there. I could feel tiny tears beginning to accumulate then slowly spill from my eyes. My whole world seemed to have slowed down, and I felt as if I were watching myself from outer space. And David just sat, stone still and silent.

He looked down at his hands, which he had clasped in front of him on the table. When he looked up, tears were shimmering in his blue eyes. "Thank-you, Katherine. Finally." Then he got up, walked the two steps to where I was, lifted me out of my chair and hugged me fiercely. "Katherine Wilson, will you marry me?"

I'm Sorry

John Denver, 1975

THE MOMENT DAVID ASKED ME TO MARRY HIM, I knew that my entire life up until then had been leading me to this moment. In the split second before I told him that I couldn't think of anything I'd rather do in my life than share it with him, my path to this moment flashed in front of me. The crushing disappointment of my father's reaction to art school; my defiance of him when I left for New York; my excitement of finally following my passion; meeting Chuck; losing Chuck; losing the baby; finding my way back to my life. And I knew that now that I had found my own way back, I was ready to share my life with David. So, I said yes.

It had been a long time since I had felt so relaxed and settled. Yet, even in the face of apparent serenity, I knew that there would always be a part of me that mourned the loss of my creative aspirations. There would always be a tiny voice in the back of my mind telling me to find a creative outlet. I told the little voice to go to sleep for a while, that I'd get back to it sometime. Then I carried on with life.

I heard the news on the radio one Saturday morning in October as I poured skim milk onto my cereal. There had been a horrific car accident—a head-on collision on the highway just outside the city. A pick-up truck and a car had collided. There had been one driver and no passengers in each vehicle. Both drivers had been killed instantly. The driver of the car was identified as Alan Davies.

I stopped pouring milk and just listened, stunned. Mr. Davies was survived by his wife, Elizabeth, the reporter said. Liz. I sat there, alone in my kitchen, and a tear escaped my eye. I knew that I should put everything behind me and pick up the phone, tell her how sorry I was for her loss. Maybe even tell her how sorry I was for how we'd left things. But I wasn't sorry—at least not for how we'd left things. There was a deep hole buried in my heart where my lost baby should have been, and somehow in my mind, I associated that hole with Liz and her decision. I knew it was irrational, but I couldn't change that right then. Maybe someday. So, I ignored the profound sadness that my former best friend must have been suffering. It was not my finest moment.

Time slipped by, and I never did move on with finding a way to forgive Liz. I chose, instead, to put her out of my mind as my life carried on. I found that I enjoyed my students and the life that David and I were building. My parents approved of David (although their approval was not paramount at that point in my life—when had it ever been?), and my mother was even excited at the prospect of helping me plan a wedding. We didn't plan to rush to the altar, so the process was leisurely. And this pace gave me time to think about my wedding dress—again.

When Chuck died, I had started—but never completed—the wedding dress I had planned to wear when he returned. Those pieces of lace still sat, folded within sheets of tissue paper, in a large, flat cardboard box, the box in which I had placed them when the devastating news had come. It was time to have a look at them.

One Saturday, early in the new year, I telephoned Mom and asked her if I could come over for coffee. While I was there, I told her I had to retrieve a few boxes or at least check on their contents. I declined her offer to help. This was something I had to do alone.

There was a large storage room in my parents' basement, and this was where they had stacked the boxes I had sent on from New York and which I had never taken to my new apartment—mostly because I didn't have space. I had scoured them only once since my return, and that was to search for the elusive red sketchbook. I knew that I should have culled them then, but I couldn't face getting rid of any of them. I also wasn't sure I wanted to be reminded of my life with Chuck. The time had come.

I found the box easily. It was not shaped like all the other square cardboard boxes that held my collection of sewing patterns I'd never used. It was a large, flat rectangle. I slid it out from between several other boxes and laid it on the linoleum floor Dad had laid himself in the basement directly over the concrete. I sat down and was quickly reminded about how cold those floors were. I stayed there anyway. I opened the box and lifted the first piece of lined lace, momentarily holding it against my face. I could almost see tear stains on the lace. I squinted, and a single tear squeezed itself out of the corner of my eye. When my eyes cleared, I realized that the stains were just in my memory—the lace was pristine. I didn't take any more of the pieces out of the box. I refolded the one I had taken out, put it back in the box, covered it with tissue paper and went in search of my father's cellophane packing tape. I remembered what Nan had said to me when I returned from New York full of anguish, desperately trying to hang onto the memory of a dead lover. "Store your memories in your heart, Kat, darling. Do not store them in your head. There will always be room in your heart to make more memories, but if you keep them in your head, you will never find new memories to make." I think Nan must have always been right.

I would make a new dress.

~

I arrived home just in time to hear my telephone hanging on the kitchen wall ringing off the hook. I scrambled to reach it before the caller hung up, and in the process, dropped it loudly on the counter below.

"Hello? Sorry for the noise!"

"Kat darling, is that you? Is anything wrong?"

I laughed. "No, Nan. Nothing's wrong. I just dropped the phone. What's up?"

"Turn on the television."

"What? Why?"

"Darling girl, just turn on the CBC news, then call me back." She hung up.

What was this all about? It didn't take long for me to realize what it was and why she called.

"South Vietnam surrenders, and the communists occupy Saigon," the news anchor was saying. The U.S. involvement in the Vietnam war was over. I sat there stunned by what I was seeing. Although U.S. soldiers had been leaving Vietnam for some time, this was the final event in the war. The communists had taken over Saigon, and they were renaming it Ho Chi Minh City. The news channels showed footage of a merry-go-round of helicopters swirling around the American embassy in Saigon, plucking the remaining Americans and desperate South Vietnamese survivors from the rooftop amid the sounds of gunfire in the background. I shivered.

So, it was finally over for the Americans. All I could think about at that moment was, *"And for what? What have you accomplished by letting so many young people die on a foreign battlefield in a war nobody wanted?"* And I thought of all the war vets I'd seen on television recently talking about how difficult it was to reintegrate into society, and I wondered if Chuck would have been one of those. Without a shadow of a doubt, I knew that I held the memories in my heart, but my mind was on the future.

~

At Christmas in 1975, David and I finally set the date for our wedding. It was to be on Saturday, July 17 of the following year. We had six months to plan the wedding and to find a house. David was adamant that we find a house before the wedding. I had no quarrel with that.

By the time spring arrived, we had accelerated our house search, but nothing was perfect. By the beginning of July, we still had not found one, and time was running out. Four days before the wedding, David and I went to see absolutely the last one we would look at until we returned from our honeymoon in the Bahamas. Yes, a July honeymoon in the Bahamas, but it's what we both wanted. Anyway, we were resigned to the fact that we would be staying in David's apartment (it was bigger than mine) until we found and closed the sale on a house. The minute we walked in through the front door of this three-year-old, ranch-style bungalow, we knew we were home. It was extraordinary. We forced the realtor to write up the offer at that very moment.

Later that afternoon, when I returned to my apartment alone, I was feeling elated. I had a couple of hours before I had to be ready for dinner with both families. The week before the wedding was so full of social activities that I hardly had a moment for anything else. It was a good thing I didn't have to worry about my dress since I had finished it three weeks earlier. I had done a variety of sketches for a personal design, but in the end, I found a commercial pattern for a sheath-style dress with a wide bateau neckline and long, slender sleeves that ended in a point over my hands. It also had a removable train. It was perfect. It was now adorning my dressmaker's dummy in my living room. Since David wasn't going to be here this week, and there was no risk he'd see it before the wedding, I had moved the mannequin into plain view so I could see it whenever I walked in the door. I was very proud of it.

I had just made myself a cup of instant coffee (I'd run out of ground coffee for my percolator) when the doorbell buzzed from downstairs. I wasn't expecting anyone.

I pressed the button on the intercom. "Hello?"

"Is this Katherine Wilson? Kat?"

"Who's asking?" You couldn't be too careful these days.

"Kat, it's Simon. Simon Carmichael."

I started to feel a bit dizzy. I steadied myself against the wall, swallowing hard. It couldn't possibly be Simon. First of all, what in the world would he be doing in Halifax? And second, why in the world would he want to see me? Third, and most important of all, why in the world would I ever want to speak to Simon again after all that had happened?

Of course, only the answers to the first two questions could possibly give me an answer to the third.

"What are you doing here, Simon?"

"Kat, please," he said with a noticeable note of pleading in his voice. It was a sound I never expected to hear from Simon Carmichael. "Could we talk, please? I've come a long way to see you."

So, he had come specifically to see me? I pressed the buzzer to open the door. "I'm on the eighth floor."

I walked into my tiny bathroom and stared at myself in the mirror as I waited for him to make his way to my door. What was going on? I couldn't help myself. I refreshed my lipstick and fluffed my hair. Then I heard a faint rap on the door.

When I opened the door, there stood Simon, perfectly coiffed and dressed impeccably. He was clutching a leather briefcase. He looked at me, smiling tentatively.

"Hello, Kat. You look marvellous. May I come in?"

I gestured him inside. He walked in and took in the entire apartment in a single glance. His eyes stopped when they reached the wedding dress. He looked at me. "May I?"

I nodded. Walking toward the dress, he dropped his briefcase on the coffee table. When he reached it, he lifted the fabric and gently swirled it between his fingers. I'd seen him do this many times. I'd even begun doing it myself. "Beautiful silk," he said. "And exquisite work." He turned and looked at me. "Yours?"

"Yes," I said. "Mine. For Saturday."

"May we sit?" he said, gesturing toward the sofa across from where he had placed his briefcase.

I sat down opposite him trying to be as dignified as possible while resisting the urge to punch him in the face.

"Kat, I'm sorry," he began. "I know that you may not want to hear this, but I am so sorry for what happened to you."

"That's lovely, Simon, that you're sorry, but it doesn't change anything. Besides, you've paid me off." I couldn't keep the snark out of my voice.

He reached into his briefcase and pulled out a red sketchbook. My red sketchbook! He handed it to me.

I snatched it from him. "So, you did have the whole sketchbook. You stole it from me. And you stole my collection!"

"That's not how it happened, Kat. That's why I'm here. I had no idea that the designs were yours. I didn't even know that we'd settled a lawsuit with you, only that there had been one, and my legal team took care of it."

"How could you not know? And if you didn't steal it, who did?"

"Theodore Lang."

"Who?" I thought for a moment. "Theo? Your assistant?" And Suzanne's boyfriend. Then I remembered. The day I heard the news about Chuck's death, Suzanne and Theo had offered to get my things home later after Theo gallantly put me in a cab. I never saw the sketchbook again.

Simon then explained that Theo had come to him with sketches for a collection that were so brilliant, he hadn't been able to turn him down when he offered them to Simon. It clinched Theo's place as second-in-command to Simon and would have led him to have his own label under the SXC brand's umbrella. Later, when he was told about the lawsuit brought by some unnamed woman, Simon had left it to his legal team to settle it as quietly as possible. Of course, he wasn't concerned. This kind of thing happened more often than anyone realized when you became as successful as Simon had.

Then, two weeks ago, one of his assistants stumbled on the sketchbook while she was helping to clear out one of the offices before renovations began.

"When she brought it to me, I was puzzled. It contained all the sketches that Theo had evidently copied. But they were all dated sometime before he brought me sketches, and then I saw your initials inside the front cover and that little cat you sometimes draw. I confronted Theo. As you might expect, he denied it at first. Then he admitted that he figured you were never going to return to Parsons, so he claimed the work as his own. I immediately fired him."

I was speechless. I almost didn't hear him when he said, "I'm here to set this right."

Then from his briefcase, he withdrew a document tube.

"There is no student we have had who deserves this more than you. This is your Parsons diploma in Fashion Design. I presented my collection based on your designs along with your sketchbook to the board of directors, and they were adamant that we award you your diploma—with distinction."

I took it from him, and all my creative longings seemed to bubble to the surface.

"One other thing, Kat. I want you to come work for me."

The Way I've Always Heard it Should Be

Carly Simon, 1971

SIMON CAME ALL THE WAY FROM NEW YORK to ask me to work for him? This was so out-of-left-field that I was speechless. I had waited all my life for this offer.

"Kat? Did you hear me? I want you to come to work for me."

"In New York?"

He frowned at me. "Well, yes. In New York."

I swallowed hard. Without any conscious thought, my eyes moved toward the mannequin where my wedding dress was hanging. "I'm getting married on Saturday, Simon. That's three days from now." Simon said nothing.

I got up and walked over to the window to look down into the street below. I could see people strolling around in the sunshine underneath the trees that lined the boulevard. There were some children playing catch in the park across the street. I turned around with my back to the window and looked at him. "Simon, do you believe that opportunity only knocks once?"

"I'm not sure I understand," he said.

I wasn't entirely sure I understood, either. This was the opportunity I'd been waiting for. This was the way I always thought my career would be—working for a famous designer. Or was it? Did I want to work for a famous designer—or did I want to *be* that famous designer?

"Isn't this what you've always wanted, Kat? Isn't this why you came to Parsons?"

I was suddenly reminded of something I read in one of my English textbooks in high school. I had even written it in the back of an old sketchbook. *Don't wait for the right opportunity; create it.* I think it was George Bernard Shaw. I was suddenly aware that I could create my own opportunity, and with the money I still had from Simon—the settlement money. And I had him to thank for reminding me of this.

I thanked him for the offer, but I was getting married, and that was also something I wanted in my life. At that time, I couldn't see myself pulling up stakes to follow him back to New York City. Something about it didn't feel right. After all, Simon was still Simon, and I still wasn't sure I could trust him.

~

Saturday dawned sunny and beautiful. David and I were getting married. My parents seemed to be very excited about this. In that way my mother had of pretending something wasn't important when it was, she murmured something about the fact that although I was thirty years old, there was still time. Time for what, I had asked her? For children, she had answered. As for my father? What can I say?

Dad was happy to be the father-of-the-bride today, but he wasn't entirely happy about the event. I had known this all along, but I had hoped he would have gotten over it before the day finally arrived.

I had finished dressing and was in my childhood bedroom with my mother when Dad poked his head around the door. After a brief moment of taking in his only daughter dressed in white for her wedding, he said, "He's here." And he scowled ever so slightly, but I noticed.

"Did you let him in, James?" Mom said.

"Of course. I'm not that rude, but Katherine," he said to me, "you know I still don't approve."

There was so much of my father bundled up in that simple phrase, "I don't approve." Where do I begin? At that very moment in time, what he didn't approve of was Eddie, but he approved even less of the fact that Eddie was my "man of honour." Dad had been scandalized when, some months earlier, I told him that I wasn't having a maid of honour since my closest friend outside of David was Eddie. So, a man of honour it would be. He protested loudly that this just wasn't done. I assured him that I didn't care. I was doing it, and he could stay home on the day of the wedding if he wanted to. But that wasn't all.

After he had grudgingly agreed to Eddie standing with me at the wedding, he had said, "But there's to be no...friend, or whatever you call them."

"Do you mean Eddie's partner?" I'd said.

Of course, that's what he meant. I assured him that, indeed, Eddie's "friend" would be there, and he would be sitting with us. And, by the way, he was also a professor, and his name was Buzz. As expected, Nan was on my side about this and told Dad, in no uncertain terms, to back off. He did so grudgingly, but even now, as we prepared to get into the waiting limousine, he still had to demonstrate his displeasure.

"I still don't know why you didn't ask Liz to stand with you," he said, casting a bit of a pall over the moment for me since Liz was still *persona non grata* to me. "I'll never understand girls."

"Women," Mom said.

I looked at her, astonished. Way to go, Mom!

Then it was time.

I swept into the living room where my man of honour was waiting to ride to the church with my father and me.

~

The wedding went perfectly. The weather had held. The flight to Montreal for our connection to the Nassau in the Bahamas was smooth. And now, David and I were a honeymooning husband and wife sitting on the *Holiday Inn* beach on Paradise Island, sipping Goombay Smash from plastic glasses.

I dug my feet into the sand and pulled my floppy-brimmed sunhat down over my eyes. I adjusted my new sunglasses that were so large they nearly covered my face. I took a sip of the super-sweet drink that was probably made drinkable only by the copious pour of rum we'd seen the bartender put in it.

"David," I said, "I forgot to tell you something."

"That you hate sand?" he said lazily from behind his own face-covering aviators.

"Simon Carmichael showed up at my apartment a few days before the wedding."

David sat up. "Simon Carmichael, the designer you used to work for?"

"The very one," I said, taking another sip. "He brought my Parsons diploma."

"What? Your diploma? And you didn't tell me? This is bloody fantastic!" Now David was sitting up very straight. "Wait. This is the Simon Carmichael who stole your designs?"

I told him the whole story, and when I had finished, he said, "You turned down the opportunity of a lifetime to marry me. Is that about right?"

I told David that it just didn't feel right for me at this point in my life and that I wondered if I might not be able to make my own opportunity when the time was right.

"Katherine, I love that you chose me over the job, but it's a heavy burden for me to carry. If you were meant to be a designer—"

"Then I'll be a designer. Someday. When the time is right."

"So, why didn't you tell me about this before the wedding?"

"Honestly? I forgot. We were so busy that it slipped right out of my mind." I looked out over the waves that were lapping the shore, leaving a line of white froth that looked like lace edging. "I guess my mind blotted it out temporarily."

We talked a bit more about Simon and his offer, and David made me promise him to always feel that he could be my sounding board. He wanted me to know that my career dreams were just as important as any family and home dreams we might have together. I was that important to him. I promised.

~

Home. We finally moved into our bungalow two months after the wedding. I was well installed in the new school year, so we had to move and settle in on the weekends. David had gone back to his apartment to retrieve a few final items he had not wanted the movers to transport, so I was alone in my new home one Sunday afternoon. My belongings that had been in storage at my parents' house had arrived, and I was left to decide what to do with the boxes of sewing and designing paraphernalia. And there was my sewing machine in its teak-wood cabinet I'd bought the year before. I made a decision.

I was going to put that all behind me—at least temporarily. That way, when the time was right, I could revisit that part of my career. In the meantime, I had lots to fill my life. It was going to take time for me to get the house the way I wanted it. And I wanted to be a good wife to David. Perhaps we would even have children. The fates would determine that.

I took the sewing machine out of its cabinet so that I could move it to the basement. There was no way I could do it while it was still in its cabinet—too awkward and too heavy. Once I got it down in the cavernous basement, I found a spot against the back wall and put the machine back in its cabinet, which I had brought down separately. I placed the large, flat box containing the wedding dress pieces I'd never finished on top of it. I then stacked the pattern boxes on top. I stood back and looked at them and wondered when I'd retrieve them. I walked up the basement steps and closed the door behind me.

My Life

Billy Joel, 1978

IT'S A FUNNY THING ABOUT LIFE. Sometimes we think we're making things happen. Other times it just happens. Throughout my life, Nan has often reminded me of this. "Want to make god laugh," she'd say. "Tell her your plans." And so, it goes. The best-laid plans—life is what happens to us while we're making plans—yes, life happens.

Every ending is a beginning, so when I put all my sewing and design trappings in the basement, it was a kind of ending that allowed me to move forward into a new beginning. And that beginning was the life that David and I created—a life that was both comfortable and adult. Yes, it felt very adult.

For the first few years of our marriage, I thought we might start a family. When that didn't happen, I was reminded once again about Nan's admonishment about making plans. So, we let that idea go. But when you let one idea go, doesn't another one often come along to fill that space? It seems so.

I hadn't allowed myself to think much about Simon and his preposterous offer the week before the wedding. Still, once I realized that it was unlikely that I would ever be a mother, it occurred to me that the time now might be right to revisit the idea

311

of fulfilling my dreams. At Christmas, just after our fifth anniversary, I thought David must have sensed it because on Christmas morning, after we had finished our first glass of mimosa, he handed me a package. It was especially beautifully wrapped in gold and silver paper with shimmering gold ribbon. It was almost too pretty to tear open. But I did.

Inside was a red-covered sketchbook embossed in gold on the front cover with my initials and a tiny cat. I hadn't even realized he'd noticed the little cat face I often sketched in the corner of my designs. David was far more in tune with me than I even imagined. I hadn't sketched in years—not since I had filled the sketchbook Nan had given me.

I suddenly realized that there was nothing I wanted to do more than start to fill it with sketches of all the ideas that had been crowding my mind for longer than I had ever acknowledged. It was time to get them out of my mind and onto paper.

~

For a long time after that, sketching was all I needed to do. I filled that red sketchbook then bought myself another one, then another. On a rainy Saturday evening the following April, David came into the kitchen where I was finishing cleaning up after dinner.

"Were you ever going to mention this to me?" he said, waving a piece of paper at me.

I didn't even need to look at it to know what he was talking about. I had left it on my dresser—perhaps hoping that he would pick it up. "Yes, I was. Eventually."

"Katherine, this is important. You know we've had this conversation about your career before."

He was holding the latest letter I'd received from Simon, who had been sending them every few months for the past several years. I'd thrown them all out except this last one. It sounded different. It sounded desperate. And maybe I was different.

"It says here he thinks there's a way for you to work with him without moving to New York. Are you going to consider it?"

I sat down at our red Formica kitchen table that I'd fallen in love with when we were searching for furniture for our new house. David sat down across from me, placing the letter on the table between us, facing me. I looked at the familiar SXC letterhead and the now-familiar handwriting. I picked it up and looked at it more closely. The handwriting didn't seem to be exactly as I remembered it over the past couple of years. As I put it back down on the table, David reached across and took my two hands in his.

"Katherine, my love, I've seen those sketches you've been doing for the past few months. More to the point, though, I've seen how happy you are when you're working on them. In fact, you're happier doing that than anything related to your teaching."

"I love my teaching, David," I said, interrupting him.

"I know you do, darling, but you love designing things much more. I think it's part of who *you are*, and teaching is just what *you do*."

I swallowed hard. Taking any steps in the direction of pursuing my dream was scary. "But it would change our lives, David. You know it would."

He smiled at me. "If it's what you're supposed to do, it can only change our lives for the better." He picked up the letter again. "He's asking you to come to New York to talk to him." He stopped and moved his finger down the lines of writing. "No, I'm wrong. He's begging you to come."

And so he was. As I reread the letter, Simon's words sounded pleading. He was imploring me to reconsider his offer, and that had never been Simon's way. If I came to New York to see his operation and talk about my future with them, and I still felt that

313

it wasn't something I wanted to do, he would stop pestering me about it. He promised.

"Call him, Kat." David rarely called me Kat. "Call him tomorrow morning and tell him that you'll come."

"Will you come with me?"

"To New York City? Are you kidding? I wouldn't miss it."

~

Because of my teaching schedule, I couldn't get away until the last week in June. David had never been to New York before and was excited. As for me, I was nervous—nervous about seeing Simon in his atelier once again, nervous about how I might react, and, to be honest, nervous about showing David around my old haunts. He had insisted that I take him on a tour of the places that I'd spent my time when I lived in New York. I wondered how I'd feel when we started retracing my journey.

Simon insisted that we stay at the Plaza Hotel and that he take care of all our expenses. As the bellman opened the taxi door in front of the Plaza, David stepped out and gazed across the street toward Central Park. People hurried along the sidewalks, and horses clopped along, pulling the carriages that took tourists for rides in the park. Sirens and car horns blared in the distance. "Wow," he said. "I think I'm going to enjoy this town."

David and I settled into our hotel room and quickly readied ourselves to begin the tour. We started with Central Park. The next morning, I would visit Simon in his atelier while David explored on his own for a few hours. Then we would make our way to Greenwich Village, where David wanted to see the apartment building where I had lived with Chuck. I wasn't sure which of those events made me more nervous.

As I walked up the steps to Simon's atelier the next day, it was as if I'd never left. His business had now taken over the entire building, with offices and workrooms on each floor, but his main atelier was still on the top floor. As I approached the door, I could see daylight spilling out from the skylights just as I'd remembered. I stood quietly in the doorway for a moment, hoping no one would notice me so that I could experience, once again, the sights, sounds and yes, smells of a fashion house at work. There were assistants and what looked like a couple of students, heads down at pattern-drafting tables, a few seamstresses at the sewing machines at the back and, in the middle of the space, just as always, was Simon concentrating on a half-finished design on a model standing still as he pinned the fabric precisely where he wanted it.

He somehow looked different, though. Older, for sure, with his hair now streaked with grey, but there was also something else. If I wasn't mistaken, his hands seemed to be shaking. Simon always had the steadiest hands when it came to his deliberateness about his designs. Perhaps he wasn't sure he liked this one? Then, someone noticed me standing there.

It seemed as if I was expected not only by Simon but by all of his employees. A young Asian woman in a lab coat left her spot at the pattern-drafting table to come over to welcome me and beckon me in. Simon looked up. His face flooded with a smile that I'd never seen before. It was so genuine and warm. I was touched.

"Ladies and gentlemen," he said, gesturing for me to come into the centre of the room. "I'd like to present Kat." He whispered to me, "Is it still Wilson?"

I was surprised that I hadn't given that particular issue any thought. Then I considered David and how supportive he was about all this. "Hudson," I said. "It's Kat Hudson."

He nodded, then looked around at his staff. "If today's meeting goes as I expect it will, Kat Hudson will become our new head designer."

My head jerked up, and my mouth fell open. Head designer? He didn't say anything about that. What in the world was going on? Where was he going?

After Simon introduced me to every single person in the room, and I'd had a chance to look at everyone's current work, my head was spinning. By the time he ushered me out of the atelier and into his private office, it was clear that he did intend for me to take over. But why? I most assuredly didn't have the experience to be head designer of anything and certainly still needed a mentor. I may have been thirty-six years old, but I was a neophyte in the industry. Just because I had terrific creative ideas, that wasn't enough.

We sat down in his office, and one of his assistants brought us coffee. Once we were comfortable and had caught up on chit-chat, an odd feeling for me to make small talk with Simon, he got down to business. I was caught a bit off-guard when he began to talk business because I was focused on the tremor in his hands and the almost imperceptible shaking of his head. His voice also seemed softer than I remembered. Something wasn't right.

Simon came straight to the point. He had always admired my work and had been baffled by my departure from the school (I didn't offer any details about what was going on in my life then). However, he had expected me to return. He had been planning to offer me a job when I graduated. Then, when he found out the awful truth about the collection he thought was Theo's inspiration, he knew he absolutely had to have me as one of his designers. (As he had told me before, he had fired Theo on the spot when he discovered the truth.) And now he needed someone to take over because he had recently been diagnosed with Parkinson's disease (*aren't you a bit young for that?* I was thinking), and he was rapidly losing his ability to hide it from his staff. It occurred to me that, based on the gentleness I'd observed when the young woman served him his coffee, they already knew.

"Kat, I need you to work with me. I urgently need you to be my hands and eventually my mind."

He had worked it all out. He would stay as long as he could, teaching me the business and guiding the collections until he was no longer able. I could work from my current home base, but he'd need me to fly to New York once a month for a couple of days, a bit longer during Fashion Week in the spring and fall. Before I left, he pressed me to make a decision before I left the city. I promised I'd think about it for the next two days while David and I played tourist, then I'd return with my answer before we flew home.

David and I spent the next day in Greenwich Village. Nothing had changed, yet everything had changed. I thought I'd feel strange taking him to see the apartment building where Chuck and I had lived and to *Urban Underground,* which was still there but under new ownership. But I didn't. I wasn't the same person who had haunted these streets as an artistic-bohemian wannabe. I knew who I was now. I didn't have to cultivate a persona just because I somehow felt it was expected in my creative industry. I could be me and still create beautiful designs. And that's what I'd do.

I'd made up my mind, and David was fully supportive of my decision. When I told Simon, he threw his arms around me, thanking me profusely. And my new life began.

I am Woman

Helen Reddy, 1972

I GAVE MY NOTICE TO THE SCHOOL as soon as we arrived home. The principal insisted that I stay on their substitute teachers' list, and I agreed since I was still a bit nervous about the new direction. What's more, I liked teaching and thought that the odd day in front of a group of teenagers might actually contribute to my creative process. But there was still the matter of precisely where I'd do my work.

David suggested that we could convert one of the three bedrooms into a workspace, but I hesitated. I think that, deep inside, I figured that the two bedrooms apart from our master bedroom might still, one day, be needed for children. I realized how ridiculous that thought was becoming, but I wasn't yet ready to let it go completely.

Eddie and I had started having dinner together once a month. Our idea was to try out different restaurants, but we always seemed to end up at a seafood restaurant called *Salty's* on a pier in the historic harbourfront area. We sat there one evening pondering the issue of my workroom problem when he had a sudden thought.

"I know this might sound far-fetched," he began, sipping his wine, "but Buzz's family owns a storage facility. We have a storage unit there ourselves, and it's kind of unique."

I couldn't quite imagine how a storage unit would be an idea for a workspace, far-fetched or not.

He continued. "All the spaces are really large—large enough to store two cars and more—and they're insulated and heated. They even have plumbing.

"Plumbing? Seems odd. Why does a storage unit need plumbing?"

He shrugged. "Beats me. I guess the original builder must have thought it would become something else other than a storage space. Or maybe he thought it would be a place for car storage and that owners might like to wash their cars? Anyway, the point is that you could have a large work area with all the facilities you'd need."

It sounded crazy to me, but at that point, I was willing to consider anything—and the price was right. David was equally nonplussed about it, but he agreed to come with me to see the space.

The facility was a twenty-minute drive from our house in a semi-industrial area on the edge of the city. It was enormous. We were greeted by the manager at the gate and escorted in to see the unit. We rounded the corner, and in front of us stretched a massively long kind of street bordered on both sides by dozens of garage doors. We were looking for two particular units that were side-by-side. According to Buzz, they had been partially converted to office space with a bathroom, a kitchenette and skylights. But the person who had planned to rent them had changed his mind, and they were left with these odd storage units. When I walked into the space, I had expected it to be dark and dingy. I was wrong. It was cavernous, but natural light flooded in from above. I could immediately picture where I'd put everything I needed—sewing machines, sergers, a large drafting and cutting table, filing cabinets, a desk. I also considered where I'd put a record player because I planned on having my old vinyl records here to accompany me while I worked. David liked only classical music and a bit of jazz, which I also enjoyed, but now I'd get back to The Brothers Four, Phil Ochs, Simon and Garfunkel and maybe even a bit of Janis.

~

It shocked me how quickly I fell in love with being back in the design field. I had wondered how I (and David) would feel about the monthly excursions to New York, but it turns out that I loved business travel, and David didn't mind a few days to himself. There were never very many women travelling alone, but I soon learned that I, for one, enjoyed it. Simon's brand, SXC, kept a company apartment on the upper east side of Manhattan—a chic address—where I stayed whenever I was in the city. Each morning, promptly at eight a.m., a driver would appear at the front door and whisk me off to the atelier. At six p.m., barring any kind of work-related social event, the car would take me back to the apartment. It was divinely decadent. And working with Simon? I couldn't have been happier.

I had some initial trepidation, given Simon's youthful proclivities for smarminess. But age and infirmity seemed to have caught up with him. Every so often, you could see a bit of the old Simon, but for the most part, each time I went to New York, he seemed frailer and more fragile. I wondered what would happen when he could no longer come to the atelier every day. I knew that there was no way I could move to New York if that's what he had in mind. I liked this arrangement just fine.

As I worked together with Simon and his assistants, I also often sketched my own designs. I loved the idea of a line of funky sportswear that had a kind of signature look about it. I even spent some time in my workroom at home, putting samples together for myself. I started working with new knit fabrics and found that they were far more comfortable for travelling back and forth to New York than my suits ever were. But make no mistake; I had long ago learned that the bohemian artistic style was not the one that worked for me. While the rest of Simon's employees wore their trendy, hip all-black outfits at the atelier, I favoured a more conservative, suit-centred aesthetic. It's just who I was. But when I started working with the knit fabrics for myself, I realized that I could create a more tailored design in a more comfortable fabric.

I was in Simon's office one afternoon when Misty (dear god, who calls their child Misty unless she's destined to be a porn star?), one of Simon's assistant assistants, rapped on the door. She was wearing unrelenting black from the velvet hairband at the top to the heavy (black) goth-inspired Doc Maartens at the bottom. Admittedly, I was also in black—a black blazer (fabricated by me in a knit fabric) over dark jeans, but I also wore a white-collared shirt to break it up a bit. And I was wearing pumps.

"Excuse me. Ms. Hudson?"

I had asked them to call me Kat, but this was a bridge too far for some of the younger ones. I beckoned her in.

"Ms. Hudson, I was wondering if I could ask you a question." I told her to go ahead. "I was wondering about the designs in that notebook you left on the drafting table. I mean, not just me. We were all wondering about it."

I hadn't remembered leaving it there. In any case, I was still waiting for her question. "Sure, Misty. What were you wondering about?"

"Are we planning on making those ones at SXC? I mean, we love them, but SXC is too expensive for most of us."

I laughed at the absurdity of working at a fashion house whose designs were beyond your paycheque.

"Actually, Misty, they're designs that I just create when I'm doodling. I sometimes make them up myself in my workshop at home, but they're not for sale."

"If you ever did manufacture them, would they be the kind of prices we could afford?" She glanced behind her at the open work area of the atelier.

I had never thought about that. In fact, I had never really thought much about producing these as a line of clothing. I hadn't thought about it *much,* but I had to admit that it had crossed my mind from time to time.

"You know what, Misty? I'm going to give that some thought. Thank-you for the idea."

She smiled broadly and left. I sat back in my chair and contemplated the possibility of a line of affordable, funky, trendy clothing under the SXC brand. But it would have to be a separate line. Later that evening, as I sipped a glass of wine alone in the uptown apartment, I started sketching out a business plan. There was a big, clunky computer in the den at the apartment, and I had recently turned my free time while in New York to learning about word processing. Now, I sat down in front of it, fired up a program called WordPerfect, and started to put my thoughts down in some kind of cohesive plan. When I had something I thought might work, I put it on a disk to take to the office and print. I then planned to add some sketches to the portfolio and present it to Simon. I was about to give birth to *Kosmic Kat,* my new label under the SXC umbrella.

~

The whole thing took more than a year—even longer than it took to give birth to a baby—but in the spring of 1984, we launched *Kosmic Kat* with a four-page editorial spread in *Vogue*

magazine. There, in the pages of the most famous fashion magazine in the world, were super-models Christie Brinkley and Brooke Shields smiling out from the pages, wearing *Kosmic Kat* designs. "The New Affordable Luxury," the headline said. There was even a picture of me to accompany the interview I gave. I knew I had reached one of the pinnacles of the fashion design world. I might not have been designing haute couture in a Paris atelier, but I created pieces that real women could wear throughout their real lives. And there in the corner of the page was the smiling little cat face I'd been sketching for years—the new logo for *Kosmic Kat*.

When Simon had asked me what I'd like to call the new brand, I knew immediately that my original inspiration for funky and cool came from that one-time meeting with Janis Joplin. Of course, she was fronting her new band then—The Kozmic Blues Band. So, that and me, Kat, would be the new brand. It wasn't too much of a stretch to figure out what ought to be part of the new logo.

David was so excited that you could be forgiven for concluding that he'd created the line himself. The day the *Vogue* magazine arrived, he told me to call Eddie and Buzz, and we'd have expensive champagne and eat caviar. It was magical.

Over the next year, my focus was almost entirely on my own line, while I helped Simon, who came into the atelier less and less often and always accompanied by a caregiver now, to find new designers to join his team. He told me that I should consider an assistant designer for *Kosmc Kat*, but I didn't think I needed one until one day, about a year after the launch, when I visited my doctor because I hadn't been feeling well.

"How old are you now, Mrs. Hudson?" my family doctor asked me as he shuffled through my chart, presumably looking for my age.

"I'm forty, Dr. Mills."

"Hmm. Yes," he said absently. He placed his pen back on the desk and stopped shuffling papers. "Well, Mrs. Hudson, it appears that you are pregnant."

My mouth dropped open. I was dumbfounded. "How...?"

He smiled at me. "I believe you know how, Mrs. Hudson."

No kidding, I was thinking. I guess I *was* going to have to hire an associate designer, after all.

Child of Mine

Carole King, 1970

DAVID WAS AS BEFUDDLED ABOUT THE NEWS AS I WAS—in a good way. We had moved on from thinking we'd ever be parents, and now this. I could hear Nan's voice in my ear again…if you want to make god laugh…

Before I even considered telling my parents that at long last, they would be grandparents, I wanted to talk to Nan. She needed to know that she was going to be a great-grandmother, and I needed to know that she'd be around to meet this little one. Since she had just turned eighty-five, though, I knew it was far from guaranteed.

Even so, Nan was still as elegant and energetic as she had always been. I didn't know how she spent her days, although I'd noticed that she had recently upgraded her computer system, insisting that it was important to her to have state-of-the-art computing capabilities. What she did in that office all day, I had never been able to figure out, but whatever it was, she seemed energized by it. I called and told her I had some news. She told me to come right over.

"Well, Nan," I said as we settled in for coffee, "I have some shocking news." I took a sip of the coffee that had just been put in front of me by Nan's new housekeeper, Marilyn, who, in my view, resembled an ageing Marilyn Monroe.

"Darling girl, there is very little in this life that shocks me," she said, fingering the pearls that she was wearing with her cream-coloured silk blouse. Nan always looked perfect. Even her new glasses matched the cream of the silk. "I'm not sure there has *ever* been much that shocked me. But go ahead. Shock me."

"You're going to be a great-grandmother."

She put her coffee cup down on the table and took my hands into her lap. "Now that is wonderful news but hardly shocking."

"Well, I have to say that it shocked me. And I think David even more so."

Nan laughed. "I suppose it might shock him. He is a wonderful man, you know. And you will both make marvellous parents."

"Thanks, Nan. I'm worried, though. I'm forty years old. I never thought this would happen." I fiddled with my linen napkin, and for a moment, my mind drifted toward my lost baby. I quickly shook that off. "I'm going to have to give up my design work. I'm not sure what I'll say to Simon. I'll be letting down a lot of people."

Nan looked at me sternly. I had seen that look before, but it was usually directed toward my father. "Katherine Hudson, I am surprised at you. I presume you're familiar with the psychologist Carl Jung?" I nodded. "He once said, '*Nothing has a stronger influence psychologically on their environment and especially on their children than the unlived life of the parent.*' Do you understand what I'm saying?"

"I'm not sure."

"One of the very worst things you can do to a child is to place your unfulfilled dreams onto them. Abandoning your passion to focus on a child is too much of a burden for the child."

"I'm not sure I'm following, Nan."

"Kat, you are an extraordinarily creative and talented woman who has endured a lot to get where you are today. Your work is important to you and always will be, child or no child. If you abandon yourself, your child will not be any happier and is likely to be a damn sight worse off." She picked up her coffee, sipped it and sat back. "Believe me, darling girl, I know what I'm talking about."

I had no idea what she was talking about, but her words did begin to resonate with me. If I abandoned *Kosmic Kat* at this point in my life, I would likely never be able to resuscitate it. Would I resent a child for this? I couldn't imagine myself doing that, but Nan did have a point. "Nan, isn't it expected that a mother makes sacrifices for her child?"

"Sacrificial love sounds like a good thing, doesn't it? The problem, darling Kat, is this. You cannot truly love another human being if you don't first love yourself." She stopped as if to let that sink into my recalcitrant brain for a moment. "Your passion and talent are fundamental parts of who you are. If you give those up for a child, you will always suffer an undercurrent of bitterness. A bitter mother, or father for that matter, is no kind of parent for a child of any age."

I thought about my father and his bitterness that had been evident to me all my life. Now I wondered what Nan had given up to be his mother. It didn't seem like the time to ask.

As I drove home, I thought about Nan's perspective and her adamance that giving up *Kosmic Kat* was a mistake. But could I do it all? That evening, as David and I discussed Nan's words of wisdom, I realized that despite not being sure if I could do it, I had to try. And so it seemed that *Kosmic Kat* would survive to live another day with Kat Hudson at its head.

There is a lot of truth to the notion of nesting. I had heard about women who went into a frenzy of home-based activity in the last weeks or days before the birth of a baby. For me, it was longer and broader. Once David and I decided that it was the best decision for all of us (including our future child) for this new mother to maintain her career, my time in my studio was frenzied indeed. I had a collection to prepare. I also realized that my best course of action would be to complete the preliminary work on the next one as well. For that, I was going to need help.

I hired a young woman named Lena, who had recently immigrated from Bulgaria with her family. Nineteen years old, Lena was an extraordinary seamstress. I knew this from the moment during her interview when she began peeling off her layers of clothing to show them to me. She had made every piece, and the quality these garments showed almost put me to shame, and I had always prided myself on my seamstress skills. Then, I asked her to see what she could do with the pattern and fabric on the cutting table. She had the pattern pinned to the fabric so fast and accurately that it made my head spin. Then, when she sat down at one of my three sewing machines, the fabric flew under the presser foot, accurately and faithfully producing the design. I hired her on the spot. The second position was going to be more challenging to fill.

I was going to need what I was planning to call an "associate designer." I needed someone who could work with me and take charge whenever I needed her (or him) to do so. The problem was that in a city the size of Halifax, the pool of potential designers with the skills I was looking for was limited.

When I talked to Simon about it, he suggested that I situate my associate designer in New York. Simon rarely went into the atelier any longer himself, and he had a new designer who was charged with the SXC label now and several assistant designers. Although he could no longer take a hands-on approach to his business, he still had most of his faculties, and I often consulted with him. I got the impression he loved it when I did. The more I thought about it, the more I realized he was right. For a few months after the baby was born, my new designer could travel to Halifax every few weeks. After that, I could once again travel to

New York from time to time, as I had always done. Amid all this frenzy of activity, I also worried about the baby.

I had heard horror stories about older mothers and their babies. I knew that there was a risk that the baby might have some kind of genetic problem because of my age. A child with such needs would change everything. The moment I met my new baby, though, was the moment I knew everything would be all right.

~

Our tiny daughter made her entrance into the world screaming at the top of her lungs. When my obstetrician placed her on my chest, she quieted down immediately and looked up at me thoughtfully (at least that's how it looked to a harried new mom who had just endured eighteen hours of ghastly labour). I stared into her beautiful, huge blue eyes and took in the mop of dark hair covering her tiny head. "Mom," she seemed to be saying, "I'm here now, and I'm in charge."

As I looked back at her, I somehow knew that this child wasn't going to let me direct her life. She was going to know precisely the direction of her life. I was so right.

We called her Evelyn after David's grandmother. My parents loved their new granddaughter, but as expected, they were controlled in their enthusiasm. It was their way. David's parents were delighted. And Nan, let's just say she thought the sun rose and set on little Evelyn.

It was a busy time in my life, juggling a baby and a fashion design label. I was forever grateful for my new designer Julie Desjardins, late of Paris, Lena, who held down the fort at the workshop when I couldn't be there in the early months, and, oddly, Marilyn.

Nan had lent me Marilyn's services as a part-time nanny, and she excelled at it. I found it endlessly amusing to see this Marilyn

Munroe doppelganger (albeit older) doting over this little child. We had found our rhythm of work and home life when I was struck by lightning for the second time.

"Well, Mrs. Hudson," my family doctor said to me during my annual check-up when Evelyn was fifteen months old, "would you like me to make an appointment for you with Dr. Lea?"

"Why would I need Dr. Lea?"

"Oh, I'm sure you know," he said chuckling. Dr. Lea, of course, was my obstetrician.

David and I were going to have another baby—and I was forty-two by this time.

~

Evelyn's little sister was more reserved than she had ever been. From the moment she was born, I could see this little one was radically different from Evelyn. Evelyn was boisterous, demanding and tenacious. Evelyn's baby sister was quiet, contemplative, and looked to me to be all-knowing. From the first moment I saw her, I could see a fellow artistic soul. We called her Charlie. I need to tell you why.

A few months before Charlie was born, David and I started that inevitable "what shall we name the baby" conversation. We had fully expected a boy this time around.

"I think we should call him Charles," David said.

I remember looking at him quizzically. The only Charles I had ever known was Chuck, and naming a baby after an old love seemed—odd. I said as much to David.

"Katherine, you've had a most interesting life. Chuck was a part of that. Honouring who you are and where you've come from might be the best way to go here. Besides," he said laughing, "my great-grandfather's name was Charles!" So, Charles it would be.

330

There was only one problem, however. The moment Dr. Lea said, "Katherine, it's another girl baby," I knew we had a problem.

"God, David," I said as I looked down at my new little daughter, all of five minutes old. "What in the world are we going to call her?"

"That's simple," he said as her tiny fingers curled around one of his, "Charlie. Short for Charlotte."

And that is how my little Charlie, the artist and dreamer, entered our lives. By the time Charlie was eight months old, Nan quoted Vincent Van Gogh one day as we watched her sit among the fallen leaves in the park, lifting each one and looking at it seemingly from all sides. "*Normality is a paved road: It's comfortable to walk, but no flowers grow.*"

"This little one will have lots of flowers in her life," she said, wistfulness apparent in her voice. Two months later, my Nan, Frannie Phillips, was dead.

It's Too Late

Carole King, 1971

I HAD NEVER CONTEMPLATED MY LIFE WITHOUT NAN, without knowing that she was there on the other end of the telephone even if we weren't in the same city. Or just a drive away now that I'd settled back in my hometown. I had considered how I would respond to Mom and Dad's deaths, but Nan was a fixture in my life that I couldn't even consider losing. The moment Marilyn called that night when Charlie was ten months old and Evelyn almost three to tell me that she had died, I collapsed in a heap on the floor and sobbed. She was gone.

I had been to see Nan earlier in the day. She hadn't been feeling well for a few weeks. Since Nan was rarely ill, this had concerned me. I was even more concerned when I left her house earlier that day because of the conversation we'd had. It had seemed so…final.

"Katherine, darling girl, come sit beside me." Nan patted the side of the chaise lounge where she was sitting in the sunshine with a fur throw over her legs. Even at eighty-nine years old, she rarely spent much time sitting with her feet up. When I had settled in beside her, she continued. "Kat, when you look at an old lady, what do you see?"

I didn't quite know what to say.

"Oh, I know," Nan said, waving her hand as if to brush away whatever she thought I might be thinking. "You see lines and sagging skin, and a sallow complexion, and wispy hair. But look deeper." She stroked my hand. "If you really look, you will discover that there is so much more. No one is born old, you know. Inside every old lady is every kind of woman she has ever been. Remember that, Kat."

~

And that is what I was thinking as I sat in the front row of the chapel at the funeral home when an old friend of Nan's began the service.

I was supposed to do the eulogy, and it occurred to me that Nan had been trying to tell me something. She seemed to be trying to tell me that she had been different women throughout her life, and perhaps, this is what I needed to say to the assembled crowd (which was larger than I had expected, I have to admit). However, the problem was that I suddenly realized how little I knew about my grandmother as a young woman. I was ashamed to admit that, to me, Nan had been only one person—my grandmother. But as I sat there listening to the mellow voice now intoning the *Desiderata* —"Go placidly amid the noise and haste…" I knew that she had once been a young mother, a wife, a daughter…but what else? I realized that I hadn't known my grandmother at all. She lived in a beautiful house that must have been costly, but I had no idea where her money came from. She had friends in the city, but I didn't know who they were. She had an album full of photographs that I'd only ever glanced through before. After all, what child wants to spend time peering at old black-and-white pictures of fusty people from long ago? And what about that house in London? She had never told me why she wanted me to see it. Then there was her visit to New

York to visit me when she'd told me she'd been here before but didn't elaborate. Who was this woman I'd called Nan for my whole life? How could I eulogize someone I hardly knew? I felt a sudden urge to flee the service and run to Nan's house to see if I could figure out who she had been.

I muddled through. My words were so inadequate. Standing up there in front of that crowd that I could see only dimly as if through a veil, I could feel tears clouding my eyes. As I spoke, though, I gained composure as if I could now see Nan as a woman who had held onto her mysteries just a bit closer than most and wondered if, one day, my daughters might say the same about me.

Finally, it was over. I hate funerals with a passion and just want to flee the moment the service is complete. However, my father, who, as far as I could tell, hadn't liked his mother much (and the feeling had appeared mutual), herded us into a kind of receiving line to greet the mourners, one at a time. And they came, each one bearing a more doleful platitude than the one before. "She's in a better place." (*Seriously? Who says this kind of drivel?*) " "She had a good life." (*How in the world do you know this?*) "Time heals all wounds." (*You don't even know me.*) And the one heard most often: "*So sorry for your loss.*" I wanted to scream, *I know exactly where she is—right here in my heart.* But I nodded and thanked each one.

As we were dispersing, I noticed a well-dressed, silver-haired man I judged to be in his eighties, lingering in the corner of the lobby. He had what appeared to be a silk scarf knotted around his neck, suggesting to me that he might be European. I had no idea who he was. He caught my eye and beckoned me over.

As I approached, he held out his hand. I took it. "You must be Katherine." Then he drew me toward him for the French double kiss, which seemed the most natural accompaniment to his beautiful Parisian accent. "*Ta grand-mère était une femme merveilleuse.* She was marvellous." He then stood back as if to salute me. "I am so sorry, my dear. I have lost all sense of my manners. May I present myself? I am Jean-Christophe Lemieux."

"Hello, Mr. Lemieux," I said. "How did you know my grandmother?"

"Ah," he said with a twinkle in his eye. "Françoise and I go back a very long time. There was no one quite like your grandmother. The world will lose a bit of its sparkle for me without her in it."

"Did you play bridge with her?" I had no idea where they might have known one another.

"Bridge? Is that what she called it?" He laughed. "*Comme c'est amusant!* I cannot imagine a more droll scene than to consider Frannie Phillips playing bridge!"

This took me by surprise since Nan often mentioned that she was going to be playing bridge. Was that some kind of euphemism?

"Mr. Lemieux, could I buy you lunch sometime? I'd love to hear more stories about Nan. I now fear I didn't know her as well as I thought I did."

He looked at me more seriously with a kind of knowing expression. "Françoise often talked of you, Katherine. She loved you more than life itself, you know. But she always maintained that not everything about a woman must become the news of the land." He looked at his watch. "*Mon dieu.* I fear I must be going. I have a plane to catch."

"Did you fly in from somewhere to be here?"

"But of course. And I must be back in Paris by the morning."

I was having a hard time trying to figure this out. "May I drive you to the airport? We could talk along the way."

"What a wonderful offer, but I have a driver waiting for me, and I have already provided the pilot with a departure time."

The pilot? With a departure time? Who was this man?

Then he handed me a small, cream-coloured, gilt-edged business card, bowed slightly then quickly, as if he were decades younger, stepped away and out through the front door, leaving me with more questions than answers. I looked down at the card in my hand. It read simply, "Jean-Christophe Lemieux" with a European telephone number.

~

Two weeks later, with Marilyn, who now worked full-time as a nanny to the girls, doting over the girls at the house, David and I sat in Nan's lawyer's office waiting for him to begin reading her will. As I had suspected, Nan had considerable assets. In addition to the house, there was money in accounts in Canada, London and Switzerland. She had left sizable donations to both the *Paris Opera Ballet* and *the National Ballet of Canada*. Nan had been a massive ballet fan—but why the Paris Opera Ballet? That was a mystery to me. Most of the rest of the money would be deposited in a trust for her granddaughters who would come into it at age thirty-five. She had left the furnishings in her house to Marilyn and her extended family, whom Nan seemed to know. The house she left to me with instructions to sell it and use the proceeds any way I wanted. Before I could sell it, though, I would have to clear it out. Oh, and she left my parents' house to them. It did seem appropriate.

I had to set aside a week to devote to the process. I arranged for a mover to take the large furniture pieces to wherever Marilyn wanted them to go. Then I was left with her jewelry and cranberry glass collections, personal papers and other intimate belongings, and her clothes. My god, the clothes!

Nan had always been well-dressed. She favoured silks and linen in the summer and cashmere and tweed in the winter. What I did not realize, however, was that she seemed to have kept every single gown and cocktail dress she'd worn since—well, I'd have to take a closer look to figure that out.

On the second floor of her house was a closet that I'd never known existed. Back when I'd moved home from New York and couldn't live with my parents any longer, I'd taken the guest room on the third floor. I walked past this double set of doors every day I was there, yet I'd never even wondered what was behind it. The key to the brass lock was on Nan's dresser in a cranberry glass candy dish. I felt almost as if I were prying as I turned the key in the lock then slowly opened the doors to a massive walk-in closet lined on two sides with long rails filled with what looked like vintage clothing. Across the facing wall was a mirror flanked by shelves filled with hats, handbags, gloves and fans, of all things. I stood in the middle of the closet, slowly turning around to take it all in.

My hands were shaking as I pulled one dress after another from the rail, feeling the softness of the silk and drinking in a slight but unmistakable fragrance that had been Nan's signature forever—*Shalimar*. I thought about the bottle of *Shalimar* she'd presented to me so many years ago and wondered why I'd never worn it. I vowed from that moment on that *Shalimar* would be my signature fragrance, too. And I never wavered from it after that.

But the dresses! As I gazed at the three I had hung on hooks that someone had thoughtfully placed on the upright dividers between sections, I was suddenly inspired. I would have to use these somehow in an upcoming collection. I was known now as a sportswear designer, but I didn't see any reason why *Kosmic Kat* couldn't have a cocktail line. I could see it so clearly in my mind's eye.

As I pulled another particularly striking full-length, gold lamé silk gown trimmed with panels of ivory satin from the rail, my eyes fluttered to the label in the back. I think I stopped breathing for a moment. *PAUL POIRET À PARIS* and beneath the designer's name was *77436 ATELIER, Mme Françoise Phillips*. I was holding in my hands a 1920s Paul Poiret original that had been made for my grandmother.

I felt a cold ghost creep up my spine as I looked at the label and wondered: *Who are you, Frannie Phillips, and what have you done with my grandmother?*

I took the dress out of the closet and into Nan's bedroom, laying it on the bed. I sat down beside it and thought for a few minutes. That's when I saw the diary.

My eye lingered on a gold-covered book tied up with a Chanel-stamped ribbon sitting atop the small jewelry box Nan kept on her dressing table, one of those art deco-styled ones made from burl wood. I was glad the movers weren't coming to take away the furniture until the day after tomorrow. I walked over and picked it up, immediately beginning to flip through the pages. I recognized the handwriting immediately—it was Nan's, and I was holding her diary. Then what appeared to be a folded letter slipped out from the book's leaves and fluttered to the floor. I picked it up and went back over to the bed to sit down. I opened it up.

"My darling Katherine (Kat to those of us who love you):

'I am too intelligent, too demanding, and too resourceful for anyone to be able to take charge of me entirely. No one knows me or loves me completely. I have only myself.' I did not write those words. They are from the pen of my dear friend Simone de Beauvoir, but they could have been written by me or at least about me. Sometimes, I'm sorry that I didn't share my life with you, but as I told you today, old ladies are not only what they appear to be. They are so much more. Thus, I leave you my diary. You may find it amusing. Some day in the far distant future, please ensure that Charlie receives it. I have looked into the soul of that tiny baby, and I know she will know what to do with it. Please always know that I have adored you, my darling girl. I am always with you. Nan."

The letter was dated the day she died. I knew she must have written it after I left her that day. And Simone de Beauvoir!

Surely, she must have been joking about being friends. I held the diary tightly to myself and could feel her looking down at me and whispering, "Life must go on, Kat. Life must go on."

Take My Breath Away

Berlin, 1986

I will spend my entire life—and beyond—wondering what's wrong with the women in my family that we cannot seem to share our lives completely with our loved ones. I was really no different from Fran. As time went on, I knew that it would be a long time before either of my daughters understood my own passion.

Evelyn grew up to be a force to be reckoned with. She won her first public speaking contest when she was only ten years old. Her topic? "Why I am going to be a world-famous lawyer when I grow up." She spent weeks researching her subject and had not a trace of stage fright about her. When she walked onto that gymnasium stage, she took control. Her audience lapped it up, and, naturally, she won, besting even students three years older.

Throughout her performance, while David and I were on the edges of our seats, Charlie sat beside me, swinging her legs beneath the folding chair, drawing in the sketchbook I'd presented to her for her eighth birthday, and writing stories about the drawings. Periodically, I could hear her sigh and yawn. Once, she tapped me on the arm and whispered, "When can we go home?" Public speaking contests were not her preferred form of entertainment. Charlie was a true dreamer.

I suppose some of my reluctance about laying bare our lives to our children must have rubbed off on David somewhere along the way. We never did take Nan's money and buy a new house. Instead, we invested it and did some renovations on our rancher, becoming the proud owners of the only house on the street with an ensuite bathroom. There was, however, a darker reason for this and how David's reticence about telling the girls about our lives manifested itself.

It began the year after Charlie was born. We had started looking for a new house when the symptoms first began to manifest. Almost unnoticeable at first—stiffness in the morning—they were easy to dismiss. We laughingly attributed them to getting older. The day David fell off the step ladder he was using to put Christmas lights on the trees out front was the day I started to worry. He wouldn't even consider going to a doctor. "Normal part of ageing," he kept saying. The trouble was that he was only forty-four years old. Age-related issues could hardly be causing anything at that stage. It was only after he couldn't get out of bed without my help one morning that he agreed to talk to our family doctor.

When David came home, he downplayed any medical concerns.

"Well, what did he say?" I said, wishing I had been there with him. He had insisted on going alone.

"He just wants to send me to some neurologist," David said. "Routine stuff. They have to cover their asses, you know."

Routine was certainly not the word I'd use when, three months later, we sat (I insisted this time) across the large expanse of desk from the neurologist. He tapped his pen on David's chart open in front of him and said, "Diagnosis is difficult in these kinds of cases."

"What kinds of cases are these, precisely?" I said. David reached over and squeezed my arm as if to suggest that perhaps I ought to wait for the doctor to finish.

"That's the problem, Mrs. Hudson. Precision. All we have to go on are these progressive symptoms." He pushed his glasses up on his face and lifted one of the pages of the chart. "I have to say I thought you were a bit young for this, but I presented your case at grand rounds on the neurology service two weeks ago. We had a fulsome discussion, and we've concluded that you're suffering from a rare disease called corticobasal degeneration."

We both looked at him, puzzled.

"CBD isn't very well known, and I have to say I've only had two other cases in my career. It's a rare neurological disorder."

"Is it fatal?" David said.

"Well, it's a progressive kind of disease, and yes, I'd have to say that eventually, you'll likely die from complications related to one or more of the symptoms. Often patients die of pneumonia and sepsis."

"What kind of treatment can we expect?" I was starting to think I knew where this was going. Words like 'progressive' and 'rare' suggested a direction I wouldn't like.

"Unfortunately…" and that's all I had to hear.

There would be no treatment. The disease would progress and take my best friend from me.

"Is it genetic?" David, always the pragmatic one, obviously needed to know if he might have passed it onto his daughters.

The answer was no, CBD was not genetic. They had no idea what caused it. David looked at me. "Well, then, Katherine, we don't have to tell the girls. They're too young to understand at this point anyway."

And so began David's struggle against this disease that changed him from a seriously outgoing man to a quiet, reserved individual and changed him into someone desperate to keep his symptoms from his girls. They would never get to know the man I had known and loved.

~

The disease progressed more slowly than the doctors had expected. So, David insisted that I not change my work schedule at all. The most difficult part of the process, though, wasn't his increasing physical difficulties. The problem was that he had a growing need to hold onto things. He refused to let me throw anything away, so began to keep and store things. Stuff. Paraphernalia. Junk. He had even bought an ancient motorcycle he thought he might one day restore, as well as tools needed to do so. All of this, and much more, now resided in box after box in our basement. Thank goodness the girls never went down there.

Evelyn was finally in law school and Charlie in her last year of undergrad when David died, taking a big piece of my heart along with him. It was such a peculiar thing. The disease was progressing, but in the end, it was a massive stroke that killed him without warning. I was with him at the end and grateful for every moment I'd had with him. My only regret was that as the girls grew up, David became more and more distant from them. The moment he died, I wanted to tell them everything, but before he died—before there was any indication he might die suddenly—David had made me promise to keep his secret. The only thing I could do was honour his wishes.

I plunged myself into my design work. With the girls both out of town studying, I was able to get to New York more often than ever. Julie, my associate designer who had now worked with me for some twenty years, was irreplaceable. I couldn't have accomplished what I had without her. She was even now designing a children's line within *Kosmic Kat*.

Eddie and I had continued our weekly dinners. He had never met my girls, but I hoped to rectify that at the funeral. As bad luck would have it, Buzz, who had been suffering for some years with the complications of HIV, died the week before David. Neither of us had been able to be there for the other as we weathered our darkest personal tragedies.

Evelyn had been entering her last year in law school when Charlie announced that she would go on to graduate school and pursue a Master of Fine Arts in creative writing. This decision didn't surprise me—Charlie had always had a creative bent—and it was more in the direction of writing than visual art, although she did like to sketch. I always supported her artistic pursuits, but her sister did not.

That Christmas, Evelyn was almost apoplectic when she heard that Charlie was going to be what Evelyn described as a "starving artist." I found this endlessly amusing since I was hardly starving: they just didn't know I was an artist. (I was still working on my plan to reveal all to the girls.) Charlie had a fellowship to cover costs (not that cost would have been an obstacle), so she went anyway. I had always provided a substantial allowance to each of the girls when they were in school. They never questioned its provenance, and I never offered any explanation. I suppose they thought it came from their father's life insurance.

When Charlie graduated with her M.F.A., she began the writer's uphill struggle to publication. She sold the odd magazine article, but I knew that she wanted to be a novelist. She asked me if she could move home for a while to save money. I agreed although I have to admit it was with some reluctance. I think she thought I needed support since it was only just over a year since David died. I'm not sure where she thought I went almost every day of the week, but I still wasn't prepared to offer an explanation. That would come eventually.

After a year, I told her I thought it was time for her to find a place of her own. I subsidized her income—she had sold a few writing pieces and now worked in one of the university libraries stacking books part-time. She found a place to share with some other struggling artists, and I think she was happy, but who really knows about their children? After all, since children rarely know their parents as people, parents can't really know their children's minds!

Evelyn found the love of her life in Michael, a law school classmate who had eschewed a legal career to become a stockbroker and was doing well, as far as any of us could figure out. They had bought a condo in downtown Toronto where they both revelled in the workaholism of the Bay Street financial and legal firms.

Charlie, on the other hand, hadn't had much luck in the love department. I worried about her whenever I had the time to think about it. Somewhere along the line, I began to consider how I would introduce the girls to *Kosmic Kat*. I never had the chance.

Every so often, the girls would express the opinion that I ought to sell the house and move to a "carefree retirement facility," as they put it. I couldn't think of anything I'd hate more. "Too many old people," I'd say to them. Besides, I wasn't old enough and was in good health. Until I wasn't.

And When I Die

Blood, Sweat and Tears, 1968

I SUPPOSE I'M ONE OF THOSE PEOPLE who always tended to ignore aches and pains. Over the years, I found myself too busy to pay attention to them. Then, one morning when I awoke, it was impossible to ignore them. I had to make an appointment with my new family doctor.

As I sat in her waiting room, I wondered what a newly minted family physician could possibly know about the perils of ageing. But she was all I had. By the time I emerged from her office, I had stepped onto that merry-go-round that is modern medical diagnostics. I would have to have an ultrasound, blood work, possibly an MRI. My head was spinning.

I was not prepared for the diagnosis. Cancer. Aggressive.

Radiation therapy might do some good. Chemo was not likely to help, but I could have it if I wanted. When I considered the quality of life I'd have if I took the chemo, and for what? Two extra months of misery? I declined. I prepared to tell the girls. But before I did, I had a lot of preliminary preparations to make.

Eddie helped me. I prepared my business for Julie to take over. I had meetings with my financial advisers and set up trust funds for the girls. I would add the money to the fund Nan had left to them, but they would not have access to it until they were thirty-five—Evelyn would have hers next year, Charlie, two years later. I had to protect their money from tax issues as much as possible. Then I prepared letters for each of them. I also wrote a letter to Liz.

I needed to apologize to her and hoped that I'd be able to give the letter to her in person. I had to put that right. It was something that I should have done much earlier in my life.

Then, I started arrangements to get the girls both in the same room so that I could lay it all out for them, and they would understand that the business had to remain untouched for a year after my death. Eddie would help me. Getting them together, though, would take some finessing since Evelyn, who lived so far away, was always so busy, and she'd have to drop everything and fly home for a visit without knowing why.

~

I never did get the girls together or give Liz her letter. I know what Nan would say as I make this last entry, and I understand her. At last.

"God? You *are* laughing, aren't you?

Charlie

The Rainbow Connection

The Carpenters, 1981

BY THE TIME I REACHED THE END of Mom's diary, I was sobbing. As I felt a tear drop off the end of my nose and splash onto the page in front of me, it seemed everything was in slow motion. I felt as if I were in a dream and couldn't wake myself up. I had no idea what time it was. Through that veil of tears, I looked up at the skylights and could see the moon and a few pinpoints of starlight. I had been there all day.

"Shit, shit, shit!" I said to no one since I was alone in the dark. "How could I have not known any of this about my mother?"

I turned on the desk light and looked around at the workshop. Yes, it was real. My phone was on the desk, and the moment I picked it up, I could see that I'd missed four calls, three from Tom, who doubtless wondered what the hell I was doing here for so long. One was from an unknown number. There were also two texts from Tom, the final one saying, "Should I come and rescue you? We're going to be late for our dinner engagement."

Damn it! I'd forgotten all about dinner with our friends Andrea and Richard. I immediately texted him back and

349

apologized for being missing in action for so long. I told him there was much more to do here than I had thought and that I'd be home in an hour or so. At least I thought I would be. I might just have enough time to change before we had to leave. Though, I seriously doubted that I'd want to make idle chit-chat over dinner at this stage in the day. Just as I clicked "send," the phone rang in my hands. It was the same unknown number.

"Charlie?" the slightly familiar voice said. "It's Ed. Everything okay in there? You've been there a long time."

I felt a shiver run up my spine as I heard his voice because now, just hours after I'd met the man, I felt as if I knew him. "I'm fine. Ed? Would you have a minute to chat with me?"

"Of course, Charlie. I thought you might have a few questions. And I have something to give you."

A few questions? That was something of an understatement. Two minutes later, Ed (Eddie?) was at the door. He took off his hat, and as I looked at him this time, I felt as if I might have seen him before. Or perhaps it was only the story I'd just read that made me see things that weren't there.

"You know, Ed, you do look familiar to me." I thought about it for a moment, and then it struck me. "You were at Mom's funeral, weren't you? As we started filing out, I remember noticing a man I didn't recognize at the back of the church. It was you. I never saw you again."

He nodded sadly. "Yes, I was there. How could I have missed it?"

"Why didn't you stay to introduce yourself to us?"

"I couldn't. I was too overcome with grief to speak to anyone. Your mother was the only friend I had left and the only person in the world who really knew me from way back when." He cleared his throat. "Your mother never expected to become so ill so quickly, or she would have told you all of this sooner. It happened so fast, Charlie. She was planning to tell you and Evelyn everything, but she wanted to have her affairs in order first. Then the opportunity never presented itself. You have to believe that. She wanted everything to be perfect."

This was only a part of what I was confused about. "Ed, Eddie? As far as I can tell, you were Mom's oldest and best friend. Why did she never introduce you to us?"

"She tried several times, but it never seemed to work out." He peered at me closely. "You know, we have met before, but you were too young to remember."

"But what about that year I lived with Mom after I finished my MFA? How could it have been possible that I never knew you existed all through that time?"

"That's an easy one," he said. "I was a visiting professor back at my old alma mater, Berkeley, for two years at that time. I was home only a few times to see Buzz." He looked down at the open diary on the desk. "I presume you know who Buzz was?" I nodded as he continued. "I always regretted that I couldn't have known you and Evelyn as you grew up."

I looked around at the space, sweeping my hand past sewing machines, drafting tables, mannequins and rails of clothing. "And what about all this? How do you fit into this now?"

"I promised your mother I'd help her. And since Buzz's parents left this mega-storage business to me when they died, it seemed natural. I don't usually work here. I'm still lecturing part-time and writing. But I knew I had to be here when you came. I had to meet you," he said, reaching inside his coat to pull an envelope from his inner pocket. "And to give you this."

Eddie handed me a small white envelope. When I opened it up, a key fell out.

"Another key?" I said. "I don't know if I'm up for any more surprises today."

He laughed. "I quite understand, Charlie. I can't imagine how you're feeling right now. Your mother and I had often discussed her reluctance to share her artistic life with her daughters—or anyone other than me, for that matter, apart from your father."

He picked up the key and stroked it. He looked to me as if he were trying to conjure Mom's ghost like Aladdin and the lamp. "Your mother left this key with me years ago for safe-keeping. She didn't want it to get lost." He put it in my hand. "It opens the closet over there." He pointed to the far corner of the workshop tucked between two sets of shelves. I hadn't noticed it before.

"Charlie, I'll leave you now, but call me when you're ready to begin all the paperwork. There's going to be a ton of it." He put a business card on the desk. "Your mother, Kat, was one of the most remarkable women I've ever known in my life. It was a privilege to know her—and it's been a privilege to meet you, Charlie." He squeezed my hand and headed to the door.

I looked down at the card. It said, "Dr. Edmund Lancaster, Professor Emeritus." I wished I'd known my mother as well as he did.

I took the key and headed over to the closet. It was a padlock key. Mom clearly hadn't wanted the contents of this closet to go missing. The lock was stiff as if no one had used it in years. When I finally got it off, I opened the door, wondering what more secrets my mother was hiding.

I was greeted by masses of dresses of all colours, but mostly of silk. Over the past year, I'd learned a lot about fabrics (I had made myself twelve dresses, but that's s story for another day), and I knew silk when I felt it. But these were no ordinary garments. These were vintage gowns. I took one off the rail to read the label.

PAUL POIRET À PARIS
77436 ATELIER, Mme Françoise Phillips

It was just as Mom had written about it in her diary. My hand shook as I looked at the cream-coloured silk. I was looking at a Paul Poiret original. And Françoise Phillips was my great-grandmother, Frannie.

I placed it back in the closet and looked at the hat boxes lining the shelf above. Tucked in the corner were two books, well, three—I took them out slowly. Two of them seemed to be two volumes of one book. The title was *Le Deuxième Sexe*. The writer in me immediately opened volume one to the copyright page. It was copyright 1949. I was holding an original first edition of Simone de Beauvoir's feminist manifesto that I'd had to read years ago in a women's studies class in university. I knew it as *The Second Sex*. This was, however, the original French edition—unadulterated.

And what's more, it was signed. "*Pour ma chère amie, Françoise. Toujours ensemble*" — "For my dear friend, Françoise. Always together"—followed by the author's signature. *Oh, my actual god,* I thought. My great-grandmother really did know Simone de Beauvoir.

The third volume was a diary. Another diary! I thought I might faint. It would have to be for another day—I could not read another diary now. But there was one more thing I needed to check. As Mom's letter had directed, I needed to find a green file folder in the top drawer of the cabinet. Then I was going home to see if I could get this spinning in my brain to stop.

I walked over to the filing cabinet and opened the top drawer. Just as Mom had said, there was a green file folder in the front. It was stuffed with papers. I opened the folder on the desk and started to scan them. *Oh my god*, I thought as I read the letter on the top. *This spinning might never stop.*

~

His name was Peter Taylor-Jackson III. He had graduated *summa cum laude* from Johns Hopkins University Medical School in 1996, after which he completed a residency in pediatric oncology at the Children's Hospital of Philadelphia. He was currently living in Boston, where he headed the pediatric oncology department at Boston Children's Hospital. *Why am I reading this professional bio of someone I've never even heard of know?* I thought as I flipped through the dossier. *And why the hell does my mother have a file about a pediatrician in Boston?* I was getting tired, I had just texted Tom to tell him I'd have to skip dinner, and my nerves were wearing thin. I flipped over a few more pages.

Staring me in the face was a birth certificate. The male child had been born in Halifax, Nova Scotia, Canada on August 9, 1970. The mother's name was Katherine Elizabeth Wilson. My mother. There was no father's name listed. This could not be possible. Then there were a few more pages of official-looking documents. I stopped flipping at a form that was clearly one a new mother would sign to give up her baby for adoption. My eyes were drawn immediately to the signature line. There was my mother's signature, and the witness was listed as James Wilson, my grandfather, except for one thing. It wasn't my mother's signature. I had seen my mother's signature many times over the years, and this was not hers. Then there were the letters.

There were several letters from Dr. Peter that my mother had obviously answered, judging from his subsequent correspondence. Somehow, this Peter had managed to get his adoption records unsealed after the death of both his adoptive parents, and he had tracked down his biological mother. My mother. A half-brother? And they had been corresponding for almost a year. The last letter from him was dated a month after she had died. Had he found her only to lose her again? In this letter, he confirmed that he would travel to visit her within the next two months. It had never happened.

My heart began to thump loudly and quickly. How could this be? How could Mom not have mentioned this? Then I realized what had happened. It was in one of Peter's letters.

"*...It breaks my heart to hear that your parents told you I had not survived, to hear that you have lived with this hole in your heart for so many years...*"

She never had even the slightest idea that he was alive. My own mother had lived with this heartbreak for her whole adult life, and we didn't know anything about it. I had to talk to Evelyn as soon as possible. But one thing was crystal clear to me: I had to meet him.

~

It took a while, but Evelyn and I finally connected with Peter. He had read Mom's obituary online, and he had wanted to meet us, but he knew from what Mom had told him that she hadn't yet mentioned his existence to us. He thought that it might be too soon. That's why, on the day I finally was able to get through to him at the hospital in Boston, he was so overcome. I could hear the tears in his voice when he told me how much he'd like to meet both of us. So we made the arrangements.

Tom promised to stay in the background until I gave him the all-clear. Evelyn would arrive from the airport a few hours before Peter, and the two of us would present ourselves as a family unit when he arrived. However, Evelyn's flight was delayed twice by bad weather in Toronto, so when the doorbell finally rang at the appointed moment, I was alone to greet our long-lost half-brother.

I checked my hair in the hall mirror and whispered, "Mom, wish me luck." I could almost hear her say, "You've got this, Charlie."

I opened the door slowly. There he stood. Over six-feet tall with a sprinkle of white in his black hair. He was so handsome, my jaw dropped. I looked at him, and before I could put my brain in gear, my mouth was off and running. "You're black!" I said.

"You're white!"

355

I guess I wasn't the only one shocked. I let him into the house, and we both tried to overcome our astonishment. When I offered him a drink, he happily accepted a martini from Tom, who I'd waved over for support.

When we finally settled down, Peter took a sip of his drink then put it down on the coffee table. "She never sent me her photo. You know, I'm no geneticist, Charlie, but I do know a bit about genetic inheritance, and if your mother..."

"Our mother," I corrected him. I was starting to get the hang of this.

He smiled. "Our mother...was white, and my father was mixed race as you say her diary says, then I should look more like you. Maybe I'm *not* your half-brother."

I had no idea where to go from here until Tom, ever the pragmatist, stepped in. "DNA testing," he said. It was that simple.

And so, we did it that same week. As Peter and I and Evelyn spent some time together (what else could we do?), I hoped against hope that he was my half-sibling. He was a wonderful man who had been brought up by two Boston doctors—one white and one black, a situation that was frowned upon in the 1970s—who had longed to adopt a mixed-race child. He was their shining light, as he put it.

A week later, the results came back. Peter, Evelyn and I sat together in my living room, looking at the envelope on the table. Finally, I picked it up, ripped it open and looked at them.

"You're our brother, Peter."

"That leaves only one question, then," he said as he raised his champagne glass. We'd had them ready for just such results. "How did this happen?"

My eyes flitted across the room to where great-grandmother Fran's diary sat on a table, as yet unread.

"'*If you cannot get rid of the family skeleton, you may as well make it dance,*'" I said softly.

"What?" they both said together.

"Oh, just something a friend said to me once. Anyway, I think I might have to find out a bit more about Fran," I said, sipping my champagne.

"Who?" Peter said.

"Frannie Phillips," I said. "Our great-grandmother."

Kat's Playlist

The soundtrack of a life

On Spotify at:
https://open.spotify.com/playlist/3HPK0qNfidvAVOWAqeC wNe

- Try to Remember…The Brothers Four, 1965
- I am a Rock…Simon and Garfunkel, 1965
- Don't Think Twice…Peter, Paul and Mary, 1963
- Downtown…Petula Clark, 1963
- Just One Look…The Hollies, 1964
- Catch the Wind…Donovan, 1965
- You Were on My Mind…We Five, 1965
- I Know a Place…Petula Clark, 1965
- Have Yourself a Merry Little Christmas…Andy Williams, 1965
- Cast Your Fate to the Wind…We Five, 1965
- The Carnival is Over…The Seekers, 1965
- Can't Help but Wonder Where I'm Bound…Tom Paxton, 1964
- Both Sides Now…Joni Mitchell, 1964
- The Way I Feel…Gordon Lightfoot, 1967
- The First Time Ever I Saw Your Face…Peter, Paul & Mary, 1965

- See You In September...The Happenings, 1966

- America...Simon and Garfunkel, 1967
- Autumn in New York...Louis Armstrong and Elle Fitzgerald, 1957
- The Times They are A-Changing...Bob Dylan, 1964
- A Hazy Shade of Winter...Simon and Garfunkel, 1968
- Too Many Martyrs...Phil Ochs, 1964
- Society's Child...Janis Ian, 1963
- Reach out of the Darkness...Friend and Lover, 1968
- Those Were the Days...Mary Hopkin, 1968
- Bad Moon Rising...Creedence Clearwater Revival, 1969
- Piece of my Heart...Janis Joplin, 1969
- Eve of Destruction...Barry McGuire, 1965
- Universal Soldier...Buffy St. Marie, 1964
- Where Have All the Flowers Gone?...Peter, Paul and Mary, 1962
- Reason to Believe...The Carpenters, 1970
- Bridge Over Troubled Water...Simon and Garfunkel, 1970
- You've Got a Friend...Carole King, 197
- Killing Me Softly...Roberta Flack, 1973
- I'm Sorry...John Denver, 1975
- The Way I've Always Heard it Should Be...Carly Simon, 1971
- My Life...Billy Joel, 1978
- I am Woman...Helen Reddy, 1972
- Child of Mine...Carole King, 1970
- It's Too Late...Carole King, 1971
- Take My Breath Away...Berlin, 1986
- And When I Die...Blood, Sweat and Tears, 1968
- The Rainbow Connection...The Carpenters, 1981

Coming soon!

Charlie learns about her great-grandmother…

The Inscrutable Life of Frannie Phillips

For years after what came to be known in our family as "the incident," my parents chose to believe that it had scarred me for life. It was convenient for them in the years that followed. It is how they explained my subsequent behaviour to friends and family, believing deeply in the necessity to maintain their good reputation. But it was not the horror of "the incident" that affected me. It was that Duff-Gordon woman. I remember every detail.

The evening before "the incident," I was dining with my parents in the first-class dining room. We had sailed out of Southampton to great fanfare a day earlier on what was proclaimed to be the world's first unsinkable ship. The RMS Titanic was a sight to behold, and the dining room was appointed in a manner that its passengers had come to expect, or perhaps to be more precise, to demand. Our dinner companions that evening were Lucy, Lady Duff-Gordon and her husband, Sir Cosmo Duff-Gordon. As I approached the table with my parents that evening, the Duff-Gordons were already seated and well into their first coupes of champagne. I observed Lady Duff-Gordon's eyes running up and down me as we advanced, no doubt finding me wanting in some way. I had met her on two previous occasions when I accompanied my mother to a dress fitting. That did not seem to matter. No doubt she thought a twelve-year-old would put a damper on the evening's festivities. I would just have to prove her wrong.

I was secretly delighted to be sitting with the famous Lucile, as Lady Duff-Gordon was known by her public. My mother, however, ever the snob, had been less than enthusiastic when she was told of our table assignment, referring to Lucile as being merely "in trade." She objected to dining with one of her couturiers. I, on the other hand, was thrilled since I, too, wanted to design and sew dresses regardless of my parents' clear disapproval. Even at the tender age of twelve, I knew that it would be essential to meet the right people.

Twenty-four hours later, I wished I had not wasted my time.

About the Author

Patricia J. Parsons has written over a dozen books, including health and business books, a memoir, two historical novels, and women's fiction. She has been a fashion design and sewing fanatic for most of her life, a passion she writes about online at *The GG Files blog*. She lives, writes and sews in Toronto.

Connect with her on Instagram @patriciajparsons or @pjparsonswriter

Join her on Facebook @patriciaparsonswriter and at facebook.com/12 dresses

Visit her web site at www.patriciajparsons.com or the *GG Files* blog at gloriaglamont.com.

Some other books by Patricia J. Parsons

The Year I Made Twelve Dresses (women's fiction—where Charlie's story begins)

Plan B (lit-for-intelligent-chicks)

Confessions of a Failed Yuppie (lit-for-intelligent-chicks)

Something More Than Love (historical fiction)

Grace Note: In Hildegard's Shadow (historical fiction)

Another 'Pointe' of View: The Life & Times of a Ballet Mom (memoir)